ASPIRATIONS
of the HEART

CASPIRATIONS
of the HEART

a novel

Katie Hart Smith

To Ann —
many
Blessings!
Katie Hart Smith

Deeds Publishing | Atlanta

Published by Deeds Publishing in Athens, GA
www.deedspublishing.com

Printed in The United States of America

Cover and text layout by Mark Babcock

Library of Congress Cataloging-in-Publications data is available
upon request.

ISBN 978-1-944193-33-1

Books are available in quantity for promotional or premium use. For
information, email info@deedspublishing.com.

First Edition, 2016

10 9 8 7 6 5 4 3 2 1

For Gigi

I

Addie wanted to be anywhere but here. She pleaded silently with God. *I'm trapped in a place where the harsh realities of life trump my aspirations of the heart and crush my dreams into a pile of dust as unfulfilled wishes. Please help me!*

"Addie, please! I'm beggin' ya. Git out of the house now and make yourself busy," Maw pleaded with Addie as she pulled out a pair of pruning shears from her deep, apron pocket. "Be a big help to me. I need for you to tend to the rose bush in the back yard."

"But Maw!" Addie resisted.

"No, Addie. Paw just got home. I can handle him, always have, always will. It's my job to look after ya. Now go!" Maw pushed Addie out the back door as Paw stumbled up the front porch steps and into the house.

With reluctant obedience, Addie ran over to the bush, knelt down in the grass and randomly snipped at branches. Addie overheard Maw and Paw arguing. It was always the same argument.

Today was no different from any other day.

"You didn't use the money I gave ya to pay the bank, did ya? Of course not! Instead, ya gambled and drank it all away, ya ol' fool! You're no good! You're drunk! Now go and git some sleep or better yet, jest git out of this house! You're no good to me and Addie in this condition." Exasperated, Maw realized her scolding was futile.

Paw, back on the farm after a four-day binge in town, hollered back at Maw causing Addie to lose her concentration and prick her right index finger on a thorn. A droplet of blood fell onto her white cotton apron. Instinctively, she stuck her finger into her mouth to stop the bleeding with the pressure from her tongue. It tasted of warm, sweet metal. *Is this all there is for me? Will I end up just like Maw? God, I want so much more. I wonder what lies beyond the corn fields of the farm, past the outskirts of town. I want to know more about life, love, and how I fit into this crazy world as a useful human being.*

"No, please stop! You're hurting me!" Maw cried out.

Maw and Paw weren't the only things stirred up on the farm. Cold autumn breezes blew Maw's handmade curtains, yellowed from the years, grit, sun, and rain, against the white-washed wooden window sills. As if on cue, freshly washed brown pants, white undergarments, blouses, aprons, linens, and black skirts appeared spirited by ghosts as they bounced and waved up and down clothes-pinned to the rope line in the back yard. Ruddy brown and white hens clucked, pecked, and darted to and fro along the side yard between the modest house and the barn.

Addie heard a loud slap, skin against skin, again and again. Maw's screams faded to yelps and whimpers. Numbed by Paw's countless insane tirades, the howls of the blustering wind seemed to deafen the sounds of his billowing voice and her mother's pleas. Grey clouds shape-shifted overhead and quickly captured her attention as a v-shaped formation of honking geese enticed her to go south and escape with them.

As the birds disappeared behind the tree line, Addie's gaze fell and focused on two small, white wooden crosses in a tiny clearing just beyond the barn. For a brief moment her heart panged for the loss of her little brother Ben and younger sister, affectionately called Sissy, who were struck down by scarlet fever a few years back.

Addie recalled how she felt a sense of immense purpose as she and Maw toiled day after day caring for them, wiping their sweaty, hot brows for endless nights as they watched death sneak in to take their young souls—first Sissy and then Ben. But now they were gone and at peace, escaping her hell on earth. Her sense of self simply dissolved when they were lowered into their final resting places. This wasn't how she envisioned her life.

After they buried Sissy and Ben, Paw never recovered, finding solace in moonshine and playing cards. He'd disappear for days and return home only when he needed a meal, more money, or to prove to Maw that he was still the man of the house. With winter setting in and Paw's predictable misappropriation of their money, the bank's threats to repossess the farm would soon be realized.

To protect her spirit and soul from Paw, Addie chose to build an emotional wall using stones made from anger, bitterness, and resentment. Other than Maw, there was only one other person who could magically turn Addie's emotional wall into a pile of rubble—Garrett. Garrett, her best childhood friend, lived on a neighboring farm located a few miles away. He could always find a way to make her laugh on the dark days.

I grow weary of the dark days. Addie stiffened as Paw opened the creaky screened door, emerging onto the front porch. He brushed off his brown hat against the leg of his grungy coveralls.

"Addie! Addie! Where are ya girl?" Paw slurred out. Using the back of his hand, he wiped spittle off of his beard.

Clad in the same red, moth-eaten, long sleeve shirt he left the house wearing earlier in the week, he clomped down the front stairs and scuffled through the grass along the side yard. Hens flittered, squawked, and scurried to get out of his way as he kicked at them. Luckily all escaped unharmed.

"Girl, what are ya doin' out here? Didn't ya hear me callin' ya? Now git up and ready my horse. I'm goin' back into town. Seems I'm not wanted 'round here." He swiped at Addie, but like the hens she too managed to avoid physical contact with her father.

"Yes, Paw! Right away, Paw!" Addie yelled back over her shoulder. She picked up her skirt and ran toward the barn. Her braided ponytail swung back and forth. Breathless, she flung the barn doors open. The aroma of hay and manure embraced her like an old friend as she saddled up the last of their livestock, an old chestnut mare. Leading the horse out the barn, Addie swore she saw a tear in the mare's left eye. Leaning closer into the horse's ear, she whispered, "Don't worry, Ol' Girl. It'll all be fine. Just you wait and see. Please take care of Paw." Addie handed over the reins to her father.

"Why are ya talking to that horse? You stupid girl!" Paw blurted out, stumbling back a few steps and letting out a deep belch.

4

Addie winced and backed away. Paw mumbled something inaudible. After two hops, he managed to get his left boot into the stirrup. He grabbed the horn of the saddle and pulled his rawbone frame up and into the worn brown leather seat. Paw clicked his tongue and shoved the heels of his boots hard into the mare's ribs. The mare let out a whinny and galloped toward town. The two disappeared into a cloud of dust.

Addie's thoughts immediately went to Maw, who still hadn't emerged from the house. After securing the barn doors for the night, Addie ran back toward the house.

"Maw? Maw? Where are you Maw?" Addie called out from the front room. Emerging into the tiny kitchen, she saw fresh blood smeared along the pine board wall. A bloody paring knife lay on the walnut-stained kitchen table. Drops of blood on the hardwood floor lured Addie from the kitchen into the back hallway toward the washroom.

From the washroom doorframe, Addie saw her mother lying quietly in the bathtub. *Why is Maw still wearing her frock dress and apron?* She stepped closer. Horrified, she raised her hands to cover her mouth and silence her screams.

"Oh, Maw! What have you done to yourself? Oh, God! Please don't leave me! Don't leave me here alone with Paw!" Addie pleaded. "Maw! No!"

Blood flowed from her mother's slit wrists and pooled in her apron.

Oh, dear God! Addie trembled. She watched the crimson stain grow. The smell of iron permeated the air. Addie's knees went weak and she dropped to the floor alongside her mother.

As Addie attempted to stop the bleeding by applying pressure to the wounds, Maw whispered, "Stop. Your work here is done, Addie. Leave this place. This place will kill you...and your dreams. Find yourself. Make your place in this world." Maw's words grew faint. Her face turned ghastly white and her lips blue. "I'll be your guardian angel."

Maw drew in shallow breaths and her breathing labored. "Money...box...buried...rosebush.

I...love...you...." Maw exhaled. She was gone.

"Oh! Maw! No! No! Don't die! Please, don't leave me!" Addie wailed. She threw her arms around her mother's limp body and drew her into her embrace. Burying her head into her mother's neck, Maw's dark auburn, lilac-scented hair provided Addie with a brief interlude of familiar comfort, but only for a moment. Reality set in. Reluctantly, Addie cradled her mother's head back to rest on the edge of the bathtub. With shaky hands, Addie brushed her Maw's hair off her forehead and positioned her hands; right on top of the left, just like she had seen Sissy and Ben's hands placed on their chests in their caskets.

Addie slowly rose to her feet and dried her eyes using the edges of her stained sleeves. Backing slowly out of the washroom, she blew her mother a kiss from the doorway. "Good-bye, Maw. I love you."

Addie crumpled to the floor outside the kitchen and passed out.

A flash of lightning followed by a clap of thunder startled Addie awake. *Why am I on the floor? Why is there blood on my hands and clothes?* She hoisted herself up using the kitchen door frame. A white flash of light illuminated the night sky through the windows. The glint of Maw's silver knife covered in blood caught her eye. The puzzle pieces fell into place. *Maw was gone. Dead. By her own hand.*

Realizing she was alone, a loud crash of thunder caused her to jump. Fear caused a tingling sensation to flush throughout her body followed by the taste of metal in her mouth. Lightning streaked across the night sky. A bad storm brewed from the west.

Addie counted aloud. "One, one-thousand, two, one-thousand, three, one-thousand, four, one-thousand, five, one-thousand..." Thunder rumbled and shook the panes in the open windows. She divided five seconds by five, something Garrett taught her to do to learn how many miles she was from where lightning just struck. *Lightning struck one mile away.*

Lighting a candle to illuminate the kitchen, Addie glanced down the dark hallway toward the back of the house. Another flash of light lit up the backyard as she caught a glimpse of the laundry whipping wildly in the furious wind. Maw's handkerchief flew off the line and got caught in the freshly pruned branches of the rosebush. The wind whistled through the door frames and slammed the bedroom doors shut, startling Addie. She nearly dropped the candle onto the floor.

Storm gusts swirled Addie's dress and apron strings in the air. She cupped her hands around the candle's open flame as she made her way around the corner to her bedroom. Maw's final words played over and over in her head and none of it made sense. *How can I leave my home? Where will I go? What will I do? How will I survive?*

Addie strained to hear a familiar whinny and galloping hooves. *Paw.* Thunder boomed. *Go! Leave this place. It will kill you. Paw will kill me. Go! Money. Box. Buried. Rosebush. Oh, God!*

In a frenzied panic, Addie pulled the black and white striped, down pillow from its white, cotton pillow case and discarded it. She absentmindedly threw clothes and undergarments into the empty case. She glanced around the room; her favorite wall caught her attention. She paused for only a moment. Old, faded magazine pictures of cosmopolitan women from discarded issues of *Ladies' Home Journal* and newspaper photos from faraway places beckoned.

Secured on the wood paneling with flour paste made using Maw's recipe of equal parts water and flour with just a pinch of salt to prevent molding, Sissy and Addie designed a large, heart-shaped collage of beautiful women in high fashion and magnificent places Addie dreamed of visiting in the United States and in Europe. Since there was never enough money to paint or wallpaper her room, the pictures, bordered with dried lavender, thistles, and roses from Maw's bushes, provided Addie with a visual sanctuary as she lay on her bed at night, trying to escape and drown out the madness between Maw and Paw that frequently occurred outside her bedroom door. Addie marveled at how immaculate and beautiful, carefree, and happy the women in the images seemed.

Now, staring back from the threshold of the bedroom doorway clutching her pillowcase, Addie found their faces unnerving as they smiled back, unscathed by the terror under her roof. She ran into the kitchen, grabbed a large metal serving spoon and blew out her candle before dropping it on the kitchen table. She bolted down the dark hallway without glancing into the washroom and ran out the back door as she heard Paw's boots shuffle-stepping up the front porch stairs.

A staccato series of lightning flashes revealed the rosebush in the darkness. Maw's handkerchief waved, starched out like a flag in the storm gusts. Addie ran to it and dropped to her knees in the dying grass. She stabbed the metal spoon into the dirt and started digging and scraping away layers of soil.

"Mother? Addie? Where are ya ingrates?" Paw's inebriated voice carried over the rumbling thunder.

Addie clawed at the earth, frequently glancing over her shoulder. A yellowish light appeared in the kitchen window and faded. Paw's black silhouette disappeared.

"Mother! Damn it, woman! Where are ya? Addie! Quit playin' games with me, ya foolish women! Damn it! Wait 'til I get a hold of ya!" Paw shouted out from the depths of the house.

A light rain fell as Addie continued to dig around the bush. She heard Paw scream.

"Mother! No! Mother! Speak to me, Mother!"

Dead silence hung in the thick, humid air for a brief moment. Addie held her breath.

Paw erupted, "Addie? Where are ya? I know you're here! I saw a light from the house! Git out here this instant! When I catch ya, girl, you're gonna regret it!"

Maw's curtains danced violently in and out of the windows. The tall Georgia pines rustled and swayed as the storm rolled in. One by one, the windows glowed amber then turned black as Paw searched for her, room by room. Addie dug faster as she heard closet doors slam shut, tables overturn, and glass break. Paw's vile profanity mixed with Addie's name filled her ears. Paw and the storm roared on. Another flash of light crackled overhead. *One, one-thousand, two...Clap. Boom.* Thunder shook Addie to the core.

Fearing it was simply a matter of moments before Paw found her in the backyard and dragged her back into the house, Addie mustered all her strength. With both hands, she stabbed the spoon into the dirt one last time. *Ting!* Metal struck metal. Raindrops speckled the lid of the box. Addie quickly unearthed it, then shoved the muddy, tin box into her pillowcase and ran toward the barn. *Crack! Snap! Thud!* Red and orange flames burst from the tree line as lightning struck and shattered a tall pine in the forest.

"God damn it, Addie! What did ya do to your Maw? I'm gonna KILL you! Jest wait 'til I git my hands on ya!" Paw's tone was demonic. "Show yourself!"

Thunder vibrated in Addie's chest and shook the ground as she opened the stall. She grabbed the golden mane of Ol' Girl and hurled herself onto the bareback mare. They darted out of the barn door, immediately becoming drenched in the sheets of rain. She directed the horse east. As Ol' Girl gained her stride, Addie glanced over her shoulder only once to see in a flash of light her father throwing down the lit candle and running toward the open barn doors.

Maw's words reeled through Addie's head. *'Go! You were meant for so much more. Leave this place. This place will kill you.'* I think she meant that Paw would kill me! *'Find yourself.'*

As the wind gusted, rain pellets stung her face, camouflaging the tears streaming down her cheeks. She and the mare rode into the night. *Who should I turn to for help?* With Maw dead and Paw's threats to kill her, Addie directed the horse to go to the only safe place she knew.

Soaked to the bone, Addie secured Ol' Girl into one of the

Darling's vacant stalls in their barn. Hiding out in the Darling's barn for the night would provide a safe haven, for now. Addie planned to tell Garrett what happened in the morning. With only two months separating her from adulthood and freedom, Addie needed to be careful whom to trust.

Addie shivered as she gathered up oats from the feeding bin, placed them into her blood-stained apron and handfed them to the mare. "You deserve a better name than Ol' Girl." Addie remarked.

Addie recalled having personalized names for their livestock until her father soured and squandered their savings. Week after week, month after month, Addie and Maw watched Paw sell the flock of Suffolk sheep, to include Sadie, Fay, Maggie, and Bob. Lazy Larry, a black mule, was sold at the town auction last summer along with the forty head of Black Angus cattle. After Sissy and Ben died, their Shetland ponies, Becky and Huck, named after characters in Ben's favorite book, *The Adventures of Tom Sawyer*, by Mark Twain, were traded in for the chestnut mare. Addie couldn't bear to name her and simply called her Ol' Girl knowing one day, she too, would be taken from her.

Like the animals, Addie watched in horror as her beloved family disappeared before her eyes. Cherished memories were replaced with nightmares and echoes of Paw's promise to kill her. She grew to despise him over the years. He was no longer the father she said, 'I love you' to, but rather he became a stranger living among them under their roof. Addie prayed at night that God would take him from this earth. *I hate him! I wish he were dead! Why has my life come to this? What did I do wrong? What can I do to fix it? How can I make it stop? What's going to happen to me tomorrow and in the days, weeks, and years to follow?* Addie's head spun with a series of questions without answers as she dried Ol' Girl and secured a red plaid blanket over her back to ward off the chill of the stormy night air.

Rain drops continued to assault the barn roof as Addie undressed in the dark stall. She hung her wet clothes over the slats in the stall walls and changed into one of Maw's hand-me-down, brown, floral dresses. Finding a spare blanket, she rubbed it over her rain-soaked hair. Using her fingers as a comb, she collected the damp, auburn strands and braided her hair into a ponytail, securing it at the end with a piece of twine. Addie wrapped the blanket around her and nested into a corner of the stall with Ol' Girl. The sweet smell of hay calmed her. Lightning flashed, revealing the open cracks and spaces in the barn walls and doors. *One, one-thousand...two, one-thousand...three, one-thousand...four, one-thousand...five, one-thousand...*

Exhausted, Addie drifted off to sleep before hearing the next roll of thunder.

2

Thursday, October 16, 1913, Hope, Georgia

Addie, leave this place. It will kill you. Breathless, Addie ran through the cornfield, through rows and rows of tall, green stalks trying to escape, but Paw was in hot pursuit and threatened.

"Addie! When I find you, I'm gonna KILL you!" Addie felt Paw's hand on her left arm.

"Addie? Are you okay? Wake up." Garrett quietly whispered as he knelt beside Addie and shook her left shoulder. Addie startled and awoke from her nightmare.

Addie gasped and shrunk back further into the corner, confused. *Am I still dreaming?*

Garrett stood up and backed away, sensing there was something terribly wrong, especially after stumbling upon Addie stowed away in their barn. He noticed that her apron had faded brown blotches all over it. As a farmer and a hunter, he had seen enough blood-stained clothes from killing, skinning, and gutting deer and squirrels to know the spots were merely diluted remainders of their former appearance.

Addie rubbed her eyes and refocused on Garrett, who stood next to Ol' Girl with his left hand on her rump to steady him.

Garrett carefully evaluated Addie as he stepped forward and knelt down beside her. He cupped his warm hands over her cold ones. The distal part of his right index finger was missing. It didn't bother her. She knew him so well and how he sustained every scratch, scar, and injury over the years. Addie ran her fingers over the scarred nub. Injuries, like Garrett's finger, were just a casualty of farm life, unforgiving and hard, always taking its share of flesh and blood.

"What happened? Are you alright?" Garrett's copper brows wrinkled with worry. Her hands began to tremble in his. "What's wrong?" He remained calm, yet was intent on getting answers.

Addie struggled to say the words. "Maw's dead! Paw...he wanted to *kill* me!" Terror veiled her face and tears flowed.

"What? Who? Who killed your Maw? Did your Paw kill her?"

Sobbing, Addie managed to swallow hard and gathered her thoughts and words. "No. Paw came home drunk again. Maw and Paw fought—again. When Paw had his fill, he rode off toward town. I went back into the house looking for her to see if she was alright. I overheard Paw beating her. I heard her screams and pleas for him to stop." Addie paused.

Garrett continued to warm her hands in his. "Go on."

Horror filled Addie's eyes. "Maw killed herself, by her own hand. She cut her wrists. I found her in the bathtub, but it was too late. I couldn't save her." Red, splotchy hives suddenly appeared on her neck and freckled chest. Releasing her hands from his grasp, she wiped her face with the front and back of her hands. Grabbing the edges of the blanket, she curled up into a tight ball. A chill ran through her bones.

Garrett gave Addie a moment before asking. "Why? Why did she do it?"

Rocking back and forth, Addie went into a trance-like state of disbelief, still trying to comprehend all of the events that unraveled her life in less than twelve hours. "Maw said my work on the farm was done. I was meant for so much more. She said to leave this place and that it would kill me!" Addie snapped back into the present moment and looked into Garrett's eyes.

She stopped rocking. "Paw tried to find me. He said he wanted to *kill* me if he caught me. Can you believe it? My own Paw! So, I ran. I just got on Ol' Girl and came here, to the only place where I knew I'd be safe...from the storm and from Paw."

"Where's he now?"

"I saw him running out to the barn when Ol' Girl and I escaped. I guess he's still there. There's no way for him to get off the farm, unless he walks."

Garrett took comfort knowing that Addie's father wasn't going anywhere anytime soon, especially in his inebriated state. "Look, we've got to go into town and tell the sheriff about your Maw."

"Oh, no! Please don't tell anyone, not even your father just yet. I won't be eighteen for two more months. They'll see that Paw's not fit and place him into the Georgia Asylum in Milledgeville. I'll be stuck into an orphanage or they'll throw me on the orphan train and sell me to some family out West."

Garrett knew Addie was right. They had heard the stories about orphaned and homeless babies and kids. Some were even loaded onto trains on the east coast and taken to various rural areas throughout the Midwest to be adopted by families needing help on their farms. While some children ended up in good homes, there were frightful stories of neglect and abuse that resulted in runaways. One such twelve-year-old boy made his way to their community in north Georgia. He called himself 'Will.' No one knew if that was his Christian name or one that he fabricated. It didn't matter. The Davis family from church adopted him after losing a son to consumption.

"I could lie about my age, but everyone in town and on the surrounding farms including the sheriff knows me."

"You're right." Garrett knew that wasn't an option.

Addie was known to all and was a bright light of beauty that everyone adored and loved. She was quick to lend a helping hand and even helped care for his ailing mother when she got ill and died from rheumatic fever last summer. Many of the town's people took pity on Addie and her mother's plight and helped them out on the farm when they could.

Silence fell over Garrett and Addie as they tried to comprehend the magnitude of all of the events that had just transpired.

At that moment, Garrett's father burst into the barn, shattering their thoughts. "Garrett? Son? Come quick!"

Garrett popped up. He brushed off the hay stuck to his pants, emerged from the stall, and rushed over to intercept his father before Mr. Darling saw Ol' Girl and Addie. "Dad, what is it?"

Standing eye to eye with his only child, Mr. Darling grabbed Garrett's broad, muscular shoulders, squaring him in front of him. "Listen. Hitch up the horses to the wagon. There's thick, black smoke comin' from beyond the trees over toward the Campbell's and Engel's farms. We've got to see what's burning. Thank God it rained last night; otherwise we'd have a complete mess on our hands. Perhaps it's just a brush fire started by a lightning strike. Who knows, but we've got to go check it out and put it out." Mr. Darling continued, "I'll grab some buckets, tools, and my rifle. Hurry up with the horses. Time is precious."

Garrett watched his father dart out the open barn doors. Once he was out of sight, Garrett ran back to Addie who was hiding under the blanket. He pulled the blanket off her head. "Father and I are going to check out a fire, possibly a brush fire started by the lightning last night. Go inside the house and get cleaned up. Feel free to fix yourself something to eat and get some rest. Stay in my room until we get back, ya hear?"

Addie nodded. She watched Garrett gather the horses and skillfully hitch them to the clapboard wagon outside the open barn doors. As Garrett closed the doors, he gave Addie a nod, wink, and a smile. Addie's emotional wall crumbled and her heart melted knowing she came to the right place, to the right person, her best friend.

"Yaa!" Mr. Darling commanded the horses. Harnesses clanked. A whip snapped. The large, wooden wheels with wooden spokes and black iron rims splashed though puddles on the damp road as the Darling men headed toward the source of the smoke.

The sounds outside faded, leaving only Ol' Girl's snorts, an occasional *moo* from one of the Jerseys, clucks from the hens, and bleats from the goats and sheep. Addie let a few more minutes pass before making her way out of the barn and into the Darling house.

While many hewed-log homes could be found sprinkled

throughout northern Georgia, the Darling's house was painted white with white trim. Every farm house looked alike in their town. Some had black shutters while others had forest green ones. The Darling's house, like Addie's, had the latter. Years back, Mr. Darling and Paw purchased the paint together in order to save money. Everyone in both families pitched in to help whitewash both homes. It was a joyous time—then. Now the two homes, though painted the exact same colors, appeared completely different from the roadside. Paint peeled from the Engel's house and siding rotted in desperate need of repair. Addie and Maw couldn't afford to keep it painted over the years. It was all they could do to keep the corn crops going to pay their bills.

Once inside, she felt safe and relieved to be in a place where she didn't jump from unannounced visits from Paw. Addie noticed there were no floral scents in the Darling house. It simply smelled of must, coffee, and wood. Familiar with the layout, Addie settled in. After fixing a small meal, she heated up a kettle of hot water on the stove and bathed in their washroom. Addie changed into one of Garrett's cotton long-sleeve white shirts, pushed up the sleeves and put on a pair of Garrett's baggy, bibbed overalls, rolling up the legs about six inches to make cuffs.

She used the Darling's washboard and a bucket to remove the mud and blood from her clothing and dirty pillowcase, hanging them up to dry on the clothesline in the backyard. Fighting off temptation, Addie addressed the muddy box last.

While the morning air was light and crisp, feelings of trepidation filled Addie as she walked through the damp grass that chilled her bare feet, sending ripples through her body. Walking over to the water pump, she rinsed the tin box and dried it. Sunshine peeked through the morning clouds and a blinding light reflected off the lid. Addie returned to the house and sat cross-legged on top of Garrett's bed. She slowly opened the box. Rolls and rolls of money were lined inside. Each roll was secured with a piece of string. Addie unrolled each bundle and organized the bills by denominations: twenties, tens, fives, and ones. Counting twice, her final count totaled seventy-three dollars. Maw had stashed the extra earnings from the farm to be used on a rainy day. *Oh, my God! That stormy, rainy day came yesterday!* Tears filled Addie's eyes.

What am I going to do? What's going to become of Paw and me? Paw would surely spend every last cent if he got his hands on this money.

Unsure of what to do next, Addie put the money back in the tin box and set it on Garrett's night stand. Next to his brass oil lamp sat his Bible and a copy of *Aesop's Fables* and *Mark Twain's Quips and Quotes*. The Twain book grabbed her attention. She picked it up and rifled through it. It contained a compilation of Twain's famous one-liners from his speeches and publications. Flipping through the pages, she came across a quote that called to her. Addie read it aloud: "The two most important days in your life are the day you are born and the day you find out why." *Well, isn't that the truth!* She closed the book and set it next to her on the bed. Pulling the multi-colored patchwork quilt that Garrett's mother made using scraps of old clothing up around her shoulders, she rested her head on his pillow. *I need to find out why.*

3

Edward Alexander II's aspiration to build magnificent hospitals and nursing schools for white people and for black people in downtown Atlanta was finally coming true. Four years ago, he secured the necessary federal, state, and municipal funds for the capital campaign. Edward and his wife Trudy held many fundraisers at their home, which he referred to as grippin' an' grinnin'. He even used a small portion of the money he inherited from the sale of his maternal aunt's multigenerational cotton plantation located outside of Savannah to reach his financial goals. With less than a year away from the grand opening of the medical facility, he had much to do.

"By God, we need to write a press release!" Edward boomed as he slammed his palm down on the mahogany desk and puffed on the cigar that was wedged in the space between his thick, greying mustache and beard. Smoke swirled over his balding head.

"A what? I'm not sure that I know what you're talking about

Mr. Alexander." Clyde nervously sat up straight in the tan leather chair and adjusted his gray vest and jacket. His long fingers skimmed his thin, slicked back, coal strands of hair. Out of his periphery, he could see the glass eyes of a mounted cougar, buffalo, and red fox staring back at him, a few of the trophies collected over the years by Edward and his father on their hunting expeditions with Teddie, a family friend and former United States President. Under his feet lay a zebra-skin rug. A thousand-pound grizzly bear stood on its hind legs with raised claws, baring its ivory teeth in the room dubbed "The Zoo" in the Alexander house. The Alexander mansion, located on Washington Street, was a few miles south of Atlanta's bustling business district.

"A press release. We need to publicize our plans to the public. It will also assist us in our fundraising efforts and help us market our services to potential patients in Atlanta and throughout the State. Boy, as Chief Operating Officer at Sacred Heart Hospital, have you not heard of a press release?"

"Uh, well no sir. I have not." Clyde uncrossed his legs, sipped his scotch, and crossed his legs again. Unconsciously, his black, leather shoe tapped the heart-of-pine floor.

"For God's sake!" Edward sighed and swirled the scotch in his Waterford crystal glass. He took a moment to calm his nerves and reflect on all of his hard work to date.

Hiring Clyde was a favor extended to Congressman Posey's son in exchange for securing the votes necessary to obtain the funding to build the private, state-of-the-art hospitals and nursing schools. More importantly, he required Congressman Posey's influence, among many other elected officials at the state and local level, to amend the city ordinances to allow Edward to build the separate buildings on the same piece of property.

Originally, the thirty-two acre lot located in the city's Sixth Ward was zoned for white businesses only. City ordinances and Jim Crow laws pushed for separate schools, churches, businesses, and even hospital facilities to be built in different zones of the city, segregating black from whites. Grady Hospital, Atlanta's municipal hospital, once housed white and Negro patients on separate wards that were connected by extended corridors, under one roof. However, because of the laws, even Grady was pressured to construct another hospital, for Negroes only, at the corner of Armstrong and Butler Streets.

Edward thought it was a ridiculous idea to build a separate hospital for Colored people in a completely different "designated" district. From a business operations perspective, Edward knew he could save millions in expenses if he could utilize the same kitchen, laundry, janitorial staff, and morgue for both facilities. He eventually struck a compromise that originated out of very heated, private debates with Mayors Joyner and Maddox.

According to the Atlanta City Council, his plans for Alexander Hall, the Negro hospital, had to meet three criteria; 1) The hospital had to be constructed on a separate street and have a completely different street address from Sacred Heart Hospital; 2) The "sister" hospital had to operate under an independent name and have its own construction timeline; and 3) underground tunnels needed to be constructed, connecting the two medical facilities and the segregated nursing schools, thereby allowing Edward to have the operational efficiencies he demanded.

Sacred Heart's groundbreaking ceremony, attended by Georgia's elite and elected, occurred in May, 1909, and included the laying of a ceremonial cornerstone by the Freemasons and a blessing from Edward's parish priest from the Shrine of the Immaculate Conception. Alexander Hall, designed to look like a palatial brick home from the street, was located around the corner. Alexander Hall also underwent the same ceremonial pomp and circumstance in August, 1912. Edward secured the best architectural firm in Atlanta, shipped in the finest construction materials including travertine stone. Building commenced on both facilities utilizing two teams from a construction company owned by Edward's childhood friend, Tom Greene.

He chose the corner of Alexander, a street named in honor of Dr. James. F. Alexander, a prominent Atlanta pioneer and physician in the mid-1800's who wasn't related to his kinfolk, and Spring Streets. Alexander Hall would be built on Alexander Street while Sacred Heart overlooked Spring. On the surface, this arrangement gave the public the perception that they were two unique complexes. Edward even had the architects develop a different brick facade for Alexander Hall and utilize a series of brick walls and landscaping to comply with the illusion.

Edward knew that building with the best supplies also meant low maintenance costs long-term. He envisioned Sacred Heart Hospital and Alexander Hall becoming pieces of Atlanta history, too. The city was the rising star of the South and Edward was ready to hitch his ambitious dreams to that star. He desired to make a name for himself and eventually step out of his deceased father's shadow. Edward, embracing all of the lessons learned while growing up in the Catholic Church, knew that Jesus' physical heart represented his divine love for all humanity. In concert with those teachings, Edward hoped that Atlanta would dissolve the segregation ordinances. But he doubted he would bear witness to it in his lifetime. Instead, he, the architects, construction company, and leadership team were bound by a non-disclosure pact that would pass along the Alexander Hall's secret to the next generation, planning for the day when the bricks would be removed from the Colored hospital, revealing the travertine tile underneath. The walls would also come down around the property and between the Colored and White nursing schools so that all of the travertine-built facilities would merge into one entity allowing the medical facility to care for all Georgian's, as one Sacred Heart.

Until that day, there was much to be accomplished and managed, to include Clyde. Focused and refueled, Edward continued. "Well, let me educate you on the matter of press releases. Do you recall reading about that train accident in Atlantic City about seven years ago?"

"Yes, sir. Didn't it involve Pennsylvania Railroad? A car jumped the tracks and plunged into a creek, killing fifty passengers." Clyde exhaled in relief, knowledgeable about the incident.

With his confidence reestablished, he sipped from his glass. His shoe continued to tap the floor.

"Yes, yes, that's the one. Well, a man by the name of Ivy Lee jumped out ahead of the journalists to squelch the rumor mills and provided the *New York Times* with a press release on behalf of the company about the accident. Brilliant move, I say! Just brilliant! So, we're going to develop a press release of our own to educate the public with the details we need for them to know about the opening of Sacred Heart, our services, the new nursing school, and to promote our ribbon cutting ceremony." He flipped through his calendar book. "We will open our doors on Friday, May 22nd." Edward looked scornfully at Clyde. "You got all that? I don't see you writing anything down or taking any notes."

Clyde set his scotch down on the maple end table next to him and quickly reached inside his jacket pocket. He removed a set of wire spectacles, a tiny notepad, and pencil. After adjusting the glasses on his face, he scribbled away, "Press release, ribbon cutting ceremony, Friday, May 22nd, next year. Got it, Mr. Alexander. On top of it, sir." He closed his notepad, removed his glasses, and put his belongings back into the pocket of his jacket.

Edward's blood boiled and his rosy cheeks turned ruby red. He got up from his chair, walked over to the fireplace, and tossed what remained of his cigar into the lit fireplace. He knew Clyde didn't share in his passion for the monumental task of building and opening Sacred Heart. Clyde was simply biding his time, ready to jump at the next opportunity when the congressman needed another favor. Over the years, he had seen many young men throw out their family names like confetti in the wind and ride on their father's coattails, but not him. Driven by a mission to make a difference in the world and fueled by scotch, he saw himself differently from men like Clyde. Edward called out, "Miss Mattie?"

A buxom, Negro woman emerged from behind the swinging pecan-stained, wooden door that separated the Zoo from the rest of the house. Dressed in a long, black dress with a white necktie, she wore a starched white, eyelet apron, and a stiff, white ruffled cap sat atop of her head. Her hair was neatly pulled back into a low bun. Her apron bow in the back bounced with each step. "Yes, Mr. Alexander?"

"Please see Mr. Posey out. We've concluded our meeting." Edward turned toward Clyde and outstretched his right hand.

Clyde was about ready to pick up his drink to enjoy another sip of the exquisite, aged selection when Miss Mattie reached for the crystal glass, swiftly removing it from his reach. She had subtle ways of dealing with people she didn't like.

Clyde, unsettled about the abrupt ending to the meeting and Miss Mattie taking his drink glass away from him, snubbed his nose at her as he glided over to Edward to shake his hand. Looking up to make eye contact, "Thank you, sir, for your time. I look forward to seeing you at our leadership meeting next week."

As founder and director, Edward hosted these separate meetings with Clyde in the privacy of his home, apart from the other hospital leaders. He wanted to keep him on track with the building project and maintain a watchful eye on him. His gut churned with acid in Clyde's presence. Edward always listened to his gut. "Have that draft of the press release ready so we can review it with everyone at that meeting. Good night, Mr. Posey."

Mr. Posey nodded anxiously ready to escape the Zoo and the grip Edward had on him. He resented the late afternoon meetings and knew Edward was keeping him on a short leash. Serving as the Chief Operating Officer at the new Sacred Heart Hospital did not include oversight of Alexander Hall and was merely a stepping stone in his career path to the State Capital. He was deeply relieved to learn that Edward had the Board appoint another man named Oliver Louis, from New York, for that job.

Clyde got into his Model T Ford and started the engine. He headed north on Washington Street. Once he reached Edgewood Avenue, he turned right. A half-mile later, he turned left onto Boulevard landing him in front of his palatial home on the corner of Johnson in an area called the Fourth Ward. Clyde owned the most desirable bachelor pad frequented by many women and men, both single and married alike. Despite his frail frame, pointy nose, and stubby ears, Clyde was perceived as attractive not only because of his father's appointed position, but as an only child, he was the sole heir to the Posey family fortune. To those seeking higher aspirations, that made him very handsome in their eyes.

Clyde came home to find that very kind of aspiring woman lying naked on a deep purple, velvet blanket on the floor of his living room in front of the marble fireplace. Feeling conquered, skewered, and skinned by Edward, Clyde was ready to turn the tables and mount a trophy of his own. His personal collection didn't consist of four-legged beasts and wild creatures. Instead, Clyde preferred the company of exotic, untamed, and uninhibited humans. He loved them all, all ethnicities, sizes, and ages. 'The bawdier, the better' was his motto.

"Hard day at work, sweetie?" Moira propped herself up on her elbows and watched Clyde slowly undress. She noticed he was particular about the order and fashion in which he folded and laid his clothes across the yellow sofa cushions.

His pale, naked body walked toward the bar that was set up on the far side of the living room. Opening the ebony wood doors of the custom-made corner piece, he pulled out a leaf which extended the serving area. He reached up and pulled a box inlaid with mother of pearl from the top shelf. He opened the lid and pulled out two sugar cubes and a silver, slotted spoon. Pulling out a bottle that contained a green liquid and partially filling two pale, green glasses, he placed the slotted spoon over one of the glasses. Clyde set a cube on top of the spoon and slowly poured ice water from a pewter pitcher over the sugar. The clear, green mixture turned cloudy. With both drinks prepared, he turned and walked toward Moira as he licked his lips ready to devour his fresh catch of the night.

Thursday evening, Hope, Georgia

Exhausted from fighting the fire, and covered in smudges of soot, Garrett and his father returned home. The pair of buckskin Quarter horses were unhitched from the wagon and returned to the stalls to be watered and fed. Neither Garrett nor Mr. Darling uttered a word until they had shut the barn doors.

Taking a deep breath, Mr. Darling broke the silence. "I don't know exactly how we're gonna break the news to her, son. I can't believe her mother took her own life. I'm at a complete loss." He pulled out his handkerchief, wiped his forehead and shoved it into his back pants pocket.

When they discovered the source of the fire, Garrett immediately told his father about what Addie had shared with him in the barn. They had found the Engel house and barn engulfed in flames. Farmers and town folk who had also seen the black smoke from the horizon came to help. Mr. Darling took the lead and focused everyone's efforts and water resources to contain and extinguish the blazing structures. When there was nothing left but rubble and smoking debris, all were shocked to discover the charred remains of a man cradling the body of a woman in his arms on what was left of the front porch swing.

"Lord, give me the strength...." Mr. Darling's lower lip quivered. He pulled out his handkerchief again and dabbed at his wet eyes. "Come on son, we've got to tell her."

4

Friday morning, October 17, 1913
Fourth Ward

"Get up! It's time for you to go. But before you do, I have a project for you." Clyde was bathed and dressed. With a snort of cocaine in each nostril to complete his morning routine, he was ready to start the day. He pulled at Moira's bare foot that stuck out from the bed covers. "Hey! Come on, wake up."

"Alright! Alright! Quit talking so loud. What the hell did you put in that drink last night? My head's about ready to explode, you bastard." Moira's dark brown curls cascaded across her face and she spit and sputtered to get her hair clear from her mouth. Sitting up slowly in bed, she readied herself for her morning routine as Clyde placed a small hand mirror containing two white powder lines in her lap. Raising the mirror to her nose, each line disappeared into a nostril. She licked her finger, gathered the residual powder on her fingertip and rubbed it on her gums. "Now that's better than a cup of coffee."

"It will help cure your absinthe hangover." Clyde got straight to his point. "Listen, I've got a project for you. And, if you do it well, I'll hire you for the concierge job you want so badly at Sacred Heart. Do you know what a press release is?" Clyde took the hand mirror from her and paddled her butt as he scooted her out of the four-poster, canopy bed.

"Sure, Clyde. I know what one is. What do you take me for, some kind of idiot?" Moira slipped into her clothes. She stepped over to his walnut dresser and brushed her unruly curls in the mirror using Clyde's silver hair brush. She twisted her hair into a knot and secured it with a large, faux jewel encrusted, fan-style comb.

As she dressed, Clyde thought her hairstyle looked like a headless peacock from behind as he picked up the hairbrush and fastidiously plucked out any evidence of her. "Great. It needs to be about Sacred Heart, its services, the new nursing school, to include details about the ribbon cutting ceremony next year in May, blah, blah, blah. Here are the details and feel free to throw in any other juicy tidbits to make it read well. Do a good job because your future job depends on it."

"Yea, yea. When do you need it?" She grabbed the note paper from his hand, as she walked out the bedroom door and made her way down the grand semi-circular foyer staircase toward the front door. Large Confederate portraits of past ancestors who fought with Lee in the Civil War appeared to give a disapproving look during her descent. Soft pastel-colored oil paintings featuring various landscapes of the South were sprinkled in so it didn't give the appearance that Clyde's scandalous activities were seen as a spectator sport by his relatives on the wall. All were selectively placed by Stephen Jones, a well-known interior designer in Atlanta and a frequent guest of Clyde's.

Leaning over the wrought iron railing at the top landing of the staircase, a masterpiece that Stephen had designed and forged by a company in Savannah, Clyde replied, "In three days. Make sure its type written."

Moira didn't respond and closed the heavy front door behind her. Adjusting the red silk scarf around her head, she had no idea what a press release was and didn't own a typewriter. But she knew who would and who did.

Friday afternoon

Hope, Georgia

Addie and Garrett sat in silence in the rocking chairs on the Darling's front porch as they waited in anticipation for Mr. Darling to return from town. She basked in the afternoon autumn sun which felt like Maw's warm hands on her cheeks. Her eyes, still bloodshot and swollen after learning the traumatic news and enduring a sleepless night, gazed upon red, golden, and orange leaves that blew across the front lawn in the breeze. *I am one of those leaves*, thought Addie. *Fallen from my family tree, lost and tumbling, unsure of where I'll end up.*

Mr. Darling returned from town on the back of one of the Quarter horses. He joined Addie and Garrett on the porch, removed his felt hat, and sat down on the white, wicker couch next to Addie. "Listen. I made a few phone calls and also made graveside funeral arrangements for your parents. I let the preacher and the undertaker know your wishes to have them buried on the farm next to Sissy and Ben. That's the proper place for them, although I'm not sure how the bank will feel about it when they learn the news." Mr. Darling paused and then added, "But not to worry, Addie dear, I'll deal with them in time. I consider you a part of the family. I made a promise to God in my prayers last night that I will do my part to look after you. So don't you worry about a thing." Mr. Darling gave her a reassuring smile which added warmth to the moment as he patted her knee.

"Mr. Darling, when will we have the funeral for Maw and Paw?"

"Tomorrow afternoon at three o'clock. The undertaker will provide the caskets and prepare the graves and the markers. The preacher will meet us at the site. Does that sound okay?"

"Yes, sir. It sounds perfect." She felt guilty. For years she had wished that God would take Paw from this earth and He did. Addie hung her head and closed her eyes. *Please forgive me, Paw. I'm so sorry.* She opened her eyes, lifted her head, and wiped away her tears.

"I've got a few more things to talk with you about, Addie. Because you don't turn eighteen until December, it's only fittin' and proper for a young lady like yourself to live with someone, er someplace, well, uh, that's more appropriate than, well, uh, say this place. With us I mean. Us, men. Uh, do you know what I'm tryin' to say?" Mr. Darling flushed in his search for the right words. He played with the brim of his hat.

"Yes, sir. I think so. Who or where or what did you have in mind?"

"Well, I had a long conversation with the sheriff 'bout everything. He promised not to report your status as an orphan if you agree to what I'm 'bout to tell you. Please know I'm just lookin' out for you and your best interests — long term. I feel obliged to your parents and to my dear wife, God rest her soul, to look after you as if you were my own daughter."

"I understand." Addie bit her thumbnail. As a wayward leaf on the wind, she readied herself to hear her fate.

"I spoke with my younger sister, Mary, who lives down in Atlanta. She's been lookin' after our older sister, Olive, who lives 'round the corner from her. Olive just became a widow last month. Her husband, Doc Gray had a heart attack and she's been actin' poorly ever since. It would be a great help to Garrett's Aunt Mary and me if you would consider lookin' after her as her caretaker and nurse her back to health. You can even stay in her home. She'll also give you free room and board. How does that sound?" Mr. Darling fidgeted with the band around his hat and waited for Addie's response.

Addie stopped biting her nail and immediately replied, "Gosh, Mr. Darling. That sounds like a grand plan. I'd be so honored to look after Aunt Olive. Are you kidding me? Really? I can live in her house in Atlanta? Oh, thank you! Thank you, ever so much!" Addie got up and threw her arms around an unsuspecting Mr. Darling, nearly crushing his hat in the process.

Garrett chuckled at the sight of his father being smothered by Addie's zealous embrace. "Well I guess that settles it. The country mouse is off to go live in the big city."

Addie sat back down right next to Mr. Darling on the couch. "Country mouse, hah!" Addie chided back at Garrett. "I remember the story from *Aesop's Fables* that you read to me down by the pond. However, I believe that this mouse will enjoy becoming a town mouse."

"Yea, right!" Garrett rolled his eyes. "Just wait until you meet the rest of the family. My Aunt Mary's got some interesting children. My cousin, Lester, is a rotten peach."

"Listen. Garrett please speak honorably 'bout your cousins, son." Mr. Darling weighed in. He watched the spark ignite between Addie and Garrett. He relished the rare opportunity to observe the spirited conversation unfolding. "Tell ya what. Let's all go inside and I'll fix us up some dinner. Garrett, you can tell Addie all 'bout the family and we'll discuss our travel plans inside while I'm cookin'. Addie, how does country ham, butter beans, mashed potatoes, and buttermilk biscuits 'n gravy sound to you?"

Addie's stomach rumbled. She couldn't remember the last time she had eaten such a grand meal. "That sounds so heavenly, Mr. Darling! Did you know that I can make the best biscuits? Maw taught me how to keep them light and fluffy so they just break apart in your hands." Addie paused, realizing that for the first time she mentioned Maw in a conversation, but referred to her in the past tense. Swallowing hard and fighting off the emerging tears, she continued. "I'd be happy to help you in the kitchen."

"I'd be honored, Addie. It's been a long time since…." Mr. Darling's lower lip began to tremble and his eye's moistened as he recalled the days when his home was filled with the aromatic cooking of Mrs. Darling. "Well, never mind. Let's all head into the house. We've got our work cut out for us and a big day ahead of us tomorrow. Now, let's remember that God helps those who help themselves." He stood up, walked over to the front door, and opened it.

Garrett and Addie exchanged a look of surprise.

Mr. Darling stopped, turned back, and grinned. "I also read Garrett's copy of *Aesop's Fables*—remember the tale about Hercules and the Waggoner? Come on, you kids. Get up and get in here." He motioned them to come inside with his hat. "We've got to put our shoulders to the wheel."

5

Monday morning, October 20, 1913
First Ward

Moira rapped her knuckles on the closed door. *Charlie Finch, Senior Reporter* was painted in black on the frosted glass in front of her. She adjusted her hat and long, blue Edwardian-style coat that had matching cloth-covered buttons down the front. A cameo pendant, a gift from a former Senator who resided in Columbus, was affixed at the base of the white, high-collared, ruffled blouse. She kicked her boot out from the bottom of her skirt, enjoying her newfound freedom in movement. She was happy to rid her wardrobe of hobble dresses and skirts. She detested the braided, elastic fetter that she wore around each leg to restrict her stride and prevent tearing of the fabric while she ambulated carefully around the city. She preferred the versatility of walking suits which were better suited for her activities, day and night.

"Come in," said a male voice from behind the door. Moira found Charlie on the phone, his hand over the microphone of the receiver. "Have a seat. I'll be with you in a jiffy," he whispered as he motioned her over to the empty chair in front of his desk. He removed his hand and interjected, "Look, sheriff, this is Mr. Finch from *The Atlanta Dispatch*. I'm calling to inquire about the details pertaining to the farmhouse fire in Hope and the two people burnt to a crisp.

Yes, yes, you can speak frankly with me and off the record. Yes, I promise to keep your name out of the paper like always. Yes, I'll be sure to thank you with a generous Christmas gift."

Charlie picked up his pencil, pulled a notepad out from a stack of papers, and began writing. "Uh, huh. You don't say. Gruesome. No survivors. Okay. Gotcha. Hey, thanks a million. I look forward to seeing you next month. What? You want what? Season tickets to the University of Georgia football games? Uh, I'll see what I can do for you." Charlie paused before saying, "No, no, you don't need to remind me about that incident. But thanks for doing so anyway. Always a pleasure doing business with you." Charlie slammed the phone down. "Fuck me!"

"Right here? Right now? Moira smiled and began to clear a stack of papers lying on his desk in front of her.

"No, no. The sheriff in Hope drives a hard bargain. Bastard!" Charlie inhaled deeply and then exhaled through pursed lips. "I take it you are here for the Sacred Heart press release or are you here to spend some quality time with me?"

"Both, Mr. Finch."

"Good, that's what I like to hear. So, do you think you will land that job over at Sacred Heart? If you do, I'll make it worth your while. For every story that you share with me, I'll pay you... provided that it pans out."

"Well, that all depends on Mr. Posey. If he likes what I've written, or rather what *you've* written, then we're on."

Charlie rested back in his chair and folded his arms behind his head. "Oh, he will. I'm sure of it. Also, I've been thinking. We've got to come up with some kind of coded language that we can use between us so that when I call you or you call me, we know that it's a good time to talk."

Charlie unfolded his arms and glanced down at one of *The Atlanta Dispatch* papers in front of him. The forecast was printed near the top of the page. A stroke of genius struck Charlie. "I got it. When I call you, I will say, 'Is it sunny out?' If there's no one around you and you're able to talk freely, then respond by saying this." Charlie cleared his throat and tried to mimic a female voice. "Yes, it's sunny out." Moira laughed at his poor attempt. He continued, speaking in his own voice. "And, vice versa. When you call me to ask the same, and if someone is in my office or I'm busy, I'll respond by saying, 'No, it looks cloudy.' How's that for a plan?"

"Sounds perfect!" Moira clapped her hands together. "You always think of everything, Mr. Finch. You are *The Atlanta Dispatch*'s best and brightest. You'll be the editor one day, just you wait and see." Moira batted her eyes at him. "Now, I've just got to get the job at Sacred Heart. I have to deliver the press release to Mr. Posey later today." Moira refrained from disclosing her evening affair with Clyde. "I'm hoping the press release will seal the deal."

"Oh, it will." Charlie stood up and unzipped his dark green trousers. "And, speaking of sealing the deal, why don't you come over here so you can seal the deal with me."

Moira stood up and made sure the office door was locked. She slinked over to him and summoned her sultry, Southern voice. "Oh, Charlie! You are so naughty. Here? Now? Well, alright then." Moira gently placed her hands on his shoulders, and coaxed him back down into his chair.

The phone on Charlie's desk rang. Charlie groaned and leaned over to pick it up. Looking down, he said to the top of her head, "Sorry, I've got to take this. Hey, this is Charlie Finch. What can I do for you?" As he continued gazing down at the dark, brown head bobbing back and forth, he became captivated by the bejeweled fan in her bun. He chuckled to himself thinking it looked like he had a beheaded peacock in his lap.

Hope, Georgia

Addie was lost in thought as she folded a long, brown skirt and placed it into the grip. She had tossed and turned again in the night. This time she wasn't haunted by Maw's final words or terrorized by Paw's threats, but rather she was filled with anticipation. In less than a week, her life had become completely unraveled. However, through the generosity and kindness shown by the Darling family, they managed to mend and repair her frayed heart and soul in a matter of days. The short time spent with Mr. Darling and Garrett reminded her of what it was like to live in a home filled with love, respect, and laughter.

Addie gazed into the suitcase, in awe of how her wishes, prayers, and dreams were finally coming true. Unfortunately, it came at a devastating price. *Perhaps, with the money Maw saved in the tin box, I could finally take a few college classes? Perhaps, I'll take a trip? Perhaps, I'll travel out of the United States and see the world?* The potential possibilities were endless and for the first time in her life she no longer felt trapped.

Addie couldn't believe she was going to live in Atlanta. She'd never ventured outside of Hope and didn't know what to expect. She'd read about the big city and seen pictures in the newspapers, but reading about it and living in it were two completely different things. Anxious and scared, her tummy fluttered with the thoughts of not knowing what life had in store for her. She was heading to a city where she had no real family and didn't have any friends.

The thought of leaving Garrett also unsettled her. He had always been her rock, a steady force, someone who kept her grounded despite her chaotic living conditions on the farm. Throughout the weekend together, she noticed something different about him. It was the way in which he acted and spoke around her. He was truly concerned about her. She'd catch Garrett looking at her out of the corner of her eye, but not like he used to do as a boy. Instead, she saw him through the eyes of a young woman, not as girl. She quickly realized how much he had been a part of her life and still was an integral a part of her, heart and soul.

In an effort to suppress her nerves, she sought comfort in her evening prayers. Addie also found contentment when she asked God for forgiveness as she bid her family a final farewell at the funeral. With each shovelful of dirt that was thrown on top of the pine caskets, Addie buried the past with them and mentally readied herself to begin anew in Atlanta.

Sensing Garrett was in the bedroom doorway looking at her in that same manner again, she said, "I'm almost done. I've got a few more things to pack." Without looking up, Addie placed the tin box deep inside the luggage. She continued to fold her clothes, putting them into the suitcase Mr. Darling gave to her. It had belonged to Mrs. Darling. Mr. Darling also let Addie pick out a few dresses, skirts, aprons, and blouses that he had packed in boxes in the attic. He knew that they would eventually be useful to someone someday.

Garrett carefully watched her as she closed the lid and buckled the worn, leather straps. Last night, he wrestled with the thought of not seeing Addie for a while. Although it had been a bittersweet weekend, he was amazed by how much he enjoyed having her stay with them in their house, how her hair smelled of lilacs, and how he noticed that it glowed with golden highlights in the sunlight. Her blue eyes sparkled like the pond when it reflected a cloudless sky. It caught him off guard that he knew that she bit her nails and hives broke out on her neck and freckled chest when she got nervous. And that she did indeed make the best biscuits that he'd ever eaten. So it pained him to utter the words, "Before you go, I have two more things for you to take with you to Atlanta. Here, this is for you." He handed her the book of Mark Twain quotations. "It's for those times when you're at Aunt Olive's house when you need to be reminded that you're a country mouse at heart."

"Oh, Garrett. I can't take your book. I know how much it means to you." She opened the cover. Inscribed inside was: *To Garrett, Merry Christmas! Love, Mom and Dad. December, 25, 1907.* Below that, read: *To Addie, Happy Birthday! Fondly, Gar-*

rett. December 25, 1913. "You remembered? This is so special! What a way to commemorate my eighteenth birthday early!" She closed the book and held it close to her chest. "I will cherish it, always. Thank you, Garrett." Addie stepped forward to give him a hug. Garrett extended his right arm and stopped her.

"Wait, I have one more thing for you, country mouse. Close your eyes and hold out your hand." Addie giggled, closed her eyes, and held out her right hand. Garrett stuck his hand into his front pocket, pulled out and placed a smooth, pebble with rounded edges in her palm. "Okay, now open your eyes."

Addie laughed, "A rock? Um, okay? Is this a joke?" Addie raised it for a closer inspection. She saw that the stone contained veins and specks of iron pyrite. *Fools Gold.*

"No, I can assure you it's no joke. Do you remember when Miss McGowan read to us about how penguins picked out a special pebble to present to their mate?"

Addie blushed at the thought. "I do remember the story. The male penguin searches for the perfect pebble with the hopes that it will be accepted by the female penguin." Her neck and chest flushed. "Why, Mr. Darling, are you saying you fancy li'l ol' me?" Addie searched his eyes and waited for a reply.

Garrett stammered and searched for the right words in his head. *I think I love you. No, that will scare her. I adore you. No, too formal. I think you're cute. No, she's not a puppy. I'm fond of you. I'm also fond of grits and my Aunt Olive, so, that won't do either.* Garrett settled on *You are my dearest and best friend in the world. I care about you a lot. I picked this particular stone because the specks of gold radiate like your hair in the sunlight.* Garrett nervously ran his hands through his thick, copper hair. *Lord, I gave her a rock!*

I'm such an idiot. Okay, it's time to recover and think of something genius to say, something from the heart. He coughed and continued. "Addie, perhaps one day..."

Mr. Darling interrupted Garrett as he called out from the front porch. "Addie, I'll be waitin' for ya out front with the horses and the wagon."

Garrett rolled his eyes. *Really? Thanks, Dad.* He knew this was his last chance to convey his feelings to Addie since he wasn't going into Atlanta with them. His father had asked him to stay behind to keep an eye on the Engel farm while he was away.

"I'm coming, Mr. Darling," Addie called back, realizing this was going to be her last conversation with Garrett for a while.

The opportunity passed. Garrett deflated. "Addie, I just want to you be safe and write to me. We'll be down to visit the family at Christmas. I look forward to seeing you then."

Confused by the sudden change in tone in Garrett's voice, Addie wrangled with the right words to say to Garrett. *I'm really going to miss you. What am I going to do without you? You are my rock. You hold my heart. I think...I really, really like...love you. Oh, God, none of that will do! What if he doesn't feel the same way?* Instead, she punched him in the upper arm and said, "You are also my dearest and best friend. I care about you, too, Garrett...a lot. I'll be sure to write you every chance I get. Now, come on, let's not keep your father waiting." Addie gave him a quick hug and darted out of the guest bedroom clutching the book and the pebble.

Garrett slowly picked the grip up off the bed. This wasn't how he envisioned the conversation going. Last night, he rehearsed the perfect words to say to her to let her know just how special she was to him. But the moment came and went.

Addie, already outside, was bundled in her grey, wool riding coat and scarf and walking toward Mr. Darling and the wagon. "Coming, Mr. Darling."

Addie smiled for the first time in a long time and she wasn't exactly sure what caused it. Her cheeks, neck, and chest were still rosy from the awkward exchange with Garrett in the guest bedroom. However, the October wind was quick to cool her radiant skin and the hives disappeared. And with each step, she was eager to start her new life, one beyond the borders of Hope.

6

Friday morning, October 24, 1913, Second Ward

While the hospitals remained under construction in the Sixth Ward, the Sacred Heart and Alexander Hall leadership meetings took place in Edward's dining room. An exquisite room in its own right, it was located on the opposite side of the foyer from the Zoo. Grand embellishments included a three-hundred-pound crystal chandelier, a reproduction his wife, Trudy, asked for after she fell in love with the original while vacationing at The Greenbrier one summer. A mahogany table comfortably seated eighteen and was adorned with silver candelabras and white candles. The buffet table hosted a pair of Tiffany lamps and sat under a large, gold leaf mirror. A cart covered with a white linen table cloth with an embroidered, pastel floral design was home to the sterling silver coffee and tea service. Decorative plant stands filled with ferns, white orchids, Philodendron, and Dieffenbachia were carefully placed throughout the room.

Edward wanted to host the meetings at his private, members-only club. Unfortunately, women weren't allowed and that would have excluded Lena Marie Hartman, Superintendent of both the White and Colored nursing schools, from the important discussions. He had also thought about holding the meetings at The Georgian Terrace, a new luxury hotel that opened down the street two years ago. But he decided against it after he calculated that he could save a bundle in expenses. As a result, he opted to keep them in the privacy of his own home, which also prevented wayward listeners from overhearing their strategic business discussions.

"Well, let's get this meeting started, shall we?" Edward began. He tapped the end of his pen against his orange juice glass.

The door between the dining room and the kitchen swung open. Miss Mattie walked in carrying a silver tray filled with a basket of piping hot cinnamon rolls, buttermilk biscuits, and blueberry muffins. Butter, assorted jams, and fresh fruit were available in a variety of cut crystal bowls. She placed it at the end of the table in front of the six-member team. "Mr. Alexander asked me to cook y'all up breakfast nibbles this mornin'. I hope y'all enjoy 'em."

Edward sat at the head. To his right, sat Dr. John Williams, Medical Director for both Sacred Heart Hospital and Alexander Hall and beside him was the Chief Financial Officer of both institutions, Alan Waxman. Oliver Louis, Chief Operating Officer of Alexander Hall sat next to him. Nurse Hartman sat across from Mr. Waxman. Mr. Posey positioned himself in the remaining chair next to Edward.

"Does anyone care for any more coffee or orange juice?" Edward inquired.

"I'll take a touch more coffee." Clyde quickly raised his right index finger in the air indicating to Miss Mattie he was ready to be served first.

"I believe I'll take a refill, too, Miss Mattie. This all looks so delicious," Dr. Williams chimed in as he placed a blueberry muffin on his breakfast plate using a pair of silver tongs. Turning to Mr. Waxman and handing the tongs to him, he asked "Alan, do you care for a roll, muffin, or a biscuit?"

"I believe I would. Why, thank you, Dr. Williams." Using his napkin, Alan grabbed the end of the tongs. He reached for a cinnamon roll, placed it on his plate, and returned the tongs to the basket. He repeatedly wiped his hands four times before refolding his napkin four times and replacing it in his lap.

Dr. Williams, Mr. Louis, and Nurse Hartman chuckled and shook their heads as they watched one of Alan's many rituals. However, it didn't bother Edward in the slightest. Alan's eccentric nature also made him the one of the best financial managers he had ever worked with.

While the rest of Edward's staff filled their breakfast plates, Miss Mattie topped off Dr. William's cup of coffee and made sure she served Clyde last. After she completed his pour, she appeared to accidently spill a few drops onto his right pant leg. Clyde reared back in his chair as he snatched the napkin from his lap to blot the coffee stain. "Oh, Mr. Posey! I'm so sorry 'bout that. Here, let me help ya."

Clyde's face reddened. "No, no. I've got it. I'm sure it was just an accident. No need to make a fuss over it."

In complete agreement with Mr. Posey, Miss Mattie returned the coffee pot to the serving tray on the cart and exited the room with her apron bow bopping up and down with her every step.

Edward agreed with Clyde in silence. "Alright then, let's get to it. Dr. Williams, would you care to start with your updates about physician recruitment and the progress of the patient units and the operating suites? Also, please include the status on the acquisition of medical equipment."

Dr. Williams pulled out his notepad and glanced down at his notes. "I've got the curriculum vitaes for two fine physicians who both graduated at the top of their classes. Let me begin with Dr. Randall Springer. He is originally from New York, having worked at New York Hospital and The Children's Hospital of Philadelphia. I think he will make a great addition to Sacred Heart, not only on the pediatric ward and the nursery, but on the adult units, too. My next candidate is Dr. David Leventhal; he is from Augusta, Georgia. He attended the Medical College of Georgia, completed his residency at Northwestern, and his surgical fellowship at The Medical College of Louisiana. He comes highly recommended by my surgical colleagues. I'd be proud to have him on our team." Dr. Williams handed the papers to Edward. "After I receive the hospital board's blessing, I'll extend an offer to them. Regarding Alexander Hall's physician staff, I plan to begin scouting for applicants in the Fall, 1915 since we don't plan to open that hospital for four more years."

Edward looked through the stack of papers before passing them to Clyde. Lena, Oliver, and Alan took a moment to review them before they landed back with Dr. Williams.

"They both look stellar, Dr. Williams. By the way, what's the status of finding a doctor for our morgue?"

"I'm still reviewing applications and plan to have someone identified by our next leadership meeting." Dr. Williams informed them.

"Great! When that has been finalized, I'll present the physician and staff appointments collectively to the Hospital Board for approval." Edward took a bite out of his cinnamon roll followed by a swig of his coffee.

Dr. Williams continued. "Clyde, Oliver, and I met with the general contractor to procure the hospital beds and the operating tables that I've picked out. I've provided them with a complete list of medical supplies and equipment that we will need stocked in time for the grand opening.

We'll store Alexander's beds and equipment in the garage facility on the backside of the property until they are needed. The cost savings for buying in bulk now will save the hospital thousands."

Oliver and Clyde nodded in agreement to the group. Clyde added. "I'm on top of it."

Alan agreed and made a notation on his notepad to document the date, discussion, decision, and parties involved. He enjoyed keeping thorough journal entries of all his business phone calls and meetings. He prided himself on meticulous record keeping, should any decision ever come into question, legally or otherwise, he could trace the origin and dispel any rumors with facts.

"By the way, has a date been set yet for the opening of Sacred Heart?" Lena inquired, directing her question to Edward.

"As a matter of fact, it has. The hospital will open in May next year on Friday the twenty second to be exact. I've provided Clyde with the details so we can publish the news about our grand ribbon cutting ceremony in *The Atlanta Dispatch* and the other papers." Excited, Edward's eyes sparkled. "Clyde, let's review the press release that you've drafted for us. Oliver, take notes, because I'll have you create a press release for Alexander Hall and the Colored nursing school when it opens."

"Will do," Oliver replied as he picked up his pen.

Clyde sat up straight and proud in his chair, put on his spectacles and cleared his throat. Pulling out the paper Moira so graciously delivered to him on Monday night, he began, "For immediate release, Sacred Heart Hospital to celebrate opening with ribbon cutting ceremony on Friday, May 22, 1914. Edward Alexander II, Sacred Heart Hospital Founder and General Director, announces today that the 40-bed medical facility for whites will open on Friday, May 22, 1914. The hospital will consist of ten-bed wards for pediatric, medical-surgical, maternity, and tuberculosis patients. Chief Medical Officer Dr. John Williams plans to announce medical staff appointments in the coming months. The Sacred Heart Nursing School, under the leadership of Lena Marie Hartman, RN, is currently seeking potential applicants and plans to begin classes in April. Inquires can be made by…."

The kitchen door abruptly swung open. A five-year old boy carrying a bow and arrow, wearing an American Indian costume, burst into the dining room and began running around the dining room table. Sergeant, the Alexander's German Shepherd, barked wildly, in hot pursuit.

"Whoo! Whoo! Whoo! Whoo!" The young Indian's hand flapped over his mouth. "Look at me, Father! I'm an Indian! I'm an Indian! Whoo! Whoo! Whoo! Whoo!" Sergeant attempted to intercept the child by running under the dining room table between the chairs.

Alan stood up and shrieked. He flipped his napkin at the young boy and the dog. "Shoo! Shoo! Don't either of you come near me."

The boy paused, ignoring Mr. Waxman. He set his sights on Clyde. He pulled his bow string back, aimed, and released the plastic arrow. The arrow bounced off of Clyde's head and fell onto the table knocking the coffee cup into his lap. "Gotcha! You're dead!" Clyde quickly recovered the cup, replacing it back into the saucer.

Clyde jumped up, "Edward, please do something about your boy, immediately!" He blotted his crotch with his napkin. Lena attempted to help him with his efforts, thought otherwise, and instead offered him her napkin.

Edward burst out of his chair and tried to console Clyde while wrangling his son and the dog. "So sorry, Clyde." He called out. "Miss Mattie? Miss Mattie?"

Dr. Williams howled in laughter as Alan and his napkin sought refuge behind Oliver.

"Come here, Trip. Look son, you make a fine Indian, but your father is trying to conduct a meeting. Will you please apologize to Mr. Posey and tell him how sorry you are for spilling coffee in his lap."

"I'm sorry, Mr. Posey." Trip hung his head. His headdress slipped forward.

Breathless, Miss Mattie rushed into the room. "I'm so sorry, Mr. Alexander. Trip got away from me. I've been looking for him everywhere."

Trip readjusted the white, feathered head piece and looked up at his father. Sensing the chase was over, Sergeant came and sat patiently by his side, awaiting further instructions.

"Trip, go and mind Miss Mattie. If you don't, I'll be sure to send you to bed without dinner," Edward reluctantly scolded him.

"Yes, father. Come on, Sergeant. Let's go." With a look of disappointment in his eyes, the Indian and his side kick were escorted back into the kitchen by Miss Mattie.

"My apologies, Clyde. Are you alright? Please be sure to send me the laundry bill for your trousers." Edward patted Clyde on the shoulder before returning to his seat. "Now, where were we? Oh, yes, Clyde and the press release."

"I'm fine." Clyde pasted a subtle smile on his face and seated himself back into his chair, sliding the coffee cup and saucer further away from him. "I'll spare you the rest of the mundane details. I included the contact information for Lena's potential nursing school applicants."

Lena patted Clyde reassuringly on the back. "Thank you, Clyde. Great job!"

"Yes, well done." Alan and Dr. Williams chimed in.

"Clyde, I'm impressed. Make sure you personally deliver it to Sam Sloan, the Editor over at *The Atlanta Dispatch*. Put it into his hands and no one else's. Got it?" Edward wanted to be sure the press release didn't get tossed and lost in a pile of papers.

"Yes, Edward. I'll be sure to drop it off to Sam this afternoon." Clyde confirmed. "I'll do the same at *The Atlanta Journal* and *The Atlanta Constitution*. By the way, I'm still reviewing applicants to run our linen, housekeeping, dietary, and pharmacy departments, and for the concierge and ambulance driver positions."

"Can you have the nominations ready to go in time for our

next leadership meeting? I want to present all our appointments to the Board by the end of the year."

"Sure, Edward. Not a problem." Clyde scribbled a note to himself.

"Lena, what's the status of the nursing school applicants? Did you get my daughter's application yet?" Edward inquired.

"Yes, I've received Opal's along with five others. That leaves four more slots to be filled. While our entrance fees are higher than the other nursing schools in town, I'm confident that with the articles, we'll have the rest of the spots filled before the end of the year." Lena shuffled through her papers. She thought back to how she wanted to set Sacred Heart's Nursing School apart from the others.

She polled the nursing schools in the city and across the United States to research their admission criteria. Almost all of them required a minimum of just one year of high school and the girls had to be unmarried. Tuition costs were waived. However, they required the students to be on duty at the hospital from seven o'clock in the morning to seven o'clock at night. The number of days they worked compared to class time varied between three, four, and five days. In return, the student nurses received between five and seven dollars on average per month to work at the hospital. Alan and Lena agreed to set the bar and the admission standards higher, knowing they needed to balance costs and expenses. As a result, in order to enroll into Sacred Heart Nursing School, an unmarried woman who had at a minimum of three years of high school or was a high school graduate was eligible. Tuition costs were set at fifty dollars for the three-year program which covered the costs of books, room and board, and more impressively, uniforms.

Lena learned that many hospital-based programs required the students to make their own uniforms. She detested the thought of seeing how the instructions could be misinterpreted, leaving the final product to creative interpretation. While that was the vein of many contentious arguments with Alan, she finally won the argument when she explained that the Citadel and United States military uniforms were issued and not handmade by the soldier's girlfriends and wives. In order to be perceived as a professional, her students needed to set a new standard and look the part. She wanted her nurses to be different, clean, crisp, and unified. She prided herself on the stricter guidelines. Pleased with the outcome, she added, "I've also met the general contractor. We're on schedule to finish the nursing school classrooms and dorms by March. That will give us a month to prep everything before classes begin in April."

Alan made a few notes on his notepad.

Lena continued, directing her comment to Edward. "I'm thrilled that the City approved the underground tunnels to connect the nursing schools to both hospitals. That will make their travels back and forth so much easier, especially in all kinds of weather. It will also allow the doctors and nurses to flow freely between the buildings without interfering with the flow of hospital visitors and operations. I appreciate your support to make that happen. Your hard work has truly paid off."

Dr. Williams and Alan concurred. Alan shuddered at the thought of coming into contact with a gaggle of giggly, female students with contaminated uniforms. He worked quickly to find the extra funds needed for the project. In addition to the underground, private passageway, Alan was happy with the placement of his office in Sacred Heart. He was insistent on making sure it was located next to a side door so he had his own private entrance, allowing him to come and go as he pleased.

Edward leaned over to Alan, "How are the books looking?"

Alan peered through his spectacles and glanced down at his notes. "According to the balance sheets, we are over this month by about one thousand dollars, but not to worry. I still have to process the nursing student's checks that Lena gave me earlier in the week and the two thousand dollar check from the Masonic fundraiser last weekend. Next month, we will receive another installment from the state and federal governments. From now on, fundraising events will be crucial to continue to supplement the coffers."

Edward pulled out a gold watch from his vest pocket, flipped it open, closed it, and replaced it. "Great meeting, everyone. Alright, let's recap. Dr. Williams, at the next meeting you will have found a candidate for the morgue. Clyde, I'll meet with you next week to go over the status of the open positions. Lena, fill those vacancies. Begin outlining plans and the staff you will need for Alexander Hall's Training School for Colored Nurses. If, you'll please excuse me, I've got to make my way uptown to the Georgian Terrace for a meeting with my attorney within the hour. Stay the course and pull me in on anything that you feel requires my help or attention. As my daddy used to say, 'let's get to it and just do it.' I'll see you again next month."

"Will do, Edward," Clyde was first to respond. The others followed suit.

Edward stood, buttoned his suit jacket, and addressed them. "Remember, opening Sacred Heart Hospital and Alexander Hall is our calling, our duty, and our responsibility to the Atlanta community and Georgia at large. And I needn't remind you about our binding construction secret, do I?" Heads around the table shook in the negative. He continued. "It is our mission to improve the health and well-being of those we serve with a commitment to providing quality care, dedicated services, and an educational platform for tomorrow's nurses."

Edward's heart burst with pride. His vision was finally becoming a reality with every passing day. He knew this was the easy part; his true success would be defined by their daily operations and outcomes in the years to follow. The architectural plans and accounting ledgers flushed out the details so nicely on paper. However, once the unpredictable behaviors of people, pathogens, and politics were factored in, their course was set for uncharted territory.

7

Nearly a week had passed since Addie left Hope. She closed the front door behind her after retrieving *The Atlanta Dispatch* from Olive Gray's porch steps. She was still adjusting to her new morning routines to accommodate Mrs. Gray's whims and wishes which no longer included gathering eggs from the hen house, mucking the stalls, and feeding Ol' Girl.

Addie glanced over at the brass clock on the fireplace mantel. *Six forty-five. I have fifteen minutes before I help Mrs. Gray dress for the day.* The fashions and accessories used on a daily basis to revamp the city woman, although foreign, fascinated her. She was mesmerized by the transformation; a hair frame made of natural hair, used to style Mrs. Gray's thinning locks into a monstrous, fluffy, and luxurious pile on her head. Mrs. Gray taught Addie how to comb the thinning strands over the mold to help achieve the popular look of a pompadour. Hair collected from the brush comprised the false bun that was secured on top. Additional stray hair was made into ringlets which hung on either side of Mrs. Gray's face. Her fabulous assortment of hats sat atop, giving the appearance that they hovered over the perfect platform.

Breakfast was served promptly at eight o'clock at the kitchen table. By nine o'clock, Addie read the highlights from the morning paper while Mrs. Gray sipped her coffee in the parlor.

"According to the forecast, today will be sunny with temperatures in the mid-sixties. There will be a chance of rain showers tomorrow and Monday." Addie adjusted the paper to read aloud. "Explosive Ending to Construction Project on Panama Canal recaps how President Wilson triggered the explosion of the Gamboa Dike which ended the construction project. The article says they plan to open the canal in August, 1914."

Mrs. Gray tapped her cane on the floor in lieu of applause as she steadied her coffee cup in her hand. "How marvelous and exciting! I love hearing stories that illustrate how this world is getting back on track and rebuilding itself after that wretched war here in the states."

"Well, if that's the case, then you'll love this one. Sacred Heart Hospital to celebrate opening with ribbon cutting ceremony on Friday, May 22, 1914. Edward Alexander II, Sacred Heart Hospital Founder and General Director, announces today that the 40-bed medical facility will open in May, 1914. The hospital located on 422 Spring Street will consist of ten-bed wards for pediatric, medical-surgical, maternity, and tuberculosis patients. In compliance with the city's segregation ordinance, a separate facility for Negroes is under construction and slated to open in 1917. Chief Medical Officer, Dr. John Williams plans to announce medical staff appointments in the coming months. The Sacred Heart Nursing School, under the leadership of Lena

Marie Hartman, R.N. is currently seeking potential applicants and plans to begin classes in April."

"Oh, dear Lena. Good for her." Mrs. Gray rested her cup in the saucer that sat on a doily-covered coffee table in front of her. "She is a remarkable, Southern soul and a dear friend of the family. She's got quite a brilliant mind and is a forward thinker, especially when it comes to a woman's role in this world. I've heard her speak at various women's group meetings. Lordy, she is so passionate about advocating for a woman's right to vote and to have a voice in our government." She leaned forward and lowered her voice to a whisper as she spoke across the table. Addie scooted to the edge of the winged-back chair, straining to listen. "She even believes that a woman can have a position in the workplace right along with men." Mrs. Gray sat back, tapped her cane up and down on the floor and shouted. "Here! Here! How 'bout them apples!" She continued. "Doc Gray was always quite fond of her and looked forward to helping her teach classes at the nursing school. We first met her at a fundraising party four years ago at the exquisite home of Mr. Alexander's. My husband..." Mrs. Gray looked up, raised her right hand and shook it in the air and paused before continuing. "...God rest his soul, was slated to be the medical director at Sacred Heart until he suffered his heart attack. Dr. John Williams, another true salt of the earth and a dear family friend, stepped in to replace him. I do hope I'm around long enough to bear witness to the opening. I'd love to see it. What else does the article say?"

"The article concludes with instructions for potential nursing school students on where to send in their applications and how to contact Miss Hartman for inquires."

Mrs. Gray noticed Addie studying the article intently. "My dear, is that something that interests you?"

Startled and caught off guard that Mrs. Gray was reading her thoughts, Addie responded, "Gosh, I've never really thought about it until just now." *I've got the money that Maw saved. Perhaps that will cover the cost?* "By the way, how much does it cost to go to nursing school?"

"I'm not entirely sure. I can place a call to Lena if you would like for me to inquire on your behalf. Would you like me to talk to her and have her mail you an application?"

"Oh, my, would you? That would be so grand of you to do." *Wow! A nurse! How wonderful would it be to be surrounded by people who enjoyed the healing arts as much as I do!*

Addie reveled in the thought of going to school to become something more than a girl who lived on a farm. *No longer just a country mouse, but a nurse! I've always felt a keen sense of purpose when I've provided help to others when they were sick. To read about this new opportunity to be someone and to do something more with my life than just plow cornfields and plant corn causes my heart to patter with excitement at the prospect.*

"Well, that just settles it, my dear, Addie! You're about to pop just thinking and talking about it. I'll ring her up on Monday morning. In the meantime, we need to head into town to do some shopping." With assistance from her cane, Mrs. Gray got up off the couch. "I'll call my nephew, Lester, who can carry us into town in that fancy new car of his. I'm still trying to get used to riding in it. He's been working hard at selling a new medicine to ailing folks in town. I think it's called Doc Gray's Nerve and Blood Purification Tonic."

"He named it after his uncle? How thoughtful of him to do that!" Addie cleared the coffee cups and walked toward the kitchen. *I wonder why Garrett referred to him as a 'rotten peach?'*

"I know. Such a sweet one, he is. He's becoming a young, entrepreneurial businessman and making his fortune. It's pretty good stuff. I've been taking it ever since Doc Gray died and it really puts pep in my step. Lester says to take a tablespoon in the morning and I'm right as rain for the rest of the day. In the afternoon, sometimes, I take a sip or two more. But don't tell him that." Mrs. Gray put her crooked index finger to her lips.

"Oh, I won't." Addie did the same. She twisted the invisible key that locked her lips and tossed it over her shoulder.

Mrs. Gray laughed, paddling Addie's behind with her cane as she followed her into the kitchen. "Addie, dear, I'm taking you clothes shopping today. No more wearing these frocks in town." She used the end of her cane to lift up the bottom of Addie's hand-me-down dress. "This will not do for a young lady in the city."

Addie's thoughts immediately went to her tin box. Unsure of how much nursing school cost, she had to be mindful of frivolous expenses. Addie began biting her thumb nail.

Mrs. Gray lifted her cane up and guided Addie's thumb away from her mouth. "Please keep your hands out of your mouth. Doc Gray used to say that was one of the most important ways to prevent infection and stop the spread of diseases in addition to good hand washing. He had a saying, 'Wash your hands and say your prayers because germs and God are everywhere!'"

Addie laughed and stuck her hands in her dress pockets.

"Now, don't you worry about needing any money. It's going to be my treat. Consider it an early birthday present." Addie looked surprised. "Yes, my dear brother told me that your eighteenth birthday was on Christmas Day just like Baby Jesus'. Since I love the holidays, let's start celebrating today. Run upstairs and fetch my coat. We're heading out of the Fourth Ward to go uptown and shop at Rich and Brothers. I'll call Lester so he can carry us in his car up to Whitehall Street. By the way, Addie, we do need to do something about your hair. A young lady such as yourself needs to have a style that befits you. You are coming of age and in my humble opinion the braided ponytail needs to go."

Addie clutched at her ponytail. "How marvelous! I can't wait! I've only known how to fix my hair into a bun and a braid. But I'm not on the farm any more, am I?" Mrs. Gray shook her head. "I can't imagine what I will look like with a new hair style!" Without a moment to lose, Addie darted upstairs. *I'm not going to be a country mouse anymore!*

Before ringing her nephew, Mrs. Gray shuffled over to one of the kitchen cabinets and rested her cane against the countertop. She pulled out the flour tin from the back of the shelf, opened the lid, and removed a bottle of Doc Gray's tonic. After drinking a few healthy gulps, she returned it to its rightful place out of view. "Wow! Now that's better than a cup of coffee!"

The squeaky, hinged mail slot in the side panel next to the front door opened and closed. Letters fell into the brass container. Olive exited the kitchen and turned left down the main hallway toward the sound of the noise. She opened the mailbox and retrieved two letters. One was addressed to her; it was from the Alexanders. She opened it and read aloud. "Please save the date. You and a guest are cordially invited to attend Mr. and Mrs. Edward Alexander II's Christmas Dinner Party at their home on Saturday, December 20, 1913 at seven o'clock." She returned the invitation into the envelope. "Well, I'm no longer up for such soirées anymore. I'll just pass this along to Lester so he can represent the family at the grand event." She shuffled the unopened envelope on top of the invitation. The letter, addressed to Addie, was from Garrett Darling, Hope, Georgia.

Addie called over the upstairs bannister. "Did I hear the mail come? Was there anything for me today?"

Mrs. Gray put the letter into her dress pocket as she replied from the downstairs hall. "No, dear. Nothing for you today. I'm going to ring Lester now." She rapped her cane on the stair rail as she walked back to the kitchen. "Please be ready to leave in twenty minutes."

"Yes, ma'am." Addie rushed off to change into her best secondhand dress, a light brown dress that buttoned down the back. She had remade it to stay current with the fashion. Addie adjusted the ruffled neck to make sure the fabric hadn't folded in on itself and tied the matching sash into a bow in the back. Sitting on the edge of the bed, Addie buttoned up her boots. She retrieved her coat and hat from the closet. Before leaving the bedroom, she glanced into the dresser mirror one last time. A freckled face smiled back.

8

Addie assisted Mrs. Gray into her bedclothes and tucked her into bed for the night. Addie returned to her bedroom. Dress boxes lay in stacks on top of her bed. Sitting down in front of the mirrored dresser, Addie stared at the young woman in front of her. All traces of the farm girl from Hope were gone. Touching her face, she thought *I can't believe how my red, rouge-stained cheeks and lips bring a new dimension to my complexion, making my blue eyes even brighter. It's funny how Sissy and I use to play dress up with Maw, using crushed red berries for rouge and lip stain and coal from the fireplace for eyeliner. I'm amazed at how much I've bloomed in such a short amount of time.*

Her long hair easily held her new transformation in place without the need for extra hair pieces or extensions. She smiled at her reflection with a new air of confidence, genuinely pleased with the day's results. *I truly look like one of the models in my pasted, paper picture collage that I had always dreamed of becoming.*

Pulling out a piece of beige stationary from the center desk drawer, Addie decided to write a letter to Garrett. Taking the pen from the inkwell, she couldn't believe it had been nearly a week since they had their unusual conversation before she left his house. She didn't have much time to reflect on it after it happened until now. The thought of writing to Garrett caused her heart and stomach to flip with excitement. She had so much to tell him. *Where do I begin?*

25 October, 1913

Dearest Garrett, What a whirlwind week it has been for me. I can't thank your father enough for allowing me to stay and care for your Aunt Olive. She is so darling and I am truly enjoying my time with her. I find her in good spirits every day, especially in the mornings after our coffee. Sometimes the afternoons and nights are hard on her, but there are days when I find that she is happier than others. I can tell that the passing of your uncle has been hard on her, but I am helping her through these difficult times. Believe it or not, she is also helping me, too. I miss my family and the farm so much especially when I stop to think about all that happened. When I begin to day dream, usually your aunt paddles me on the behind with her cane to get me unstuck in my thoughts. She is a character! Speaking of characters, I've become acquainted with your older cousin, Lester. He carried Aunt Olive and me into town in his new car so we could go shopping, of all things! I couldn't believe how fast we could go and how smooth the ride was compared to horse and buggy. Aunt Olive says he is an entrepreneur, making a fast fortune selling a medicinal tonic that he named after your uncle. I can't say that I've tried it yet, but your aunt swears by it.

How are things on the farm? I'm sure the bank has repossessed our property by now. Is anyone asking about me? I surely hope not. If they do, tell them I went to go live with relatives. It isn't lying; they don't need to know I'm living with your family and not mine. I didn't have any one to live with anyway.

Oh, Garrett, being a town mouse is so much fun and yet very dangerous. I'm still trying to get used to looking both ways before crossing the road. In Hope, maybe we had one person travel our roads during the day. Here, I stepped off the sidewalk and nearly got hit by a speeding car. Thank goodness a man pulled me back by the collar of my coat or else I would have been a goner for sure!

By the way, how's your father? I can't thank you both enough for all you have done for me. Please give him my warmest regards. I look forward to seeing you over the Christmas holidays. We'll have so much to catching up to do. Until then, may God and his angels watch over you.

Fondly, Addie

P.S. Look forward to hearing from you soon!
P.S.S. Did I tell you how much I love being a town mouse!

Addie opened the desk drawer in front of her and pulled out an envelope. The Twain book rested next to her box of stationary. The pebble Garrett gave her rolled around inside the bottom of the drawer, catching her attention. Addie watched the gold flecks catch the light and sparkle. When it stopped moving, she picked it up, clutched the rock, and closed her hands to her chest. She smiled. *So, that's what Garrett saw in me in the sunlight.*

9

Wednesday afternoon, November 12, 1913, Third Ward

Lester steered his Pope Hartford 33 Roadster off of Factory Road, east of Oakland Cemetery and into the gravel parking lot next to Newman's Painting and Supplies Company. He shut off the engine, pulled out his snuff box from his coat pocket, and inhaled a scant amount of white powder. He brushed off the excess from his coat as he exited the car and walked up the side porch steps, proceeding through the front door. A tinkling bell announced his visit. Fumes permeated the air along with the smell of stale hay. The workers acknowledged his presence as he walked toward the back of the warehouse.

"Hello, Mr. Schwinn. How are you this fine day?" A teenage boy inquired as he passed him carrying a gallon of paint in each hand.

"Fuck off." Lester kept walking.

Caught off guard by Lester's response, the boy scurried off and made his way to a line of children sitting on wooden stools on the far side of the building filling containers with product.

Lester approached a man in his mid-thirties sitting at a

desk in the back of the building. He watched him shuffle invoices from one pile on the left side of the desk to the right side as he made check marks in a forest green ledger book. Lester only noticed his pinkish-purple scarred hands and fingers void of nails. The third, fourth, and fifth digits on his right hand were webbed. "Looks like your hands are healing nicely."

"I guess so. There's nothing like having a constant reminder of having lost my youngest son."

"Well at least you have your older daughter and your health." It had been eleven months since the gruesome accident when the two-year old toddler wandered off and fell into a chicken scalding pot. His death was instantaneous, Lester hoped. Uncomfortable and quick to switch the topic, he asked. "So, how are paint sales going?"

"What? The sight of my hands still bothers you?" He held them up. He displayed his fingers out like a fan as the sunlight illuminated the webbed ones. I'd wear gloves, but as you can see, they don't make any for this hand." He tried to wiggle the stiff, scarred fingers.

"Knock it off, for fucks sake. Try wearing mittens."

The gentleman laughed. "Orders are coming in from Tennessee, Ohio, Alabama, and even the Carolinas. I'm just double checking the invoices to make sure we are on time with the fulfilment schedule. So far, we're keeping up with the demand. Paint is very popular these days."

"Good. Good to hear it. I'm glad to know that the kids are doing their job."

"Be glad that we can get away with employing ten year olds for eleven hours a day. If the business was in North Carolina, they'd have to be at least twelve." He rolled a yellow pencil between the bumpy palms. "Lower wages for us means a better bottom line for the company."

"There's nothing better than a healthy profit margin. Allows one to reinvest into the company, expand business, and provide for bonus potential."

"Now you're speaking my language. What brings you in today?"

"Alvin Martin asked me to pick up a few gallons of paint for him. Thought I'd stop in, check in on you and drop them off to him at the pharmacy on my way to the Capital City Club."

"Sure thing. Got just what you need over here." He pointed toward a stack of silver paint cans against the wall. "How many gallons does he need?"

"Six gallons will do for now. If he needs more, he knows where to get it."

"Any specific color?" The man winked and laughed.

Lester laughed along with him. "White will do just fine. What colors are your best sellers this month?"

"Green is our most popular, followed by white and red. How would he like to pay for it?"

"Put it on my tab. I'll take care of it for him."

"No problem. Let me get a couple of kids to help carry those out to your car for you. Billy, Todd, and Mary, get over here now!" He commanded.

Three young kids stiffened and hopped off their stools. They ran across the room in a full sprint toward the gentleman.

"Great! I'd appreciate it. You know how I hate to get my hands dirty." Lester held up his hands and twisted them in the air.

The young man mimicked Lester's gestures. "I'd lend you a hand or two if I could." He directed his comments to the young, breathless laborers standing in front of his desk. "Mr. Schwinn needs six gallons of paint taken to this car immediately."

Lester laughed as he watched two boys and a young girl scurry off and pick up the cans, two apiece. "On one hand, I can see you are a shrewd businessman. On the other, I can see you are a big asshole." Lester turned to leave.

"Lester, my man, I can see you're still a bit...touchy." Bending his left thumb, second, fourth, and fifth fingers down with his right hand, he flipped Lester a bird behind his back with his left one.

Lester followed the children toward the front door. The front bell rang out as the door was opened. The sun cast a shadow on the brick wall in front of him. He saw the reflection of the man's extended middle finger. He looked back. "Nice, smartass. You're lucky I like you." Lester winked at him as he closed the front door behind him.

A cloud passed over the sun; the bird disappeared.

10

Friday morning, November 21, 1913, Second Ward

Edward tapped his pen on his orange juice glass to get everyone's attention. Miss Mattie emerged from the kitchen carrying sausage and egg biscuits on a white, porcelain platter in one hand. In the other, she carried a plate of freshly sliced bananas and strawberries. She carefully placed them on the table in front of the group who all sat in their respective chairs for every meeting.

She chuckled to herself as she recalled how everyone even has their favorite seat in their favorite pew at church. "Would anyone like more coffee or juice?" Miss Mattie rested her hands on her wide hips.

Alan responded, "I'll have a touch more coffee. Thanks, Miss Mattie. By the way, those cinnamon rolls you made for the last meeting were just divine. My mouth still waters thinking about them."

Miss Mattie clutched her hands. "Oh, that jest makes my day when my food touches someone's soul. I'll be sure to make some special jest for ya for the next meetin', ya hear." She retrieved the coffee pot and topped off Alan's cup. She looked over at Clyde who put up a hand in protest, indicating he had had his fill.

"Alright, let's get going. I've got to be uptown for my weekly meeting with my attorney by eleven o'clock. Dr. Williams, what's the status of finding a doctor for the morgue?" Edward passed the platter of biscuits around the table.

Dr. Williams pulled out the curriculum vitae for his potential candidate and gave it to Edward to review. "I've selected Dr. Morgan Paine for that position. He comes to us by way of St. Joseph's and Grady Hospital, having graduated from Atlanta Medical College."

Clyde hammered the table with his fist and laughed out loud. "Talk about what's in a name!"

"Huh? I'm not sure I follow you Clyde. I fail to see your humor." Dr. Williams looked perplexed.

"You're kidding me, right? Dr. MORG-an Paine? That's hysterical, just plain hysterical!" Clyde stopped for a moment and changed the timber of his voice to sound ghoulish and raised his hands in the air for effect. "Where ever did you find Dr. Death?"

Edward, Lena, and Alan caught on to what Clyde was insinuating. But they resisted joining in his laughter for fear it would come off as offensive to Dr. Williams.

Mr. Williams clearly understood what Clyde was saying, but failed to appreciate Clyde's juvenile humor. Taking a deep breath, he exhaled slowly. "As I was saying, Dr. Paine use to work at St. Joe's and Grady and has teaching experience. His knowledge of forensic medicine is first rate. With your approval, Edward, I'd like for us to add him to our staff."

Dr. Paine's papers rounded the table. Dr. Williams returned them into a folder. "His credentials are impressive and with fifteen years of experience under his belt, he will bring a level of expertise that will rival the other hospitals in town. I also believe he will be an asset to Lena when it comes time to teaching the nursing students AP classes."

"What the heck are AP classes?" Alan questioned.

Lena explained. "Anatomy and Physiology, Alan. You remember the dollars we earmarked to procure cadavers for the students? Well, they will be housed in the morgue. The students will receive their AP training not only in the classroom, but they will require practicum experience under the supervision of the morgue physician."

Alan turned a pale shade of his usual pallor. He waved his face with his hand and swallowed hard, preventing the sausage and egg biscuit that was rising from his stomach into his esophagus from making a quick reappearance in front of his colleagues. Regaining his composure, "I've heard enough. I completely understand. Thank you, Lena."

"Are you alright, Alan?" Dr. Williams scooted his chair a few inches from Alan after a quick assessment of his appearance and mannerisms.

"Yes, I'm fine. Please, let's move on with this meeting, shall we?" Alan wiped the beads of sweat that had popped up on his upper lip.

Dr. Williams handed the file folder to Edward.

"Fantastic work, Dr. Williams. I'll present all three of your recommendations to include, Dr. Paine, Dr. Springer, and Dr. Leventhal at the Board meeting next month." Edward flipped through his calendar book. "Looks like our next Board meeting is on Monday, December eighth."

"Clyde, what do you have for us today?" Edward already knew the answers, having met with Clyde on two other occasions to finalize the resumes of applicants and make the best selections for the vacant positions. Unconventional. It pleased Edward that he was hiring a Chinese couple and a Jewish woman.

Clyde removed a stack of resumes and began reading. "Maybelle Reed would be ideal to be in charge of the kitchen, better known as our Dietary Department. Mr. Joshua Goode came highly recommended by Edward and will serve as the head of housekeeping and maintenance. Mr. and Mrs. Wei and Ying Wu will oversee the laundry service. Moira Goldberg will serve as Sacred Heart's concierge. Alvin Martin is a well-known pharmacist...*my personal supplier*...in town and I'm looking forward to having him join the staff. The McDaniel Brothers, Brice, Rob, Tim and Jim will serve as our ambulance drivers. We purchased their private company to include two vehicles. Their existing contracts with a few of the city hospitals expire on March 31, 1914. Sacred Heart's ownership will begin effective April 1st."

Edward interjected. "That will give us a little over a month to get their uniforms ready, paint, and refurbish the trucks so they will be in good working order in time for the grand opening. In the meantime, I've also had them sign a confidentiality statement preventing them from talking about their acquisition. I don't want the other places to get any ideas about stealing them away from us."

"They are the best in town. Reliable, reputable, and responsive—everything you'd ever want in an ambulance service. By the way, which ones are the twins? I can never remember." Dr. Williams asked.

"Hey, I like that catchy slogan, Dr. Williams—'reliable, reputable, and responsive.'" Edward pointed at Clyde. "Please make a note about that and be sure to have that tag line added to the sides of the vehicles." Edward beamed with pride to have not one, but two motorized ambulances at his facility.

"Tim and Jim are the twins. Brice is the oldest followed by Rob according to the birthdates on their resumes." Clyde passed the resumes around the table before returning them into their respective folders and handing them to Edward.

Edward stacked the personnel folders next to him. "Lena, how's it going with our enrollment numbers?"

"I'm thrilled to announce that we've achieved our goal to fill the remaining four spots. Our ten students, to include your daughter, Opal, have been identified. Since the articles ran in the newspapers last month, I received ten more applicants. However, I had to reject more than half for not meeting our minimum entrance requirements. I've given Alan the reminder of those checks to be deposited. We'll be ready to begin classes in April." Lena relished the thought and looked forward to educating and training the new generation of nurses at Sacred Heart.

Friday afternoon, Fourth Ward

Addie tended to her afternoon chores, which included serving tea to Mrs. Gray in the parlor at three o'clock. Addie, lost in thought while dusting, remembered that she hadn't received any mail from Sacred Heart Nursing School or from Garrett for that matter. She stopped dusting and turned toward Mrs. Gray who sat behind her on the couch.

"Mrs. Gray, did you ever get a chance to talk with Nurse Hartman about Sacred Heart's Nursing School?" Addie resumed dusting, removing the bone china vase with hand-painted, blue irises that sat on the fireplace mantel in the parlor.

Mrs. Gray stopped sipping her cup of tea and promptly set it back down. "Oh, my Lord, dear Addie. I completely forgot to call Lena. It absolutely slipped my mind. Come to think about it, I'm having trouble these days keeping track of my thoughts. Thank you so much for reminding me. Let me go and place a call to her right now."

Mrs. Gray got up from the sofa, grabbed her cane, and walked into the kitchen to the Western Electric wooden wall phone. Picking up the ear piece and placing it next to her ear, she spoke into the mounted receiver. "Hello? Operator? Yes, please ring Miss Lena Hartman for me. Yes, I'll hold. Thank you." A few moments passed. "Lena? Lena is that you, dear? Oh, it's wonderful to hear your voice. It's Mrs. Olive Gray. I've got a question for you, dear. It's about your nursing school." Mrs. Gray stopped to listen while Addie strained to overhear the conversation from the parlor. Chuckling, she said, "Oh, no, dear. Not for me. I'm making the inquiry on behalf of my nursemaid. Yes, since Doc Gray passed on, I've needed some help. Her name? Addie Rose Engel. She's just a delight and will be turning eighteen next month. Yes, a December baby. Actually, she and Baby Jesus share the same birthday. Isn't that so special! Uh, huh. I couldn't agree more. Listen, we read about your new nursing school and I wanted to see about enrolling Addie into your program. What? You don't say. Oh. Well then. When will you begin recruiting for the next class? In the Winter of 1914. Okay. I will pass that information along to Addie. She was really hoping to get into your upcoming class. How much schooling does she have? Well, I'm not quite sure, let me ask her. Hold on for just a minute." Mrs. Gray covered the received. "Addie, dear. Can you come here for a minute? Lena wants to know how much schooling you've had."

Addie rushed over to join Mrs. Gray in the kitchen. "Tell her I graduated from twelfth grade in June of this year. I was a good student and completed my required classes. I have my diploma…." Addie paused then added. "I *had* a diploma, but it was lost in the house fire."

Mrs. Gray nodded. "Addie said she graduated high school in June of this year. Where? Hope, Georgia, dear. But unfortunately, she lost her diploma in a house fire. Yes, it was unfortunate. By the way, how much is tuition, dear? You don't say. Fifty dollars and that will cover room, board, books, and uniforms. And, how long is your program? Three years. Got it. Well, would you please mail an application to the house? Yes, I'm still at the same address. I love getting your Christmas cards every year. What? You moved? You don't say. I hear that the Ponce de Leon apartments are very exquisite. Yes, dear. Fantastic! Great chatting with you. You, too. Good-bye for now." Mrs. Gray returned the ear piece into the holder.

"What did she have to say?" Addie fiddled with the feathers in the duster.

"I've got good news and I've got bad news. The good news is that you meet their strict admission requirements and with my recommendation, you would be able to enroll. The bad news is that the Spring, 1914 class is full and you will have to wait and enroll in the Spring of 1915. It's a three-year program and they have tuition set at fifty dollars."

Addie clapped her hands together with excitement. "That's just wonderful news! I do have enough money saved up and I truly don't mind waiting a year and a half to get into her program." Addie threw her arms abound Mrs. Gray and hugged her. "Oh, thank you ever so much. It has always been a dream of mine to go to college and learn more about medicine and science. I just never thought about becoming a nurse until I came here. This is just remarkable. My Maw would be so proud of me."

"Oh honey. I'm sure she's looking down on you right now as your guardian angel. You have your whole life in front of you. You need to make it your own."

While still in Mrs. Gray's embrace, Addie envisioned her Maw smiling from above, recalling Maw's final words. *'I'll be your guardian angel.'* *Thank you, Maw! Oh, thank you!*

Friday evening, Hope, Georgia

Mr. Darling walked back from the barn and into the house. Garrett was stirring the beef and vegetable barley soup in a cast-iron pot on the stove.

"Smells grand! I'm starving. It was a chilly ride into town this afternoon."

"Was there anything at the post office for me today?"

"Sorry, son. There wasn't a letter from Addie. Don't worry. I'm sure she's got her hands full caring for your Aunt Olive. She did write you last month."

"Did you mail my other letter?"

"Yes, son. I gave the second letter to the postmaster today. We're going to be heading to Atlanta to spend the Christmas holiday at my sister, Mary's house this year. You'll be seeing Addie in a month. Don't worry."

"I know, Father. I really miss her. It's just so quiet here without her. I miss seeing her smiling face and hearing her laugh at my silly jokes." Garrett ladled out two bowls of soup and placed them on the kitchen table. "Sure would be good to have some of Addie's biscuits to go with our meal."

Mr. Darling ruffled the top of Garrett's head. "I'm sure she misses you, too, son."

"How'd your discussion go at the bank today? Will they sell the Engel farm?"

"Yes, they will. With the profits from our farm this year and the additional income selling the ginger root for Doc Gray's tonic, I had enough money to put a downpayment on the place. It was great to have Mayor Miller there with me and sell the bank executives on the collaborative plan we had to convert the farm into Hope's Guardian Angel Cemetery. With the Engel family plots already on the land, the town had been looking at sites to expand the town cemetery. The timing was perfect. The Mayor will hold a fund-raiser after the first of the year with plans to pick up the remaining monthly payments in 1914. We considered my part a donation which will help offset our taxes this year. The bank was ready to finalize the deal, close out their open 1913 accounts, and work with a 'dependable,' I think they meant, a *paying* client."

"What a great way to utilize the land and bring honor and dignity back to the Engel family.

Addie will be so touched by your generosity." Garrett reached out his hand across the table. Mr. Darling took his son's hand in his.

"Make me a promise, son, that you won't tell her about our plans for the family farm, not just yet. There is still some paperwork between the Mayor, the bank, and me that has to be finalized. I'd hate to tell her and then have something unforeseen unravel the deal."

"I promise."

While still holding hands, Mr. Darling and Garrett bowed their heads to pray before enjoying their evening meal.

II

Monday afternoon, December 8, 1913, Fourth Ward

Addie stoked the pile of wood in the fireplace. Reddish-orange embers flew up the chimney as the wood popped and crackled in the flames. She repositioned the ornate fireplace screen. Mrs. Gray had fallen asleep while enjoying her afternoon tea. Addie took the cream-colored, crocheted blanket from the arm of the sofa, unfolded it, and placed it on top of Mrs. Gray. There was a knock at the front door. Addie walked into the foyer and peeked through the sheer curtains on the sidelights. Lester, wrapped in a black, wool coat with a blue, wool scarf around his neck, stood on the front porch.

Addie opened the door. "Lester, good to see you. Come on in. What brings you here today?" Lester walked in the house and Addie closed the front door behind him. The frigid wind sent a chill through her body. "Are you here to see your Aunt?"

Hugging and rubbing his arms in an effort to warm him, Lester said, "Actually, I'm here to see you. I have a question to ask you, Addie. And, may I say you look radiant today. I believe your new hairstyle is most becoming."

Addie patted her hair, a bit self-conscious of the compliment. "Thank you, Lester. I still find myself getting used to the new look. But it's getting easier and easier for me to manage." Lester removed his overcoat and handed it to Addie. "I'd invite you into the parlor, but your Aunt has fallen asleep. Let's step into the kitchen so we don't disturb her. Can I offer you some coffee or tea?"

Lester followed behind Addie. He noticed she was no longer wearing her simple country clothes. She sported a new tailored, burgundy suit that accentuated her narrow waist. Her walking skirt accommodated her new gliding gait. He also observed that she carried herself with an air of sophistication that she had not shown when he first met her almost two months ago.

"No, I'm good. Thanks for the offer, though." Lester sat down at the kitchen table and pulled out a silver flask from his vest, uncapped it, and drank a few swallows. Addie frowned as she thought about bearing witness to her Paw's self-destructive consumption of the substance. Lester immediately sensed her disapproval. "Not to worry. It's medicinal. It's not alcohol, but the special tonic that I sell."

"I'm familiar with it. I've seen Mrs. Gray take it in the mornings, although I've never had reason to take it myself. She mentioned that your product was selling quite well."

"Yes, as a matter of fact sales are going through the roof. I just got back from Augusta. I'm thrilled that they're going to put Doc Gray's tonic on the shelves in their apothecaries." Lester handed her the flask. "Here, why don't you try some for yourself?"

"But I'm not sickly." Addie thrust her right hand out in protest.

"You don't have to be. Doc Gray's Nerve and Blood Purification Tonic promotes health and vigor." Lester released his sales pitch. "Can you believe that one hundred percent of my consumers report that they experience marked improvement in their levels of energy? They feel more productive during the day. The testimonials from over one hundred women state that Doc Gray's tonic helps calm their nerves and they don't feel anxious and stressed anymore. Tell me what product can deliver on those kinds of claims? Why Doc Gray's tonic can! It cleans your body of unwanted toxins and purifies your blood."

Addie recalled Paw running off a traveling salesman who tried to peddle pots and pans out of his old prairie schooner. He yelled at the man, 'Our cow died last night, so we don't need your bull!' Intrigued yet repulsed by the slimy pitch, she probed. "How?"

"Huh?" Lester was on a roll and completely caught off guard with her question. He didn't want to divulge how a sprinkle of cocaine, a jigger of spirits, ginger, food coloring, flavoring, and water were dispensed into a brown bottle with a label slapped on it that contained the name of a reputable physician could cure all.

"How exactly does it do all of those things you mentioned? What's in it to make it so special and unique?" Addie seated herself across from him.

Lester fidgeted in his chair at the kitchen table searching for an answer. "Well, uh, it's proprietary."

"Proprietary? I'm not sure what you mean by that."

"Meaning that the tonic consists of a top secret blend of special ingredients to do what it says it does and legally, I am bound from revealing them to you." Addie looked at him suspiciously. Lester needed her for the Alexander's Christmas party and selected his next words carefully so that she would trust him. "Because if I did tell you, it wouldn't be special and everyone would replicate it on their own. See?"

Not entirely convinced, but reassured that Mrs. Gray and Lester were still alive and breathing after taking the tonic, she convinced herself to try it. *What harm could it do?* Addie took the flask from him and drank from it.

"Woah! Don't drink too much." Lester pulled the flask from her lips and reclaimed it.

Addie winced as she swallowed. "Oh, my God! My insides are on fire." She clutched at her belly.

"Not to worry, give it a minute to work its magic." A few minutes passed. Lester waited with bated breath to see what she had to say next. He watched Addie's facial expressions change. She went from looking like she just ate a bitter lemon to a look of relaxed surprise. Her cheeks flushed and her eyes sparked with a surge of energy.

"Holy cow! I feel invincible and energized to go and clean the entire house and do the cooking and laundry. Wow! That's remarkable! I had no idea I could feel this way."

Pleased with the results, Lester returned the flask to Addie. "Here, take this. Ideally, take a tablespoon first thing in the morning and whenever you feel yourself overcome by nerves."

Addie touched her chest and neck, knowing the red blotches were always a tell-tale sign to anyone that she was nervous or anxious. *Maybe this will help?*

"Great! I have made a new customer today. I'll drop off a few more bottles for you and Aunt Olive tomorrow. Feel free to talk it up to anyone you know. They can purchase their supply from Alvin Martin's Pharmacy located on the corner of Whitehall Street and Hunter Street, two blocks south of the train depot. In the meantime, let me get straight to the point as to why I am here. I'd like to invite you to come with me to the Alexander's Christmas Party. You know who they are, right?"

Addie's head buzzed and words spilled out rapidly from her mouth. "Yes, he is the founder of the new Sacred Heart Hospital being built in town. Mrs. Gray and I read about their ribbon cutting ceremony in the paper last month. Me? Really? You want me to go to a party with you? Well, I'm not sure about that. Besides, I've got nothing fancy to wear for such an occasion."

Addie had never been invited to an extravagant party, let alone to step inside a mansion. Mrs. Gray described the place in great detail to her in previous conversations. But it never dawned on her that she could be a part of something so grand. It paled in comparison to going to simple town gatherings in Hope to feast together and sing Christmas songs while Mayor Miller played his fiddle, Mr. Darling strummed his guitar, the preacher played the washboard, and Garrett plucked his jaw harp.

Lester sensed Addie was completely unaware of her natural beauty and radiant charm. He noticed she lit up a room with her presence and easily engaged in conversation with others. She was polite and gracious, a far cry from the ladies of the night he typically associated with in deep, dark recesses of town. He recalled while they were shopping at Rich & Brothers, he observed men taking a second glance at her. Women, too, studied her fine features and relished her statuesque frame. While a farm girl walked into the department store, an elegant, young lady strolled out wearing an emerald green dress with a high collar. White ruffles peeked out from the edges of the sleeves. A matching wool wrap and felt hat, accented with peacock feathers, completed the look. Lester immediately concluded that Addie would make a stunning escort for him so he could get noticed by Edward Alexander. He wanted to be taken as a serious businessman and needed Alvin to get the pharmacy job so the tonic could be supplied to Sacred Heart patients. He knew that would solidify his reputation and standing in the Atlanta community, allowing him to expand his enterprise not only to other hospitals in Georgia, but in medical centers, infirmaries, and sanitariums across the country. Not one to take 'no' for an answer, Lester pressed. "Please come with me. The party is on Saturday, the twentieth at seven o'clock."

"I'm not sure." Addie fumbled for reasons while questions flew through her mind. *I've never been asked out on a date. What would Garrett say? Would that be too weird? Garrett's not here, is he? Have I received a letter from him, yet? No. Maybe he's set his sights on someone new. Perhaps one of the girls in town has struck his fancy? How would I know? He's there and I'm here. But he seemed so dejected when I left Hope. What am I worried about? Hurting Garrett's feelings? Oh, Lord. My head's buzzing and my heart's racing. I'm overthinking this.*

Mrs. Gray made her presence known in the kitchen doorway with the tap of her cane against the door frame which immediately shut off Addie's stream of consciousness. "Yes, you can surely go with my nephew, my dear, Addie. Between Lester's mother, Mary, and my closets, we have plenty of formals for you to choose from, plus some fabulous fur coats and jewelry. So, you don't need to worry about not having anything to wear. I believe you both will have a grand time together. It's high time you get out of this house and kick up your heels a bit."

"Are you sure about that?" Addie looked at Lester and Mrs. Gray.

"Absolutely! In fact, it will be a great opportunity for you to meet the Alexander family. And I bet Nurse Hartman will be there too. All the Atlanta movers and shakers will be at that party. I received my invitation from Trudy, but passed it on to Lester and asked that he represent the Gray family. Please do me this honor and go."

"I can't argue with you. I guess that settles it." Addie palmed the flask in her hand and stuck it in her skirt pocket.

Lester got up, walked over to Aunt Olive and planted a kiss on her cheek. He turned back to Addie. "Great! I'll pick you up next Saturday at six thirty sharp. Oh, by the way, Aunt Olive, I'll drop off a few more bottles of the tonic to you and Addie tomorrow."

Addie blushed, afraid of Mrs. Gray's reaction. But there wasn't one.

"Perfect. I look forward to seeing you tomorrow. Please give my love to your mother and father. I'm overdue for a visit with Mary. Tell her I'll ring her tomorrow."

"I will. No need to see me to the door. I'll see myself out." Lester pulled his coat on and wrapped his scarf around his neck before stepping out of the house. Once inside his roadster, he decided to drop in on Alvin at the store before it closed for the evening. It was located in the Second Ward.

Twenty minutes later, he pulled up in front of Martin's Pharmacy. The marquee was prominent. Tall, gold letters read clearly from blocks away. Bells clanged when he opened the door. "Alvin? It's me, Lester."

"In the back. Hey, will you flip the store sign to *Closed* and lock the front door for me?"

"Yea, sure." Lester did as he was instructed and proceeded to the back of the store. The interior was immaculate. The display cabinets were painted white and contained rows and rows of various pills, powders, compounds, pastes, and elixirs, including Doc Gray's tonic. He parted the heavy, tan curtains that separated the front of the store from the back and found Alvin grinding a substance into a fine, white powder using a grey marble mortar and pestle.

"It's good stuff. Here, try some." Alvin offered the bowl to Lester.

Lester licked the tip of his right index finger and stuck it into the bowl and tapped his tongue.

"Wow!"

"It's imported from China. Their heroin is the best."

"Hey, have you heard anything about your role at Sacred Heart yet?" Lester pulled up a chair and continued to watch Alvin grind away at the substance.

"Your timing is perfect. As a matter of fact, I have. I just got a call from Edward. My appointment as Sacred Heart's pharmacist will be approved at the next hospital board meeting, which will take place in two weeks." Alvin looked up and smiled, still grinding. "Looks like I'll help them get the pharmacy up and running in time for their grand opening next year. I've got to find a choir boy to run the store for me while I set up shop in the hospital. If you think of anyone, let me know."

"We've got to go out and celebrate your new position and the expansion of your pharmacy services! This is turning out to be a great day! What are your thoughts about kicking it off with a few drinks at O'Malley's pub, then heading down to Mr. Chang's for some entertainment?"

"Count me in. In fact, Mr. Chang is my supplier for this new stuff. I need to thank him for his assistance."

"If you mind me asking, how's he smuggling it into the states?"

"He's using bags of coffee beans to get his heroin supply into the country. He's a genius, I tell you." Alvin tapped the pestle against the bowl.

"Hey, by the way how did those six gallons of paint work out for you? Was it enough?"

"Yes, they worked out perfectly. I'll probably have to get some more in a few weeks." Lester watched Alvin pour the contents into an airtight container and write *ASA* on the label. "I'm ready to call it a day, how about you?"

"ASA?"

Alvin laughed. "It stands for acetylsalicylic acid — *aspirin*." He unlocked a cabinet door, placed the container on a shelf, and relocked it.

"I heard a story from my friends who worked at the large pharmaceutical companies about how it got its name. Did you know that they thought about calling it *Euspirin* because they feared consumers would associate the word *aspiration* with the product?" Lester shook his head, indicating he was unfamiliar with it. "I guess stronger minds prevailed and they settled on the name *aspirin*."

"Ah, but to *aspire* can also mean to rise up, to hope for something greater does it not?" Lester countered.

Alvin laughed as he put on his winter coat. "Yes, it does, my good man. Yes, it does. And, on that note, I have great aspirations in store for us this evening on Hulsey Street!"

12

Saturday afternoon, December 20, 1913, First Ward

Moira reached out to Clyde and tried to pull him back down into the bed with her. "Please don't go yet. We've got the rest of the day to spend together."

Clyde slipped out of her grasp and reached for his clothes that were folded neatly on her bedroom chair. "Actually, I don't. I need to get ready for Edward's Christmas party this evening."

As he bent over to pull up his trousers, Moira leaned out of the bed and threw one of her boots at him. It struck him in the buttocks.

Clyde spun around. "What the hell was that for?"

"I'm still pissed at you for not taking me as your date to the Alexander's party."

"For the last time, I told you why I can't take you with me. You will be my employee as the Sacred Heart concierge. You know that I can't be seen in public cavorting with you. It will give the appearance of impropriety. We can't risk that, can we?" Moira conceded and shook her head.

"Edward trusts me and I need his trust." Clyde stepped over

to her side of the bed as he adjusted his neck tie. He leaned over and grabbed the back of her hair with his left hand. Moira let out a yelp. While he pressed his lips to hers, he cupped her left breast in the other and pinched her nipple. Standing back up, he reached into his pants pocket, pulled out a handful of bills, and sprinkled them over her. "Look! It's snowing! Go and treat yourself to something nice. Consider it an early Christmas present."

"But you know I'm Jewish!" Moira laughed as she lay back down and swung her arms and legs in and out which spread the bills all over the bed.

"What are you doing?"

"I'm making a snow angel in this heavenly pile!"

Saturday evening, Fourth Ward

Addie didn't recognize the beauty in the mirror staring back at her. After trying on numerous dresses, the consensus was for one of Mary's deep purple, velvet formals with beaded capped sleeves. It suited Addie's tall frame best and the location of the beaded empire waist was perfect on her. The v-shaped neckline framed an amethyst tear drop necklace, an anniversary gift to Mrs. Gray from the late Dr. Gray. Addie clipped on the matching earrings. Mary helped her put on the cream, full length, silk gloves and attached the amethyst bracelet to her right wrist which completed the three-piece set.

"Oh, and for the finishing touch, I have the perfect tiara for you, my dear, Addie." Mrs. Gray said as she and Mary placed and pinned the silver and crystal encrusted accent on the top of Addie's head which already contained purple tinted, ostrich plums. Mary insisted that Addie's hair had to be higher for the evening affair so feathers were added to give it extra height. Copper curls abounded and a few cascaded down her back. Mrs. Gray reached for her atomizer and spritzed Addie's neck and all around her head.

Addie sniffed the air. "It smells like gardenias. How delightful!"

"And I have one more thing for you so you don't catch your death out there in this winter night air." Mrs. Gray left Addie's bedroom and returned carrying a full length, reddish-brown ermine coat. Addie slipped it on. Since the coat accommodated Mrs. Gray's buxom bodice, it gapped a bit in the front. "Not to worry, dear. Simply close the front lapels together and fasten the elastic band around the button located under the left collar." Addie secured the coat at the neck. "There, no more gap!" Mrs. Gray prided herself with the quick fix and tapped her cane on the floor in approval.

Mrs. Gray and Mary took a step back and marveled at their afternoon's work. "You look like an angel, Addie." Mary said, "I wish your parents could see you now." She wiped the tears from her eyes with a lace handkerchief. "They wouldn't even recognize you."

Addie gazed back at the image in the mirror. *They wouldn't recognize me. I don't recognize me. I look like a princess!* Addie embraced both women as they all dabbed their eyes.

"Hey! I'm here!" Lester called upstairs from the front hallway. "Is Addie ready yet? It's time for us to go, so y'all can stop primping now."

Mary pivoted on her heels and was the first to leave the room, followed by Mrs. Gray. They made their way downstairs to greet Lester. "Son, I did not raise you to shout and raise your voice in our house and that rule applies while you are in Aunt Olive's home. Do you hear me?"

Lester's cheeks flushed. "Mother, I'm nearly twenty years old. Please stop treating me like I was your little boy." He directed his next comment to his aunt. "Sorry for yelling upstairs, Aunt Olive."

His aunt gave him a swift pat on the behind with her cane. "You know you're never too old to mind your manners and your elders, Lester."

Before Addie started her descent down the front staircase, she reached into her dresser drawer. *Come to think of it, this is my first real date! How weird is it that it's with Garrett's cousin? God, I hope I don't mess it up.* She uncapped Doc Gray's tonic bottle. She took a big gulp. *I think I need a little more liquid courage.* Addie downed another swallow, secured the cap before replacing the bottle, and proceeded to make her way downstairs.

"My goodness gracious, Addie! You are a sight for sore eyes. You're really gussied up. You look like an angel." Lester was enchanted, his mouth agape.

"That's what we said, too." Lester's mother leaned over and lifted his chin to close his mouth. "Lester, please take good care of Addie and enjoy your time at the party."

Lester opened the front door and Addie walked out onto the front porch. He caught the fresh scent of gardenias and pine and quickly realized that Aunt Olive's Christmas tree was responsible for the smell of pine. He loved this time of year and looked forward to seeing his cousin Garrett in a few days. He thought about talking Garrett into helping him sell his tonic in North Georgia. He knew the Darlings didn't need the money. His uncle did quite well from the farm and from the ginger root that was used to make the flavoring for the tonic. Lester wondered if Garrett would want to make his own mark and have an opportunity to gain his own financial freedom. Realizing it was a discussion for another day, tonight he had to focus on gaining Edward's trust and help capture the Sacred Heart account.

Once in the car, Addie wrapped herself in a blanket that Lester gave her. She lost herself in thought. *I can't believe how in a matter of months, my life has been so drastically altered. I miss Maw, my family and Garrett so much. Why hasn't he written me yet?*

Hope, Georgia was a mere memory, a dark past that paled in comparison to this new, bright one in the city. The street lamps were ablaze illuminating their way uptown to the Alexander's Christmas party. They rode through town in silence, each lost in their own thoughts. Lester concentrated on what he was going to say to Edward while Addie gazed at the signs of Christmas as they passed each block. Wreaths dressed with red and green ribbons adorned the front doors and some houses even had wreaths hanging from red ribbons in each window. Garland and red bows wrapped porch banisters, columns, and store fronts. There was so much to look at. Each house was unique and beautifully different when compared to the one next to it.

A left turn off Houston onto Courtland led them into a sordid and lively part of town at the intersection of Decatur Street. The smell of food and sex filled the night air. Ladies of the night prowled the streets as Addie observed cars slowing down to let their hourly companions get in. Red lights blinked from windows. A Negro man blew on his trumpet, while another accompanied him on his sax and a drummer kept the rhythm of love stirred up from a nearby alley. Electric street cars clanged. After crossing over the railroad tracks south of the city, Courtland turned into Washington Street in the Second Ward where the mansion windows glowed white from within and lit candles flickered in the window sills. The street corners were void of loiterers and gas street lamps illuminated their route. The decorations, like the houses, were on a grander scale than she had seen in the Fourth Ward and other parts of town.

Breaking the silence from the twenty-minute drive, Lester announced. "We're here!" Lester pulled the car up to an attendant, who was dressed in a black tuxedo with a heavily starched white shirt and black bow tie. He wore a black top hat and stood on the sidewalk of the monumental mansion.

He opened the passenger side door for Addie. "Good evening, ma'am. Welcome to the Alexander's House. I do hope you have a memorable time here."

"I will. Thank you, sir." Addie tried to soak it all in as she stood in front of the house while Lester instructed the attendant on where and how he wanted the car parked. *I didn't realize that parking a car could be such a mammoth task. Lester sure is a strange and persnickety little fellow. Even though they are all related, he is a completely different man than Garrett.* Then she saw Lester take out a tiny, circular snuffbox. He inhaled, wiped his nose, and returned the box to his coat pocket.

"Are you ready to make our grand entrance?" Lester took

her arm in his as they walked up the front steps that had a red carpet laid down just for the event. Massive, white pillars were wrapped with red ribbons. Wreaths decorated with Baby's-breath hung from red velvet ribbons from every window.

Addie had to know. "What were you were doing by the car?"

Lester knew she wasn't referring to the conversation with the parking attendant. "It's purely medicinal." He added. "It's for my sinuses."

Addie looked at him suspiciously. She knew in her heart he was lying. Addie had observed their family doctor in Hope use cocaine for a variety of ailments, but concluded Lester's use was recreational. Addie recalled that he gave her the same look when he described Doc Gray's to her at the kitchen table a few weeks ago. *He was even lying to me about* Doc Gray's. *What does he have to hide?*

Addie's questions were immediately dismissed once they walked through the colossal, double-front doors that Edward had Tiffany custom design with stained-glass windows. Another pair of attendants dressed in formal attire acknowledged their presence and took their coats. The sights and sounds overloaded Addie's senses. A fourteen-foot spruce, decorated with gold and silver Christmas ornaments, bows, and ribbons, stood in the foyer. Plums of white feathers were carefully placed throughout the tree. A gold star encrusted in various jewel-toned crystals sparkled on top. Conversations buzzed from every space in the mansion. The aromas of fresh meats, prepared dishes, and desserts permeated the air. The aromatic scent of pine added another fragrant layer. Alternating red and white poinsettias cascaded down the foyer stairs. Fresh garlands simply dressed with sprigs of Baby's-breath was strung along the semi-circular, wrought iron staircase rails and hung from fireplace mantels in the Zoo, dining room, and the Great Hall, a room located in the back of the house that stretched the entire length of the residence. Lester and Addie made their way through the throng of guests in the various rooms and emerged into the Great Hall.

"I still can't get over Edward's office and all of those stuffed animals! And, that bear! I had no idea their fur was so soft."

A pianist playing Christmas carols on a black, grand piano was accompanied by a string quartet in the far corner of the left side of the room next to the two-story, Georgia granite fireplace. On either side of the room were two separate, yet identically decorated seating areas that contained two Celadon-colored sofas that faced each other with matching chairs capping the ends. Bookshelves on the far right-hand side of the room, next to the kitchen door, were decorated with various books, plants, and figurines.

A waiter offered Lester and Addie a glass of champagne from his silver tray. They took a glass.

"Cheers! Here's to a fabulous night." Lester raised his glass in a toast.

Addie took a sip and rubbed the tip of her nose. "The bubbles tickle my nose."

"Have you ever had champagne before?" Lester asked raising an eyebrow.

"No, this is my first time." Addie took tiny sips, savoring the popping sensation as it danced on her tongue.

"Enjoy it! Drink away!" Lester scanned the room and locked his sights on a man. "Hey, if you will please excuse me, I need to go talk with Mr. Alexander, that gentleman over there." Lester discretely pointed to a distinguished man who appeared to be in a deep discussion with three other men as they stood by the fireplace. All were dressed in a tuxedo suits and were smoking cigars. "Why don't you see your way into the dining room so you can fix us a plate of food?"

"Alright, if that's what you want. I'll be happy to." Addie and Lester parted ways and she made her way to the doors on the right that led through a hallway that connected the various rooms and ran end to end through the middle of the house. The entrance to the dining room was in front of her. She emerged into another grand room. *Wow! This is where they eat their meals every day? It even has a fireplace in it!* The dining room table caught her eye. It was the longest she had ever seen and it sat under an enormous crystal chandelier. Gazing at it, she remembered the tiny kitchen table that use to have five happy people sitting at it by candle light. *Gosh! We used our kitchen table to play jacks, make home-made, egg noodles, mend, and sew clothes, and jar jams and jellies.* Then the memories faded, replaced with the image of the bloody knife lying on the table. A young lady standing next to her interjected, which immediately erased the horrible image from Addie's thoughts.

"It's pretty large, isn't it? Mother had the chandelier replicated after seeing one she loved at the Greenbrier. It's a real thing of beauty. Father had to have the ceiling reinforced to accommodate its weight," said an eloquent young lady who appeared to be about the same age as Addie. She was dressed in an emerald green, beaded gown with a black, satin ribbon cinched around her waist and tied into a bow in the back. She noticed

Addie studying the style of her strawberry-blonde hair. "Don't you just love it? It's called a *chignon*. Sounds fancy, doesn't it? Hey, my name is Opal Alexander. What's yours?" Opal extended her white, gloved hand.

Addie, still reveling over the size of the table, the extravagant room, and light fixture, graciously shook Opal's hand. "I'm Addie Rose Engel. It's a pleasure to meet you."

"I've not seen you here before. Are you new to Atlanta?"

"As a matter of fact, I am. I use to live in...*Hope, no pick something a bit more glamorous...*North Georgia. *That narrowed it down a bit!* Addie took a sip from her glass and proceeded to empty it.

"Do you mean near Rome or Athens?" Opal waved over a waitress carrying a full tray of assorted cocktails. She lifted two glasses of champagne from the tray. "Thank you, Eve."

"Um, yes. That's correct. I lived somewhere between Rome and Athens." Addie took the glass from Opal; they toasted and proceeded toward the dining room table that was covered from end to end with an assortment of food the likes of which Addie had never witnessed before.

A thirty-pound roasted turkey filled with stuffing sat on a fine, china platter. Orange slices garnished the breast bone. Sliced ham and roast beef led to various side dishes to include green beans, corn, peas, mashed potatoes, gravy, yeast rolls, followed by a bowl of mixed fruit, and cheese trays. Iced pound cakes, pumpkin, peach, and apple pies sat beside a silver tray of cookies, petit fours, and macaroons.

Opal reached for a black cookie. "These are my favorite. They're a new kind of cookie. I think some of our guests would be completely flabbergasted if they knew that they're made by Yankees from New Jersey. Isn't that just simply scandalous?" She twisted it apart to reveal a white, creamy filling. She licked it. "It's so yummy. Here, you've simply got to try one. They're heavenly. Father likes to dunk them into his glass of milk at night." Opal handed Addie the black confection.

"But it's burned." Addie studied it.

Opal howled. "No silly. It's supposed to be black on purpose." She touched Addie on the shoulder. "My, you are a funny one."

Overcome, Addie recalled the paper heart collage surrounded by dried flowers on her bedroom wall. She had read and heard about such magnificent residences, but to step inside and see how these people lived marveled her. Addie twisted apart the treat and licked at the filling inside before crunching on the hard wafer. *Opal didn't have to grow up and learn how to plow cornfields, do chores, let alone birth a cow! I can't even imagine what it would be like to wake up to servants, prepared meals, and live in a place where all you did was fret about how to fashion your hair or what to wear. So, this is what it's like to be a wealthy, city mouse just like those smiling, effortless, paper women on my old, bedroom wall.*

Staring at the spread on the table, hunger pangs pained Addie's stomach. With the combined side effects from Doc Gray's tonic, the champagne, and tasting the sweet, delectable treat, Addie was ravenous. Using silver tongs, she and Opal plated samplings from the various dishes and filled their plates.

"Addie, Come with me. I'd like to introduce you to my older sister, Pearl, and her friends, Laura, Michelle, and Abigail. I must forewarn you, they can get a little catty, so don't take it personally," she whispered.

Addie's head buzzed as she followed Opal to the corner in the front of the room, close to the windows that overlooked the side porch. Pearl, in sharp contrast to her sister, had dark, black hair, and harsh features.

She cackled with her girlfriends, giving the appearance that they were gossiping about something outrageous. "You should go to the New Year's ball with Lester, especially since he asked you," Pearl said to Abigail.

"Why don't you come with us, Pearl? I heard you like *balls!*" Abigail fired back, threw her red head back, and snorted with laughter.

Miss Mattie, catching the word 'balls' as she set a fresh cheese tray down on the table, immediately flew over to quiet down the raucous conversation. "Young ladies, you need to be aware that you are talkin' entirely too loud and people can hear what y'all are saying." She glared at Pearl. "Now, please simmer down before somethin' is said to your parents. They would be completely mortified by your behavior."

"Yes, Miss Mattie. We promise to be good girls from now on." Pearl smirked behind Miss Mattie's back as she walked away.

Miss Mattie, keen to Pearl's and her girlfriend's ways, quickly turned back to catch Abigail thumbing her nose at her. Miss Mattie glanced up at the ceiling. *Lord, grant me the patience to deal with those ungrateful girls. Amen.* Then she turned her back to the girls and her attention back to the guests.

Abigail excused herself from the group. "I believe I saw Lester come in here earlier. I'm going to find him to let him know I'm going with him to the *BALL.*" She set out to find Lester in the crowd, exited the room, and headed toward the Great Hall.

Opal introduced Addie to the remaining group of ladies.

Curious, Addie picked up the conversation where it left off. "Did I overhear that Abigail is going to a New Year's Eve Ball with Lester? Did she mean Lester Schwinn?"

"Yup. That's the same one. I hear he's making a fortune selling his medicine. Hey, didn't I see the two of you come into the party together? Are you with him as his date tonight?" Pearl inquired. The remaining friends strained to hear Addie's reply.

"Yes and no. Yes, I came with him to the party. No, we're not dating, if that's what you mean." Addie thought it best to refrain from explaining the whys and hows of their relationship and knowledge of each other especially with this group. She agreed with Opal. *They are a catty bunch at first blush.*

Ready to size up Addie to see if she was a threat or any kind of competition, Pearl interjected, "Do you know who my daddy is?" She continued without waiting for Addie's reply. "He is the founder of the new Sacred Heart Hospital that is being built in Atlanta. It's going to be the grandest hospital in the South, in the country, even."

Not to be undone, Laura chimed in. "Well, my daddy founded Georgia Bank that helped loan the money to your father for his project."

Addie emptied her glass as the third bird on the wire started chirping about her father's accolades.

Michelle's head wobbled as she spoke. "Well, my daddy saves lives and is one of the top surgeons in Atlanta. He's going to be the Medical Director at Sacred Heart."

Pearl and her girlfriends stared inquisitively at Addie. "So, what does your father do?"

Addie felt the room beginning to sway and her chest flushed. *Well, my daddy...drank too much, smoked, spent all our hard earned money, vanished for days, beat my Maw and me, burnt the house down, and died. Did I leave out the part where my Maw killed herself and my Paw held her dead body in his arms on the front porch swing while the house went up in flames?*

Feeling tipsy, Addie lost her balance, fumbling her plate. She tried to recover it and instead watched food fly all over Pearl, Laura, and Michelle. The plate crashed to the floor and miraculously didn't break. Instead, it rolled across the dining room floor while guests jumped out of its way before it came to a stop under Miss Mattie's foot.

The shrill shrieks of three women pierced through the entire house, stopping the musical ensemble in the Great Hall and all conversations in the house came to an abrupt halt.

Miss Mattie, quick to salvage the situation, directed. "Carry on, someone just dropped a plate. Not to worry," Miss Mattie called out to the crowd as she picked up the plate. Mrs. Alexander and Lena, who had been conversing in the foyer, also came in to investigate the matter. Since the origin of the screams was not a matter of life or death, the music and conversations resumed. Upon seeing the three girls she just previously reprimanded covered in gravy, powdered sugar icing, peas, mashed potatoes, and bits of meat, Miss Mattie bit her lower lip and glanced up at the ceiling again. *Oh, Lord, I am in awe. You do answer prayers mightily quick like.*

A small crowd gathered around the girls to see the site and all watched a piece of sliced ham slide slowly down Pearl's décolleté, disappearing under the bodice of her dress. A piece of mashed potato flopped out of Michelle's hair onto the floor.

At that very moment, the door the kitchen flew open. Trip and Sergeant burst into the room. Sergeant barked and followed Trip. "Mother! What's going on? Did I miss anything? Did someone die?"

Sergeant ran over and began jumping on Pearl eager to find the slice of ham or any kind of remnant to savor. "Get this mangy mutt off of me!" Pearl cried out.

"Pearl, you and your friends are such a mess! Look at you!" Tripp pointed and howled in laughter as Pearl and her friends burst into tears.

Trudy ushered her son back into the kitchen while Lena lured Sergeant out of the room with a slice of roast beef.

Before Miss Mattie had a chance to help Pearl and the others, she observed the color drain out of Addie's face. Mattie grabbed Addie's arms to prevent her from collapsing onto the floor. As Lena returned from the kitchen she also observed Addie passing out and quickly grabbed a dining room chair and assisted Miss Mattie. Together, they placed Addie into it.

"She's got the vapors." Miss Mattie said to Lena. "I'll go and fetch a cool cloth and some water. Be right back."

Opal fanned Addie with a napkin and helped Lena prop her up in the chair.

With all the attention going to Addie, Pearl wailed at the top of her lungs, "What about me? Don't you see it's all about me?"

Trudy returned from the kitchen carrying a cold cloth with Miss Mattie in tow, carrying a glass of water. Trudy along with the rest of the guests in the foyer and dining room heard Pearl's outburst. Trudy handed the cloth to Lena and approached

Pearl. Discretely, she asked, "What about you, Pearl? Even if you are standing in high cotton, don't get above your raising." She shooed them out of the room. "You girls go on upstairs and get cleaned up. You're old enough to take care of yourselves. There are plenty of other dresses in your closets for the three of you to change into." Trudy dismissed them and rejoined Lena, Opal, and Miss Mattie as they tended to Addie.

Pearl and her friends glared at Trudy before stomping out of the room and made their way upstairs.

"She's comin"round. I can see it in her eyes. What's her name? Did she come here with anyone?" Miss Mattie asked Opal.

"Her name is Addie Engel. I just met her a few minutes ago. Yes, she came with Lester Schwinn. I believe he's in the Great Hall. I'll go and get him." Opal ran into the Great Hall and quickly spotted Lester talking with Abigale on the couch closest to her. Making her way to him, she stuck her head in between their faces. "Hey, sorry to interrupt, but your date passed out in the dining room. It's probably best that you take her home now."

Lester looked mortified and then embarrassed. Realizing that the shrieks from the dining room were probably caused by Addie, he jumped to his feet and tried to rally. "Abigale, if you'll excuse me. I'll ring you later this week so we can finalize our plans for New Year's Eve."

Lester followed Opal into the dining room where he found Addie propped up in a chair supported by Trudy, Lena, and Miss Mattie.

Lena was trying to remember why the name Addie Engel sounded so familiar to her. She had heard it before. It dawned on her that Addie was Mrs. Gray's nursemaid.

"Lesss-ter. Is that you?" Addie squinted and slurred. She reached out to him, but he took a step back.

"Oh, dear God! Is she drunk?" Appalled, he panicked, realizing Addie may have ruined his standing with Edward and the possibility of getting the Sacred Heart account as a front door attendant handed Lester their coats. Lester was not happy about leaving the party so early, especially with Governor Slaton and Mayor Woodward somewhere in the crowd and he had not yet made their acquaintance. Gruffly, he said. "Come on, Addie. Can you stand? It's time for us to go."

"Shhhuure, I can sss-stand." Addie rose to her feet and wobbled into Lester's arms.

"Here, let's put on your coat." Lester fed her arm in one sleeve, then the other as the guests stared at them and spoke to each other in hushed voices.

Bearing witness to many inebriated guests, elected officials, and aldermen over the years, Miss Mattie, Trudy, and Lena didn't give Addie's incident a second thought. Trudy surmised she was the first of many casualties of the evening and rejoined the party while Lester managed to carry Addie into the foyer. Addie caught a glimpse of the bear on her way out the front door.

"Grroowl. I can snarl like a bear." Addie hoisted the ermine coat over her head, disappearing inside it. "Did you know that? Grroowl. Can you snarl like a bear, Lesss-ter? I bet you can!"

"No, I will not. Now shut up," he said between gritted teeth as he pulled the coat down. Addie's head reappeared. Growing more impatient, Lester hastily helped her down the front stairs and waited for the valet to retrieve his car. When it arrived, he shoved her into the passenger seat and threw the blanket over her head.

"Hey, who turned off the lights?" Addie uncovered herself and waved at the valet who closed her door. "I'm having a truly memorable time tonight!"

He chuckled to himself, knowing that she was the first of many tonight.

"That was a fan-tas-tic party, Lesss-ter." Addie bobbed her head and it came to rest against the passenger side door. She passed out.

Lester sped down the street and turned left onto Crumley. He came to a stop at the corner of Capitol and Crumley and looked up at the converted former mansion of S.S.S. tonic's tycoon, Charles Thomas Swift, now called Piedmont Sanitarium. Tempted to leave Addie on the doorstep, he knew he wouldn't hear the end of it from his mother and Aunt Olive. He surmised that Aunt Olive would probably remove him from her will and put an end to Doc Gray's tonic. His foot slammed on the accelerator and he sped off through the Atlanta streets, heading his roadster toward the Fourth Ward. Thirteen minutes later, he pulled up to Aunt Gray's house, kept the car running, and ran around the front of the car. "Addie, wake up. Get out of my car." Lester slapped her face to arouse her.

"Hey! That hurts. Why are you slapping me?" Addie got her feet under her and walked with Lester's assistance to the front door.

He grabbed the inside of her arm and squeezed it hard. His eyes sparked as he viciously whispered in her ear. "I haven't begun to hurt you, yet, you ungrateful little tramp. All you had to do was look pretty and play your part. But no! You had to ruin my night, you ungrateful little farm girl bitch!"

Horrified, Addie's head spun. *Who are you? Why do I feel so weird? What happened to me tonight? I remember being at the party and now I'm on Mrs. Gray's front porch. I met some nice people, like Opal, Mrs. Alexander, Miss Mattie, and Lena. Oh, God! Not Nurse Hartman. Oh, my God! Have I blown my chances for to enter nursing school? Did she know who I was? Will she make the connection? I don't feel so well. He's hurting me. Like Paw hurt Maw. I'm not going to stand for this...not any more. He's really making me mad. How dare Lester or any man for that matter treat me in this manner? I've had enough!* Fire pulsed through her veins. Addie opened her mouth and whispered into his ear. "Lester, go to hell! You're a weasel, a chameleon. You have everyone fooled, but not me. You're a snake charmer. You're a fast talker, but I've got the goods on you, don't I?" Addie pulled back and studied his face. She read his eyes and spotted his tiny, dark soul. She had discovered his weakness and knew her truthful words were piercing his heart. She surged on. "I've seen plenty of your kind fly through Hope, selling this and that. All claim they work miracles, but in fact many people I know ended up sick, addicted, or dead from whatever elixir, medicinal or not, they were peddled. I think your Doc Gray's tonic is bad for people." Addie took in a deep breath and slowly exhaled. "I don't feel...." Addie tried to take a step back, but he grabbed her arm tighter and pulled her to him. With that last bit of motion, she threw up all over him.

"What the hell? What the hell is wrong with you, Addie?"

Addie couldn't believe the verbal vomit that flew out of her mouth let alone the real vomit that followed. Feeling better for the moment and clear headed, she left Lester standing on the front porch. She entered the house and walked upstairs to go to bed. *I think I've experienced enough for one night as a town mouse!*

Lester fumed. He ran to his car, removed his coat, and wrapped it in the blanket before he got back into the driver's seat. The car tires screeched as he did a U-turn in the middle of the street and headed around the corner to his home on Jackson, where he lived with his parents. He slammed his fists down onto the steering wheel. "Fuck you, Addie Engel!"

Addie undressed and slipped on her nightgown. After drinking a glass of water, she sat on the bed and recounted the evening's events. *God! I am so embarrassed for passing out at the party, but I know in my heart that* Doc Gray's *tonic isn't restorative or medicinal, especially if it's combined with alcohol.* Addie's cheeks flushed at the thought. *Did I ruin my reputation and standing to enter into Sacred Heart's Nursing School? In the morning I need to explain to Mrs. Gray what happened to. Perhaps she will know how to address the situation and deal with her wayward nephew.*

Though she was proud of herself for speaking her mind to Lester, the words she'd used shocked her. *All the years of seeing and experiencing Paw's wrath came out tonight as pent up rage. I didn't realize how much anger and resentment I harbored, until now. So much pain and so much loss spilled into Lester's ear — and onto his coat! There's one thing I know for certain and that is I am right about* Doc Gray's *tonic. I saw fear lurking in Lester's eyes. He's hiding something. But what is it?*

Addie wrestled with her thoughts and concluded that typically family tends to side with family. She was an outsider. But it was a risk worth taking. Mrs. Gray needed to hear her concerns about Doc Gray's tonic especially since her husband's good name was attached to it. More importantly, Addie also needed to address Lester's behavior and she would have to be cautious in her discussion with Mrs. Gray. She felt compelled to tell her the truth, yet feared how Mrs. Gray would respond. *Mrs. Gray has been so gracious to me. However, this could potentially cause a great divide between us. I could lose everything. Garrett isn't here to talk to and I still can't believe I've not received a letter from him. Without a true family of my own, who else do I have turn to?*

13

Sunday morning, December 21, 1913, Fourth Ward

Seven o'clock came way too early for Addie. Sunshine peeked through the lace curtains, alerting her that she had only an hour to get breakfast fixed for Mrs. Gray. Her head throbbed from the evening before. Addie decided her first order of business was to make a strong pot of coffee. Her second was to discard any bottles of Doc Gray's. She collected various bottles in the house to include the one Mrs. Gray had hidden in the flour tin in the kitchen cabinet and the one tucked away in her dresser drawer. Addie dumped the remaining contents into the bathroom sink before tossing the bottles into the garbage can outside the back of the house.

At eight o'clock, Mrs. Gray descended the stairs from her bedroom. Addie could tell that she was walking slower than usual as evidenced by the sound of the cane taps on the floor.

Mrs. Gray stepped into the kitchen and greeted Addie with a hug. "Good morning, dear."

Without skipping a beat, "Did you enjoy your time at the Christmas party last night? I can't wait to hear all of the details." Mrs. Gray sat down at the kitchen table.

"Yes, ma'am. I did. I do have a lot to tell you over breakfast. But first, may I ask are feeling okay this morning?" Addie scrambled the eggs and flipped fried slices of bacon in the cast iron skillet.

"I had a fitful night and a hard time sleeping. I just tossed and turned. When I did drift off to sleep, I had some vivid nightmares. Nothing that I can recall, just that I didn't have a peaceful night's rest. I did get up at some point in the night to take some pills that Lester gave to me to help me sleep. But I hate to take them. I tend to wake up foggy headed and as a result I move slower than usual."

Lester and his cure-alls. Addie huffed. She poured a cup of coffee for Mrs. Gray and returned to the table, setting down two plates of eggs and bacon. As she pulled out the chair to seat herself, there was a knock at the door. "Who could that be at this hour?" Addie said. She walked down the front hall, opened the door, and gasped. "Lester, what brings you to the house at this hour of the morning?" Addie stepped aside to let him in and closed the front door. He was already halfway down the hallway, making his way into the kitchen.

"Good morning, Aunt Olive." Lester leaned over and kissed his aunt.

"To what do we owe the honor of your presence this morning? Oh, I know, you *both* want to share with me your stories from last evening. How delightful! Do sit down and pour yourself a cup of coffee."

Flustered, Addie's cheeks and neck broke out in hives. She was unsure why Lester was here. *Oh, God! Is he going to tell Mrs. Gray about last night? If he tells her what I said to him, I'm fired for sure!* Aware that her hands were shaking, she stuck them in her dress pockets. "Can I make you some breakfast?" Addie asked. *I'm amazed at how well-groomed and composed you are this morning compared to the filthy-mouthed, vomit-covered, urchin I left on the porch last night!*

"Why, thank you for offering, Addie. But I've already eaten breakfast at Mother's." He stood up and pulled out the kitchen chair for Addie. "Have a seat while I pour you both some more coffee."

Lester and Addie locked eyes. She searched them to find the shriveled soul, fear, and fire she saw in them last night. Instead, she saw a reflection of herself and reluctantly took her seat.

While Addie and Mrs. Gray enjoyed their morning meal, Lester fiddled with the coffee pot. "Let me gather your coffee cups so I don't spill anything on Aunt Olive's lovely linen tablecloth." Lester removed the cups and saucers. With his back turned to the kitchen table, he discreetly removed a vial containing a clear liquid and poured half of the contents into one cup and the remaining amount in the other. He topped it off and returned to the table. "Here you go, fresh and hot."

Addie refrained from saying a word and waited for Lester to speak. "Has Addie talked with you about our evening together last night?"

"Why, no. Not yet. She was just about to tell me all about it." Mrs. Gray took a sip of coffee.

Addie did the same, holding the cup with both hands, fearing Lester would see her trembling.

"We had a wonderful time together. Addie looked stunning and the Alexander's house was decorated to the nines. Did you know they had a fourteen-foot Christmas tree in the foyer that had silver and gold Christmas ornaments on it? And, the food, well the spread of food covered one end of the dining room table to the other. Didn't it, Addie?"

Addie nodded in agreement. Fear settled in her eyes as she observed the exchange between the three of them. *What is he doing? Why is he acting so calm? Surely, he's going to turn the tables on me any moment.* A cold chill rippled through her body, causing her to spill the remaining contents of her coffee cup onto the kitchen table.

"My goodness, I'm such a clumsy one this morning." Addie rose to her feet to reach for a dishtowel and fell unconscious onto the floor.

At that very moment, Mrs. Gray finished her second cup and her head fell into her breakfast plate.

Lester picked up his aunt's head by the back of her hair and released it to fall back into her remaining scrambled eggs. "Aunt Olive, I'm *not* sorry for shouting in your house last night and let me remind you that you will *never* paddle me with your cane again."

Lester calmly got up and kicked Addie in the stomach. Her body remained lifeless on the kitchen carpet. "Addie, you came from nothing, you are nothing, and you will be nothing. You will never amount to anything in this world." He kicked her again.

Then he made his way through the rooms of the house, closing the parted white lace curtains in the parlor and the dining room. He walked upstairs and rummaged through Aunt Olive's bureau. Inside one of the drawers were boxes of jewelry. Removing them one by one, Lester settled on a strand of pearls with matching stud earrings. He returned the boxes to their original location and walked into Addie's room. He found nothing of interest in her dresser drawers. He turned his attention to the mirrored desk, sat down, and pilfered through the drawers. In the center, he found a copy of *Mark Twain's Quips and Quotes*. He took it out and flipped open the front cover. Inscribed inside he read, *To Garrett, Merry Christmas! Love, Mom and Dad. December, 25, 1907.* Below that it read, *To Addie, Happy Birthday! Fondly, Garrett. December 25, 1913.* He snickered as he closed the book and stuck it back in the drawer. Lester also saw the rock, picked it up, glanced at it, and threw it back into the drawer before closing it. Moving to one of the side drawers, he found a shiny, silver tin tucked in the back; he opened it to find rolls of money wrapped in twine. *Jackpot!* Lester emptied the tin and put the money into his coat pocket. He put the tin back where he found it and shut the drawer. Looking at his image in the mirror, an evil grin emerged. Pleased with his plan to thwart Addie's confession to reveal anything about last night to Aunt Olive, he was glad he intercepted the situation before it got out of hand. He glanced at his gold pocket watch. *Eight-thirty.*

Lester walked down the stairs and secured the front door, making sure it was locked. He decided to wait an hour before he would return to the house to find them passed out and save the day by calling an ambulance. He would be a hero in his Aunt Olive's eyes. Addie would know it was a warning to keep her mouth shut and to never to make inquiries about Doc Gray's tonic again, especially if she still wanted to be employed by his aunt. He also knew that once she discovered that her money was missing, she wouldn't dare report it to the police.

Her job was too important to her. Now she really had nothing. He liked having that power over her. He returned to the kitchen and stood over their bodies. He prided himself on the execution of his plan and his attention to detail.

Lester spoke to the unconscious bodies. "This is just a warning." He exited out the back door of the house and walked home.

True to his plan, Lester returned to Aunt Olive's house an hour later to discover Addie and his aunt still unconscious. He made a big production of calling the telephone operator, who summoned the motorized ambulance. He made sure the two ambulance attendants took them to Grady Memorial Hospital, giving them each a handsome tip. He thought he heard one of them singing a hymn as he pulled away from the curb. He wasn't sure and didn't care. His fetched his mother, Mary, who accompanied him to the hospital in his car.

Insisting he take charge of the situation, Lester secured his mother in a waiting room on the first floor. He made his way through the building, making inquiries until he found the admitting physician, a high school friend, Dr. Mathew. Lester spotted him in a hallway on the second floor and called out.

"Why, if it isn't Lester Schwinn? How are you my dear man?" Dr. Mathew tucked a patient's chart under his left arm and shook Lester's hand.

"Good to see you, Dr. Mathew. I understand that you admitted my aunt, Olive Gray, and her nursemaid, Addie Engle."

"Yes, I sure did. They're in a ward down there," he replied, pointing toward the end of the hallway.

"Great. Thank you so much for looking after them. I must tell you that in my humble opinion, I believe they have been battling the flu. As a matter of fact, Addie told me not to come by the house yesterday because she was sick to her stomach and complaining of severe stomach pains. Aunt Olive must have caught the bug from Addie and it was too much for her system to handle at her frail age." Lester was pleased with the fabricated story.

"Thank you for that information. It's always hard to determine the exact causes of illness especially if your patient is unconscious. Your information is very helpful and we'll be sure to take good care of Doc Gray's widow and her nursemaid. I've got them in a room together.

Would you care to check in on them? I believe you will see that they are more alert and resting comfortably now." Dr. Mathew handed the patient's chart off to a nurse passing by.

"Sure. I'd love to see them. Thank you." Lester followed Dr. Mathew down the hall and into the ward.

The room contained a total of six beds. There were three on one side and three on the other. Two of the beds on the far side of the room closest to the windows housed his aunt and Addie. Dr. Mathew pulled apart the curtains separating the beds. The sound startled Addie awake; Aunt Olive remained asleep.

"Aunt Olive? Can you hear me? It's Lester." Lester tapped on her shoulder to arouse her.

Aunt Olive awoke, confused by her strange surroundings, the sight of Dr. Mathews, and that of Addie lying on the bed next to her. "Where am I? What happened?"

"You're at Grady Hospital. I found you and Addie passed out in the kitchen. It must be from the side effects of the flu," Lester said reassuringly.

"The *flu*? I don't have the flu? Weren't we all just having breakfast at my house?" Aunt Olive rubbed her forehead and tried to sort out the facts as she remembered them.

"Heaven's no. I wasn't with you for breakfast. You must be delirious. You did hit your head...*on your breakfast plate*...when you passed out. I'm sure Dr. Mathew will take good care of you." Lester kissed his aunt's cheek and strolled over to Addie's bed. "So how are your stomach pains? Are you feeling any better?"

Addie clutched her stomach. Her insides ached. *Why? What did he do to us? Aunt Olive was right. He was with us at breakfast.* Addie tried to piece the events together. *I opened the front door; he sat with us in the kitchen. He poured us more coffee. The coffee! He must have drugged us with the coffee.* She wasn't sure why she hurt so badly. She rubbed her belly.

Dr. Mathews watched Addie wince as he palpated her abdomen over the sheets. "I see you're still tender? Not to worry, I'll have the nurse give you something for the cramping and pain. When I examined you when you came in, I noticed you had some bruising on your belly. You must have struck something when you collapsed." Addie remained silent as he flipped through the chart that hung from the foot of her bed. Lester paced the floor behind him. "It looks like your vital signs are normal and you don't have any evidence of a fever. While that isn't common for the flu, perhaps you contracted a stomach virus of some sort instead. I believe you got dehydrated and passed out." He scratched his head and walked over Aunt Olive's bed. He reviewed her chart, his admission notes and vital signs again. Aunt Olive had drifted back to sleep. "I can't explain why she would have passed out. Do you know if she experienced any vomiting or diarrhea yesterday?"

"I'm not sure," Addie stammered as she watched Lester glare at her while he paced the floor behind Dr. Mathew.

Lester stopped moving and interjected. "You know, my aunt is a very discreet woman about those matters. If she was experiencing those symptoms, we'd be the last to hear about it."

Dr. Mathew accepted Lester's response. It seemed logical. In his experience, elderly women were stoic and not forthcoming about their ailments, especially their bowel habits. "I plan to keep you both overnight for observation. If you can tolerate clear liquids and we can advance your diets to solid food, then I'll send you home tomorrow." He replaced Aunt Olive's chart on the hook. "Come, Lester, let's step into the hallway so the nurse can administer their shots. I'll have one of the nurses ring you in the morning to update you on their status so you can pick them up and take them home tomorrow afternoon, that is if they do well tonight."

As Dr. Mathew and Lester walked out of the room, Lester turned back and stared at Addie. He lifted his index finger to his lips then proceeded to swipe his index finger across his neck.

Addie wanted to scream *Lester is pure evil! He tried to kill us! Dr. Mathew, please come back!* She feared for their lives. *Lester will stop at nothing to make sure I stay quiet about his tonic!*

A few minutes passed. A nurse entered the room and administered the shots, but not before Addie had a chance to lift the sheets and slide the gown over to one side to see that her abdomen was bruised in several places. Before she drifted off to sleep again, Addie couldn't believe it. *Bastard!*

Addie awoke hours later as a nurse adjusted the covers on her bed. She glanced out the window and saw the stars in the night sky. "What time is it?"

"It's eight o'clock. You and Mrs. Gray have had a very restful day. How are you feeling?"

"Just fine, thank you."

"Are you interested in eating anything? I brought Mrs. Gray some chicken broth. Would you like some?"

Addie glanced over at Mrs. Gray who was sitting up in bed sipping broth from her spoon. "Yes, please. I'd love some. Thank you."

The nurse left the room.

Addie swung her feet out of the bed and sat on the edge. "Mrs. Gray, what happened to us? Are you feeling alright?" Addie held her stomach and rubbed her head.

Mrs. Gray set her spoon down on the tray. "Addie, dear I may be an old woman, but my bulb still burns bright. Do not mistake me for a dim-witted individual. I know for a fact that Lester was with us this morning at breakfast. Am I wrong about that?"

"No, ma'am. You aren't wrong about that and we don't have the flu." Addie got up and excused herself to use the restroom. While washing her hands and face, she glanced at her reflection in the mirror. *I've got to tell Mrs. Gray the truth and run the risk of uncertain consequences. Lester scares me and he is getting out of hand with his unpredictable behavior. He's willing to harm his aunt and me in the process. He must be stopped!* Addie returned to sit on the edge of her bed. During her absence, the nurse had set up a bedside tray with a cup of hot tea and chicken broth. "I need to tell you what really happened last night at the Christmas party."

Mrs. Gray adjusted herself to sit on the side of her bed to face Addie. "Go on, dear. When you finish, I admit that I have a bit of a confession to make to you, too."

Addie couldn't imagine what it had to do with, so she continued. Addie ate her soup and drank her tea while she recounted every last detail, including Lester covered in vomit on her front porch, to Mrs. Gray, who sat on the edge of her bed listening in amazement. Addie decided to leave out her foul-mouthed rebuttal. She tried to stay strong while retelling the story. However, her emotions took over. She started crying. "I...I...I think we're here because Lester wanted to try and stop me from talking to you about my concerns about Doc Gray's tonic. It made me so sick last night and caused me to pass out. I'm so embarrassed! I think Nurse Hartman was there. If that's the case and she connects the dots, I fear I may have ruined my chances to get into her school."

Tears streamed down Mrs. Gray's cheeks too as she tried to process all of the information. "Addie, it took a lot of courage for you to tell me the truth. I applaud you for your bravery. You have been through so much. It breaks my heart that my nephew would act in this fashion. I know my sister; Mary tried to raise him under strict rules, but that boy knows how to bend them to his advantage." Mrs. Gray smiled a sweet smile. "I've taken to you, Addie. You know that, don't you dear?"

Addie nodded her head. "I've taken to you, too." She wiped her tears.

Mrs. Gray took a deep breath and exhaled. "Based on what

you've told me, there are three issues to be addressed. First, apologies must be made on behalf of the Gray family to the Alexander's and Lena. We'll explain that you simply got the vapors after sampling champagne on an empty stomach. That will clear that matter up and I predict it will have no ill effect on your status with Lena and your entrance into Sacred Heart's Nursing School. Please remind me to contact them tomorrow afternoon when we get home. Don't give that occurrence a second thought. I'm sure you were one of many who passed out at that party. Just be glad they didn't find you behind a potted plant wearing a lamp shade on your head! Ha! Oh, my goodness!" Mrs. Gray clapped her hands together. "That reminds me of the time when they found Alderman Cotton dressed in one of Mrs. Alexander's dresses in bed with a waiter in their guest suite at their New Year's Eve party about five years ago. Lordy! Addie, there are so many stories that pour out of every pore of this city when the lights go out at night. Believe me when I say that your fainting episode doesn't even register as a memorable event. Now, if you are an elected official and have eccentric sexual habits, then you may be worth talking about." She winked at Addie, who giggled in relief and marveled at Mrs. Gray's candor. Mrs. Gray continued. "Second is how to address your concerns about Doc Gray's tonic? When Lester was getting started, he had me sign some paperwork that allowed him to use his uncle's good name. When I pressed him about the ingredients, he dismissed me and explained it away saying it was proprietary information."

Addie jumped in. "When I asked him the same question, he gave me that exact same answer!"

Mrs. Gray nodded her head. "He further explained that he

was working with one of Atlanta's well-known pharmacists, Alvin Martin, and not to concern myself about it. Doc Gray never liked Mr. Martin and I never knew why. I always trusted my late husband's judgment about people. It sounds like there may be more to the story than Lester lets on."

"So, you do believe me?" Addie waited to hear Mrs. Gray's response. Her fate hung in the balance. *Will she trust me? Does she see Lester for who he really is or will she side with him in order to protect the family name and reputation?*

"Addie, I'll have his head on a spike if I find out he's ruined Doc Gray's reputation with a tainted product. Yes, my gut tells me he's up to no good and after this morning's shenanigans that landed us here—with the *flu?* I do believe that your concerns are valid."

Relieved, Addie popped up from the bed, threw her arms around Mrs. Gray, and hugged her.

"What's all this for?"

"I was so afraid that you wouldn't believe me. Worse, that you'd fire me for speaking ill of your nephew."

Mrs. Gray looked at her lovingly. "Addie, if there is one thing I know, it's that I've come to love you as if you were one of my own. I think Doc Gray sent you as my angel on earth to look after me. I was so lost when he died. But when you came to my home, you were a radiant ray of sunshine that filled my days with purpose and hope again. I pray for good things to come to you, Addie. You have endured enough pain for a thousand life times. I want to see your wishes and dreams come true. That's what is inspiring me to get up out of bed every day. It's you, Addie. I never want to lose you let alone fire you."

Both women embraced and cried. The night nurse walked in. "Everything all right here? I heard someone crying. Are either of you hurt or in pain?"

"No, we're just fine. These are tears of joy." Mrs. Gray waved her away.

"Okay. Please let me know if you need anything. It's not often that I find my patients crying happy tears. It's a big relief to know that you both are feeling better," the nurse said as she departed the room.

Addie sat beside Mrs. Gray and took her hand. Mrs. Gray cleared her throat and took a sip of water. "That brings me to the third and final issue that is troubling me, and that has to do with Lester's strange behavior. He did this to us, didn't he? He gave us something that caused us to pass out."

Addie squeezed her hand. "I believe it to be true. And, truth be told, he scares me. I'm so afraid that he tried to send me a message to keep my mouth shut. He's afraid I'll say something or discover something about the tonic. What are we going to do?"

Mrs. Gray pondered the question for a moment before she spoke. "It's apparent that he intends to cause us harm. I think it's best that we not say anything to anyone in the family at this time, and that includes Garrett. But I do have a plan that I'll not reveal to you so you can have pure deniability if Lester were to ask you probing questions. Leave it to me and I'll take care of the details."

Addie nodded in agreement. "I understand and I completely trust you."

"There's one more thing I need to tell you. Please don't think poorly of me. I was afraid of losing you or that you would leave me to go back to Hope."

Addie was unsure of what she was trying to say. "I love being with you. I don't have any plans that include returning to Hope."

Mrs. Gray patted Addie's hand. "You need to know that Garrett has been writing to you every couple of weeks."

Addie shrank back.

"I've got three unopened letters in my wardrobe closet for you. I know your heart pines for him because every time you speak his name your eyes light up. I was so afraid you would leave me for him. I'm so sorry." Mrs. Gray hung her head and lifted it to look into Addie's eyes. "I truly apologize for my bad behavior and for withholding his letters from you. When we get home, I'll give them to you. I promise. Can you forgive this old, foolish woman?"

Bewildered, Addie struggled to respond. *Garrett did write to me after all. I'm sure he wonders why I haven't responded to him. How could she have kept them from me? This is such a strange family. I need to give full consideration to the circumstances. More importantly, she believes in me and trusts me. Dear God, grant me the strength to be just as understanding and forgiving. Mrs. Gray and I are going to need each other now more than ever, especially if we're to discover Lester's secret.* Touched by Mrs. Gray's sincerity and relived to know Garrett still cared enough about her to write, Addie responded. "I forgive you. But let's promise to not keep anything from each other again. As crazy as these as these past few days have been, I think it has actually brought us closer together."

"I couldn't agree more!" Mrs. Gray extended her hand to

seal the deal with a handshake. "Tomorrow is a new start to a brand new day and we'll need all our energy to get ready for our Christmas company and your birthday. Promise me that you won't speak a word of this to Garrett—not about the Christmas party, the tonic, or Lester."

"I promise."

Mrs. Gray sat back in the bed and tucked her feet under the covers while Addie placed a blanket over her. For the first time, Addie kissed her on the forehead. "I love you too, Addie."

Addie's heart melted. It pained her to hear the words and she remembered that the last time she said 'I love you' was to her Maw a few months earlier. She turned off the lights, got into bed, and glanced up at the night sky. She imagined the day when she would wear a white uniform and have the opportunity to care and comfort patients like the nurses were doing for her and Mrs. Gray today. She felt sure that these life experiences were testing her resolve and seasoning her for the road ahead in order to make her a better, stronger person. She had left Hope without a family to call her own and now she had Mrs. Gray. That was the best Christmas and birthday present she could ever wish for, and she had learned that Garrett did indeed write her back. *Thank you, Maw. I know you are watching over me. I love you, too.*

14

Edward passed file folders containing information about the proposed personnel out to the Sacred Heart Hospital Board members. "I'd like to present for your final approval our physicians and staff who will be an integral part of Sacred Heart Hospital. Believe me, gentlemen, when I say that we have done our due diligence when it comes to presenting you with the best candidates."

The businessmen sat around a large, walnut table that was polished to a high gloss. The smell of fresh paint, stain, and cut lumber still hung in the air. Fragrant scents of flowers and gaiety lingered from the frolic and festivities from the Atlanta Capital City Club's grand opening celebration the previous Wednesday. Tall, white French doors were closed, separating the conference room discussions from the rest of the members-only patrons who now housed their gentlemen-only discussions on the corner of Peachtree and Harris Streets.

A spindly, elderly gentleman adjusted his black necktie, tucking the loose ends back into his black vest. "Edward, thank you. Your recommendations are impressive. Gentlemen, it's time to put this matter up for a vote."

"I move to accept Edward's personnel recommendations for said Sacred Heart positions," said a cheery man with a bulbous, ruddy nose who was wearing a blue, windowpane suit.

"I second it," a man said as he adjusted the gold-framed monocle over his right eye.

"All those in favor, say 'Aye.'"

"Aye," all voices said in unison.

"Any opposed?"

The question was met with silence.

"Well, the 'ayes' have it." He reached up and shook Edward's hand. "Congratulations, Edward. You have your staff appointments for Sacred Heart."

After the Sacred Heart Board meeting concluded, Edward directed his driver to his next meeting, a newly formed group of like-minded businessmen who met once a week on Mondays at lunchtime. Members represented various areas of the Atlanta business sector and called themselves the Atlanta Rotary Club. Edward embraced their motto, "Service Above Self—He Profits Most Who Serves Best."

Edward's dream of building Sacred Heart and Alexander Hall medical centers answered the call for Georgians to have access to better medical care. He had witnessed the Atlanta population nearly double since the turn of the century to approximately 175,000 people. Atlanta was in transition, struggling to become the "New South" and aspiring to shed its traditional rural overtones for a new metropolis with an emerging skyline. The recently opened Winecoff Hotel, now the tallest building in the city, stood at sixteen stories.

Despite the growth, it troubled Edward that Georgians

were still dying at nearly twice the rate of the national average. Economic development revolved around cheap child labor and Georgia law permitted children as young as ten years of age to work up to eleven hours a day. This enticed many mills and factory owners to set up their businesses in the southern city. Shanty towns emerged and tens of thousands of workers lived without the luxuries of indoor plumbing, gas, or electricity. Edward shook his head in desperation at the thought that the city employed only fifteen "honey" or "honey pot" wagons to collect the raw sewage from such locations.

In an effort to educate himself about the earliest hospitals, Edward read numerous books about how the best ones, built in ancient Greece and Rome in the third and fourth centuries, were first called *asclepeions*, or healing temples. They were built in homage to one of Apollo's sons, the god of healing, Asclepius. His staff entwined with a snake remains the symbol of medicine to this day. The most famous asclepeion was built using travertine stone in Epidaurus, Greece.

Edward also read John Howard's book called *Hospitals and Lazarettos*. An English philanthropist and a well-known prison reformer in the mid-1700's, he investigated and described the deplorable medical conditions of hospitals and the quarantine methods used for sailors who were on ships docked at port, secluded on islands, or detained in buildings. Barbarism, terrorism, darkness, and inhumanity were the premier choice of treatment for that time.

Edward preferred to run and operate Sacred Heart and Alexander Hall Hospitals like the knights and sisters of St. John's hospitals did in 1100 A.D. The Knight Hospitallers' approach to the healing arts and patient care was through their thoughtfully and beautifully constructed buildings, organized grand rounds, discipline, compassion, and formality. They even served their patron's meals on silver dishes. While Edward wasn't going to those lengths, he refused to operate his facilities like some hospitals he had seen across the country where patients' food was thrown on wooden tables without dishes. Lice, maggots, and bedbugs crawled through the patient's filthy bed sheets. Incompetent, untrained, barely-reformed prison employees drank and stole during their shifts. Edward rubbed his forehead. There were so many people who needed help, including many innocent children.

He knew it wasn't uncommon for the madams or *mamasans* to even pimp out young children from their brothels for quick money. As a result, drug addiction, sexually transmitted diseases, and unwanted pregnancies flourished in the cesspool. Despite the police chief's attempts to quell the sex trade, Edward hoped that the leadership at the city and state levels would be able to rise above the new challenges facing them.

As Edward stared out the window, he abruptly said to his driver. "Did you know action speaks louder than words?"

"I'm sorry, sir. I didn't quite catch that. Can you repeat that?"

"Sorry, I just opened my mouth while I was deep in thought. A quote from Mark Twain came to mind. He once said, 'Action speaks louder than words but not nearly as often.' Do you believe that to be true?"

The driver paused a moment before responding. "Yes, sir. I do believe it to be true. I believe that man has the best of intentions, but for reasons unknown, those intentions may fail to be realized. Inaction causes empty words which are simply unfulfilled goals, dreams, or promises. There's a big difference between *talkers* and *doers*. And, you, Mr. Alexander are a *doer*."

"I couldn't agree with you more. And, that's why I am a proponent of action over words any day." Edward smiled as he continued to gaze out of the car, confident of the course of action he'd plotted for Sacred Heart Hospital and Alexander Hall.

Monday afternoon, Fourth Ward

That afternoon, Mrs. Gray and Addie were discharged from Grady Hospital. Mrs. Gray managed to convince Lester to allow them to take a taxicab back to her house. She told him that the open air roadster was not an appropriate vehicle for two women to ride in, especially those recovering from the flu. He conceded and decided to make a visit to Alvin to check on the status of securing the Sacred Heart account. After abruptly leaving the Alexander Christmas party, he didn't have a chance to follow up with Alvin after his initial discussion with Edward.

When they returned home, Mrs. Gray was true to her word and gave Addie Garrett's letters. She also called Trudy Alexander and Lena Hartman to thank them for looking after Addie at the Christmas party. All agreed that "these things happen." Lena reassured her that the fact that Addie had fainted didn't impact her ability to apply to nursing school as long as the cause wasn't related to an underlying medical condition. She did comment that once enrolled into the program, the consumption of alcohol was strictly prohibited.

Addie sat in the parlor and was deep into Garrett's second of three letters, reading about the common routines of daily life on the Darling farm. She was getting the feeling that Garrett was wishing that she would come back to North Georgia and settle down. *I am so torn. My heart wants to be with Garrett, but not yet. I'm just not ready to settle down. I know that by remaining single and seeking out an education, I am bucking the conventional and social expectations that even Paw had outlined for me. Maw knew my heart and that I was different from the other farm girls. Marriage and children are not what I desire at this time in my life. I want so much more. Perhaps I'll get the chance to see those places I had pasted on my bedroom wall, like the Grand Canyon, the nation's Capitol, or even the Eiffel Tower.*

Finding Garrett's letters mundane, she was thrilled and relieved to hear the news from Mrs. Gray that her chances to get into Sacred Heart's nursing school were unaffected. With the first order of business out of the way, Mrs. Gray proceeded to the second. She called her attorney, Mr. Thompson, to discuss her concerns about Lester's possible misrepresentation of the tonic.

"Mr. Thompson? Yes, this is Mrs. Gray. I have some grave concerns about my nephew, Lester, and Doc Gray's tonic. In my personal opinion, I don't think he's fully disclosing the real ingredients on the label."

"I would agree with you that could be problematic. If your theory is proven true, it would be a violation of The Pure Food and Drug Act, a series of federal laws implemented to protect consumers from mislabeled products."

Mr. Thompson further explained that drugs used in products that were sold to consumers had to be compliant with the strength, quantity, and quality as outlined in the *United States Pharmacopeia* and the *National Formulary*. By law, variations needed to be plainly stated on the product's label. Mrs. Gray learned from Mr. Thompson that the law identified ten dangerous drugs, including alcohol, morphine, cannabis, opium, and coca, that if used in the tonic had to be mentioned on the label.

"Do you believe Lester is in compliance?

"My gut tells me he's probably not being compliant with the law. He's been working with pharmacist Alvin Martin on the formula."

There was a long pause before Mr. Thompson added. "I have a feeling your suspicions may be valid. I've been hearing rumors about Mr. Martin that pertain more to his pharmaceutical practice of out of the back of his store than through the front of the apothecary."

Fearing the worst, Mrs. Gray asked. "Mr. Thompson, will you utilize your resources so that Lester could be discreetly investigated? I willingly agree to fund the private investigator's expenses to look into the matter and report his findings to you."

"That would be just fine. I'll take care of the details."

"Depending upon the outcome, will you also draft a cease and desist letter to Lester to stop him from using Doc Gray's name on the label? Threaten to sue him if you have to." Mrs. Gray knew it would potentially bring bad press, or worse. However, she was ready to get out ahead of the problem and the story if it did break. It was her marriage vow to Doc Gray, "...for better, for worse, for richer, for poorer, in sickness and in health, until death do us part. I will love and honor you all the days of my life." She was compelled to honor her good husband's name and reputation. As much as she loved her sister, in her mind, Lester was no longer considered her nephew.

"Consider it done."

"I have one other task for you, Mr. Thompson. I need to amend my will. Regardless of the outcome of the investigation, I have decided to change my will to remove Lester as an heir. I need it revised to include Addie Rose Engel, my nursemaid."

Mrs. Gray had already named Garrett as a recipient of her inheritance while Lester's older sister, Susan was never originally a part of the will. Married with a family of her own in Charleston, South Carolina and very well off, Mrs. Gray knew that Susan was being taken care of by her husband and his family's money.

"I'll be happy to draft up the new papers and send them to your house next week via one of my law clerks. I need him to bear witness to your signature and to ensure that you are not under any duress and are of sound mind and body."

"I completely understand. Next week will be just fine with me. Thank you."

"Even though the holidays are upon us, the investigation will begin before the first of the year. Please note it may take a few months to gather enough evidence and conclude a finding," Mr. Thompson added.

Without putting their concerns into words, both knew there was a problem. Only time and the facts would reveal what Lester was trying so desperately to cover up.

"Again, that will be just fine. Thank you, Mr. Thompson. I wish you and your family a very Merry Christmas."

"A Merry Christmas to you, too, Mrs. Gray."

Across town, Alvin was having an intense discussion with Lester about how to get Sacred Heart Hospital to stock Doc Gray's. "Look, Lester. Edward isn't going to give you an answer one way or the other about stocking the tonic at Sacred Heart. So don't get so impatient yet."

Unsure if Alvin was putting the squeeze on him, Lester was prepared to seal the deal today. He wanted go into 1914 with a new marketing strategy for more hospital-based customers. Sacred Heart would be the first, in the long line of many more to come. He just needed one to start the domino effect for the other medical facilities to fall in line. "Don't you understand that profit margins will increase tremendously?"

"Of course, I do. As a silent partner with you, I have to be careful. Edward is going to look to Sacred Heart's Medical Director, Doctor Williams, to determine which drugs the hospital will stock. Ultimately, he will be picking the drugs that he and his team will be ordering and using."

Lester anticipated where the discussion was going. "I got it. You need Doctor Williams to make the recommendation to you and not the other way around. I've got to hand it to you. You are a clever one."

"I don't really know him well enough to have that discussion with him at this time. The Chief Operating Officer at Sacred Heart, my friend Clyde Posey, plans to have staff meetings beginning in January to make final preparations for the hospital, complete the build out and make sure everything is in working order by April."

"I thought I read in the paper the hospital doesn't open until May?"

"It doesn't. The nursing school starts classes in April. They plan to conduct mock operations beginning in May so when they do open the doors at the end of that month, they will be fully functional and optimally staffed."

"In the meantime, how do you recommend we get more attention for Doc Gray's?"

Alvin threw *The Atlanta Dispatch* at Lester.

Lester flinched, barely catching the paper. "What the hell?"

Alvin laughed. "We'll put a combination article and advertisement in the paper. I'm sure I can get an out-of-state physician to put his name to a piece that I draft up and submit to the paper. I know the assistant editor."

"Sounds like a great plan."

"If I thought of it, it is! It won't be cheap. I'm tapped out right now. I had to pay Mr. Chang an installment for my last shipment of opium. How are you on access to cash?"

"How does fifty dollars sound to you? Will that be enough?"

"Yea, I think that will do it. Twenty-five dollars apiece should take care of them."

Lester pulled out a few rolls of money wrapped in twine and threw them on the table in front of Alvin.

"You work fast. Where did you get this? Did you rob a bank on the way over here?" Alvin held out his hand in protest. "On second thought, I really don't want to know where it came from, do I?"

"Let's just say I found it in my Christmas stocking. It's an early present from Santa."

Alvin took the money and secured it into his locked cabinet.

Lester pulled out a black jewelry box and handed it to Alvin. "Here, this is for you to give to Mrs. Martin. I'd say you've been a good boy this year and earned it."

Alvin opened the box and pulled out the pearl necklace and earrings. "Where ever did you find these?" Alvin looked suspiciously at Lester. "Oh, wait. Let me guess in your Christmas stocking?"

Lester chose not to respond. He figured it was a rhetorical question, anyway.

"She will love these. Nothing says, 'Merry Christmas, darling,' like a marvelous strand of pearls with matching earrings. Don't worry, Lester. I'll do my part at the staff meetings. I'll have Clyde bring a copy of *The Atlanta Dispatch* that will have our *article-tisement* to one of the staff meetings when it comes time to discuss stocking the pharmacy. I think I'll even have Clyde say that he is an avid user of the product, too."

"How do we want to market it to the hospitals?"

"Based on the ingredients, I'd call it a restorative."

"I like that." Lester got up to leave. "Well, I'm off to run a few more errands around town. I wish you and your family a very Merry Christmas!"

Lester shook hands with Alvin. "Merry Christmas to you, too."

As Lester exited out the back door of the store, bells clanged indicating that someone had entered through the front door. Peering out from behind the curtain, he saw Clyde walking toward him.

"Merry Christmas to you, Alvin. How's my favorite supplier and soon-to-be pharmacist at Sacred Heart doing?"

Alvin shook his hand. "Fantastic! How's everything going with you?"

"Fine. Absolutely fine. I'm just stopping by to pick up my medicine." Clyde wasn't sure if they were alone or not and never took any chances. "I figured you'd be closed through next week on account of the holidays."

"Great timing! You just missed Lester Gray. We were talking about how to get Sacred Heart to stock Doc Gray's in the pharmacy." Alvin jumped straight to the point and debriefed Clyde on the plan to include the article in *The Dispatch* and Clyde's personal testimonial. "To sweeten the deal, I've got an early Christmas present for you from Santa."

Alvin walked over to his cabinet, unlocked it, and counted out twenty dollars from one of the rolls Lester had just given to him. He also pulled out a small vial of white powder.

"Santa said you have been a very deserving chap this year." Alvin handed him the money and the vial. "Today's supply is on the house. No charge. Just be sure Dr. Williams makes the recommendation to stock and use Doc Gray's."

"Wow! I really appreciate Santa's generosity. Thank you. Nice doing business with you, Alvin. I look forward to what 1914 brings. It should be a stellar and unforgettable year for us. Have a Merry Christmas."

"I sure will. Merry Christmas."

Clyde exited the store. Alvin locked the door behind him and flipped the door sign. *Closed.*

15

Lester, his father, Mr. Darling, and Garrett sat comfortably by the fire in the living room of the Schwinn house. The grandfather clock in the hall tolled twelve. Mary toiled away in the kitchen, anticipating the arrival of her sister and Addie. Frustration grew as Lester continued to press Garrett about selling Doc Gray's tonic in North Georgia.

Mr. Darling, sensing Lester was pushing the issue too hard, weighed in. "It's a mighty fine offer you are proposin' to Garrett. I'm not sure that Garrett will have enough time to commit to sellin' your product. Between the two of us, tendin' to the livestock, crops, and harvestin' the ginger root for your elixir, to put in plainly, there aren't enough hours in the day to provide any kind of dedication to your sales there." Mr. Darling also knew that the project to renovate the land on the Engel farm to accommodate the town's new cemetery would also require a lot of work on their behalf once the deal was finalized after the first of the year. He anticipated clearing the debris from the house and barn beginning in the spring.

A knock at the door interrupted their conversation.

Shaking off the scant amount of snow from her boots, Mrs. Gray gave the front door another quick knock with her cane handle before she proceeded to open the door and step inside. "Merry Christmas!" Addie and Mrs. Gray walked into the Schwinn's house carrying baskets filled with Addie's homemade biscuits, assorted jams, a pumpkin and pecan pie, and Christmas presents.

Garrett was first to jump up from the living room couch to greet them. Lester, Mr. Schwinn, and Mr. Darling got up from their chairs and followed him to welcome the new arrivals.

Taking the baskets from them, Garrett placed them on the hall floor and took Addie in his arms. "I've missed you so much. Are you and Aunt Olive alright? Lester was just filling me in about your recent hospitalization with the flu or some kind of stomach ailment. Gosh, you don't even look like yourself. Look at you." He twirled her around. "You've become quite the town mouse!" Garrett couldn't get over her new hair style and the garnet red velvet dress, a birthday present from his Aunt Olive.

"I've missed you, too, Garrett." Addie sank into his arms. She didn't want to let him go. She looked at Mrs. Gray and winked. "We're just fine. The doctor said it was a mild stomach virus."

Addie went on to hug Mr. Darling and Mr. Schwinn. She avoided making any contact with Lester.

Garrett had to know. "Why haven't you written me? I received your letter and mailed three back to you."

"I did receive them...*yesterday*. They were lovely and I appreciate you taking the time to tell me how you and your father were spending your days on the farm."

Lester interjected. "Addie's been so busy with Aunt Olive.

She's really had her hands full. By the way, did I fail to mention to you that I brought Addie as my date to a Christmas party this past weekend?"

Garrett's smile disappeared and he stepped back from Addie as Lester moved in next to her.

Mrs. Gray sensed Lester had an ulterior motive and she wasn't going to let Lester have the last word. "Oh, come now, Lester. You and Addie haven't been dating. You simply attended the Alexander Christmas party in my stead." Mrs. Gray wanted to take control of the conversation and redirect it. "We mustn't let our food get cold out here in the hallway. Come on, everyone! I'm sure Mary's ready to get dinner on the table."

Mrs. Gray picked up a basket and handed it to Addie. "Let's get these into the kitchen." Mrs. Gray picked up the other and followed Addie.

Mr. Schwinn, who was deaf in his right ear and hard of hearing in his left as a result of being an avid hunter who loved using his shotgun, leaned over to Lester and shouted. "What about a kitten?"

Lester shouted back. "No, father. Not a KITTEN. We're going into the KITCHEN."

"Oh! Good, 'cause I hate kittens and I'm hungry."

Addie looked back at Garrett who stood motionless while everyone made their way down the hall.

Following the blessing, Addie made sure she sat across from Garrett. She missed seeing his warm smile and sun-kissed face. Addie was looking forward to having a meaningful discussion with him. Lester made it impossible, having seated himself right next to her. Addie purposefully inched her chair away from him, attempting to create the illusion of some distance between them. Dissolving the illusion, Lester adjusted his chair closer to her. *That bastard! I need to figure out a way to talk with Garrett alone after dinner.*

Plates were filled with mounds of delectable foods and emptied, some more than twice. Garrett raved multiple times about Addie's delicious biscuits. Not to be outdone, Lester did the same. Following the Christmas Day feast the Darlings, Schwinns, Mrs. Gray, and Addie adjourned to enjoy a glass of eggnog by the living room fire. Mr. Darling settled into one of the wingback chairs closest to the fireplace. Olive sat across from him. Addie seated herself on the sofa and became uncomfortably sandwiched between Lester on her right and Garrett on the left. Mr. Schwinn hated trying to converse with multiple people and found it extremely difficult to keep up with the conversation. Instead, he opted for a postprandial nap. He purposely chose a chair in the corner of the room next to the Christmas tree, a Douglas fir that was decorated with a variety of ornaments including handmade ones from Susan and Lester when they were young. Strands of popped corn and cranberries accented the tree. A white angel with spread wings adorned the top. Mary lingered behind in the kitchen. The sound of clanking dishes and a crackling fire permeated the room.

Addie started to get up from the sofa. "It sounds like your Mother might need some help in the kitchen."

Lester pulled her back down. "No, she really doesn't. The kitchen is her domain and she is very particular about how she cleans her porcelain. She has a method and no one interferes with it."

Mrs. Gray laughed. "It's true, Addie. Why do you think I'm sitting out here? I've learned over the years not to mess with my little sister and respect her rules while I'm a guest in her home."

A few more minutes of dish clinking ensued before it stopped. Mary entered into the living room carrying a crystal pedestal cake dish with a white frosted birthday cake on top. Red poinsettia flowers with green leaves made from icing bordered the round cake. A simple candle was lit in its center.

The group erupted. "Happy birthday to you! Happy birthday to you! Happy birthday, dear, Addie. Happy birthday to you!"

Clapping and hollering followed.

The commotion startled Mr. Schwinn. He awoke from his nap. "Happy birthday, Baby Jesus!" He nodded off back to sleep.

Addie's cheeks flushed and red hives popped out above the collar of her dress. "Oh, my goodness gracious! How did y'all know that today is my birthday?"

Garrett noticed her hives and began to speak.

Instead, Lester interjected. "I told Mother."

Garrett's mouth closed.

Lester continued. "She wanted to bake you a special cake for your eighteenth birthday today. Now, make a wish and blow out your candle."

Addie shifted nervously in her seat, closed her eyes, and blew out the candle. When she opened her eyes, she looked at Garrett and smiled. She took his hand in hers. "I'm so glad you are here with me. We've got so much to talk about."

Lester squirmed at the sight. His face reddened. A knock at the front door startled everyone.

"I'll get it." Mary walked into the hallway and opened the door. "Oh, we have carolers!

Everyone, please come to the door."

With the exception of Mr. Schwinn who continued to rest peacefully by the Christmas tree, everyone clambered into the hall.

The youthful carolers sang out. "We wish you a Merry Christmas. We wish you a Merry Christmas. We wish you a Merry Christmas and a Happy New Year. Good tidings we bring for you and your kin. Good tidings for Christmas and a Happy New Year. We wish you a Happy Birthday. We wish you a Happy Birthday."

Addie, realizing the carolers were singing *to* her and *not* for the family, began biting at her thumb nail. She fidgeted. *Why is Lester going to such great lengths to give the appearance that we are dating? What is he doing?* Then it dawned on her. *He's trying to stake his claim and make Garrett jealous. He is ruthless!*

Garrett noticed Addie's reaction.

"We wish you a Happy Birthday and a Happy New Year. Merry Christmas! Happy Birthday, Addie!" The carolers added. They started singing the song over again.

I want to wring Lester's neck for embarrassing me in front of his family! Addie was struck with an impulsive idea. She pretended to be overcome with emotions and the residual side effects of her recent hospitalization. She swooned, purposefully landing into Garrett's arms. As Addie lay in his arms, she squinted out of one eye and saw Mary slam the front door shut on the singing carolers.

"Addie, are you alright?" Concerned, Garrett scooped up Addie into his arms. "I believe you still are recovering from your stomach virus."

Mary insisted. "Garrett, she's got the vapors. Please take her upstairs to the guest bed so she can get off her feet and get some rest. I'll be up in a minute with a cool cloth and some hot tea."

Garrett began the ascent. Lester tried to follow.

Aunt Olive noticed. "Lester, would you be so kind as to run down to my house to get my shawl. I feel the touch of a chill coming on."

Miffed, Lester reluctantly descended the staircase. "I'm sure Mother has one you can borrow."

"No, no. I can't wear hers. They're too itchy for me. I need my cashmere one lying in my parlor on the back of the sofa. Be a dear, would you?"

Lester begrudgingly complied while Mr. Darling escorted his sister into the parlor. He opened the front door and walked into the carolers who remained on the front porch.

The oldest boy of the group spoke out. "Hey, mister! You said you'd give us a tip when we were done. We did what you asked of us. You need to pay up."

Lester pulled out a few bills and tossed them into the air behind him as he hurried down the front porch to Aunt Olive's house. The children scurried to capture the flying money.

Garrett laid Addie on the guest bed. "Addie? What's wrong with you? You're acting so strange and I'm so worried about you. You're not behaving like yourself."

Addie opened her eyes and propped herself up on her elbows. She looked around the room. "Are we alone?"

"Yes. Aunt Mary is getting you a cold compress and some hot tea."

"I don't need any of that. I'm just fine. Trust me." Addie sat all the way up and leaned up against the headboard. "Lester is making me so mad and he's getting under my skin. He's trying to make you jealous and convince you that we're dating."

"Well, are you...dating him?" Garrett hated asking the question, afraid of her response.

"Gosh, no, Garrett!" Addie punched him in the upper arm. "I don't have time to date." Addie watched Garrett's face change. "That didn't come out right. What I meant to say was that I am not searching out anyone to date. I'm staying so busy with your Aunt and helping her keep up the house. When I do have time for myself, there is only one person I think of and it's you."

Addie's cheeks flushed.

"Really?"

"Yes, really." Addie reached out to hold his hand.

"I'm going to pop him in the nose for acting like a fool today."

"Please, don't you dare. Garrett, trust me when I say that he's an interesting character. I know he's your cousin and you think you know him, but you really don't."

Garrett grew concerned. "What did he do to you? Did he hurt you in any way?"

Addie hated being untruthful to him. "No, no." But she was curious about his question. "Why do you ask?"

"I remember playing with him when we were kids. He always seemed to have a dark side to him. He enjoyed killing anything that was tiny and defenseless, like frogs, squirrels, and one time there was this cat...." Garrett stopped. "Never mind.

I'm just saying he can be a bit odd, to say the least. I can't blame him for taking a fancy to you. Look at the young woman you've become. You are just stunning. Being a town mouse suits you." Addie blush deepened. "Thank you. Well, I guess it's official. I am legally an adult today."

"I'm sure your family would be so proud of you."

"I have to tell you, I do love living with your Aunt. She is the sweetest, most loving individual, and I can't thank your father enough for sending me here. I can only imagine what my life would have been like...." *Now, your cousin, Lester on the other hand is a complete scoundrel and there is so much I want to tell you about him. But I made your Aunt a promise not to tell you.* "I can let you in on a little secret. Your Aunt has a friend who is in charge of the new Sacred Heart Nursing School. She has put in a good word for me and I plan to enroll into the program in Spring, 1915."

"That's absolutely wonderful news. I'm so happy for you. You will make the best nurse. I think back to the time when you took such good care of my mother. You're a natural." Garrett paused. His heart was bursting at the seams. He wanted to tell her about the plans for her family farm, but he made a promise to his father to keep it a secret. He couldn't contain himself any longer. "I have a birthday gift for you." Garrett leaned over and kissed her.

Addie responded passionately to his kiss. Then they heard footsteps up the stairs.

Garrett stood up and rushed over to greet his Aunt in the doorway. "Addie's feeling so much better now."

"Good. Addie, here's a cold cloth for your head and some hot tea to soothe your nerves. It's my special recipe and I even added a pinch of some of Lester's special medicine to it."

Addie was still touching her lips with her fingertips. "How thoughtful of you. You really shouldn't have." *No, you really shouldn't have!*

"Wasn't any trouble, Addie." Mary set the cup and saucer down on the side table and placed the cloth on Addie's forehead. "Come now, Garrett. Let's let her rest for a while. I'll be back up in an hour or so to check on you. We'll exchange Christmas presents when you're feeling better."

Garrett and his aunt left the room, closing the door behind them. As soon as Addie heard them talking downstairs, she took the cloth off her head, got up off the bed, and opened one of the windows a few inches. She ran back over to the side table, grabbed the cup, and tossed the tea out the window. Closing the window, she returned the cup to the saucer and sat on the edge of the bed.

Addie couldn't believe that Garrett had kissed her. *What a marvelous birthday and Christmas it has been today.* Addie glided her fingertips back over her rosy, bow-shaped lips. She yearned for more, to feel his bare skin pressing against her skin. It was her first and their first real kiss. It wasn't like the one he pecked on her cheek when they were six years old and playing with frogs and turtles down by the pond. *How can a kiss be so soft and passionate, yet spark a flame inside my soul that begs for me to unravel in his arms?* Overcome by a rush of warmth, Addie picked up the cool cloth from the bed stand and blotted her face and the back of her neck. *I know he wants so much more from me, but I want so much more for myself in this life. I'm not ready to settle down yet. There's so much that this world has to offer and there are so many places I wish to explore. For the first time in my life, I'm officially in charge of my destiny—the choices and direction are finally mine to own. Nursing school is the key to unlocking my potential. I need to remain focused. Only God knows what my grand plan is. I know I have lived through hell. I may be scared, but I survived with the gracious help of Mr. Darling and his family. I just need to let go and trust God, follow my heart, and chase after my dreams. After all, that's what Maw's final wish was for me. She knew there was so much more in store for me in this lifetime. While I could turn into my father and use all of my anger and strength to strangle Lester to death with my own bare hands right now, that will only show this world that I perpetuated my family's cycle of violence and land me in the hoosegow condemned to death. Instead, I am taking lessons from Mrs. Gray and trust her plan to use her resources, influence, and money to take care of Lester. While the results won't be immediate like a shooting or a stabbing, Mrs. Gray is mitigating the drama, because whatever the results, it will affect the family's name and reputation. Justice will be served to Lester on a silver platter in the end.* Addie chuckled. *It's just another difference between country and town mice.*

Addie still relishing Garrett's kiss, reflected on a Twain quote she read in Garrett's book. *"The hard and sordid things of life are too hard and too sordid and too cruel for us to know and touch them year after year without some mitigating influence, some kindly veil to draw over them, from time to time, to blur the craggy outlines, and make the thorns less sharp and the cruelties less malignant."* Addie smiled as she hopped off the bed to rejoin the rest of the family downstairs to open Christmas presents.

Second Ward

Edward paced back and forth while talking to Clyde on his office phone in the Zoo. He glanced out the window to see that the dusting of snow that fell overnight still lingered on the front lawn in patches. "Clyde, we have got to be vigilant to our timelines. Be sure Tom knows to have Mr. Chen's excavation team complete the tunnel project by March. Let's set Monday, March 2nd as their deadline."

"Damn, Edward that's really pushing them. I believe Tom was shooting more for the first of April when the nursing school is slated to open. Tom said the farmers are seeing a thicker coat on their cows and livestock this year. We may be in for a harsh winter."

"Have them light bonfires near the site to keep the ground from freezing, if that's his concern. You know how fickle Georgia weather can be. We may have a sprinkle of snow today and then find ourselves basking in seventy-degree sunshine by next week."

"Do you want to offer them an incentive for finishing early?"

Edward's pacing stopped as he mulled over the idea. "Yes, since the project has been subcontracted to Mr. Chen and his men, a highly experienced and reputable group known for their expedient work out West dynamiting tunnels for the railroad." Edward returned to his desk and scribbled a few figures on his notepad. "As my daddy used to say, 'let's get to it and just do it.'"

"What's your offer?"

"According to my calculations, let's plan for an extra twenty percent on top of the project cost. If I need to, I'll have Trudy organize another 'grip and grin' at the house to offset the costs. I know I'll catch some flak from the Board members, but the cows aren't the only ones with thick hides around here. Speaking of thick hides, did I ever tell you about the time Daddy and Teddy went on a safari in Africa to hunt elephants back in 18..." Edward tried to recall the exact date.

Clyde interrupted Edward's moment of silence. "Edward, I hate to cut you short, but I've got to get to my parent's house. They are expecting me for Christmas dinner."

"Yes, yes. Sorry my dear, man. Give your folks my best regards. Merry Christmas to you."

"Merry Christmas, Edward." Clyde hung up the phone before Edward had a change of heart and rekindled the conversation. He leaned over and pulled out a small vial from the bedside table drawer. After uncapping it, he clenched his left hand into a fist, and poured out a small amount into the space between his thumb and index finger. He inhaled deeply and offered the remainder to Moira, who did the same. He recapped the vial and set in on top of the table.

Moira pulled her hair up above her head and twirled it into a top knot before resting her head back on the pillow. "Does that man ever stop working?"

Clyde rolled over and propped himself up on his elbow. "No, I don't think so. But that's what makes him annoyingly respected. He's always thinking about the bigger picture and he even pays attention to the smaller details."

"What did he want this time?"

Clyde rolled over on top of Moira. "He wants to be sure Tom's Chinamen get the tunnel project completed by the beginning of March. He's planning to pay them a decent bonus if they finish early."

"Doesn't that run a risk and incentivize sloppy construction?"

The cocaine kicked in and Clyde was eager to quell the conversation. "Not my problem, is it? I'm just delivering the message. What they do on their end isn't my concern."

"So, what is your concern?"

"Right now? I plan to undertake a drilling project of my own."

Moira giggled. She spread her legs and wrapped them around Clyde, pulling him into her.

Second Ward

A few blocks down from Armstrong Street, sat a small, whitewashed Methodist church. An undecorated wreath made from fresh pine hung on the red front door.

"Can I get an amen?"

"Amen!" the Negro congregation responded. Many women raised their right hands into the air while they fanned themselves with their hand fans.

"Please join me in singing 'O Holy Night.' Mrs. Glover, will you get us started?"

A frail, elderly woman dressed in a sage green dress and a ruby red hat nodded and turned toward the upright Steinway, a gift to the church from the Alexander family last year. She began the prelude of the song in the key of C. Candles on the simple altar flickered and glowed while the congregation sang.

When the song concluded, Reverend Goode opened his eyes. "Thank you, Mrs. Glover. My, how that song does move me to hear y'all sing it with such passion and praise for our Lord and Savior Jesus Christ! Can I get an amen!"

"Amen!" The congregation shouted back and clapped.

One woman on the second pew jumped up and hollered out, "Praise Jesus!" She jumped around and nearly lost the hat on her head. Others joined her.

Reverend Joshua Goode prayed aloud, reflecting on the origin of the hymn. "Thank you, dear God for this beautiful song. Mighty is the verse, 'Chains shall He break, for the slave is our brother, and in His name all oppression shall cease.' You are a powerful and most merciful father to put all of these angels on earth and gather us together in this place tonight to sing your praises on this of holiest of nights. May your wonders never cease to amaze us. Amen. Go in peace my brothers and my sisters."

"Amen! Praise Jesus! Praise the Lord!" various voices shouted out.

The Reverend stepped down from the pulpit and walked toward the narthex of the small church to open the front door. Mrs. Glover played a medley of Christmas carols as church members followed the preacher and filed out the sanctuary. He shook hands with various individuals as they exited.

A wiry old man looked up at Joshua. "Thank you, Reverend. You gave a mighty fine sermon tonight, son. Your pappy would have been proud to have heard you, may God rest his soul."

"Thank you. I appreciate your kind words and for coming tonight to celebrate our Savior's birth."

"By the way, congratulations! I heard from your mother that you got the lead housekeeping and maintenance job at the new Sacred Heart hospital."

"My goodness. Good news travels fast around here, thanks to her. I'll start working there when the nursing school opens in April. I plan to work there during the weekdays and preach here on Sundays."

"The Alexanders have been so good to you, your mother, and now to our church. We may be tiny, but we sure are mighty! Does she still work as their mammy?"

"Yes, she does. She's been there for almost twenty-eight years. She started with them when she was seventeen, a year before I was born."

"My, my, that's a long time. She's a fine woman, she is." The woman standing next to him nudged him in the ribs with her elbow. "That's my cue. We best be going. My wife is anxious to get dinner on the table. Blessings to you and Merry Christmas."

"Merry Christmas."

16

Friday morning, December 26, 1913, Fourth Ward

Clyde sat in his office at home with the phone receiver in his ear, his appetite sated from a fine Christmas meal at his parent's home last evening. The scent of evergreen surged into the air as he watched a few of his housekeeping staff carry the undecorated Christmas tree out of the back door. A mocha-skinned young woman followed behind the crew, sweeping up the fallen needles. Clyde watched her hips swish and sway to the rhythm of the broom. While his appetite for food was suppressed, he hungered for her.

"Hello? Hello? Is anybody there? This is Tom Greene? Hello?"

"Sorry, Tom, I just got a bit distracted. This is Clyde Posey."

"Yes, Clyde. I hope you had a great Christmas. What can I do for you?"

"I did, thank you." Clyde didn't care if Tom did and didn't inquire. He had more pressing matters to attend to. "In a conversation that I had with Edward, he expressed that he would like to make sure you complete the tunnel connecting Sacred Heart Hospital to the nursing school by the first of March."

There was a temporary lull in the conversation. "That's quite an aggressive timeline. I was thinking more along the lines of the end of March, in time for the opening of the nursing school."

"Look, let me get straight to the point. Edward is prepared to pay you an extra twenty percent above the projected cost as a bonus for completing the project early."

"That's a very generous offer." There was a moment of silence before Tom added. "We can do it. Tell Edward he has a deal."

"Great. I'll let Edward know you will comply with his wishes." Clyde hung up the phone.

"A Happy New Year's to you, Clyde. Hello? Hello?" Tom placed the receiver back into the holder. "Fucker."

Clyde's next call went to Edward's home. Miss Mattie answered the phone and promised to relay the message to Mr. Alexander, who was out with Miss Trudy having morning brunch with friends. Clyde didn't care what Edward and Trudy were doing this fine morning. He had other things on his mind.

Sixth Ward

Tom left his home, got into his truck, and drove down to the Sacred Heart construction site located in the Sixth Ward. Scanning the property from his vehicle, he spotted Mr. Chen and his co-workers who were busy excavating the dirt to make the first of three tunnels. The first was going to connect Sacred Heart Hospital to its nursing school. The second was slated to begin next spring, connecting Alexander Hall to Sacred Heart Hospital. The third tunnel would connect Alexander Hall to the Colored nursing school, creating an underground triangle connecting the four buildings together. Only a thin brick wall would divide the schools on the surface.

Tom got out of his car and walked toward Mr. Chen and his crew. "Mr. Chen. Can I speak with you for a minute?"

Mr. Chen bowed at the waist. "Sure Mr. Tom. What you need?"

"Is it possible to have this first tunnel completed by March first?"

Mr. Chen removed his hat and scratched his head. "A minute." He walked toward a Chinese man wearing a dark, brown coat who was directing other men as they picked away at the dirt while others shoveled and threw it onto the back of a horse-drawn wagon to be hauled to another area of the property. They bantered back and forth in Chinese then bowed to each other. Mr. Chen returned. "Yes. No problem."

"Great!" Tom opted not to tell Mr. Chen about the incentive bonus. He decided to check on the status of the southern half of the excavation and most completed part of the project.

He continued to smoke his pipe, feeling comforted by the fact that he was on an excavation instead of an underground tunnel endeavor. He knew he wasn't going to run into hazards like dynamite or pockets of methane gas that had the potential to cause unpredictable explosions. Once the floor of the tunnel was dug out, the walls and ceiling of the tunnel would be constructed around it, enclosing the area. The removed dirt would be reused to encase the structure and leveled off for landscaping.

The slope of the tunnel caused him to hold onto the lumber-sided walls to prevent slipping. The dusting of snow the city received yesterday had moistened the ground just enough to make the ground muddy underfoot. As he inspected the walls shored up by timbers, he noticed where one of the pieces of wood had slipped out of alignment with the others. He stood outstretched to adjust the end piece back into place. Before he knew it, dirt spilled out from behind the wood wall. He quickly raised his arms, attempting to stop the avalanche of soil. The entire wall collapsed on top of him. Mr. Chen and his men felt the rumble under their feet and ran toward the rubble with shovels in hand.

An hour passed before Edward's house phone rang and Miss Mattie burst into the Zoo. "Mr. Alexander, Sorry to interrupt you but a man by the name of Mr. Chen is on the phone for you. I had a hard time making out what he was trying to say. Something about 'green dirt?'"

"Thanks, Miss Mattie." Edward picked up the receiver. This is Mr. Alexander, how can I help you, Mr. Chen?"

Mr. Chen had run across the street to use someone's house phone. In the best English he could muster, he breathlessly tried to sort through his Chinese and English words. "Mr. Alexander? Mr. Greene got DEAD by dirt."

"What? What do you mean 'Mr. Greene got dead by dirt?' I'm not following you."

"I say, Mr. Greene got DEAD. Dirt falled on him. Falled on him at work. In tun-nuh. You hear what I say?"

Edward pieced together the words and phrases. "Good God, my dear man! I'll be down there as soon as I can." Edward clicked the receiver button and dialed Clyde's home number.

He found Clyde still at home. He was addressing his hunger for a mocha-colored woman and reluctantly agreed to meet Edward at the site.

Thirty minutes later, Edward and Clyde walked around the fallen wall with Mr. Chen. Edward heard the sound of a police siren making its way along the street toward them. Edward noticed something in the dirt and kicked at it with his boot. Recognizing the shape, he bent over and picked up Tom's pipe. The top of the bowl of the pipe was filled with soil. He turned it over, dumping the contents into his palm. The tobacco ashes were still warm. "Where's the body?" Edward brushed the dirt and leaves out of his palm and onto the ground before sticking the pipe into his coat pocket.

Mr. Chen said. "Come. Over here." He ran toward the horse drawn cart that contained a tarp-covered body on the bed of the wagon.

Edward and Clyde followed. The sound of the police siren stopped. Edward climbed up on the back of the wagon, bent down, and uncovered the corpse. Clyde gasped and walked away. Tom's expression was grotesque. His eyes and mouth were open, filled with red Georgia clay and pebbles. A bloody, white rib bone with shards of muscle tissue and skin pierced through the left side of his forest green, corduroy coat. Edward imagined that the other part of the rib had probably punctured Tom's lung and possibly his heart, too. He prayed his friend went quickly. Tom's extremities and trunk were contorted in an unnatural manner that indicated he had sustained multiple compound and open fractures due to the crushing nature of the incident. Edward recovered his friend's face and said a silent prayer. Mr. Chen clasped his hands and said something in Chinese. Edward climbed off the wagon and walked toward Clyde and the approaching policeman. Clyde quickly rubbed his nose after inhaling a hefty pinch of white power from his snuff box while Edward attended to his dead friend.

The police chief shook Edward's hand. "Morning, Edward. Sorry to hear about Tom. The neighbor across the street called me after Mr. Chen asked to use their phone. Mind if I go take a gander for myself to make sure there wasn't any foul play?"

"Not a problem. From what I can glean from Mr. Chen and his men, Tom walked down to the southern end to inspect their progress. Before the men knew it, the wall was falling on top of him. Looking at his injuries, he didn't suffer and went quickly." Edward stuck his cold hands into his coat pockets and fumbled with the pipe in his left pocket.

The chief walked down to the rubble and then over to the wagon where he inspected the body. He returned to Edward and Clyde who were still standing where he had last left them.

"You sure you don't want my job? Looks like you are right on the money about this. What a hell of a way to go. Here one minute and gone the next."

Edward reached out to Clyde. "Come on, Clyde. Ride with me."

"Where are we going?"

"We're heading over to the First Ward to see Mrs. Greene and to give her proper notification about her husband."

"Chief, will you follow us over there to make sure she knows that you inspected the site and that you have deemed it a misfortunate accident?"

"Sure. I'd be happy to. I'll expedite the paperwork, too. I know you'll need it to show cause of death and release you from any liability for the business' insurance company. I'll do what I can to squelch the story with *The Atlanta Dispatch* and the other papers, too. Sacred Heart doesn't need any bad press."

On the walk back to the cars, Edward thought about how to assuage any potential litigation by Mrs. Greene. He decided to share his plan aloud with Clyde and the chief. "I'll let Mrs. Greene know that we will honor Tom's memory by dedicating this tunnel to him. Clyde, make a mental note to make sure Mrs. Greene and their family are invited to the ribbon cutting ceremony. Be sure to get a commemorative plaque with a cross on it so that we can affix it to the wall where he died. I'll also be sure to have the funeral home send me the charges for his funeral. Luckily his brother Peter is in partnership with him. The construction company will fall solely into his hands. I'll have a talk with Peter to see if he'll purchase Tom's shares of the business and give that money to Tom's wife and kids. That should provide her with an adequate nest egg."

The chief opened the car door to his police vehicle. "That's a generous offer, Edward. I'm impressed how you manage to put others first. You're a good Christian gentleman."

"Thanks, Chief." Edward and Clyde got into the car. As Edward started the ignition, he sensed that Clyde was still unsettled. "Don't worry, Clyde. Tom won't come back to haunt you. Working at Sacred Heart, you'll get a chance to see a lot more dead bodies for a variety of reasons. It reminds me of the time when…"

Clyde's secret snuff was working its magic. He mentally checked out as Edward droned on about an African safari expedition, sponsored by the Smithsonian to collect animal specimens for the new Natural History museum, and a side-trip gone awry in 1909 with Teddy and his father. He appeared interested in the one-sided conversation as they followed the Chief's car, which navigated its way through the city streets toward the Greene's house.

17

Sunday night, December 28, 1913, Fourth Ward

Clyde was still trying to erase the image of Tom's post-mortem face from his memory. With the help of Alvin's medicinal therapy and Mr. Chang's opium and massage emporium, Clyde spent the rest of Friday afternoon, Saturday, and most of Sunday in a semi-conscious state. After a myriad of canoodling sessions with a variety of Asian woman and restorative sessions with noodle soup, he eventually made his way home Sunday night to find Moira sitting by a roaring fire, smoking a cigarette on his living room couch. Her legs were crossed and a shoe dangled from her right big toe as she took a swig from an open bottle of champagne. Clyde stumbled in front of her and she flipped her shoe up into the air at him, narrowly missing his head.

He attempted to avoid it and fell onto the floor.

Apparent that she, too, had been imbibing for a while, Moira cackled, "Where have you been? I've been calling and calling. You were supposed to come over last night." She looked him over. "You look like hell." Moira took another big gulp from the green bottle. "When I say you look like hell, I mean it looks like you have been to hell and back. You reek of booze, drugs, and sex."

Still on the floor, Clyde rolled over onto his back and clutched his head. "Shut the fuck up, would you. I don't think the servants can hear you."

"Not to worry. I sent them home early tonight. I made sure they fixed you dinner. It's on the stove, just ready to heat and eat."

Clyde's mouth watered. He desired to chew on something more substantial than rice noodles, vegetables with bits of poultry floating in a watery, chicken broth. "Will you fix me a plate? I promise to tell you all about it."

"What do I look like, your fucking maid? Get up off your ass and fix it yourself."

"I can't. I'm too tired and exhausted. Please? Pretty please? If you are a good girl, I've got a little present for you. It's some new stuff compliments from Mr. Chang." Clyde wriggled out of his coat and suit jacket. He reached inside his suit coat and pulled out a tiny vial filled with a beige powder.

Intrigued and a bit hungry herself, Moira gave the bottle to Clyde and complied with his request. She returned a few minutes later with two plates of food, silverware, and napkins. Clyde stayed on the floor and propped his back up against the sofa. Moira sat down next to him. Clyde was silent as he shoveled forkfuls of mashed potatoes and gravy into his mouth. He was ravenous. He picked up the pork tenderloin with his fingers, ripping and chewing on the meat.

Moira set her plate down. She lost her appetite watching him eat and swig champagne from the bottle. She observed gravy dripping onto the front of his shirt and vest. Clyde let out a loud burp, passed gas into the oriental carpet underneath him, and laughed out loud. "Ah, I feel so much better now."

Disgusted, Moira put her plate on the side table next to the sofa and sat in a chair across from him. "God, for a man of such wealth, you sure do act like a crass little boy sometimes. I hate seeing this side of you.."

"Back at cha, you inebriated wench." Clyde opened his mouth and stuck out his tongue which held a mound of partially chewed food on it.

"You are such a clod!" With that, Moira hoisted up her tan skirt to show him that she wasn't wearing any undergarments. "Eat me, instead!"

Clyde smiled, chewed, and swallowed. "Thanks, but no thanks. I've already got a mouth full."

Moira laughed along with him. "We make such a pair, don't we?" She knew he didn't have to answer. She loved him just the way he was. She knew about his sordid ways and didn't care what he did away from her. As long as he always came back to her, that's all that mattered. "What did you want to share with me?"

Clyde spoke between chews. "God, you wouldn't believe what happened on Friday morning at Sacred Heart."

Moira was intrigued. "What? Do tell."

Clyde pointed his three-tine, silver fork at her. "Now what I'm about to tell you is a secret to be kept between you and me. Do you hear?"

Moira waved her hand in the air indicating to him to proceed. "Yea, yea. It goes without saying. Go on."

"Well, I got a call from Edward to meet him down at the Sacred Heart construction site.

Apparently there was an accident of some kind. You know Tom and Pete Greene who own Greene's Construction?"

Moira nodded.

"Tom was killed on the site Friday morning. It appears that a portion of the tunnel wall fell on him, crushing him to death. Edward asked me to join him at the sight to investigate the situation. The Chief of Police met us there. There doesn't seem like there was any foul play by Mr. Chen and his men. It's just a freak accident, pure and simple."

"So why are you so shook up and messed up?"

Clyde drank some champagne. "Because...I saw the body and the expression on Tom's face was gruesome. His eyes, his mouth...the bones poking out of his clothes, the blood...I can't seem to un-see it. It's haunting me." Clyde finished what remained in the bottle. "I had just spoken with him on the phone about moving up the construction timeline to complete the tunnel before March of next year. And, now he's dead. God, life is bizarre. He was here among us and now he's not. Poof! Just like that, he is gone!"

"Ain't life a bitch! That's why you make the most of your days. Tomorrow isn't guaranteed to us."

"Yea, I know. Edward, the chief, and I also made the notification to Mrs. Greene about her husband. That was such a gut wrenching experience. I still hear her screams. And, when the kids overheard the conversation and saw their mother go into a conniption fit, they became hysterical and wailed. That's all I hear in my head."

"Jesus Christ! What did you expect? This woman just learned that her husband wasn't coming home anymore. The kids just lost their father. Show some compassion for God's sake. That's just an awful way to die—to be crushed to death and suffocate under a mound of dirt. That's not my idea of a fun way to leave this earth."

"Not mine, either. Edward plans to honor his memory and name the tunnel after him at the grand opening next year."

Moira laughed. "That's a nice way to keep the family quiet and from raising too much of a fuss about it. How do you know that crappy construction isn't to blame for the accident?"

"Common sense tells us that the ground probably got nice and hard when we had below freezing temps last week. Then, when the sun came out and temperatures warmed the ground, the ice crystals melted and softened the soil. The timber walls can constrict and expand as the weather changes, too." He pointed his fork back at her. "So don't go jumping to some kind of conspiracy theory conclusions, missy."

"Ah, ha! How do you know that another hospital didn't send a gang of hooligans over to sabotage the site in the middle of the night?"

"Now that's completely absurd. I think that's the champagne talking." Clyde set his plate down and crawled over on his hands and knees toward Moira. "I'm done talking about it. It's time to move on and investigate a site of my own." Clyde pulled up Moira's skirt and disappeared underneath it.

18

Monday morning, December 29, 1913, First Ward

Moira dressed in silence early Monday morning, leaving Clyde in bed. She returned to her apartment across town. She was anxious to relay the news she learned about the construction accident to Charlie Finch.

She rang his office. She heard him pick up the receiver on the other end. "Charlie?"

"Yes? This is."

"Hey! It's me, Moira." Excited to use their code phrase for the first time, she blurted, "Is it sunny out?"

Charlie laughed as he snuffed out his cigarette and grabbed a pencil and pad of paper. "Clear, blue skies for as far as I can see. What do you have for me so early on this fabulous Monday morning?"

"Well, you didn't hear this from me, but...." Moira looked suspiciously around her apartment as if someone lurked in the shadows before proceeding. "Well, there was a fatal accident at the Sacred Heart construction site on Friday morning."

"You're kidding me? Really? I've not heard a thing about it. Usually, I get a tip from the police about stuff like that."

"Well, that's because Mr. Alexander is keeping it hush hush. You know how close he is to the police chief. He doesn't want any bad press, you see."

"Who's your source?"

"I can't say. Let's just keep it that way, Charlie. Trust me when I say it comes from a reliable source, I mean a very reliable source. It's from someone who's very close to the action."

"You better be good with this information. Our jobs depend on it. Tell you what, I'll send Scout out to the site to see what he can stir up. Someone will talk if they have enough of an incentive to do so."

"So, what's my incentive, Charlie?"

"How about a nice steak dinner at Roscoe's?"

"And..."

"And...if it pans out to be good, then let's say three bucks on top of that."

"Three bucks? Are you kidding me? I'd rather forgo the steak dinner and pocket that change, too. Let's say the steak dinner and five dollars. You know this is a good story, Charlie, especially since you haven't caught wind of it yet."

Charlie knew she was right. If the story was valid, then *The Atlanta Dispatch* would be the first to report on it before *The Atlanta Journal* or *The Atlanta Constitution* picked it up. "Deal. You drive a hard bargain, Miss Sunshine. What's your schedule like this week? How about getting together for dinner tomorrow night? I'll come pick you up at the apartment around seven?"

"Oh, Charlie! I love the name, 'Miss Sunshine.' It sounds so fetching. It's so me. Tomorrow night will be grand. See you then, Charlie dear."

"See you then."

"Toodles." Moira hung up the phone. She undressed and poured a perfumed bubble bath. She had a big shopping day planned at Macy's uptown. She knew Charlie would make good on his promise to her and with her first mission accomplished, Miss Sunshine had new money to spend.

It wasn't until a quarter past four o'clock when Charlie finally heard back from Scout. He reported back to Charlie's office as instructed. The young lad sat down in a chair in front of Charlie's desk and removed the tweed cap from his sandy, blonde head.

Charlie shuffled around a few stacks of newspapers on his desk so he could make eye contact with the kid. "How'd your expedition go, Scout?"

"Mighty fine, Mr. Finch. Mighty fine. Seems like your hunch paid out in spades."

Charlie sat back in his chair and enjoyed a good belly laugh. "Spades, that's a good one, kid. Dirt, construction, excavation site, I get it. That's a good one. So what did you learn? What can I go to press with?"

"Seems like all your facts were spot on the money. I used your 'incentive' to get an Irishman with eight kids who worked on the site next to the tunnel to open up and corroborate the story. It's all just like you said, word for word."

Charlie smiled and lit up a cigarette. "Finally, I have something that *The Atlanta Journal* or the *Constitution* doesn't have yet."

"There's one more thing. Rumor has it that Mr. Alexander told Mr. Greene's widow that Sacred Heart will memorialize her husband and dedicate the tunnel to him when they open next year, calling it 'Greene's tunnel.'"

"Sounds honorable." Charlie inhaled deeply and blew out smoke rings. "I bet his widow is glad her last name wasn't...Hiscock or Willy."

The kid roared back in laughter and not to be outdone added. "How about Doomey?"

Charlie loved words and word play. He was into the name game, hook, line, and sinker. "Or, Nutters?"

Hysterical, the kid slapped his hat on his knee and added. "Oh, I've got it! How about Rockaway?"

"Oh, God, kid! That's priceless. I should put you at an editorial desk. You're killing it today. I haven't laughed that hard in a long time. You know, they say laughter is good for your health. Damn! I just had a week's worth of medicine." Charlie wiped tears from his eyes. He opened up his desk drawer and pulled out an envelope. He sifted through the bills, picked out two dollars and tossed them between two stacks of papers toward his guest. "Here, this is for all your hard work and the extra is for making my day."

"Gee, thanks, Mr. Finch. You're the best!"

"Now, be gone with you. I've got a story to write." Charlie flipped his right hand at the teen motioning him toward the door.

"No problem, Mr. Finch. Just call me again when you need me."

"Will do, kid. Will do." Charlie didn't bother to look up as Scout left his office. He was already past the main headline and well into the first paragraph by the time he heard the door latch close.

19

Tuesday morning, December 30, 1913, Fourth Ward

The clock in Mrs. Gray's parlor struck nine bells while she sipped her morning coffee. The fireplace was aglow. Yesterday, they spent the majority of the day taking down the Christmas tree. Mrs. Gray said it was bad luck to keep the holiday decorations up past New Year's Day. Addie had never heard of that tradition, and recalled many farmhouses in Hope, including their own, that kept their Christmas trees on display through mid-January. Addie chalked it up to being an old wives' tale and then recalled how she lost her younger brother and sister, Maw, and Paw. A chill ran through her body. Perhaps there was something to that tradition after all, she concluded as she removed the remaining decorations throughout the house and stored them away in the attic, ready to reappear in twelve months.

Addie sat in a chair closest to the fireplace. She relished the early mornings where she and Mrs. Gray had the opportunity to engage in conversation about current events, politics, and any other matter that popped into Mrs. Gray's head. Addie adjusted and folded *The Atlanta Dispatch* and gasped as she read aloud the morning headline in big, black, bold letters. "Oh, no! *Tragedy Strikes Sacred Heart Construction Site.*" She didn't wait for

Mrs. Gray to respond and kept reading. "Last Friday morning, Mr. Tom Greene, co-owner of Greene Construction Company, died tragically at the Sacred Heart Hospital Construction site. A tunnel wall under excavation collapsed on top of him, crushing him to death. Mr. Greene leaves behind his wife, Sarah, and his three small children, Tom, Jr. (5 yrs), Elizabeth (4 yrs), and Emily (3 yrs). While the Atlanta Police Department ruled the unfortunate event as an accident, an unidentified source commented that Sacred Heart's Founder and Director, Mr. Edward Alexander II, was incentivizing the construction crew to complete the tunnel project before its scheduled date of March 16, 1914. Upon learning the news, the widow Greene only added that Mr. Alexander plans to honor her late husband's memory by naming the tunnel after him when the hospital opens next year. She declined further comment. Mr. Alexander was not available for an interview; phone calls were unreturned. Sacred Heart Hospital is scheduled to open its doors on Friday, May 22, 1914 and will provide a myriad of services. The hospital will consist of ten-bed wards for pediatric, medical-surgical, maternity, and tuberculosis patients. In compliance with the city's segregation ordinance, a separate facility for Negroes called Alexander Hall is being built by Alexander and is currently under construction, slated to open in 1917."

Second Ward

Across town and compliant with his morning ritual, Edward sipped his coffee at the dining room table and scanned the headlines from *The Atlanta Journal* and *The Atlanta Constitution*. He hollered when he opened up *The Atlanta Dispatch*, startling Trudy. She dropped her partially eaten muffin onto her breakfast plate.

Edward erupted. "God damn it! I'm going to kill Sam for running this story."

Miss Mattie hustled into the dining room after hearing the commotion.

"Edward, what has gotten you so riled up?" Trudy picked up what remained of her crumbled muffin and took a bite.

Edward threw the paper at Trudy. "Here, see for yourself. I've got some damage control to do." Edward stormed out of the dining room, marched through the front hall, and burst into the Zoo to join the other wild animals. Picking up the phone, he dialed Sam Sloan, *The Atlanta Dispatch* editor.

The phone on the other end rang only once before Sam picked it up. "Hell..."

"Let's cut straight to the point, Sam. What the hell is going on down there at your paper? I thought we had an agreement? I thought that before you ran any, and I mean any kind of article about Sacred Heart Hospital, you'd give me a heads up about it first."

"Edward? Is this you?"

"For fucks sake, of course it's me."

Blindsided, Sam stammered as he quickly sorted through the facts in his head that Charlie relayed about the story before they agreed to go to press with it. With everything in order, he was prepared to tackle Edward. "Edward, it was my understanding that my reporter tried to contact you on a few occasions yesterday. According to my notes, the messages were given to your son to give to you."

"God damn it! My son? My son? Do you know how old my son is?"

Sam didn't answer. He knew it was a rhetorical question.

"Trip is only five years old! Did you hear what I said?" Edward slammed his fist on his desk.

"He's only FIVE. Your reporter gave those messages to a five-year old? That message is as lost as last year's Easter egg! What were you thinking?"

Sam knew Edward had a young son, but didn't realize he was only five. The reporter said the kid promised to relay the messages to his father. Sam's face flushed. "I'm so sorry, Edward. I tried. I really tried to get a hold of you."

"Where the hell did you get the information about the tunnel's construction project?" Untrusting, Edward opted to remain tightlipped about the details.

Sam closed his eyes and remembered that Charlie said he used Scout to get the rest of the details from an Irishman on the site. "Look, Edward. The details came from one of Greene's construction workers. I don't know his name, but he was an Irishman. That's all I know."

Edward inventoried all the people that would have been privy to the construction incentive, to include Clyde, Tom, possibly Pete, and the tunnel foreman. Any or all of those parties could have said something in passing to anyone. But since Tom was a childhood friend, he trusted him like a brother. He wouldn't have mouthed off to just anyone about a bonus. That kind of a business deal was usually kept close to the vest. "Here's what I need from you, Sam. Let me be crystal clear. Moving forward, you will track me down and personally talk with me about any future story. Got it?"

"Got it." Sam waited before interjecting. He knew there was more.

"And, you will run a nice cover piece tomorrow about Sacred Heart with an emphasis on its new nursing school. Contact Miss Lena Hartman for an interview. She'll be happy to give you all the details about how we plan to serve Georgia with excellence and provide skilled nurses to our patients. I'll make my daughter, Opal, available to you, too, so you can profile a young nursing student."

"I didn't know your daughter enrolled into Sacred Heart's nursing school? That's terrific.

Congratulations. I'm sure you are very proud of her."

Edward knew Sam's comments were meant to pacify him and he responded in kind by deescalating the conversation. "Yes, I am very proud of her. She'll be in the first class. It's quite an honor. She does make her father proud."

"I'll send a reporter and a photographer over to your home this afternoon, let's say two o'clock."

"Fine. I'll have Miss Hartman and Opal available for you."

"You've got a deal. Again, my apologies. I am so sorry." Sam knew he wasn't being sincere as he hung up the phone. He was ecstatic that he got the story published before his counterparts did. And, there was truth in that story, enough to cause Edward heartburn over it. He didn't care if Edward got heartburn. Sam was used to getting threats of all kinds, every day. This was just another typical news day in Atlanta.

Edward concluded the call with Sam and then dialed Lena. He received a busy signal. He gave it a few minutes before he reattempted the call. Her phone rang.

"Hello?"

"Lena? This is Edward. How are you this morning?"

"I'm fine. But I believe the more important question is how are you doing? I know you've already seen *The Atlanta Dispatch's* headlines this morning. That was shocking, to say the least."

"Yes it was and that's why I'm calling. I've made arrangements with Sam to have him run a cover piece in tomorrow's edition on the nursing school and to profile a student. Can you free yourself up and be here at the house for a two o'clock interview and photo shoot? Opal will be joining you." Edward stretched the story and included. "Sam wants to interview a nursing student, too."

"Sure. It won't be a problem." She paused. "The story will do us some good. I just got off the phone with an upset father who is pulling her daughter from our nursing program. I've got to call Alan so he can refund their tuition check. But there's no need to worry. I've got another call to make. I learned that Mrs. Gray's nursemaid is anxious to enroll into our program. When I spoke with her last, the program was full and she was told that we'd accept her into the 1915 class. I'll just put her into this vacant spot."

"That's a great plan. So when you are interviewed this afternoon, you can truly say that our nursing program is full and now accepting applications for the Spring, 1915 class." Relieved, Edward smiled for the first time today. "Lena, that's what I love about you and that's what makes you such a great nurse. You are always thinking ahead and are two steps ahead of me."

"Thanks, Edward. While we aren't blood relatives, that's what family does. We're a team and we've got to be able to see the bigger picture." Lena decided to throw in a medical metaphor to amuse Edward. "It's like when a patient begins to bleed out on the operating table. Simply clamp off the affected artery with your hemostats, mitigate and repair the damage, and move on to salvage the patient. We're just mitigating the damage and moving forward. Your vision is becoming a reality in less than a year. I'm just so proud to be a part of it."

Edward chuckled. "Thanks, Lena. I wouldn't have it any other way. While I won't be here this afternoon, Trudy will be here to greet you. Again, thanks for everything. I look forward to reading all about it in tomorrow's headlines. After all, today's paper is just tomorrow's liner for a birdcage."

Lena laughed as she hung up the phone. She reached for her notebook on the desk and looked up Olive Gray's phone number. She dialed the residence.

"Hello! You have reached the Gray residence. Happy holidays!" Addie sang out.

"Hello. Happy holidays to you. This is Miss Lena Hartman. Is Mrs. Gray home and available to speak on the telephone?"

"Yes, ma'am! Please wait for just a moment while I get her."

Addie put the receiver on top of the wooden phone mounted on the kitchen wall and ran into the parlor. "Mrs. Gray, it's Nurse Hartman. She wants to speak to you."

Mrs. Gray set her coffee cup into the saucer and stood up with assistance from Addie. With her cane in hand, she made her way into the kitchen. "Did she say what the call was about or what she wanted?"

"No, ma'am, she didn't. She simply asked if you were available to speak with her."

Mrs. Gray picked up the receiver. "Hello? Lena is that you?"

"Hello, Olive. How are you? Did you and your family have a merry Christmas?"

"Oh, we did! The family gathered at my sister's house and we had a delightful time together. And, you?"

"Yes, I sure did. I traveled down to Macon to be with my brother and his family. I just got back two days ago. Listen, the reason for my call is to see if your nursemaid, Addie, is still interested in enrolling into Sacred Heart's Nursing School? We had a student drop out of the program." Lena opted to not explain the details as to why the student's father had a change of heart. "If she is, I'd love to have her in the upcoming 1914 class that begins in April."

"Wow! That's remarkable news. Will you hold for just a moment while I ask her?"

"Sure. I'll hold."

"Addie?" Mrs. Gray called out toward the parlor.

Addie's heart pounded as she stood in the hallway between the kitchen and the parlor overhearing the one-sided phone conversation. She waited a few seconds before responding to Mrs. Gray. She wanted Mrs. Gray to think that she was sitting in the parlor and she squelched her excitement. "Yes? What is it?"

"Nurse Hartman has an opening in this Spring's nursing school program. Are you interested in signing up?"

Addie couldn't contain her emotions any longer. She was emphatic. "Yes! Yes! A thousand times, yes! Please tell her I would be honored to be in her program." Tears pooled in her eyes as she leaned back against the kitchen counter.

Mrs. Gray also welled up at the sight of Addie's priceless response. "Lena, Addie said, 'yes!' She'd love to be a student in your program. You have just made our day!"

"Wonderful! I'm thrilled to have her be in our first class. Olive, I trust your judgment in people implicitly. I know Addie wouldn't be working for you if she wasn't a top-notch individual. While my interaction with her at the Alexanders' Christmas party was brief to say the least...." Both Lena and Olive laughed, knowing the embarrassing details didn't need to be rehashed. "I would like her to make an appointment with me next week, let's say on Monday morning at ten o'clock at my residence. I will need for her to complete an application, make payment, and I will review the course curriculum and expectations at that time, too."

"Lena, I can't thank you enough for the call. I really appreciate you extending this offer to Addie. She will be at your apartment on Monday at ten o'clock. I'll be sure to have her bring her payment, too. Happy New Year."

"Happy New Year to you, too, Olive."

Mrs. Gray hung up the receiver, turned, and found herself engulfed in a huge embrace. Addie cried on her shoulder. She shed a multitude of tears—for excitement, for joy, for a dream coming true, for the loss of her family, for the gratitude shown by Mr. Darling and Mrs. Gray, for the pent up anger, for Lester's sadistic antics, and for the day when Garrett would hold her in his arms and never let go.

Later that evening, soon after Mrs. Gray went to bed, Addie

sat at her desk to write a letter to Garrett using stationary he had given to her for her birthday. She was anxious to share her new news with him.

30 — December, 1913

Dearest Garrett, It was simply wonderful to see you and your father last week. I must confess that I love writing to you on my birthday present. The scarf and gloves you gave me for Christmas were also appreciated. We country mice must think alike. I hope that your new scarf and glove set keeps you warm and you think of me when you wear them.

I can't believe how my life has changed so much in the short course of two months. It has been a bittersweet journey. I pray that 1914 will be less dramatic. Speaking of the New Year which is nearly upon us, I wanted to share with you that I received a call today from Nurse Hartman at Sacred Heart's Nursing School. I am thrilled to tell you that I have been accepted into the Spring, 1914 program. Because they had a student drop out, she invited me to fill the empty position.

Garrett, I can't tell you that despite all of the tragedy that has befallen me, it seems like the grey, cloudy skies have parted and my tears have dried. My days are now filled with sunshine and laughter. My dreams of becoming a nurse are finally coming true and everything is falling into place. I meet with Nurse Hartman on Monday morning to find out more about the curriculum.

Garrett, please share my news with your father, too. None of this would have been possible without his wise judgment and his caring heart. I finally have options and possibilities that I never knew existed beyond the borders of Hope. My future is but blank pages yet to be filled in with new adventures. I'm thrilled to begin this new journey. I pray that you and your father are well. Give Ol' Girl an extra carrot for me. Please write and tell me of the news in Hope.

I wish you both a very blessed and Happy New Year.

Until we see each other again.

Fondly, Addie

Addie reached into her desk drawer for an envelope. She folded her letter and placed it inside, addressing it to Garrett. She then reached down and pulled out the drawer that contained the silver, tin box in the back of it. As she pulled it out, it seemed much lighter in her hand than it had in the past. She opened the box to find it empty. Stricken with panic, Addie flushed. Only a garbled reflection of her horrified face stared back at her from the bottom of the container.

"Oh, no!" Addie shrieked. Addie closed her eyes and tried to remember when she had last checked the contents. *Who could have taken my money?* She remembered taking out some money to purchase Christmas gifts for Mrs. Gray, Mr. Darling, Garrett, and the Schwinns the week before she and Mrs.Gray were admitted to Grady Hospital. *Who would have been in the house while we were gone...or unconscious?* She was hit with a revelation. *There's only one scoundrel who is low enough to steal from his own family and that would be Lester! Oh, God! I feel sick. What am I to do? I don't have any proof that he stole my money and I have nothing to give Nurse Hartman for payment when I meet with her on Monday.* Addie started to cry. Her dreams were crumbling before her eyes. All of her possibilities and desire to go to school vanished just like Maw's savings. *I don't even have anything of value that I could sell.*

Addie threw herself on her bed, buried her head into her pillow, and screamed. Through gritted teeth, Addie hissed. "I hate you Lester! You are the devil incarnate! There is a special place in hell waiting just for you, I swear it! Mark my words, the truth will come out. And, when it does, I hope you suffer painful consequences."

Feelings of guilt washed over Addie for wishing ill will on Lester, recalling how she had wished her Paw dead. Addie bowed her head and clasped her hands together in prayer. *Oh! Dear Lord, Please, I beg of you to help me see my way clear out of this dilemma. Please help me find a way to fight off these feelings of anger and resentment against Lester. I know you know he is a very bad man. I need to trust in you that you will put a stop to him and his corrupt and harmful ways. Can I put a rush on that request? I am fearful of him. I know that you see what he is capable of. I need to trust and let go that you will deal with him with swift and just action. While you are aware of the bigger plan, I am stuck again. Lester has stolen Maw's money and I don't have a way to earn that kind of money in time for the upcoming school year. Lord, I just can't bear anymore heartache. I need your help!*

There was a gentle knock on Addie's bedroom door.

"Addie, dear are you okay? I thought I heard you cry out."

Addie jumped off her bed and attempted to dry her eyes on her nightgown sleeves. "Coming." She opened the door to find Mrs. Gray standing in front of her.

Mrs. Gray studied her face. "My dear, you've been crying. What's the matter? Are you sick or hurt?" Addie opened the door wider and let Mrs. Gray enter the room. Mrs. Gray steadied herself on her cane and took inventory of the room. She noticed an envelope on the desk and next to it was an open, silver container. She walked over to it to find it empty. "What was inside?"

Tears streamed down Addie's face as she sat on the edge of her bed. "It was Maw's savings. It was the money she had saved for the family for a rainy day. She told me to take it after she kill..." Addie swallowed hard and chose to replace the word. "Died. It was all I had. I had seventy dollars in there a few weeks ago and now it's empty. I was going to use it to pay for nursing school."

"Who do you think took it?" Mrs. Gray sat down in the chair at the desk. She saw the letter addressed to Garrett and smiled. Looking back at Addie, she added. "No, don't tell me. I know who it was. It was Lester, wasn't it?"

Addie shook her head in the affirmative. "I believe in my heart that he did. He's the only one who would have had access to the house and who is evil enough to commit the crime." Addie didn't hold back. "Mrs. Gray I am sick. I don't know how I am going to pay for school now. What am I going to do? I guess I will need to call Nurse Hartman in the morning and cancel my meeting with her."

"You will do no such thing!" Mrs. Gray snapped back as anger fired from her eyes and she banged her cane into the floor. Mrs. Gray let a moment of silence pass before continuing. "You know, I tried to find my favorite pearl necklace and earrings to wear on Christmas Day to Mary's house. They were a gift from Doc for our twentieth year wedding anniversary. I couldn't find them anywhere. I had been storing them in the same place ever since I received them. I thought I was losing my mind or being forgetful. This concludes only one thing. Lester is at the root of this theft. That son-of-a-bitch!" She banged her cane hard on the floor again.

Addie gasped. She had never heard Mrs. Gray use profanity, nor had she ever seen her angry before. "What are we going to do about him?"

"*We* are going to do nothing. *I* on the other hand am done with that rat bastard of a nephew! As I told you, I am dealing with him in my own way, and trust me when I say that he will pay for his crimes." Mrs. Gray closed the lid on the tin box. "Addie, I am so sorry for all of the pain he has caused you. I need to make things right." Mrs. Gray looked back at Addie. "In the morning, you and I are going to the bank. I am going to make sure you get a real bank account, not this tin one here. The account will be in your name only and only you will have access to it. You'll be able to write checks against it and pull out money when you need it for school expenses. You will even be able to deposit your hospital paychecks into it, too."

Confused, Addie fired back. "What are you talking about? Did you not hear what I said? Thanks to Lester, I don't have any money to open up a bank account or to pay for school."

"I clearly heard what you said. I will make sure you have enough money in your account to write a check to Nurse Hartman and you'll have plenty left over to call your own."

Shocked, Addie covered her mouth with her hands. Shaking her head in complete disbelief at what she was hearing, *God? My you sure did work a miracle tonight!* Addie ran over to Mrs. Gray and embraced her. "Oh, Mrs. Gray! Thank you! Thank you! You are too good to me." Addie fell to her knees and sobbed, burying her head in Mrs. Gray's lap.

Mrs. Gray patted the top of Addie's head and then soothingly combed her hair with her fingers. "There, there my dear girl. Everything will be alright. Just you wait and see. I may not be your mother, but I am going to make sure you are given every opportunity as if you were my own daughter. I love you, dear one."

Addie looked up and wiped her cheeks with the sleeves of her light blue, flannel nightgown.

"I love you, too." She consoled herself and stood up to help Mrs. Gray up from the chair. "You are truly my angel on earth. I don't know what I would do without you."

"I believe that God put us together for a reason, so that we'd be there for each other when times get tough. I'm sure Doc and your Maw are looking down on us right now from heaven." Mrs. Gray touched her heart. "I feel the warmth of his smile in my heart right now. It's his way of telling me everything is going to be alright and that I'm making the right decisions for us."

"I truly believe you and trust you as if you were my own mother."

Mrs. Gray smiled in appreciation. "Best we get back to bed. We've got a big day tomorrow. We'll set out for the bank about nine o'clock in the morning. I'll call for a taxi and have them carry us uptown."

"That sounds grand."

"Dress in your best, Addie, dear. We're going to make a day of it to include a little shopping and champagne lunch at The Georgian Terrace. We're going to end this year on a bright note if I have anything to say about it." Mrs. Gray raised her cane in the air and spoke to the ceiling.

"Hear that, Doc? We girls are headed out on the town tomorrow! Isn't that a hoot! Out with the old and in with the new, I say! We're going to ring in this New Year with some bubbly and a bang!" Mrs. Gray laughed and danced, tapping her cane on the floor all the way down the hall until she closed her bedroom door.

Addie laughed at Mrs. Gray. The more she got to know her, the more she just loved her to the core. Addie closed her bedroom door, turned off the lights, and returned to bed. She clasped her hands in prayer and spoke softly. "Maw, guess what? My wish is finally coming true! I'm going to nursing school! I can't believe it. I'm going to be a nurse! I know you are proud of me. I can feel it. Like Mrs. Gray said, I can truly feel the warmth of your love in my heart." Comforted by the thought, Addie touched her heart, closed her eyes, and fell asleep before she heard the clock chime twelve bells in the parlor.

20

Across town, Frank Stone crouched in an alley off of Factory Road out of sight and under the cover of darkness. He inhaled the stale stench of cigar smoke from the wool fibers in his black scarf and slowly exhaled, preventing the vapors of his breath from betraying his location across the street a half of a block away. He retrieved a silver pocket watch from the breast pocket of his black wool coat with a gloved hand. *Three o'clock.* There were only three more hours until he saw the last sunrise in 1913. Frank wondered if 1914 would be a more prosperous New Year for him, or if it would bring more of the same — booze, broads, and bad men. His heart settled on the latter.

Glancing left diagonally across the street, he watched Lester Schwinn smoking a cigar as he supervised a group of Negro men carrying wooden crates out of the front door of Newman's Painting and Supplies Company. The sound of boots walking across the plywood front porch echoed under the white, aluminum awning. They walked away from him, down the side porch steps, and stacked the crates into the beds of four black trucks that were located in the gravel parking lot next to the store. Frank pulled out a pair of mother of pearl opera glasses with gold embellishments from another coat pocket and observed that each truck had *Newman's Painting and Supplies Company* painted in white on the driver's side doors. He assumed the same was painted on the passenger doors, too.

Approximately another half hour passed before the last of the boxes were loaded. The men placed tan tarps over the boxes and secured the cargo with ropes. When all of the men returned into the paint store, Frank snuck toward the alley on his left which was located directly across the street from the two-story, brick building. He pulled out his notepad and pencil and scribbled down the vehicle registration numbers from the porcelain plates. He shoved his pad and pencil back into his coat pocket as he scanned the street for other cars. He darted across the road toward the trucks. Lifting up the tarp on the truck furthest from the street, Frank climbed into the back bed and pried off the lid from one of the crates with a putty knife that he had in his back pants pocket. From another coat pocket, he pulled out an Eveready flashlight. A dull, yellow light illuminated the silver lids of six paint cans. Holding the flashlight with his chin, Frank jimmied open one of the cans. The smell of fresh hay wafted into the air. He blindly reached inside and groped around to find ten small bottles nestled inside. He pulled out one of the bottles closest to the top. The label read, "Doc Gray's Tonic & Cure-all."

Frank heard Newman's squeaky, wooden, front door open. The tinkling of a bell was a signal to Frank that he needed to make himself as small as possible to avoid being seen by the approaching men. Frank said a silent prayer. *God, I'm not ready to die yet. I vow to give up one of my vices. I'm not sure which one, just yet. I'll have to get back to you on that. But if you let me live to see another day, your will be done. Amen.*

Frank could make out the voice of Lester and a colored man. He watched them walk out onto the sidewalk in front of the store. Lester placed his black bowler on his head as the two men conversed. They were too far away to make out what they were saying. Lester quickly turned toward the trucks and pointed. Frank's heart jumped into his chest. Then, Lester turned away and pointed in the opposite direction down the street. Frank sighed in relief and surmised that Lester was giving the man directions on how to leave the city. The two men shook hands and Lester strode off away from view. Frank heard the sound of boots as they made their way up the front porch steps. The wooden, front door creaked and a bell jingled. A car engine on the opposite side of the building whined as it started up. Frank remained motionless as he watched Lester's car drive past the lot and take a left turn. He surmised he had only a matter of seconds before the driving teams emerged. He quickly replaced the paint lid and the top of the wooden crate. He secured the tarp and ran toward the back of the building. He dove behind a row of high azalea bushes.

The front door opened and the bell rang out again. Frank counted a total of eight men filing out to the trucks, a driver and a passenger for each truck. The passengers were easily identified. They toted the new Smith and Wesson semi-automatic pistol. Frank was impressed with their firepower. This band of brethren were unlike the moonshiners he'd run into who preferred to carry 20-gauge shot guns, like the 14-inch barrel Winchester. Frank tapped his right hip. His trusty Colt .45 was by his side.

One of the men, wearing a short, brown coat and matching hat, pulled out a piece of paper from his bib overalls. He read it, wadded it up, and threw it toward Frank. He was the last driver to get into the truck. All four engines turned over. One after the other they filed out, turning left onto the main road. Once out of sight, Frank emerged to retrieve the discarded paper. As he did, he heard the sound of multiple motor car engines driving toward his location. He shoved the paper into his coat pocket before scurrying behind the bushes again. A car pulled into the lot. Rocks crunched under tire wheels. The second car, a police car, approached and pulled into the lot from the opposite direction so that the driver's side windows faced each other. Frank cautiously peered through the branches. The police car was closest to him; there were two officers in the car. Lester's car was next to it. This time Frank was close enough to overhear the conversation.

Lester was first to speak. "Thanks for all your fine work, officers." Lester handed the officer behind the wheel a cream-colored envelope. He, in turn, handed it to his partner. Frank watched the passenger bow his head; he assumed he was counting the payoff. The policeman raised his head and nodded. Frank didn't need words to know that the money was in order.

The officer behind the wheel adjusted his hat. "Where are your boys headed?"

"They're off to Alabama and are taking the route you told me to use."

"Great. We'll catch up to them and discreetly escort them out of town. Just wanna be sure they don't run into any trouble."

The passenger rolled down his window and spat tobacco onto the gravel. He chimed in. "Yea, we've got a few boys on the west side of town who belong to the KKK. It seems like they like to play night watchmen of the roads. It's rumored that they lynched a few colored boys last month who were caught transporting moonshine to Villa Rica."

The driver added. "I've told them to leave Newman's Paint trucks alone. But you never know if the message gets passed along to the new recruits."

Lester slammed his hands down on his steering wheel. "My boys better not run into the Klan!

If they do, it will affect your monthly stipends!"

"Now pipe down, Lester. We'll make sure the dog wags the tail 'round here and not the other way 'round." The driver reaffirmed.

His partner spat, wiped the dip drippings from his chin, and laughed. Frank laughed at the analogy, too, silently.

"Happy New Year to ya, Lester."

"And to you."

The two cars pulled away and headed in opposite directions. Frank breathed a sigh of relief as he pulled out his notepad and pencil. He scribbled down the patrol car number and plate numbers. *25. 21798.* He pulled out his watch again. *Four thirty.* Concluding he still had enough time to check the inside of the building before the break of day, he finished his prayer. *It looks like I will see 1914 after all. God, thank you. I owe you one!*

Frank was determined to collect as much evidence as he

could for his client, Mr. Thompson. He despised men like Lester who made a living by selling empty promises in a bottle by preying on the poor, stricken, disadvantaged, and gullible. Instead of improving and curing all that ailed them, Lester was robbing them blind and creating addicts.

Old copies of *The Atlanta Journal*, *The Atlanta Constitution*, and *The Atlanta Dispatch* were taped to the inside windows, preventing him from getting a peek inside. Frank walked to the back door and reached inside his breast pocket, pulling out a lock pick. With a few twists, the backdoor bolt retreated inside its iron casing and he entered the premises. Although the windows were occluded, the light from gas street lamps streamed through the spaces between the newspapers. Frank took a few moments to allow his eyes to adjust before proceeding into the darkness.

He made out a wooden desk in the back of the store. Numerous invoices were laid in stacks on top of it. Using his flashlight, he picked up one of the white invoices. Newman's Painting and Supplies Company was printed at the top of the paper, followed by the address and phone number. "Recipient" was printed in a blank fill-in the box that provided enough space to write in the person or company's name, address, and phone number. There was a table below that with two columns. "Order" was typed into the first column and "Quantity" was printed in the second.

This invoice was designated to go to Kentucky. The order was for fifty gallons of green paint, below that read "white paint, 10 gallons," and the next line read "red paint, five gallons." The "Total" printed in bold, black ink at the bottom of the table tallied "65 gallons."

Frank figured they were keeping the operation simple. One gallon of paint held ten small bottles of tonic. Ten bottles multiplied by sixty-five totaled an order for six hundred and fifty bottles of tonic. He was unsure if the paint colors mean something more, but he'd find out. He had plenty of time on his hands to dedicate to this case. He scanned the invoice further. At the bottom of the page was printed *Delivery date* and handwritten next to that read, *January 5, 1914.* Below that was typed, *Payment Method: Cash, Check, COD.* COD was circled in pencil.

Frank grabbed the next invoice. This shipment was going to All Rite Pharmacy in Tennessee. The order was for thirty gallons of green paint, ten gallons of red paint, and ten gallons of white paint. The grand total was for an order for five hundred bottles of Doc Gray's tonic. The order was due to be delivered on January 8, 1914. COD was circled in pencil at the bottom.

Frank flipped through the remaining stack of invoices on the desk. The deliveries were headed to apothecaries or pharmacies in Alabama, Tennessee, South Carolina, North Carolina, Kentucky, and even to Indiana, Illinois and Ohio. All deliveries were slated for January and all payment methods indicated that they were being paid in cash or cash on delivery. Frank noticed that the word "check" was never circled as a method of payment. He quickly surmised that the district attorney's office would love to get their hands on this open and shut case.

Frank took an invoice from the bottom of the stack. It was an order to be delivered to Stewart's Pharmacy in Rome, Georgia. Frank deduced since Rome was a couple of hours drive northwest of Atlanta, he could set out in the morning. With enough pressure and impressive language he could watch the small town seller roll over before lunchtime. Frank knew that an investigation and a trip out of state wasn't ideal, especially to a state north of the Mason-Dixon Line. In his experience, the Yankees were tougher to turn and tight-lipped. As a Southerner, Frank was considered an outsider. He could quickly disappear during his travels, unfamiliar with the territory, roads, and local police. No one would miss him. There wasn't a wife, kids, family, or even a pet. Mr. Thompson and a few drinking buddies probably would be the only ones to mourn him.

He once wore the badge earlier in his career in Columbus, Georgia. However, the accidental shooting of a colored teenager who he thought had a gun in his hand, which actually turned out to be a horse brush, ruined his chances of ever wanting to be happy, find love, and live the "happily ever after" dream. While the incident went undisputed, it left him with deep emotional scars and a small hand tremor. The invoice shook in the night air as he folded it and placed it into the same pocket as the crumpled piece of paper the Negro driver discarded. Like the paper, he pushed the painful memories into a dark recess and focused on his mission at hand.

Moving from the desk to the other side of the building, Frank saw boxes of empty brown, corked bottles in large, medium, and small sizes. Against the far wall under the other set of papered out windows, he made out two large, capsule-shaped, copper vessels that were housed on a wooden base. Each container had a total of twenty spickets, ten on each side. A small wooden stool sat in front of each faucet. After a quick calculation in his head, Frank concluded the tiny stools were made for children. He counted a total of forty spickets which meant there were a minimum of forty kids employed to fill those bottles with Doc Gray's tonic eleven hours a day, every day. Frank looked up at the ceiling. Two copper pipes fed each container and appeared to originate from the second floor.

Frank pulled out his pocket watch again. *Five o'clock.* He glanced at the wooden staircase in front of him that led to the second floor. Knowing he was pushing his luck, Frank ran up the staircase and emerged into another vast room He immediately inventoried the contents to find bales of hay, wooden crates, empty paint cans, label makers, and what appeared to look like a large kitchen with counters, cabinets, spoons, ladles, scales, and bowls. Four large, copper vessels with lids sat on the floor on top of their respective pipe. Frank lifted the lid of one of the containers. The pungent odor of the tonic overcame him and he hastily recovered it.

Ever mindful of the ticking seconds, Frank concluded he had gathered enough evidence for one night for Mr. Thompson. He promptly retreated back down the stairs, out the back door, and secured the lock. He figured he could type up his report and have it ready for Mr. Thompson by Monday. As he made his way along the back alley and crossed the street to return to his Chevrolet Series C, Frank glanced down at the morning edition of *The Atlanta Dispatch* that had been tossed on the front stoop of a neighboring cotton mill. He grabbed the paper and removed the elastic band that held it together.

As he walked to his car, he scanned the front page. One of the headlines read, *Sacred Heart's Nursing School Focused on Educating Tomorrow's Nurses.* Below that were photos of an older woman with sharp, dark eyes and a structured nose. Her hair was pulled tightly back and it appeared dark in the black and white photo. The younger girl had a beautiful head of apparently blonde locks that were piled high on her head. A few tendrils framed her heart-shaped face. Although she didn't smile, she looked happy and full of hope. Without reading the article, Frank assumed the former portrait was the nursing school's director and the younger, a prospective student.

Frank got into his car and threw the paper into the passenger seat. He turned the engine over and headed the car out of the alley, onto the road. As he glanced over his left shoulder, the sun crested over the horizon. Frank welcomed the dawn of the new day, the last day of 1913. He didn't see patrol car #25 ducked into the alley on his right.

"Did you get the plate number?" the driver asked.

"Yup. Got it." The passenger spat tobacco from his open patrol car window.

21

Monday morning, January 5, 1914, Sixth Ward

It was a day of firsts for Addie. It was the first Monday of 1914, her first time to ride in a streetcar, the first time she ventured uptown alone, and the first time she ever had to sit for an interview, one with Nurse Hartman. She bit her thumbnail as she waited behind a rotund man who moved as slow as a sloth to climb up the two stairs and enter the car. Once on board, she paid the streetcar conductor five cents and found an empty seat in the middle of the electric vehicle. She overheard the black-capped conductor directing the two Negro women who stood behind her in line to find a seat at the back of the car. Addie made sure she followed Mrs. Gray's instructions to the letter to include making sure she didn't set her purse down, let it out of her sight, or carry it with one hand for fear of it being pickpocketed or stolen. She clutched her bag that contained her future — a check made payable to *Sacred Heart Nursing School* for the full amount. Until the bank readied and printed her own checks, this one was issued directly from Mrs. Gray's account.

As the car glided along the track and headed uptown, Addie

gazed out the window at the well-dressed men wearing over-coats, scarves, and bowlers. The women, dressed in their best fur coats, some with matching hats, and carrying muffs, strolled the sidewalks with a sense of purpose in front of the various dry goods, shoe, and dress shops. At one point during the journey, the streetcar nearly hit a man who stumbled out in front of the tracks as he weaved his way to the liquor store in front of him.

"Next stop, Ponce de Leon Apartments and The Georgian Terrace Hotel." The conductor called out.

The car came to a quick stop in the middle of Ponce de Leon Square and Addie departed, making her way to the front door of the apartment building. She stood on the corner of Ponce de Leon Avenue and Peachtree Street. Before entering, she gazed over her left shoulder at triangular-shaped Georgian Terrace Hotel which opened a little over two years ago. Not to be outdone, the new eleven-story, luxurious, high-rise apartment building that held its ribbon-cutting ceremony four months ago stood one story higher. Addie chuckled, shook her head, and thought. *My, oh, my! Men must love boasting about how tall their buildings are. Size surely must matter to them!*

Warm and intimate, the Ponce de Leon Apartment's lobby was constructed out of Caen stone, a creamy-yellow limestone that was popular in Europe in the construction of castles and cathedrals, and Formosa marble. Addie walked between four large, yellow-hued columns, two on each side which had in-laid bench seats between them. The lobby hallway opened up to a ro-tunda surrounded by wooden columns that connected the lobby and the mezzanine to a Tiffany dome above it. Addie was mes-merized by the light blue ring that had an intricate, diamond pattern, floral design on it that encased the glass structure with gold filigree embellishments. On the outer part of the stained-glass structure, Addie counted nine separate yellow-toned, square panels that were subdivided into two rows of four smaller squares that housed a diamond pattern in the center of each one. They were framed in dark-chocolate colored, carved wood. As Addie stared up and turned in a circle, glass panels boasted varying shades of amber that faded to a pale sunflower as the design moved out from the multi-colored epicenter.

To rid herself of her nerves, Addie opted to take the stairs and ascended up the main spiral staircase to the eleventh floor. Once at the top, she leaded over the stained, wood railing and paused for moment to catch her breath. *Gosh, it looks like the inside of a nautilus shell from up here. It's so beautiful!*

Addie adjusted her scarf and hat before knocking on Miss Hartman's apartment door. Addie heard the sound of footsteps coming toward her from inside. When they stopped, the door opened.

"Why, hello. You must be Addie. Come in my dear and welcome to my home," Miss Hartman said. Her dark, no-nonsense eyes met with Addie's. Addie thought she saw a glimmer of a smile, but she wasn't quite sure.

"Why, thank you." Addie removed the gloves that Garrett gave her for Christmas, shook her hand, and entered the apartment. "This building is so posh! And, the stained-glass ceiling in the lobby is magnificent. What an extravagant sight to come home to every day."

"It is quite an architectural showplace. I moved into it when it opened in September. My father wasn't happy when he found out that I was living in tenement housing off of Decatur Street. He insisted that…" Mimicking the voice of an old, Southern gentleman, she continued.

"A proper, professional woman needs to reside in a respectable, less colorful part of town."

Addie laughed as Lena cleared her throat and resumed in her tone. "So, in an effort to appease my father, I moved uptown. I'm now within a few blocks of the hospital, so that works out nicely." Miss Hartman took Addie's coat, hat, and scarf, and placed them in the coat closet in the hallway. "How was your ride on the shorts? Did you encounter any difficulties?"

"Shorts?" Realizing Miss Hartman was referring to the streetcars and after bearing witness to a humorous side of Miss Hartman, Addie dropped her guard a little. "Oh, no ma'am. It was no trouble at all." Addie thought. *Should I bring up our brief encounter at the Alexander's Christmas party?* Addie immediately squelched the idea as soon as it popped into her head. *My past has passed. It's time to focus the conversation on the present and my future.*

"Please come and have a seat in my living room. I've prepared a pot of Earl Gray for us. Would you like a cup?"

"Please. Thank you." Addie noticed the apartment was located on the curved front of the building overlooking the square where the streetcar had just dropped her off.

Addie took a seat on the sofa and inventoried the room while Lena poured the tea. Deep, cream-colored walls and off-white trim cast a golden hue, providing the sense of instant warmth which complemented the burning embers in the fireplace. Addie quickly surmised that the meticulously decorated room, complete with fresh cut white roses with Baby's-breath and green fern accents in a crystal bowl on an end table next to her, was where Miss Hartman spent the majority of her time. A built-in bookcase was amassed with a variety of medical, science, biology, and nursing textbooks on one side. On the other, poetry books, books about foreign countries, a brass clock, and a copy of the *Official Program, Woman Suffrage Procession, Washington D.C., March 3, 1913* was proudly displayed on one of the shelves. The cover appeared to have a prince or a princess on it. Addie studied the program. Addie couldn't tell if the individual printed on the program was male or female. The individual was riding a white horse, blowing a trumpet, and wore a blue and purple flowing cape as they marched in front of the White House. A dark blue "Votes for Women" banner hung underneath it. A procession of women dressed in white gowns adorned with red, white, and blue sashes followed behind.

Nurse Hartman interjected. "Would you care for any milk or sugar in your tea?"

Addie refocused on Miss Hartman. "Yes, a cube of sugar, if you please." Addie watched her take the silver tongs and daintily added a cube to both cups.

"Here you go." Lena served her tea in a white bone china cup that had a vibrant floral design hand painted around the lip of the cup and matching saucer. "Mrs. Gray tells me you are an excellent nursemaid and that you will make a fine nurse one day. Tell me a little bit about yourself." Lena settled into the chair across from Addie.

Addie appreciated Miss Hartman's ability to set her at ease from the moment she stepped into her home. She respected her for that and elected to be candid. "I grew up in a small town, north of Atlanta, called Hope."

"I've heard of it. It's a farming community just outside of Lawrenceville."

Addie lit up. *Hope is such an inconsequential speck on the map compared to the city of Atlanta. I can't believe she is familiar with my hometown!* "Yes, it's located northeast of the city, on the border of Gwinnett as you head toward Winder."

"I pass through there on my way to visit friends who are professors in Athens. Tell me more about you, your family, and how you came to live with Mrs. Gray."

Addie felt her neck flush and struggled to find the right words to explain to Miss Hartman the details without having to divulge too much. "A series of tragic events befell our family and I am the sole survivor. I lost my younger brother and sister to scarlet fever a few years ago." Addie paused, and then said, "My parents died last year in a house fire."

"Oh, Addie. I am so sorry for your losses. I believe I read about a farm house fire in Hope this past fall in *The Atlanta Dispatch*."

"That's the one."

"But if I remember the story correctly, the sheriff said there weren't any survivors."

Addie knew that whatever she said next could be the linchpin in her future with Miss Hartman. "I was two months shy of turning eighteen. The Darlings, who are kin to Mrs. Gray, were also dear friends of my family. After the accident last year, Mr. Darling made an arrangement with the sheriff to let me live with Mrs. Gray rather than become a ward of the state." Addie waited with bated breath to hear Lena's response. Her hands trembled and her tea cup rattled in the saucer. She held it tightly as she lowered it to rest in her lap.

Lena's sharp, dark eyes softened. "That was a mighty kind gesture and probably the best decision they could have ever made on your behalf. They must really adore and love you. You have endured much at such a young age. In my humble opinion, it appears that you have landed on your feet and have a sensible head on your shoulders. Those are admirable qualities, Addie. Adversity can define us, it is in the *how* that is most important. I've seen people rise like a phoenix out of the ashes and I've seen others consumed by the flames." Lena studied Addie. "I believe you to be the former."

Lena polished off her tea and rested her cup on the saucer before placing it back on the silver tray on the coffee table in front of them. "So, why are you drawn to the field of nursing?"

"I really enjoyed caring for the sick people I knew in Hope. I helped my Maw care for my brother and sister when they got ill. I also took care of Mrs. Darling after she got consumption. I learned a little about roots and herbs from some of the women in our community and a little bit about medicine from the country doctor when he'd ride through town on his Standardbred. I even learned about health and science in school. Of course, living on a farm had its merits, too."

Lena raised an eyebrow. "What did farm life teach you?"

"As a young girl, I was amazed to see how humans and animals healed after sustaining injuries. To educate myself about the body, I'd examine the internal organs of Paw's killed deer.

After it was skinned, I'd manipulate the bones, muscles, ligaments, and tendons to see how they all worked in concert to make a joint bend."

Lena enjoyed watching the countenance on Addie's face change as she sparked with passion and exuded an unbridled enthusiasm while telling her story. "Go on."

"I wasn't like other girls in school. I loved learning about nature, animals, science, and biology. I'd gaze out the schoolhouse window at maple tree. I didn't see a tree, but I saw how it resembled the circulatory system."

"How so?"

"It's easier to see in the fall when the tree doesn't have its leaves." Addie set her cup and saucer down on tray on the coffee table and used her hands to illustrate her answer. "The trunk represents the aorta, the limbs are the veins, and the tiny branches are the capillaries. I also think the structure of the tree mimics the inside of the lungs as the bronchial tubes branch out and lead to the alveolar sacs." Addie thought she saw Lena's eyes moisten. "Did I say something wrong?"

"No. You didn't say anything wrong. I can tell you are going to make a fantastic nurse.

To be quite frank, you remind me of me when I was your age—full of life, hungry for knowledge, and eager to learn more. By the way, Mrs. Gray said you graduated from the twelfth grade?"

"Yes, I did. I made all A's and B's, or satisfactory scores in school. I did graduate and receive a diploma, but unfortunately it was lost in the fire."

"Not to worry. I'll just call your school this week and have a copy reissued and mailed to me so that I can put it into your file."

Addie reached for her purse. "I have a check made payable to the nursing school for the full amount."

"Wonderful. Thank you. I will give this to Mr. Waxman to be deposited and have him mail a receipt to Mrs. Gray." Lena took the check and placed it into a file folder on the table. "How would you like to stretch your legs and go on a tour of this place with me? Afterwards, would you join me for lunch?"

"Yes! That sounds wonderful, Miss Hartman. I'd love to!" Addie followed her.

Lena walked into the hallway and retrieved Addie's coat and her full length, brown sable coat from the closet. "Come on. We're going to explore everything from the belvedere where we have a terraced garden and spectacular views of the city to the basement." Lena read Addie's face. "Just kidding, I'm not going to take you to the basement where the ice maker and laundry service is located."

"You have an ice maker and laundry service in this building?" *Gosh! I had to fetch blocks of ice from town with the Ol' Girl and the wagon for our ice box and had to hand wash and line dry our clothes outside.* "This place is so fancy."

"We do! There's even a central vacuum and air is pumped in from the roof into each apartment providing fresh ventilation. I can say, as a nurse, that having access to ventilated air is vital to one's health and well-being. That is surely one thing I didn't have when I lived downtown. My stars! It would get so hot and stuffy in my old apartment. That warm and stale environment was a breeding ground for illness and disease. Mr. Alexander made sure a similar unit is going to be put into place at Sacred Heart and Alexander Hall."

Addie and Lena stepped out into the hallway and exited a rooftop door. Addie's senses were overloaded. While walking through the winter garden, Addie reveled at the thought of being on top of the world. This was the first time she had ever been in a high rise building overlooking the most exquisite panoramic views of the city she had ever seen. To the east, Addie could easily see Stone Mountain. Across the street was the roof of The Georgian Terrace Hotel. On the west side of the building, Kennesaw and Red Top Mountains accented the horizon north of the city. Somewhere in between, to the northeast, was Hope. Addie stared out into the distance in its general direction. She was so far from home and from Garrett. Addie pointed out her finger as if she could touch it and touch him.

Lena observed Addie for the moment. She turned and headed back toward the door, talking all the way. "Come on, before you catch a chill out here. Let's head down to the first floor to the cafeteria. That's where I take all my meals. On occasions, I'll arrange for room service, but not today. We have so much to talk about to include my expectations, the curriculum, and I'll be happy to answer any questions you have about the three-year program."

Addie snapped out of her trance. "Coming."

Addie retreated from the balcony and followed Miss Hartman back into the building. Based on their first brief encounter, Addie knew Miss Hartman was the key to her future and that she was going to be a fantastic mentor for her. Addie filed in behind her through the hallway and they stepped into an awaiting open elevator. As the doors closed, Addie decided she'd follow Miss Hartman anywhere.

Monday late afternoon, First Ward

Frank remained sequestered in his apartment on Hulsey Street over the weekend. He typed up his report from his findings at Newman's Painting and Supplies Company for Mr. Thompson. He phoned the law firm six and a half hours earlier, securing a four-thirty appointment at the practice in the Sixth Ward. He closed and locked the door to his apartment, carrying two envelopes, one with postage stamps and one without. Before he left the building, he ran into Madam McGuire on the stairs and gave her the envelope with the stamps on it.

"If you don't see me in a week's time, please mail this for me."

"Will do. Are ye in some kind of trouble, Frank? She appeared genuinely concerned. She hated the thought of losing him as a tenet and a lover. He was good to have around the brothel and he kept the bad customers at bay.

"Not sure. But please. I'm begging you to do what I ask, without questions." He hoped he'd be back. He had grown accustomed to seeing her red hair on his bare chest at night.

She nodded in agreement.

He kissed her on the cheek and exited the premises. He got into his car, driving past the city incinerator on Elliott as he made his way toward Peachtree Street. Blue lights caught his attention in his rear view mirror. He pulled the car over.

An officer stepped out of the driver's side of the vehicle and approached him. His weapon was drawn. His partner exited the vehicle, but hung back by the car.

Frank saw the patrol car number on the door. *25. Thank you, God for letting me see five days of 1914. Forgive me for my sins. I'm ready to go home.* Gunfire was the last thing Frank heard, before everything went silent and dark.

"Did you get it?" The policeman spat tobacco on the side of the road.

"Yup." The other office handed him a manila envelope spattered with bits of brain matter, hair, skull fragments, and blood. "Nice."

The two walked to the rear of the patrol car and pulled out a can of gasoline from the trunk. Frank's body and his car were doused. With the flick of a tossed lighter, the car burst into flames.

With the first part of their mission completed, they focused on the second and last for the day. They got back into the police car and turned left off Elliott, pulling into the city incinerator parking lot. The officer in the passenger seat got out of the car, holding the bloody envelope. He took out another lighter, set the package on fire, and threw it into a smoldering trash pile. He watched the flames consume the contents before returning to the car.

"Is it done?"

"Yup. It's done." He removed the wad of dip from his lower lip and tossed it onto the ground, spitting one last time before getting back into the car and closing the door.

Mr. Thompson buzzed his secretary in the front office. "Miss Bishop? What time was Frank's appointment?"

A sweet, voice with a Southern twang spoke over the intercom. "His appointment was for four-thirty, Mr. Thompson. I've haven't received a phone call from him to indicate that he's running late or cancelled the appointment. Would you like for me to try and ring him at home?"

"Please." Mr. Thompson glanced at the clock hanging on his wall. *Four-forty-five.*

The voice sang back, "Mr. Thompson. There's no answer at Mr. Stone's home."

"Thank you, Miss Bishop. That will be all."

Mr. Thompson, his empty glass, and a half-full bottle of bourbon waited in his office on Peachtree Street until eight o'clock before he decided to leave for the night. His four-thirty appointment never showed.

22

The clock in the living room struck nine bells. Addie retrieved *The Atlanta Dispatch* off of the front porch, removed the rubber band, and opened the paper. She returned to the parlor and took her usual place. Mrs. Gray waited to hear the news. Addie read the front page headline silently. *Man's Charred Remains Discovered.* She read the article further to learn that the police found an unidentified man in a Chevrolet Series C Classic Six in the First Ward last week. There weren't any leads in the case. Addie's thoughts wandered and returned to Hope to the moment when Mr. Darling and Garrett informed her about finding her parent's burnt bodies. *What a horrible way to die.*

"Is there anything of interest in the paper today?"

Addie flipped past the front page and folded the newspaper on itself, hiding the photo of the scorched car from Mrs. Gray's view.

"Oh no!" Addie furled her eyebrows. "There's an article about Doc Gray's tonic on page three." Addie flipped the paper around to show Olive the black and white photograph of a physician wearing a white lab coat holding a stethoscope in one hand and a bottle of Doc Gray's Restorative outstretched in the other.

Miffed, Olive pressed. "What does it say?"

"Doc Gray's Restorative is the number one recommended medication for Dr. Otto Barringer's patients. It goes on to say he is the Medical Director for Charleston's Infirmary and Sanitarium. There's a quote from him that says, 'I highly recommend Doc Gray's Restorative to all my hospitalized patients.' He makes sure that the hospital keeps it stocked in the pharmacy."

"Doc Gray's Restorative? I thought he was calling it Doc Gray's Nerve and Blood Purification Tonic? Mrs. Gray tapped her cane on the floor. "Barringer? Barringer? Why does that name sound so familiar to me?" She continued to tap the cane on the floor as the name rolled off her tongue. The cane stopped and she locked eyes with Addie. "Oh, dear God!"

"What? Who is Dr. Otto Barringer?"

Olive slammed her cane into the floor causing Addie to jump and the coffee cups to rattle on the table. "It's Mary's daughter, Susan's father-in-law!"

Second Ward

Edward and Clyde stood in front of the new Sacred Heart department head hires who sat on the couches and chairs in the Great Hall. Miss Mattie scurried through the room, making sure everyone had what they needed before the meeting began. She patted her son, who sat in the chair closest to the kitchen door, on the shoulder before she returned to her culinary duties. Edward watched their exchange as the grandfather clock against the far wall by the piano chimed ten o'clock.

Edward cleared his throat. "It is my absolute pleasure to have you on the Sacred Heart and Alexander Hall hospital team. I wanted to bring you all together so that you have a clear picture of where we were going in these next few months. As you wind down your other jobs, I want to relay to you my expectations. Now, if at any point you find this is not going to be the ideal place for you, then please confer with Mr. Posey." Edward took a sip of water from a nearby glass. "It has been a life-long dream of mine to build a state-of-the-art medical facility dedicated toward the treatment and care of all Georgians, white and colored alike. With that said, you are part of a new medical facility that will focus on providing the best medical care and teaching tomorrow's nursing students. I have drawn up for you the organizational chart for Sacred Heart and Alexander Hall so that you have a bird's eye view of our operational structure, including everyone's names, roles, and responsibilities at my institutions." Edward motioned to Clyde to pick up the stack of papers on one of the end tables and hand them out to the new hires.

The first one went to Moira, who glanced up at him and smiled. Obeying Clyde's strict instructions to her the night before, she refrained from speaking and tossed him a wink.

Once everyone had a piece of paper in hand, Edward continued. "In the top box, you will see the names of Sacred Heart and Alexander Hall, the hospital for Colored patients. It's not slated to open until 1917. I'm sure you've read in the papers and in your interviews with Clyde, you learned that Sacred Heart will open its doors in May of this year." Edward observed heads nodding in agreement and understanding.

Holding up the paper, he took his index finger and ran it down the line connecting the box with his name on it to the next line containing five boxes. He pointed to the first box. "In the first box is the name of our Medical Director for both hospitals. That's Dr. John Williams."

His finger continued to follow the line and pointed to the box below his name. "This one lists the names of our medical doctors under his direction, including Dr. David Leventhal, Surgeon, Dr. Randall Springer, Pediatrician, and Dr. Morgan Paine, our morgue physician."

A black woman sitting on the sofa wrinkled her face. Clyde pinched the side of his thigh to prevent him from laughing out loud at the mention of Dr. Paine's name, again. Moira shifted in her seat, aware of the comments Clyde made at the previous leadership meeting.

"In the second box, next to our Medical Director, is our Chief Financial Officer, Alan Waxman. He's in charge of our finances, payroll, billing, and medical records departments, and our fundraising efforts." He pointed to the third box. "Lena Marie Hartman is our superintendent for both nursing schools. She is also in charge of our nursing staff and volunteers." Edward skipped over the next box and pointed to the last one. He made a note. "I'll come back to this one. The last one is for the Chief Operating Officer for Alexander Hall. His name is Oliver Louis." Edward's finger went back to the skipped one. "This box lists Clyde Posey's name. He's our Chief Operating Office for

Sacred Heart and your direct boss." Edward turned to Clyde. "You can take it from here."

Clyde held up his piece of paper and pointed to the box under his name. "As the COO of Sacred Heart, I am responsible for all of your respective departments. Let's go around the room and have you introduce yourself to everyone. Let them know a little bit about yourself and which department you are in charge of." He turned toward Moira, who sat next to him in an end chair. "Miss Goldberg, would you go first." He had never seen her wear black before and thought she looked like she was going to a funeral. Clyde held his breath, anticipating her next words. He instructed her to keep it brief. He prayed she would.

Moira sat up tall, adjusted the cameo affixed to the lapel of her black jacket and spoke. "My name is Moira Goldberg. I am originally from New York City. I have been hired to serve as Sacred Heart's concierge and will manage the main desk, mail, and phone calls for the hospital."

Pleased with her response, Clyde released his breath. "Thank you, Miss Goldberg." He pointed to the Chinese man who sat on the couch next to Moira.

Moira's hand shot up into the air.

Clyde flinched. "Yes, Miss Goldberg? You have a question?"

"Yes, I do Mr. Posey. When do we get paid?"

Clyde felt like he'd been punched in the gut. He coughed, rustled his paper, and glared at her.

Edward stepped up and answered. "Great question, Miss Goldberg. You will officially become a part of the Sacred Heart payroll effective Monday, May 18th. According to my attorneys, the day you step into the hospital is the day we are financially and legally obligated to you. We will open our doors to you on that Monday so that you can familiarize yourself with the layout of the hospital and get your departments set up and organized. We'll hold mock operations until our grand opening celebration on Friday, May 22nd. The exception to that will be Miss Maybelle Reed and Joshua Goode, who will be assisting us with the nursing school when it opens on April 1st."

Heads around the room nodded.

Clyde avoided making eye contact with Moira and again pointed to the Chinese man. "Please, let's continue."

He stood up and bowed to the group. "My name is Mr. Wei Wu. My wife, Ying, and I are in charge of laundry service at hospital." He bowed and sat down.

A tall man sitting across from Mr. Wu interjected in a Scottish brogue and pointed at Mr. Wu.

"'Ey, don't you own a laundromat in the Second Ward? I believe me brother Rob and I picked up a stiff in the alley next door to your wee shop." He stroked his red mustache and beard that covered a pocked and ruddy complexion.

"Yes, actually it's father's shop. My wife and I work there."

"Ya speak good English, there, my good man." The Scotsman noted.

"Thank you." Mr. Wu touched his chest with his hand. "My wife and I are Americans. We born here in Atlanta. Our parents immigrated from Peking, China in 1866 just after big war here."

Clyde nodded and looked at the black woman sitting next to Mr. Wu.

She fiddled with her purse handles and looked at the floor. She spoke softly. "My name is Maybelle Reed. I was born in

Birmingham, Alabama and moved here with my momma and sister when I was a young 'un. I'll be your cook and run the kitchen at the nursing school and the hospital for Mr. Alexander and Mr. Posey." She raised her head and continued to clutch her purse.

Joshua Goode stood. His amber eyes sparkled. "My name is Joshua Goode. I'll be in charge of the Housekeeping and Maintenance Department. It's a pleasure to make your acquaintance and look forward to working with all y'all." He sat and refrained from adding that he was also Miss Mattie's son and a preacher on Sunday. Since that wasn't pertinent to the discussion, he thought it ought not be said.

A tall, spindly man on the sofa closest to Joshua arose. He smiled at Clyde and adjusted his glasses. "My name is Alvin Martin. I will serve as the pharmacist for Sacred Heart."

The Scotsman added. "'Ey! I know you, too. Don't ye have a place also in the Second Ward.

What's the name?" He twisted the tip of his beard between his index finger and his thumb.

"Martin's Pharmacy." Alvin sat back down.

"That's the one. Picked up a man one night who 'ad his brains bashed in. Someone found 'im dead on the side street outside your store. Been a few years back. He reeked of whiskey. Police thought he stumbled out into the middle of the road and a truck hit 'im."

Alvin shifted his eyes to Clyde and back to the Scotsman. "Gosh, that sounds horrible. I had no idea."

Alvin silently recalled the name and the incident clearly. Richard Steele. He beat that welcher with a baseball bat in the back of the store when he tried to skip out the back door without paying for his drugs. Alvin pulled the body out the rear door and dumped it onto the street alongside his store. He remembered pouring whiskey on the man, cleaning up the mess, and letting the police officers driving patrol car #25 do the rest.

Ready to shift the focus of the discussion off of him, Alvin redirected. "Alright, Scot. Who are you and what's your story?"

The stout Scotsman stood. His black boots shifted underneath his girth to steady him while a gold watch chain swung from his vest. "Me names Brice McDaniel. Me brothers and I own McDaniel's Brothers Ambulance Service. Our clan is from Atlanta by way of the west coast of Scotland. We've been 'ere since we was wee lads. Proud to be a part of the new Sacred Heart family, we are." He pounded his chest and sat down with such a force that Alvin rode the sofa cushion wave up and down.

Maybelle broke a smile at the sight. Joshua wasn't looking at Alvin or Brice. Maybelle caught Joshua's eye and blushed.

Clyde stepped forward. "Thank you all for those introductions. Mr. Alexander thought it was important to start the New Year with this social gathering so that you could put faces to names and begin to spread the word in your wards about the opening of Sacred Heart. If there is anything specific that you need in addition to the equipment and supplies you have already requested, please let me know. I need ample time to procure everything before we open our doors."

"Oh, let me set my expectations for you as my employees." Edward reached for another piece of paper. "There will be no drinking, smoking, or drug use on my property. I expect you to show up fifteen minutes before your shift begins. Breakfast and lunch will be provided to you. If you'd rather bring your own meals, then that's fine with me, too. But you can't eat in your department. You must eat in the staff kitchen or if the weather is nice outside, there will be picnic tables out back. I expect you to dress appropriately for your job. If uniforms are required in your area, then you will wear them. You will not mingle and cavort with the doctors, patients, or families. You will call each other by your surnames in public passing. While in public, you still represent this hospital. I better not hear about you frequenting bars, bordellos, or be seen in areas of ill repute. If Clyde or I don't like what you are doing or if we find you incompetent in any way, we will fire you on the spot. We have standards and a reputation to uphold. Georgians will hold us to higher standards because we are dealing with the health and well-being of their loved ones." Edward sipped from his glass. "If I sound strict, I am. I make no apologies for it. Running a hospital is like running a church because taking care of others is a holy and sacred business."

Joshua said silently to himself, *Amen to that!*

"You are seeing them at their worst and most vulnerable states. You will treat them with dignity and respect, no matter if they are rich or poor, and regardless of their color or creed.

People's perception of Sacred Heart is their reality." Edward folded the piece of paper. "Well, as my daddy use to say, 'Let's get to it and just do it!'" He clapped his hands together.

Clyde rolled his eyes.

"If there's nothing more, I look forward to seeing you all in May." Edward took a moment to shake their hands before leaving the Great Hall through the kitchen door.

Miss Mattie washed her hands in the sink and dried them on her apron. "Is the meeting over?"

"Yes. We're all done now. They can be shown out."

"Be happy to."

Edward stepped in front of her. "Does he know?"

"No." Miss Mattie removed her flour-covered apron. "Does she?" she fired back.

"No. It goes with me to the grave."

"Good. Me, too."

Edward swallowed hard. "Joshua has my eyes."

"I know." She left the kitchen to retrieve the coats and hats of the guests and their son.

23

Madam McGuire refused to betray Frank as she cowered in the corner of her apartment. A black boot reared back and kicked her again in the abdomen. This time she threw up on the floor.

"Nice." The police officer spat on the door which was laying on the floor.

After reading the papers, Madam McGuire knew the charred Chevrolet found on Elliott was Frank's. She was thankful that she had the sense enough to mail the envelope he gave her that morning. While he asked that she mail it if she hadn't seen him in a week's time, she decided to let another one pass, hoping he would walk through her apartment door once again. Instead, two angry police officers burst through her door tonight, knocking it completely off its hinges.

"What did Frank tell you?" the other officer asked.

"Nothing, I swear it. He never spoke to me about his work. He was a payin' customer, just like any other." She lied.

"We understand he used to live here. Take us to his apartment."

Madam McGuire pushed herself up on her elbows. Her

lower lip was split and bleeding. Red lipstick streaked up to her left cheek. "What do ye mean, 'used' to live here. He still has an apartment upstairs. Come. I'll take ye to it."

The officers exchanged glances, opting to refrain from speaking about Frank in the past tense.

"Fine." He spat at her feet as she passed by.

The policemen followed her up the stairs to the second floor. A key unlocked apartment 8-B. She stepped aside. They brushed passed her as they entered the premises.

"I'll be downstairs if ye need anything else." She refrained from adding, *Ye evil bastards! I hope ye demons burn in 'ell for what ye did to me Frank.*

An hour passed. Franks apartment was turned upside down. The chair and couch pillows were torn apart. The few decorative pictures that hung on the wall were removed and destroyed. The twin mattress and down pillow were also tossed. Dresser drawers were emptied; rugs were flipped.

"I can't find a thing." He spat on the sofa cushion stuffing at his feet. "You?"

"Not a damn thing. The place is as clean as a whistle. No nooks, crannies, or hiding places of any kind."

"Come on. Let's get out of here."

The policemen walked down the stairs. As they passed Madam McGuire's apartment, they observed her front door lying on the living room floor.

"Nice work, tonight, Seth."

"Back at cha, Lamar."

"I'll be right back, Mrs. Gray," Addie called out from the kitchen. "I'm just taking the garbage out for the night." Addie flipped on the light illuminating the back stoop. She carried a paper bag in her hands and lifted the lid to the aluminum incinerator. Tossing in the paper refuse, she retrieved a matchbox from her skirt pocket. Lighting the wooden stick, she tossed it in and replaced the conical lid with a mesh top. She looked up, startled to find Lester standing in the shadows.

"How's it going, Addie? Are you behaving yourself?"

"What? Are you just checking on me to make sure I haven't told anyone that you stole my money from my tin box?" *Thief!*

"Well, have you?"

"No." She lied.

"Good. Keep it that way. It appears that we have an understanding. Has my aunt brought up her recent hospitalization again?"

"No." Addie lied again. "She believes she passed out as a result of an illness of some sort." The third lie slipped out.

"Good." Lester stepped into the firelight. He reached out to stroke her flushed cheek.

Addie stepped back.

"You fear me. Good. I like having that control over you." Lester smirked and cautiously eyed her as he swiped his hands over the flames licking the top of the canister.

She acted intimidated on the outside. But on the inside, she was telling herself *little do you know, Lester. Little do you know. Maw always said, "If you play with fire, you will get burned." I hope that when Death robs you of your tiny, dark soul one day, you leave this world with all the pain and anguish you have bestowed on others. Lester, you will reap what you sow and I pray harvest comes soon for you. Forgive me, for that is my wish and my prayer. I pray for a miracle that will vanquish you from this world.*

Pleased with his perceived results, Lester retreated into the darkness.

24

The phone rang. Addie jumped up to answer it. "Hello, this is the Gray residence. May I help you?"

A gentleman replied in a rather curt manner. "Yes, is Mrs. Gray there? It's Mr. Thompson. I need to speak to her at once."

"Why, yes she's right here. Just one moment please." Addie covered the receiver and whispered. "It's for you. It's a Mr. Thompson."

Mrs. Gray nodded and got up to take the call. She whispered back to Addie. "Dear, will you please give me a moment of privacy?"

"Sure. I'll be in the living room if you need me. I've got some dusting to do in there anyway." Addie sought out the feather duster from across the hall in the laundry room and proceeded to the living room.

Mrs. Gray watched Addie leave before responding to her caller. "Hello, Mr. Thompson. How are you this afternoon?"

"Fine. Thank you. Listen. Let me get straight to the point. I had my private detective follow Lester and I just received the report of his findings this morning...*in the mail*. I've had a chance to read it and...." Mr. Thompson wanted to blurt out

based on Frank's report, Lester is in a lot more trouble that just sim-
ply mislabeling a tonic bottle. Frank believed that in addition to
sales outside of the state, there are a few bad policemen on his payroll
doing his dirty work for him. I believe Frank stepped into a hornet's
nest...and he got stung...to death.

Impatient, Mrs. Gray said. "Don't beat around the bush, Mr. Thompson, I'm sure this call is costing me money. Tell me what he found out."

Instead he said, "I'll spare you the details, but your concerns about Lester's *Doc Gray* tonic business were valid. The detective learned that the tonic does consist of cocaine and alcohol. Unfortunately, those ingredients and amounts aren't listed on the label. He's even smuggling the tonic across state lines. Per your instructions, I need to issue a cease and desist letter to stop Lester from using the Doc Gray name and threaten him with a lawsuit if he fails to halt production. In addition, I'm turning my evidence over to the U.S. Attorney's office so they can open up an investigation for prosecution. Mrs. Gray, your fears are founded. Your nephew is violating the laws of the federal Pure Food and Drug Act...*among other things.*"

Mrs. Gray swayed and tried to steady herself with her cane. She leaned up against the door frame between the kitchen and the dining room. Filled with rage, she yelled, "Shut him down now! You make sure he can't tarnish my husband's good name ever again!" She slammed her cane hard into the floor. Mrs. Gray felt a sharp pain behind her left eye. The right side of her face drooped and her right arm went numb. "Lessssh-tas gonna pa-pa-pay..." Olive collapsed onto the floor.

"Hello, Mrs. Gray? Are you there? Hello?"

Addie heard Mrs. Gray yelling followed by a loud thud. She rushed into the kitchen and found Mrs. Gray slumped across the threshold. The phone receiver swung back and forth against the wall.

Addie grabbed the receiver and screamed into it. "Mr. Thompson? Are you there? Please call an ambulance for me. Mrs. Gray has collapsed. Hurry, please hurry!" She hung up the phone before she heard his response so she could tend to Mrs. Gray.

Addie turned Mrs. Gray over and noticed she was still breathing on her own, although her face was pale and sweaty. Addie positioned her on her side, using the door frame to prop her. She learned from the country doctor that sometimes people vomit after they collapse. She recalled him saying, "If they are kept on their back, they can aspirate the emesis into their lungs causing them to suffocate and die." Addie tried to rouse her. "Mrs. Gray! Mrs. Gray! Can you hear me? Mrs. Gray!"

There was no response. Addie began crying and took Mrs. Gray's cool hand in hers and started to pray. "Please dear Lord, Don't take her from this world yet. Please send Maw and your angels to watch over her. Please, God, hear my prayer. I need you now!"

The sound of multiple sirens in the distance calmed Addie. "Mrs. Gray. Help is on the way. I'll be right back."

Addie ran out the front door and into the street to flag down the approaching ambulance and police car. Glancing up, she saw that dark clouds covered the sky. She directed the ambulance drivers, who were identical twins, into the house. One of them carried a rolled up canvas stretcher that was attached to two wood poles in his hand. The police officer followed.

"She's in here. Her name is Olive Gray. She was just talking on the phone and then I heard a loud noise. I came in to find her lying on the floor. She's breathing on her own, but she's unresponsive. I turned her on her side just in case she threw up."

"How did you know to do that? That's good thinking on your part," the attendant said in a Scottish brogue as he unrolled the stretcher next to Mrs. Gray.

"Just something I learned from our country doctor."

"You said her name was Olive Gray? Why does the name 'Gray' sound so familiar?" the strawberry-blonde attendant said to the other.

"She's the widow of Doc Gray. We knew 'im well." The red-headed twin said.

"Great man, he was. And he was an excellent doctor," the other twin added.

The twin with fair hair placed his hands on either side of Mrs. Gray's head. "I'll stabilize 'er head and maintain 'er airway." The policeman slid his hands palm up under her back while the other brother grabbed her legs. "Lift, on the count of three. One...two...three." Mrs. Gray was gently lifted onto the stretcher and the twins lifted her off the floor.

The red-headed brother at the foot of the stretcher began singing as they carried Olive out of the house and placed her into the back of the ambulance. "Blessed assurance, Jesus is mine! Oh, what a foretaste of glory divine! Heir of salvation, purchase of God, born of His Spirit, washed in His blood. This is my story, this is my song, praising my Savior all the day long. This is my story, this is my song, praising my Savior all the day long."

"Why are you singing?" the policeman asked as he watched them secure her stretcher.

"When I was a wee lad, I remember our Presbyterian minister telling us that 'He who sings, prays twice.' If I remember right, Saint Augustine said it first. Anyhow, I figure I'm doublin' up on me prayers for the sick and dying when I sing. I also sing to make 'em happy on their journey, where ever they may end up." As he hopped out the back of the truck and walked toward the driver's side of the vehicle, he lowered his voice and added. "More importantly, I don't want to be haunted by any ghosts of the disappointed, if you know what I mean." He elbowed the officer in the ribs and laughed heartily. "By the way, me name's Tim. That's me brother, Jim in the back. He shook hands with the officer while pointing toward the back of the ambulance. We're taking 'er to Grady. We'll see ya there." He got into the vehicle and with sirens blazing they drove off; the baritone began singing the first verse of "Amazing Grace."

A light rain began to fall. Addie shivered as she stood on the front porch steps and observed the policeman approaching her.

"Come on, ma'am. Grab your overcoat and handbag. I'll take you to Grady so you can be there for her."

"Do tell, why on earth was that man singing?"

"He's just singing his prayers, ma'am." Unsure of the prognosis for Mrs. Gray, he decided not to upset Addie and tell her the part about warding off the ghosts of the dearly departed and disappointed.

Mr. Thompson's hands trembled as he hung up his phone. "Dear God. I pray that Mrs. Gray is alright." He buzzed Miss Bishop.

"Yes, Mr. Thompson?"

"Will you ask the Chief of Police to meet me at the Winecoff Hotel in the rathskeller at six o'clock?"

"That's in an hour, sir."

"Yes, I know. Tell him it's important and it's my treat."

"Yes, sir."

"Also, will you get U.S. Attorney's office on the phone for me?"

"Yes, sir."

"That will be all for now. Thank you, Miss Bishop."

An hour later, Mr. Thompson made his way through the hotel lobby to the elevator carrying his brown leather brief case in one hand and his black umbrella in the other. He and Mrs. Thompson had attended the Winecoff's grand opening celebration three months earlier. He appreciated the tastefully decorated green and white lobby with mahogany woodwork throughout. He pressed the basement level button. The doors closed.

Exiting, he stepped into the bar to find the chief, wearing a blue suit with a crimson vest underneath, seated at a corner table. "Evening. Thanks for meeting me here tonight, Chief. May I say you look mighty dapper and patriotic." They shook hands.

A waiter came over to their table. Mr. Thompson looked over at the chief's drink. "I'll have what he's having." He removed his overcoat, handing his derby, coat, and umbrella to the young man.

The chief sipped his drink as he watched Mr. Thompson sit down and retrieve something from his briefcase. He laid the stamped envelope in front of him, pulling out the contents that included a typed report, invoices, and a crumpled piece of paper.

"This oughta be good."

"Oh, it is, Chief. It is."

The waiter returned with Mr. Thompson's drink. Mr. Thompson took the glass from him before he had the chance to set it on the table. Taking one continuous gulp, the chief and the young man watched him empty it. He returned it to the waiter saying, "Please bring me another."

"Me too." The chief pointed to his empty scotch glass. Turning to Mr. Thompson, he asked "What the hell is going on? I've never seen you this unsettled before."

Mr. Thompson heard the chief and preferred not to respond. He flipped past the cover page on Frank's report and slid it over to the chief.

The waiter returned with their drinks, sitting the chief's down in front of him. He offered Mr. Thompson his beverage. However, Mr. Thompson motioned for him to set it on the coaster on the table, waiting for the young man to leave before speaking.

"Listen. I've got a tale to tell you."

"Does it begin with 'once upon a time'?" the chief chided.

"I wish it did. But it will be up to you to make sure there's a happy ending."

"I'm intrigued. Please, continue. I like happy endings."

Both men laughed, raised their glasses, toasted and sipped.

Mr. Thompson set his glass on the coaster and scanned the

room. He spoke quietly. "I got a call from one of my clients to look into the operations of Doc Gray's tonic." He paused, scanned the room again, and proceeded. "The bottom line is that Lester Schwinn, the owner of the company, is breaking the law by not properly labeling the bottles with the drugs they are using in it. He's also smuggling the product across state lines to sell it."

Confused, the chief asked. "So, what's that got to do with me? You know that's a violation of federal, not state laws."

"Yea, I know. But there's more. I believe my investigator, who wrote and mailed this report to me, was murdered as a result of his investigation."

"Okay. Murder is something I can address."

Mr. Thompson emptied his glass again. "My private detective, Frank Stone, observed two Atlanta police officers taking a bribe from Lester. Frank suspected these officers were the muscle behind the operation and doing the dirty work."

On the defensive, the chief asked, "I'd like to speak to this Frank character about what he witnessed exactly. Otherwise, it's hearsay."

Mr. Thompson squirmed in his chair. "You can't. He's dead." Mr. Thompson tapped on the report in front of the chief. "Look. It's all in here. Read it for yourself. I have the original Frank mailed to me in this envelope back at my office. Frank was supposed to meet with me a few weeks ago to review this in person. He never showed. Instead, this package came to me in the mail. I just received it this morning."

"What makes you think he's dead and that he just simply didn't skip out of town?"

"Frank drove a Chevrolet Series C Classic Six."

The chief took a swig and immediately spit the ice back into his glass as if it were on fire. "Jesus! The burnt man who we found in the First Ward...is...was Frank Stone?"

"I believe that to be the truth. Here are the names of the two officers that are on Lester's payroll." Mr. Thompson handed the chief the crumpled piece of paper.

He unfolded it, reading the handwritten note scrawled in pencil silently. *If you get stopped or run into any trouble, ask for Officers Lamar Davis and Seth Adams—Patrol car #25.* "Where did Frank find this?"

Mr. Thompson tapped Frank's report again. "It's on page seven. One of Lester's runners tossed it. Frank picked it up and then witnessed the money exchange between Lester and these two officers." Mr. Thompson pointed to the crumpled paper in the chief's hands. "He even documented their vehicle registration number in his report, too."

"Fuck me." The chief stuck his finger between his white Arrow collar and his neck. He wanted to rip it off, but refrained. Instead, he fiddled with his tie.

Mr. Thompson watched the agitated chief. "I know. Frank even drove up to a pharmacy in Rome. He typed up the meeting with the pharmacist who rolled over on Lester on page eight." He tapped the report again.

"Where is all this taking place?"

"Page one of the report. Newman's Painting and Supplies Company, located in the Third Ward. I already spoke with the U.S. Attorney's office before I came over here. I asked them to get in touch with you."

The waiter returned. "Two more?"

"Please," they said in unison.

"Make mine a double."

"Ditto." Mr. Thompson concurred.

They sat in silence until their refills landed in front of them. Raising their glasses, they toasted.

"I'm not happy to hear about this sordid tale, but I'll look into it. To happy endings, Mr. Thompson."

"To happy endings."

25

The Sacred Heart and Alexander Hall leadership team gathered around Edward's dining room table. All sat in their usual spots. An hour into their discussion about their progress on their respective projects, construction updates, and plans, Lena discussed the status of her interviews with registered nurses to fill the fifteen positions to cover the twelve-hour day and night shifts on the units at Sacred Heart. Clyde debriefed them about the Sacred Heart department head social gathering that he and Edward had conducted two weeks earlier, reviewing the names, their roles, and responsibilities. Alan grabbed the tongs with his napkin, helping himself to a third cinnamon roll. He wiped his hands four times before folding and refolding his napkin four times, finally replacing it in his lap. Lena chuckled to herself as she observed Alan.

Edward pulled on his gold watch fob, noted the time, and returned it to his green vest pocket. "I believe Clyde's social went very well. We have a great team assembled, thanks to Clyde," Edward acknowledged.

"And thanks to Edward," Clyde countered.

Edward nodded to his left and turned to his right, to Dr. Williams. "Any updates about your physician staff?"

"Actually, there are. Dr. Randall Springer, our pediatrician has given his notification to the Children's Hospital of Philadelphia that his last day with them will be tomorrow. He plans to take a vacation abroad, cruising to Europe during the month of February and the first part of March, before returning stateside and relocating to Atlanta the last week of March. He inquired about housing. He prefers to rent a house first, so he can become acquainted with the area before buying one."

"Sowing his oats, huh?" Clyde chimed in, recalling from his curriculum vitae that Dr. Springer was unmarried.

Edward leaned away from Clyde, tilted his head, and looked at the rest of his team. "Sounds like a solid and well-thought out plan to me." The rest of the group knew he was referring to Dr. Springer's decision to rent a home and not his European trip. "Please let Dr. Williams know of any suitable homes."

Alan Waxman jotted an entry on his notepad. Lena and Oliver did the same while Clyde watched them. Edward noticed Clyde. He cringed and his gut churned.

"Oh! And one more thing." Dr. Williams pulled out a copy of *The Atlanta Dispatch* from his black leather doctor's bag that sat on the floor beside him. He flipped to the third page. "I saw this article about Doc Gray's Restorative tonic in this issue dated January 12th. It appears that Dr. Otto Barringer, who is the medical director at Charleston's hospital, uses this on his hospitalized patients and stocks it in their pharmacy. I propose doing the same."

Ecstatic, Clyde interrupted. "That's a superb medicine, if I do say so myself. As a matter of fact, our new pharmacist, Alvin Martin, can't keep it in stock in his pharmacy."

"Is that a fact?" Oliver asked, wiping his hand over his smooth, bald head.

"Isn't that the tonic that Doc Gray's nephew developed and sells?" Edward questioned Clyde.

"One in the same. Lester Schwinn is his name." Clyde pounced on the opportunity to close the deal.

"I was very fond of Doc Gray. God rest his soul," Edward commented.

"So was I. I miss my dear friend," Dr. Williams said sorrowfully. "Speaking about the loss of dear friends, I just learned about the loss of another colleague who was in charge of the roentgenology department at the University of Pennsylvania. He seemed to have succumbed to cancer last year as a result of receiving severe burns from his work with skiagraphs." He wiped a tear from the outer corner his eye with his napkin.

Uncomfortable with Dr. William's public display of emotion, Alan shifted in his chair, folding and refolding his napkin in his lap — four times.

"Skiagraphs? What are those?" Clyde inquired.

Lena jumped in to answer while Dr. Williams collected himself. "They are images taken of the insides of the human body and put on a special film using radiation. Skiagraphs are a very important diagnostic tool used by doctors. They can help locate foreign objects swallowed by young children, detect broken bones, some masses, and even kidney stones."

"You may have seen them used by carnival barkers in one of their side shows," Oliver added.

Obvious that he was not the sort to be seen at a carnival, Clyde glared at Oliver. He turned away, rolling his eyes.

Alan observed Clyde's response to Oliver.

Dr. Williams cleared his throat, keen to keeping the original discussion on track. "May I continue and clarify what I was about to say about the use of Doc Gray's tonic at Sacred Heart? I propose stocking it in our pharmacy only *after* I have sampled the tonic, queried its ingredients, and qualified its use with my colleagues in order to validate its usage at Sacred Heart."

"Great!" Clyde said sarcastically. Then he was struck with an idea. "Dr. Williams, why don't I have Alvin, er, I mean Mr. Martin get in touch with you so that you can hear about the medicinal from a qualified source and supplier? No time like the present to begin conferring with the Sacred Heart's soon-to-be hospital pharmacist."

"I like that idea. Thank you for reaching out to Mr. Martin for me, Clyde. I look forward to learning more about Doc Gray's Restorative."

Clyde adjusted his spectacles and pulled out his tiny notepad from his breast pocket. Removing the miniature pencil, he scribbled a notation.

Edward observed and smiled.

Friday evening, Hope, Georgia

Mr. Darling read from the family Bible in his handmade rocking chair while sitting by the crackling fire. Mrs. Darling's red, wool, plaid shawl was draped over his lap. Candles flickered on the mantel. Taking a break, he looked up and called into the kitchen.

"Garrett, how's your letter to Addie comin'? By the way, you have my permission to tell her 'bout the plans for her family's farm becomin' Hope's Guardian Angel Cemetery."

Excited, Garrett poked his head out from the kitchen doorway. "I do? I can?"

"Yes, son. You can. The Mayor and I finalized the details with the bank. I'd like for her to hear it from you. Please be sure to give her my love, will ya?"

"Yes, sir. I sure will."

The whinny of a galloping horse caught Mr. Darling's attention first. Garrett also heard it. He joined his father in the living room. Garrett opened the front door as Mr. Darling reached for his 12-gauge resting against the wall.

Emerging on the front porch, they watched the rider dismount from a beautiful ebony stallion. He brushed off his tan duster and adjusted his hat as he made his way up the cobblestone walk to the bottom of the front porch steps. "Evening Tom. Evening Garrett. Sorry to race up here unannounced, but I knew you didn't have a phone. Got a call at the store from your sister, Mary. She told me to tell you that your sister Olive had a stroke yesterday. She's at Grady Hospital."

"Oh, my goodness gracious. Did Mary say how she was doin'?" Mr. Darling grabbed his son's hand. He leaned on his shotgun.

"Tom, it sounds like she's pretty poorly. Mary asked that I tell you to come to Atlanta. She'll be expecting you and Garrett at her house in the morning. She gave me her number so I could ring her back after I spoke to ya."

"Tell Mary we'll see her at first light." Mr. Darling retrieved his handkerchief dangling from his back pocket. He wiped his eyes. "Thank you for comin' out at such a late hour."

"Anything for you, Tom. Happy to help." He added. "By the way, I heard from the Mayor that you are helping him turn the old Engel farm into the town's new cemetery."

"Yup. That's a fact."

"Good for you. Let me know how I can help."

Mr. Darling walked down the porch steps and shook the man's hand. "Much obliged to ya. Thank you for passin' along the message."

The man nodded and tipped his hat to Mr. Darling and Garrett. He turned away and got back on his horse. The saddle creaked underneath him as he found his seat and adjusted his boots in the stirrups. "Godspeed to you both," he called out as he disappeared into the night.

26

Mr. Darling and Garrett arrived at Mary's house as promised by dawn's first light on Saturday. Mr. Darling decided during their travel to Atlanta to refrain from telling Addie about the plans to turn the Engel family farm into Hope's Guardian Angel Cemetery. Both agreed; with Olive gravely ill, it wasn't the proper time to learn about such news.

For the next two days and as the physicians and nurses allowed, Mr. Darling, Mary, Addie, and Garrett took turns sitting by Olive's side at Grady Hospital. The physicians placed Mrs. Gray in a bed closest to the fireplace in the unit so that she could conserve her energy for healing and not expend it trying to stay warm in the dank, brick house.

At three o'clock, Addie arrived at the infirmary to relieve Garrett, taking her turn by Mrs. Gray's side. She found him reading aloud to his aunt from *The Atlanta Dispatch*. Addie corrected Garrett's routine in her head. *No, I read the paper to her at nine while she takes her morning coffee. At three o'clock, I serve her afternoon tea.*

"I wonder if Punxsutawney Phil saw his shadow this morning when he emerged from his burrow. You know if he did, we're in for another six more weeks of winter. Father says we should always make sure we have at least half our hay remaining for the cows, lest spring doesn't come early." He spoke sweetly to his aunt as he caressed her cool, rigid arms and clenched hands.

Making her way to Garrett, Addie observed a fair-haired doctor and a nurse in a cleanly starched uniform visiting with the various patients on the eight-bed ward as they went about their afternoon routines dispensing medications and changing bandages. The smell of body fluids mixed with sulfur from a recently lit wooden match that reignited an effusion oil lamp used to dissipate odors didn't bother her, either.

Approaching Garrett from behind, she placed her hand on his shoulder and spoke. "How's she doing today?"

Relieved to hear the sound of her voice, he said, "The doctor is concerned about the residual side-effects of the stroke."

"What do you mean?" Addie searched his eyes for answers.

"Meaning, when she recovers…if she recovers…."

Addie gasped. "Tell me."

"He said she awoke in the night. She moved the left side of her body, but was unable to move her right arm and leg." Garrett hesitated. "Then she fell into unconsciousness. He's been unable to rouse her ever since." His eyes welled up. "I need some fresh air. Will you step outside with me? Let's take a walk."

Deeply concerned, Addie leaned in and whispered. "What is it Garrett? What aren't you telling me?" Her cheeks flushed and hives emerged on her neck.

He loved having Addie that close to him, her soft breath on

his skin. He noticed that her hair still smelled of lilacs. Garrett didn't reply. He simply took her hand in his and led her out of the hospital.

Sixth Ward

Mr. Thompson sat at his desk and hastily signed the letter handed to him by Miss Bishop, who stood by his side. Completing the last stroke, he blew on the ink before returning it to her.

"Please see that the courier serves this in person today to Mr. Schwinn at his residence."

"Yes sir. Anything else?"

"Please get the Chief of Police on the phone for me and close the door on your way out."

"Yes sir. Will do." She stepped out of his office, closing the heavily ornate, hand-carved, pecan door behind her.

Mr. Thompson reached into his desk, pulled out a scotch bottle and a glass from the deep bottom drawer, pouring himself a double. His gut ached and rumbled. Ten minutes later his phone rang.

He set his drink down and picked up the black phone. Lifting the receiver, he placed it to his left ear. He spoke into the mouthpiece. "Chief? Hey, it's me. Listen. I'm having the *Doc Gray* tonic cease and desist letter hand delivered to Lester Schwinn at his home this afternoon." He paused and listened. "Right. As we discussed, it's not going to Newman's Painting and Supply Company. Have you started your investigation yet?" Mr. Thompson's stomach and intestines gurgled and danced in uncoordinated peristaltic waves. He squirmed in his chair. "Good to hear. Has someone from the U. S. Attorney's office contacted you yet?" Mr. Thompson stood up, making his way around to the front of his desk. "Great! Glad to hear that. Yes, I'll be happy to meet with you sometime next week. Great! Hey, listen, I've got to go. Huh? No, I *really* have to go, now! Yes, I agree with you it's a huge fucking mess." He abruptly hung up and darted out of his office, nearly colliding with Miss Bishop in the hallway as she handed an envelope to their courier.

"Mr. Thompson must be going somewhere important." The courier watched him run down the office hallway as he secured the letter into his satchel and buckled it closed.

"Oh he is, the poor man." Miss Bishop whispered. "He's working on a big case. It's his eighth time today." In a very matter-of-fact fashion, she added, "He's got the trots."

Turning beet red after learning this new bit of information about his boss, the courier hung onto his tweed cap with both hands as he scurried down the hallway in the opposite direction, his feet slipping out from under him as he skidded around the corner.

Monday night, Fourth Ward

Lester crept through Grady's lobby and wound his way to the medical unit where his aunt lay sleeping. A nurse stationed at a desk in the hallway snored loudly as he tiptoed by her. Her nursing cap remained secured to her light brown curls as her head rested on her arms atop a pile of patient charts and an open textbook. Lester slipped into the patient unit undetected. Without making a sound, he walked over to his aunt's bed. She remained asleep. Lester noted four other patients tucked into their beds for the night. He walked over to a cabinet that contained fresh linens and extra pillows. Removing a pillow, he stepped back and stood over her. He watched her breath. It wasn't smooth and rhythmic, but labored and staggered. He whispered over her. "Damn you, old woman. I will see my way clear out of this jam. You can't stop me." Clutching the pillow, Lester fumed. A hand touched his back. He jumped and whipped around to find the nursing student he passed in the hallway wide awake and staring at him.

She glared at Lester, at the pillow in his hand, then back at him. "What the heck are you doing here? Do you know what time it is?"

Lester chose to answer the first question. The second was rhetorical. Composing himself, he answered, "I'm here visiting my poor, sick aunt. I was just saying a prayer over her because…I…just miss her so much and want her to get better. I was going to put an extra pillow under her head." He looked back at Aunt Olive. Drool spilled out of the corner of her mouth. "See, I was going to prop her head up so she wouldn't choke." He threw the pillow at the night nurse. "Here, since you're up now, why don't *you* do your job? You wouldn't want me to report you to your head nurse for sleeping, now would you?"

Though still suspicious, she answered resignedly, "No."

"I didn't think so. When she wakes, please give her my regards."

"I will. But you do know she isn't long for this world. She can't speak or swallow."

Lester began his retreat out of the ward and whispered aloud, "Good."

She spun around. "What did you say?"

Lester smiled back at her and bowed. "I said goodnight."

27

The days seemed endless, one bleeding over into the next as Addie now split the shifts at Mrs. Gray's bedside with Mary. Unsure if his sister had days or weeks remaining, Mr. Darling and Garrett reluctantly headed back to Hope the evening after Addie's walk with Garrett. Although Mr. Darling asked a neighboring farmer, Mr. Campbell, to look in on the property while they were gone, the Darling farm and their livestock needed tending. Addie's thoughts of Garrett, their conversation about his Aunt Olive's grave condition, and her former life in Hope became clouded when she couldn't help but overhear the day shift nurse arguing with the female patient behind her.

"Listen. I have to give you your medicine now. If I don't give you your afternoon dose, you're going to be experiencing a lot of pain within the hour."

Addie turned to watch the interaction between the spirited nurse and a young woman who appeared to be in her mid-twenties.

The post-appendectomy patient fired back. "I don't want to take my pain medicine. I don't like how it makes me feel. I don't want to end up like her." She pointed at Olive, who lay pale and unresponsive in the next bed. She grimaced as she watched Olive gasp for air. She looked toward the ceiling and cried out, "I don't want to die!"

Agitated, the nurse picked up her silver tray.

Addie interjected, speaking to the nurse. "Wait! Don't go. Let me help you." Addie turned her attention to the woman in the bed. "Ma'am, you are simply recovering from surgery. My...." For the first time, Addie didn't know how to refer to Mrs. Gray. Keeping it formal, she said "Mrs. Gray suffered a catastrophic stroke. You don't have her condition. Please take your medicine so that you can recover quickly and can go home. You are fortunate to be able to leave this place on two feet." Addie turned back to Mrs. Gray and took her hand. "Mrs. Gray." Tears flowed down her cheeks.

"Alright! Alright! Give me my medicine if it will get me out of here quicker." She rolled over toward Addie, pulling the sheet and blankets over her head.

Addie turned to watch the nurse, who caught Addie's eye and mouthed, "Thank you." Setting her tray down, she prepared her supplies. She lifted under the covers, exposing a small area of the lady's backside, and swabbed the target site with an alcohol-soaked cotton ball. The nurse let a minute pass to let it air dry. She made a v-formation with her left index finger and thumb, placing it over the hip and buttock area. She poked the stainless steel needle into the space between her fingers. In a swift series of moves, the nurse steadied the glass syringe with her left hand, pulled back on the plunger ever so slightly with her right and injected the liquefied narcotic. In a matter of seconds, it was over.

"Is it over?" the young woman called out from under the covers.

"It's all over. I'm done now." The nurse massaged the injection site with another cotton ball.

"Now get some rest." The nurse collected her supplies, placing them back on the metal tray. She retreated to wash her hands in a nearby sink and returned to her desk in at the far end of the room. Facing the patients, she scanned the ward before sitting down and flipping open a file to chart a patient note.

Fifteen minutes later, the nurse came over to check her patient who was fast asleep. Stepping over to Addie, she said, "Thank you so much for helping me. This stuff comes so naturally to you. I've been watching you interact with Mrs. Gray this past week. You have a kind and gentle way about you. Have you ever thought about becoming a nurse yourself?

"As a matter of fact, I've been accepted into Sacred Heart's new nursing school. I begin classes this April."

"We can use more people like you in the profession. Me, on the other hand, I tend to have a short fuse and sometimes I have a tendency to be quick-tongued." She shook her head. "It's something my head nurse and I are working on."

"I've been watching you too. You are a good nurse. You anticipate the doctor's requests and are skillful with your techniques and dressing changes. Don't shortchange yourself. You're a natural too."

The nurse's brown eyes sparkled. "Thank you. I needed a

kind word today." She tucked a stray strand of her brunette hair back over her right ear. "My shift supervisor is always getting on to me about my wayward strands. We have to fashion our hair in a Grecian-style bun so we can properly wear our nursing caps. We have to make sure our ears are covered, too. Despite the fact that I've got so many pins and a palm full of pomade in my hair, the strands still slip out. It's hopeless."

Addie laughed and extended her hand. "Hey, my name's Addie Engel."

"It's pleasure to make your acquaintance, Addie. I'm Claire Scott. I've been admiring your beautiful hair color all week. I've been referring to you as 'Red' to my nursing colleagues."

Addie blushed. "Why, thank you. Where did you go to school?"

"I graduated from Grady's School of Nursing three years ago. I've been working on the medical-surgical unit ever since. So, you start classes at Sacred Heart in two months? You're going to love the strict rules. No smoking. No boys. No dating. No drinking. No fun." Then she whispered, "But we did manage to stir up a bit of harmless mischief when we were in the Grady dorms. Just you wait and see. How many are students are going to be in your class?"

"Ten."

"That's a good size. My guess is that there will be a few drop-outs along the way."

"Really?"

"Yes, some young ladies will realize the strict rules aren't for them, especially if they've got a beau back home. Some find the work too hard and others aren't prepared for what they see." She glanced over to her patients in the unit. "The realities of dealing with disease, sickness, and injuries can be overwhelming." She walked over to the other side of Mrs. Gray's bed and adjusted the pillows under her head. Reaching into her uniform pocket, she pulled out a small jar. She uncapped it, swiped a tiny gauze pad in it, and blotted Olive's lips. "By the way, I see you got a beau of your own. It's going be hard on you both." She recapped the salve and returned it to her pocket.

"I don't know what you mean. I don't have a boyfriend."

"Really? I assumed that you and that handsome young man who sat with Mrs. Gray from noon to three earlier in the week was your boyfriend based on how the two of you acted around each other."

Addie flushed, waving off the notion. "Oh! No. No. We're just best childhood friends." Touching her lips, she recalled Garrett's birthday kiss and the sweet taste of his lips on hers two months ago. Removing her hand from her mouth, she dismissed any thoughts of being romantically tied to Garrett. *Too much has changed. For the next three years, my place is with Nurse Hartman.*

The fair-haired doctor entered the patient ward carrying bandages and tape and called out to Claire. "Nurse Scott, I need your assistance."

"I'm coming." Nurse Scott acknowledged the physician and then smiled back at Addie. "Duty calls, Red."

Alvin paced on the front porch steps of Newman's Painting and Supply as he watched Lester spin his roadster into the gravel parking lot.

Lester hopped out. "Thanks so much for meeting me here on such short notice."

"This better be good. I had to close the store early to get down here."

"Come with me."

Alvin followed Lester into the warehouse, passing the children seated on the wooden stools at the spickets. They made their way upstairs to the second floor.

"You have the new prototype ready?" Lester asked the webbed-fingered young man who stood behind the printing press that sat on a long wooden table in front of them.

"Yes. I've been working on the new label ever since I received your call two days ago." He handed Lester a small, cream-colored piece of paper.

"What's this?" Alvin snatched it out of Lester's hands. "Why does this say Doc Otto's tonic?"

He snapped at Lester. "What happened to Doc Gray's label? What the hell is going on?"

"I am severing our tie with the *Gray* name."

Alvin reeled, waving the label in his hand. "What the hell are you talking about? We've spent two years branding and peddling this medicine."

Sidestepping the details outlined in Mr. Thompson's cease and desist letter with threats of a lawsuit, Lester remained unwavered by Alvin's question. "My aunt had a stroke last week. She's not expected to live. In honor of my late uncle's memory, I've decided to put his good name to rest and begin anew under a new name."

"First of all, I'm sorry to hear about your aunt. Second, what the hell are you thinking? Why didn't you consult with me about this? After all, I am a silent partner."

Lester grinned. "Exactly. My job is to run the company and make you rich," he countered. "It's time for Doc Gray's to undergo a name change with a new and improved version."

"Who the hell is Doc Otto?" Alvin slammed the mock label on the table.

The man with the red, scarred hands spoke. "We couldn't fit 'Barringer' on the label. Lester decided to use his first name instead. I think it has a nice ring to it. Don't you?"

"I wasn't asking you, freak." Alvin poked Lester in the chest with his finger. "I'm asking you."

Embarrassed, the man hung his head and slipped his hands into his trouser pockets.

"How dare you talk to him that way." Lester removed Alvin's finger from his coat lapel.

"Didn't you read the *article-tisement* we placed in *The Atlanta Dispatch* last month? Doctor Otto Barringer is my sister's father-in-law. He's the medical director at Charleston's hospital who's profiled in our picture."

"Oh, yea. Right. I remember now."

"He has agreed for a small fee...*and twenty percent of his perceived sales*...to be the new 1914 face of our improved tonic. Since he's stocking it in his pharmacy and using it on his patients, he has a better professional reputation than my dead uncle's name. We stand a greater chance of elevating this tonic to a new level than we ever did before."

Alvin paced the floor. "What changes do we have to make?" Stopping, he added, "Or have you already made those, too?"

Lester, anticipating the question, had had a few days to rehearse his response, so reeled them off in numerical order. Using his hands, he counted off. "First, we've tweaked the recipe just a bit, basically just adding cinnamon so it tastes a bit different. Second, we will include a cover letter with orders going out to our existing customers in which Dr. Otto Barringer will explain the name change and improved recipe based on his medical experiments and scientific study. Third, we will run a new *article-tisement* in the papers at the end of this month touting our new version. Fourth, fulfilment for the paint colors remains the same. Green, our best seller, is Doc Otto's *Nerve and Blood Purification* tonic, followed by white, Doc Otto's *Cure-all*, and red, Doc Otto's *Restorative*. Fifth, slap on the new label, raise our price two cents, and reap the rewards."

Alvin stopped pacing. "You raised the price, too?"

"Perception is reality. People are willing to pay a little extra for a better product."

"A better product? You heel! You simply added cinnamon! It's all the same fucking stuff with different labels on the bottles! "

"We know that, but our consumers don't. The bottom line is that they don't care. As long as they believe the scientific experiments, who cares?"

"Scientific experiments? What experiments has Dr. Barringer conducted so quickly?" Alvin demanded. "You better not land us in the hoosegow for your bonehead antics."

"Trust me, will you? Don't be such a grouser. All of our paperwork is in order and can be reviewed should anyone ask. By the way, who's going to question the stellar work and reputation of Dr. Barringer?"

Alvin resigned. "Fine, with more profits, you say?"

"Yes, there will be much more for you to pocket at the end of the day."

Alvin picked up the label and examined it again. "By the way, I got a call from Clyde. He said Dr. Williams wants to talk with me about using the tonic at Sacred Heart. I've got a meeting with him on Tuesday, March 3rd after I return from visiting my in-laws in Palm Beach. I'm taking a break from the store before I start working at Sacred Heart in May. What do I tell him now?"

"Tell him the truth and show him this study." Lester picked up a file folder off the table.

Alvin opened it to find a signed letter from Dr. Barringer explaining the new and improved tonic, the rationale for the price increase, and use and dosage suggestions. Behind the letter was a twelve-page, typed report of a study using his new formula, comparing it to *Doc Gray*'s and other tonics currently on the market. Everything appeared to be dated and signed. Closing the folder, he said "It looks official. Everything seems to be in order. I even see that he didn't divulge the family recipe. Well, it looks like you've thought of everything. But, may I add, I don't want to be blindsided again by you and your freak over there." He pointed across the table without making eye contact with the young man.

"Calm down, Alvin. Like I said, everything is in our capable hands, isn't that right?" Lester winked at his colleague who still had his hands hidden from view.

Nodding, he removed his hands from his pockets and smiled.

28

Friday evening, February 13, 1914, Fourth Ward

The chief, boasting a brown suit with an emerald green vest, sat at his usual table in the corner of the basement bar at the Winecoff Hotel. He was already working on his second single malt when Mr. Thompson walked in.

"I have to make this meeting brief. I learned this afternoon that Mrs. Thompson has invited Alderman Swift and his wife over for dinner. I've got to be home by six-thirty at the latest, so let's make it snappy." He took out his pocket watch. "I've got thirty minutes."

As the waiter approached the table, Mr. Thompson waved him off.

"The investigation into Doc Gray's formula and Lester Schwinn's interstate commerce is underway by the Feds. Suffice it to say that investigation is under their control and timeline. I have no idea how long it will take them to gather what they think is enough evidence. That is going to be completely up to them."

Mr. Thompson nodded. "How's it going with your investigation? I served Lester with the cease and desist letter and threatened a lawsuit if he didn't stop using Doc Gray's name and selling the tonic. That should put the brakes on their operation."

The chief emptied his glass. "Do you want the good news first or the bad?"

"Give me the good news first."

"Okay. Lester has stopped distributing Doc Gray's tonic."

"That's great! What's the bad news?"

"He is redistributing it under a brand new name called Doc Otto's."

"Oh, for the love of God!" Suddenly desperate for a scotch, he flagged the waiter down. "Bring us two doubles, posthaste."

"No shit. He is legally within his rights to sell his product under a new name. It happens all the time. Now if he's still selling a product that contains ingredients that have to be listed on the label and he's not, then that's still a matter for the Feds."

Perturbed, Mr. Thompson snapped, "You don't have to tell me how the law works. I'm familiar."

The server returned, placing their drinks down.

Mr. Thompson stared at his. "It's not like he's breaking any laws by using a paint store as a front for his tonic business. Any Tom, Dick, or Harry can hang a shingle on their front door, name their business whatever they like, and conduct any kind of business under its roof, whether it's related to their signage or not." He swigged half his drink. "I digress. I swear this case is causing me to come unglued, literally. I'm stepping off my soap box, please go on."

The chief grinned. "Regarding my two officers who are allegedly on Lester's payroll, I have trusty eyes on them. Nothing has popped up yet, but if and when it does, my men will let me know. Don't worry, I'm on it."

"You know, if you need a nugget of information, I'm sure Frank's girlfriend would be happy to help you out. Her name is Amy McGuire."

"Madam McGuire is, or was, Frank's girl?"

"Yes. Actually, he kept an apartment in her building. He helped her keep the deadbeats out. Why don't you shake things up a bit at your precinct by bringing her into your office for questioning?"

"Say, that's not a bad idea. I appreciate that bit of information."

"I want Lester's hooligans and Frank's killers put behind bars. You know I'm a sucker for happy endings."

The chief raised his glass. "Me, too."

Friday night, Fourth Ward

Addie was getting used to the unnatural combination of sights, sounds, and aromas on Grady's medical-surgical unit. A middle-aged woman at the other end of the room continued to vomit black emesis into a bucket by her bedside. The activated charcoal forced into her stomach through a red, rubber nasogastric tube fifteen minutes earlier was doing its job of inhibiting the absorption of the near-lethal dose of sleeping pills she had ingested after learning that her lover was leaving her for another woman. Nurse Scott enjoyed providing mini-tutorials to Addie during her vigils with Mrs. Gray. Addie made thorough notes of her lessons when she returned home to the empty house on

Houston Street. The logs crackled and popped in the fireplace as Nurse Scott placed white, cotton screens between Mrs. Gray's bed and the sleeping appendectomy patient.

"I just called Mrs. Schwinn. She is on her way over here now." Nurse Scott watched Olive's gasps for breath slow down. "She is inhaling and exhaling with longer and irregular intervals now. She has fought a good fight, but her body is surrendering to death. It's merely a matter of time."

Curious, Addie asked, "How do you know?"

Nurse Scott pulled up a chair and spoke softly. "When people begin to die, they lose the urge to eat and drink. That's why we use a wet washrag on the mouth and balms on their lips to prevent them from drying out and cracking. When the extremities begin to turn a mottled bluish-purple, starting at their most distal ends, then death is usually imminent within a day. The breathing becomes very labored, irregular, and noisy. You may have heard it referred to as the 'death rattle.'"

Addie nodded and continued listening.

"Sometimes people have a moment of clarity before they die. Others experience hallucinations; some get very upset, combative, and agitated to the point where we have to heavily medicate and restrain them. Each person has their own personal experience and dance with death. It can be very difficult for family members to witness if they have never seen someone die before. I know it was hard on me to watch my father die from pneumonia. He passed away in that bed over there just before Christmas." She pointed to an empty bed on the other side of the room closest to the sink.

"I know what you mean. I lost my Maw." Addie refrained

from disclosing the details. She took Mrs. Gray's stiff, cold hand in hers. Her fingers, hands, and arms were blotchy and purple. There were longer gaps in her breathing. Addie felt for a radial pulse in Mrs. Gray's wrist. It was absent. She leaned over and whispered into her ear. "Mrs. Gray, I can't thank you enough for letting me care for you. It has been a privilege getting to know you." Tears welled in her eyes.

"You have a wonderful family, with the exception of you know who." She wiped the tears from her cheeks and retrieved a handkerchief from her pocket to blow her nose. "Mrs. Gray, I have one more thing to tell you before you go with God. I love you dearly, too." She gently kissed her forehead.

Mrs. Gray exhaled. Her chest failed to rise. There was only silence.

"Would you like to say a prayer?" Nurse Scott reached out for Addie's other hand.

"I would, but I prefer to say a silent prayer. I...don't think I can speak the words...aloud...right now."

Squeezing Addie's hand, she said, "I completely understand. I will do the same." Nurse Scott bowed her head.

The shadow of the night cast its dark cloak over the windows as the flames flickered in the fireplace, providing an amber glow in the room.

Addie, filled with mixed emotions, gazed lovingly at Mrs. Gray. *Watching Mrs. Gray die was such a reverent and spiritual experience. It was so different from Maw's departure from this world.* She sobbed quietly as tears ran uncontrollably down her ruby cheeks. Holding Olive's hand with her left hand and Nurse Scott's with her right, she prayed. *Dear Lord, thank you for bringing Mrs. Gray into my life. I was so lost and unhappy, but she brought me to place where I found my purpose and joy again. I am ever so grateful for your abundant grace and mercy. God, please watch over her as she rejoins her loving husband in heaven. Bless and care for my family. I know one day we will be rejoined and we will rejoice. Until that day, I walk this earth serving you and others. In your name I pray. Amen.*

29

A light rain fell on Oakwood Cemetery as the procession of black vehicles followed the Ford Model T hearse from The Shrine of the Immaculate Conception through the main wrought iron gates. Addie chose to ride with Mr. Darling and Garrett in one of the two cars provided to Mrs. Gray's family by the funeral home. The Schwinn family rode in the other.

The procession passed a small brick guard post and turned left. Addie quietly stared out the window, watching the small raindrops being absorbed by bigger droplets as they cascaded down the pane. A red rose, clutched tightly in her gloved hands, shook as they drove over the granite cobblestone road.

Pointing to the large, white building on his right, Mr. Darling broke the silence. "Did you know that the bell tower on that house was used by Confederate General Hood during the Battle of Atlanta in June, 1864?"

The wake at the Schwinn house the previous day, with its parade of visitors paying their respects, followed by the hour-long mass today left Addie numb. "I'm sorry, Mr. Darling. My mind was adrift. What did you say?"

"It's been a rough couple of days, huh?" he replied.

"Yes sir. All of this is a bit overwhelming to say the least. My family's funerals were so simple. I'm not use to all of these ceremonial services for the dead."

Garrett leaned over and took her hand in his. "Are you going to be alright?"

"I'll be fine. I'll have plenty of time to rest up after today."

Addie faked a half grin and patted his hand reassuringly.

Mr. Darling asked "Addie, what do you plan to do with yourself now that Mrs. Gray is gone? You are an independent young lady now. You are free to do as you please. Do you think you'll come back and live in Hope?"

The car came to a stop in front of a large granite marker that had the family name, Gray, engraved on it.

With her hand on the handle of the door, Addie sadly replied, "I don't know yet." Before exiting the car, she pulled down the black lace veil over her face and joined the awaiting funeral attendant under an umbrella. Addie followed behind Mary to the tented area that shielded them from the inclement weather. As she was escorted to the plot, she recalled the time when she anxiously sat on the Darlings front porch with Garrett waiting for Mr. Darling to arrive to inform her of her fate after her parent's deaths. *I am lost and adrift again like the fall leaves that tumbled through the front yard that day. This time, the next choices are my own to make.* Addie tried to seek out a bit of humor to keep her sane through the pain. *It's days like today that remind me that I think it's easier being a kid.*

Mr. Darling and Garrett peeled off toward the hearse to join Dr. Williams, Mr. Schwinn, Mr. Thompson, and Lester, who served as the other pallbearers.

Observing that there were only a handful of people present, Addie took a seat that faced the empty dirt hole that was dug next to Dr. Gray's headstone. The rain struck the canvas overhead. It reminded her of when she listened to the rain assault the Darling's barn roof as she and Ol' Girl stowed themselves away in a spare stall, lost and unsure. As she watched the men carry the polished, oak casket, she struggled to answer the surge of new questions facing her. *What am I going to do now that Mrs. Gray no longer needs me? Where will I live until nursing school begins in April? What kind of job can I do to earn enough money to put a roof over my head and food on the table? These are adult questions that I've never had to deal with before. For the first time in my life, I feel truly alone in this world.* Addie began to cry as she listened to the priest say a blessing for Mrs. Gray before they lowered her remains into the ground.

Garrett, taking a seat beside Addie, gently touched her shoulder. He whispered in her ear, relishing the familiar scent of lilacs. "Are you alright, Addie?"

Turning toward him, she whispered, "No."

"What is it? What's got you so bothered?"

"It's everything and nothing."

"I'm not sure I understand."

"My life in Hope was so simple. The world seemed so out of reach for me. There were no endless possibilities and choices. I lived a restricted life filled with pain and drama. Maw's death was so tragic and unexpected. She had a life yet to live. Mrs. Gray's death was so peaceful and calm, having lived a long life. I left my family in the ground in a corn field while your family is buried with dignity, priests, and pallbearers in a real cemetery."

Addie sobbed and Garrett put his arm around her, pulling her to him.

Mary, carrying a handful of red roses, walked over to the burial plot and threw them on top of the casket before rejoining Mr. Schwinn under his umbrella. They turned to make their way back to the car. They watched Mr. Darling, Mr. Thompson, and Dr. Williams do the same. The men shook hands with the priest as they departed from the tented area.

Addie pulled away to dry her tears with her handkerchief, one that Mrs. Gray had given to her that had pink flowers cross-stitched on the corners.

"Let's go back to the car. Father and I have something important to tell you."

Before she had a chance to rise from her seat, Lester brazenly walked over to Addie and said. "Addie, your services are no longer required by my family any more. Please return to my aunt's house immediately, pack your bags, and vacate my premises."

Garrett hopped up and said through gritted teeth, "How dare you speak to Addie with that tone of voice, Lester? She doesn't deserve to be treated that way. You're going to do this here? Now?"

"Yes, I am!" Lester shoved Garrett hard enough that he stumbled backwards out from under the tent and into the rain.

Like a charging bull, Garrett lowered his head and shoulders, ramming Lester hard in his gut. "What do you mean by *your* premises? Our aunt's will made provisions for both you *and* me.

Lester buckled over only for a moment before rising up

with raised, clenched fists. "We'll just have to see about that, won't we?" Lester's right hook hit Garrett's left cheek.

Still holding her rose, Addie jumped up, attempting to break up the fight, but not before Garrett struck Lester's jaw with an upper cut. Petals flew and blood spattered. Furious, Lester shoved Addie hard. She lost her footing in the wet grass and fell into the freshly dug grave on top of the rose-covered casket. Completely oblivious, Garrett and Lester continued brawling.

"Lester! Garrett! What the hell is wrong with you two? Have you completely lost your minds?" Mr. Darling shouted out as he, Mary, and Mr. Schwinn ran over toward the commotion. "Where's Addie?"

Mr. Thompson, the priest, and Dr. Williams also ran back to join the others gathered under the tent.

"Jesus, Mary, and Joseph!" the priest cried out as he peered over the hole. Addie lay motionless on top of the casket, her tattered rose still in hand. "She's fallen into the grave. Someone, please help me get her out." The priest, wearing his white robe, jumped on top of the casket, making a loud thud. He picked up Addie's crumpled body and lifted her up so that Mr. Thompson and Mr. Darling could hoist her out and place her flat on her back on the ground.

Dr. Williams ran over to assess her. He leaned his ear over her mouth. "She's breathing." He quickly palpated her arms and legs to make sure she didn't have any obvious broken bones. He gently tapped her cheeks. "Addie, can you hear me? Addie, wake up! It's Dr. Williams. Can you hear me?"

Addie roused and reached to clutch the back of her head. "What happened?"

Dr. Williams' hands felt the back of Addie's head. "She's got a nice goose egg back there," he said to the onlookers. "Addie, do you hurt anywhere? Are you in pain?"

"The back of my head hurts. That's all."

"Do you know where you are?"

Addie looked around. "I'm on the ground?"

Dr. Williams laughed. "Yes, yes you are."

Addie struggled to sit up. The priest knelt behind her to support her back. "It's a miracle you didn't break anything, Miss."

Dr. Williams held his finger in front of Addie's eyes. "Watch my finger." He moved it slowly across her gaze to the right, back to center then to the left. "Squeeze my fingers with both of your hands." Addie took his fingers and squeezed them. "Good."

"Wiggle your arms and legs for me." Addie moved her upper and lower extremities with ease. "Excellent."

Lester leaned over Dr. Williams' shoulder and whispered, "You're lucky you didn't die from the fall." He slinked back to rejoin his parents, who were huddled together.

"You go to hell, Lester!" Addie fired back.

The priest made the sign of the cross. Mary shuddered and fell back into her husband's arms. Mr. Thompson, Mr. Darling, and Garrett gasped. Lester laughed.

"I'll be right back." Dr. Williams dashed to his car, retrieving his black leather doctor's bag.

"You nearly killed me again." She shook her finger at Lester as she tried to scramble to her feet, pushing the mourning veil away from her face. "You tried to kill Mrs. Gray and me."

"Dear God, she has gone mad." Lester smirked and backed away.

Garrett grabbed Addie's elbow. "What are you talking about? How did he nearly kill you before?"

Addie struggled to free herself from Garrett's hold as she lurched at Lester. Dr. Williams frantically rummaged through his bag.

"I've got just the remedy she needs." Dr. Williams pulled out his supplies. He injected a small vial of medicine with air and pulled out the clear liquid into the glass chamber of the syringe by retracting the plunger. He grabbed a cotton ball soaked with alcohol and pushed up Addie's sleeve. Swabbing her arm, he quickly administered the shot. "There, that should calm her down."

He stepped back, speaking to the group as if he were lecturing to his medical students on grand rounds. "It happens all the time. Sometimes, people get a bit agitated and confused after they hit their head."

"I'm not agitated or confused!" Addie screamed out, trying to wiggle out of Garrett's grasp.

Dr. Williams calmly continued. "Women can be very frail and emotional, especially after a traumatic incident. I should dare say that this qualifies as one."

"I'm not frail or emotion...." Addie felt a warm flush surge through her body. Her knees collapsed under her weight.

Garrett caught her in his arms. He swiftly scooped her up and carried her back to their waiting car. Mr. Darling and the priest followed in hot pursuit. The priest pulled out his rosary beads, making the sign of the cross in the air behind Garrett while saying a prayer.

Before Garrett got into the car, Mr. Thompson called out

and rushed over. "Garrett! May I have just a quick word with you before you go?" Breathless, he held up his index finger. Catching his breath, he resumed. "There will be a reading of Mrs. Gray's will in my office tomorrow afternoon at four o'clock sharp. If Addie is feeling up to it, please make sure she is in attendance. I must stress that it will be important for her to be there. She needs to get plenty of rest tonight."

"Yea, sure. Anything you say, Mr. Thompson." Garrett disappeared in the back seat. The car door closed and it drove away.

Mr. Thompson returned to the tent to find the Schwinn clan still huddled together like lost ducklings.

Mary spat on her handkerchief and tried to wipe away the blood from Lester's chin. "What was that all about, my dear boy? Lester, why were you and Garrett tussling?"

Mr. Thompson interrupted. "Excuse me, but I need to inform you, Mrs. Schwinn and Lester, that there will be a reading of Mrs. Gray's will tomorrow afternoon at four o'clock in my office. Please be prompt." Not interested in hearing their response or carrying on any further conversation with Lester, he turned on his heels and walked back through the rain to his car.

Lester had had enough of his mother's doting attention and stormed off into the rain toward their car. "God damn it!" he screamed out. He was enraged from his fight with Garrett, still reeling from being issued the cease and desist letter from Mr. Thompson that stopped him from using the *Gray* name, and his blood boiled after hearing Addie's remarks to the crowd about him. Soaked to the bone, Lester looked up at the cloudy sky and raised his middle finger. A bolt of lightning streaked across the sky. Thunder boomed. Lester tossed his head back, raised his hands into the air, and screamed as he threw open the passenger door, got into the back seat, and slammed the door shut.

Mr. Schwinn observed his son's behavior. Gravely concerned, he turned to Mary, and inquired. "What's gotten into Lester?"

"Oh, you know how sensitive our boy can be," Mary replied as she tucked her handkerchief back into her purse.

As Mr. Schwinn opened his umbrella, he mumbled. "That boy is touched. Sensitive, my ass!"

"What did you say?" She nuzzled under the umbrella with him.

"I've got gas."

She laughed aloud. "Mr. Schwinn. I may suffer from a lot of things, but being hard of hearing actually isn't one of them!"

Monday night, Fourth Ward

Addie awoke in her bedroom at Mrs. Gray's house with a headache. Glancing around the room, she made out a dark shadow rocking in the corner. The person stopped and leaned forward as she sat up in bed. The gas lights from the sidewalks illuminated Garrett's concerned face.

"How are you feeling? You took quite a tumble." Garrett stood up and walked over, taking a seat on the edge of her bed.

"I just have a bit of a headache." She rubbed the back of her head. "What a fiasco that turned out to be. I'm sure Mrs. Gray is looking down on us, raising her cane, and threatening to give you and Lester a swift kick in the hind end for your shenanigans this afternoon." She tenderly reached out to touch his bruised, swollen cheek. "Thank you for standing up to Lester for me." Noticing she was dressed in her nightgown, "By the way, who undressed me?"

Garrett chuckled. "Don't worry. Aunt Mary came over and readied you for bed. Father and I thought it best to spend the night over here and keep watch over you. She's not pleased with my behavior today. I can't say I blame her. I'm not proud of how I acted today. I'm so sorry." Garrett poured her a glass of water from the glass pitcher that sat on her bedside table. He handed it to her. "Why were you so angry? I've never seen you filled with such rage or heard you spout profanity before. What did you mean when you said to Lester that he tried to kill you, *again?*"

Addie drank from it, deciding how to answer his question. *With Lester still on the loose, I'm afraid that if I tell Garrett the truth, Lester will find a way to harm both of us. I can't risk putting Garrett or Mr. Darling in harm's way. I can't tell him right now.* Innocently, she replied, "Whatever are you talking about? I don't recall what happened."

He studied her face, searching for answers in her eyes. "Are you sure? You don't remember anything after falling into Aunt Olive's grave? You woke up and screamed at Lester, accusing him that he had tried to kill you and Aunt Olive."

Addie shook her head. "No. I don't remember. It all just seems like a bad dream." Addie hated lying to Garrett. Anxious to switch the topic, she said, "Hey, you told me that you and your father had something important to tell me. What was that all about? Can you tell me now?"

"Actually, I have two important things to tell you. First, Mr.

Thompson wants to do the reading of Aunt Olive's will tomorrow afternoon at four o'clock. He asked that you be present for it."

"Really? How odd is that? I can't imagine what I have to do with the reading of her will. But if Mr. Thompson made the request, then I will be there."

"Good. As for the other matter, I know father wanted to tell you this news too. However, he's fast asleep next door in Aunt Olive's room. He did give me permission to tell you in a letter I started to write to you a few weeks ago." He stopped, taking a moment to watch her face fill with curiosity. "So, I guess there's no harm in spilling the beans."

"Go on. Quit teasing me and tell me." She punched him in the upper arm.

"After you came to Atlanta, Father and Mayor Miller met with the bank and presented plans to turn your family farm into the new Hope cemetery."

Addie gasped.

"Father is working with the town to refurbish the land. He proposed to call it Hope's Guardian Angel Cemetery; the town agrees. We'll begin working on the entrance this spring. Father and some volunteers plan to work the land so it is fit for use by the summer. By the way, he has even replaced the old, wooden crosses that had your family's names painted on them with proper, engraved granite headstones."

Replacing her glass on the bed stand, Addie threw her arms around Garrett and sobbed. "I am in shock! I can't believe your father's generosity and the lengths he has gone to help me and my family. I was so worried that I left my family behind and that the bank would foreclose on the property, leaving them abandoned and alone. You have put my heart at rest, knowing they are truly in their final resting place on our family farm. Oh, Garrett!"

"Father loves you, Addie." Garrett stroked her hair and whispered in her ear, "I love you, Addie."

Addie pulled away, recalling the awkward exchange in the Darling guest bedroom before she left Hope. She knew in her heart and soul that he was trying to express his feelings of love toward her. But the quick shift in their conversation made her question his original intentions and think otherwise. Addie's pent up feelings for Garrett spilled as she blurted out, "I love you too, Garrett." She leaned in slowly, kissing him passionately on his sweet, tender lips.

Garrett held Addie in his arms as he lay down beside her. "I've been in love with you my whole life. You are the only one for me, Addie Engel."

In stark contrast to the stolen kisses down by the pond as children, Addie continued to kiss Garrett. Her body was ablaze as his hands explored every inch of her underneath her nightgown. She knew him so well, yet she shuddered with nervous energy. He helped her wiggle out of her bedgown, tossing it on the floor.

He gazed upon her ivory skin in the pale night light. Garrett lowered himself on her and gently kissed her neck while he caressed her breasts, making her nipples hard. Intoxicated by his passion, Addie unbuttoned his shirt and he removed it. He lay back down on top of her. For the first time, she felt her breasts touch his chest, skin to skin.

Intertwining, becoming one, Addie whispered in his ear, "Take me, I'm yours."

30

During their ride on the shorts uptown to the Sixth Ward, Addie and Garrett repeatedly exchanged glances that made Addie blush as they remembered their intimate union. Addie, relieved that Garrett snuck out of her room during the early morning hours so that Mr. Darling wouldn't catch them together, kept the conversation focused on his acts of generosity by making serial confessions of appreciation for converting the Engel farm into Guardian Angel Cemetery. She even discussed making travel plans to Hope to pay her respects when the cemetery opened in the summer.

As Addie stepped off the streetcar in front of Mr. Thompson's law firm, she turned back to Mr. Darling. "Again, I am so overwhelmed. Thank you. Words fail to express my sincere gratitude." She placed her right, gloved hand over her heart. "I can't believe you even replaced those hand-painted, white cross grave markers for such fancy granite ones. Whatever can I do to repay you?" Addie asked.

"Not a thing, my dear child. After all, shouldn't we all be guardian angels on earth and look after one another?" Mr. Darling winked as he reached out and touched her cheek. "You can do me the honor of doin' somethin' that neither Mrs. Darling nor I ever had the opportunity to do in our lifetime." Mr. Darling opened the front door of Thompson, Chandler, and Davis Law Firm.

"What's that?" Addie said as she stepped into the main hallways of the building and they made their way to the elevators.

Entering an empty elevator car, Mr. Darling waited for the doors to close. "Addie, follow your dreams and go to nursin' school. University or college was never an option for a farmer like me. I inherited the family farm and continued to do as my Pappy and his Pappy did before him. We didn't have the choices you do now, let alone the financial means at that time, either. Go wherever your heart leads you, my child. Be a good servant to God and always help those less fortunate than you. That's all I ask in return."

"I promise." Addie smiled lovingly at Mr. Darling. The doors opened on the third floor.

Addie, Garrett, and Mr. Darling made their way to Miss Bishop's office. Mr. Darling knocked on her door and announced their arrival for the four o'clock appointment with Mr. Thompson.

"Please follow me." Miss Bishop got up from her desk and curled her right index finger over her shoulder, motioning them to follow her down the long hallway. Her blonde, spiral curls bounced and her shoe heels clicked with every step on the cold, black and white checkered, marble floor. Stopping in front of two large, heavily hand-carved doors that mimicked the one in Mr. Thompson's office, she opened one of them. "As you can see, the other party has already arrived. Mr. Thompson will be in momentarily."

Mr. and Mrs. Schwinn and Lester sat on the opposite side of the conference table. Mr. Darling stepped over to shake Mr. Schwinn's hand and kiss his sister on the cheek. As he walked behind Lester, he patted him on the shoulder and tousled his hair as he made his way back around the table to find a chair across from Mr. Schwinn. Garrett noticed the bandage under Lester's chin as he pulled out the chair next to his father for Addie. She took her place as he took his seat across from Lester, who appeared miffed as he raked his light, brown locks back into place with his fingers.

The white, plantation shutters covering the windows were positioned to allow the afternoon sunlight in without blinding those who faced them. As they sat in silence, Addie shifted nervously in her seat. She could feel hives emerging under the high-collared, pink dress. To calm her nerves, she took a moment to appreciate the beautifully decorated room. A gold chandelier hung from the middle of the white, coffered ceiling overhead. Hand-painted portraits of partners past and present graced both sides of the long walls. She caught her reflection in the grand, gilt mirror hanging on the far end of the short wall over a decorative waist-high, chestnut table. Dried, purple, pink, and blue hydrangeas were artfully arranged in a sterling silver bowl on top. She barely recognized the young woman staring back at her. The conference room door swung open. Mr. Thompson entered carrying a manila folder. Miss Bishop filed in behind him, taking a seat in the chair against the wall. She took out her steno pad and began taking notes as Mr. Thompson spoke.

"Afternoon, y'all." Mr. Thompson took the seat at the head of the table. "Thank you for meeting me here today. I am so sorry for your loss. I know how much you will miss Mrs. Gray. She was a lovely woman, God rest her soul." Glancing over at Garrett's shiner and Lester's bandaged chin, he added, "Boys, there better not be any brawling here today. Do you hear me?"

Garrett sheepishly said, "Yes sir." He touched his swollen and tender cheek.

Lester quipped, "Let's get on with it, Mr. Thompson. I'm sure this session with you is costing the estate more time and money, so let's not waste another penny, shall we?"

Mr. Schwinn and Mary, although mortified by their son's comment, opted to remain quiet, silently concurring with him.

Mr. Darling began to clear his throat to speak, but Addie reached out and placed her hands on Mr. Darling's and Garrett's arms to prevent either one of them from engaging with Lester.

Unnerved by Lester's interruption, Mr. Thompson took command of the meeting. "Please know that Mrs. Gray appointed me as the executor of her estate."

"Of course she did," Lester grumbled.

Mr. Thompson removed the will from its folder and read aloud. "Last Will and Testament of Olive Eve Gray. I, Olive Eve Gray, of 382 Houston Street, Atlanta, Fulton County, Georgia, being of full age, sound mind and memory and under no restraint, do make, publish and declare this instrument to be my Last Will and Testament and hereby revoke all Wills and Codicils ever before made by me. At the time of executing this Will, I am the widow to Dr. Robert Asa Gray and have no children.

"ITEM 1 — I direct my Executor to pay all of the expenses of my last illness, of my funeral and burial, and of the administration of my estate.

"ITEM 2 — I direct my Executor to pay any and all inheritance, transfer, estate and similar taxes (including interest and penalties) assessed or payable by reason of my death on any property or interest in property which is included in my estate for the purpose of computing taxes. My Executor shall not require any beneficiary under this Will to reimburse my estate for taxes paid on property passing under the terms of this Will.

"ITEM 3 — I direct my Executor to bury my body in keeping with my station in life in Oakwood Cemetery in the plot next to my deceased husband.

"ITEM 4 — I give, devise and bequeath the my entire estate, whether real, personal, or mixed, of every kind, nature and description whatsoever, and wherever situated, which I may now own or hereafter acquire, or have the right to dispose of at the time of my death, by the power of appointment or otherwise, including, but not limited to, any right or interest I have in my home and real property at 382 Houston Street, Atlanta, Fulton County, Georgia, any and all financial accounts, and all other items or property, real or personal, I own at the time of my death to Addie Rose Engel."

Addie gasped, "What?" *I thought Lester was getting his Aunt's home and property?*

Garrett grabbed her arm. "Addie, can you believe it? What wonderful news!"

Lester slammed his fists down hard on the table. Addie jumped, terrified by his unpredictable nature. "What the hell? Addie gets Aunt Olive's house, belongings, and bank account? Are you fucking kidding me? That house and money was promised to me! Do you hear me, Mr. Thompson? The majority of her estate is supposed to go to me! I'm her nephew, for God's sake!" He lunged across the table at Addie. "You aren't even family!"

Miss Bishop stuck her pencil behind her ear and popped up from her seat. "Mr. Thompson, I'll get security."

Mary pulled at Lester's suit coat. "Lester you have embarrassed your father and me enough these past two days. Now sit your behind back down in that chair before I jerk a knot in your tail!"

Mr. Thompson chuckled inside as he cautiously watched a flustered Lester return to his chair, then added, "No, security won't be necessary at this time. Thank you, Miss Bishop." He motioned her to take her seat.

Taking her hand off the door handle, Miss Bishop sat back down. Removing her pencil, she waited for Mr. Thompson to resume reading the will.

"Please continue, Mr. Thompson." Mr. Darling took Addie's hand in his.

Mr. Thompson cleared his throat.

"ITEM 5—I give, devise and bequeath my life insurance policy in the amount of five hundred dollars to be split evenly between Thomas Darling, Mary Schwinn and Garrett Darling, if they survive me.

"ITEM 6—I nominate and appoint my attorney, Jefferson Levy Thompson of Thompson Chandler Davis, LLP, as Executor and give to said Executor all the rights, powers and immunities set forth in this Will, including but not limited to the requirement that said Executor serve without bond and make no return to any Court whatsoever."

Mr. Thompson paused and put the paper down on the table. "The rest of the will outlines my role and responsibilities in compliance with the Georgia laws. Shall I continue reading?"

Lester stammered. "That's it? What do I get out of this? What did Aunt Olive leave for me?"

Mr. Thompson calmly replied, "Nothing, Lester. At her request made on...what was the exact date, Miss Bishop?"

Miss Bishop flipped through the pages in the notepad and stopped. She tapped her pencil at a spot on the paper. "Her request to change her will according to her new directives was made and executed on Monday, December, 22, 1913."

"Thank you, Miss Bishop. So, as you can see Lester, absolutely nothing was left to you." Mr. Thompson bit his inside lip to prevent a smile from eking out.

Lester pounded the table again with his fists. "I'm going to appeal this will, you bastard!" He shook his index finger across the table at him. Spit flew and white foam emerged near the corners of his mouth. "You can't stop me from making my tonic." Lester shifted his rant toward Addie. "You're a good for nothing farm girl from North Georgia."

Protectively, Mr. Darling and Garrett got on their feet and stood next to Addie. She grabbed their hands.

Miss Bishop ran out of the conference room door, yelling, "Security! Security! I need security!" Two men in black suits emerged from behind closed doors and followed her back into the conference room.

Lester watched the men split and walk toward him from either side of the conference room, preventing his escape. They each grabbed an arm. He writhed and screamed out, "It will be over my cold, dead body before you see one dime from my Aunt's estate! Do you hear me? I will tie you up in court and it will cost you the entire fortune! I will fight you over this, Addie!"

Mr. Schwinn and Mary stared at their son, mortified and in disbelief. It was Mary who spoke first. "Lester, for heaven's sake! Please lower your voice! Get a hold of yourself! We will handle this matter in a civilized manner. Why are you bringing the tonic into this discussion?" Tears emerged and she started crying as she watched Lester being escorted out of the room. She called out, "Has something happened that you have neglected to tell us about? What did you do to your Aunt Olive that made her cut you out of her will? Oh, dear Lord, Lester. What have you done?" She turned and buried her sobs into Mr. Schwinn's shoulder. "Take me home. Please take me home right now. I don't think I can bear to hear any more."

"Yes, my dear." Mr. Schwinn took Mary's arm. They gathered their belongings.

In an effort to comfort his sister, Mr. Darling walked over as they approached the door. Mr. Schwinn raised his hand, motioning him to stop. The door closed behind them.

Mr. Thompson, who remained seated through the ordeal, handed Addie a copy of the will. "Here, this is for you."

Miss Bishop, who took refuge behind Mr. Darling, took her seat. Garrett and Mr. Darling did the same.

"Do you have questions for me, Addie?" Mr. Thompson asked.

"Why me?" She attempted to study the paper, but her hands shook. She set it back down on the table.

"She loved you like a daughter. You were very good to her

and she wanted to make sure she looked after you. Her final wishes were to secure your future so that you could pursue your dreams and go to nursing school. She never wanted you to worry about feeling lost and abandoned again. Mrs. Gray wanted her home to be your home, to be filled with new, joyful memories. That's what she wanted for you." He rustled through the file. "Oh, this is for you, too. May I suggest that you place this in a bank safe deposit box?"

"What's this?" She took the certificate from his hand.

"It's the deed to the house."

Mr. Darling wiped his tears. "Addie, I knew when I asked you to take care of my sister, that you would be her guardian angel. You deserve all good things that are coming your way. I can't thank you enough for making her so happy in her final days. You never left her side. For that, I am eternally grateful." He reached down and hugged her.

"Addie, there's another matter to be addressed here this afternoon, too. If you don't mind, would you follow me to my office where we can speak in private?" Reticently, Mr. Thompson stood up, walked over to the door, and opened it for her.

"Uh, sure. Can you tell me what it's all about?" Addie stood and looked back at Mr. Darling and Garrett. She pointed to Garrett. "Can he come with me?"

"If that's your wish, then that's fine by me. Mr. Darling, you can wait here if you would like. Miss Bishop will be happy to get you anything to drink, eat, or read while you wait."

Addie and Garrett followed Mr. Thompson down the long hallway as Miss Bishop tended to Mr. Darling, who remained in the conference room. They entered his office to find the

Chief of Police seated comfortably in a chair at a small, round table by the bookshelf.

Mr. Thompson motioned to Addie and Garrett to take a seat as introductions were made. "I'll get straight to the point. Addie, you made some comments yesterday during the scuffle at Mrs. Gray's funeral. I have reason to believe you. Would you please tell the chief what Lester tried to do to you and Mrs. Gray?"

Caught off guard, Addie stuttered. "Wha...what? I'm not sure what I said. It's all such a blur." *What will happen to me if Lester finds out I talked with the police? What will Garrett say? I could ruin our friendship over this. He'll be so mad at me for hiding the truth from him. Oh, Maw, what should I do?*

Immediately, Addie recalled the time when she tried to lie about breaking one of Maw's cherished vases, a gift from her grandma. *Maw cautioned me not to touch it, but I didn't listen to her. I just wanted to see the beautiful butterflies and hummingbirds painted on the sides. I thought I knew best. I was a big girl—all eight years of me. As I lifted the vase off the fireplace mantel, it slipped from my hands and broke into a thousand pieces on the hardwood floor. When I tried to play dumb and innocent, Maw knew better. She saw the truth in my eyes. She said, "Addie, as God as my witness, I didn't raise you to be a liar. If you broke it, you need to own up to your mistake. Do not make me wash your mouth out with soap for spouting filth from your lips. Do not become your father's daughter!" Maw's words stung. She was sore with me because I wouldn't come right out and tell her the truth. I don't want to be like my Paw, a con and a cheat. Who is Addie Engel? I am my own woman who needs to rise like a phoenix from the ashes from my family farm and forge my own reputation in this world. After all, when I stand naked in front of a mirror before God every night, the reflection staring back at me is all I own at the end of the day. Will I be able to make eye contact with myself with the choices I make in this lifetime? Or, did I sell my soul to the devil?* Addie took a deep breath in and slowly exhaled. *I need to make Maw proud. I can't let Lester's threats or even the memory of Paw's fear and intimidation rule me. Better yet, I need to honor Mrs. Gray and make myself proud for standing up and telling the truth.*

With confidence restored and aware of all the risks, Addie continued. "Chief, I'll tell you everything I know."

31

Thursday morning, February 26, 1914, Fourth Ward

Addie swirled her coffee in her cup, staring into the mocha abyss as she sat in Mrs. Gray's spot on the sofa. A copy of *The Atlanta Dispatch* lay on the coffee table, unread. *I wish Garrett would write a letter back to me. It's been nine days since the reading of Mrs. Gray's will and nine days since I confessed all that I knew to the chief and Mr. Thompson about Lester's maleficent intentions toward Mrs. Gray and me. It's been eight days since I wrote Garrett a letter to apologize and explain why I agreed to let Mrs. Gray handle matters with Lester.*

Restless, she walked to the living room window, parted the white lace curtains, and stared out into the cloudless, blue sky. *When I shared with them my thoughts about Doc Gray's tonic, especially when combined with alcohol, they concurred. I even disclosed the debacle at the Alexander's Christmas party followed by vomiting all over Lester on Mrs. Gray's front porch. The chief and Mr. Thompson had a good laugh and thought that was an ideal way to end the night. I have to admit, looking back, it was rather funny. However,*

Garrett failed to see the humor. To see the hurt in his eyes when he found out that I wasn't completely honest with him pierced my heart.

Addie closed the curtain and paced the floor, still replaying the events and discussions over and over in her head. *The chief and Mr. Thompson asked Mr. Darling into the room. They inquired about his role with Lester's tonic company. After learning that he simply sold ginger, harvested from his Hope farm to make the product, the chief swore us to secrecy while Mr. Thompson made us sign a confidentiality agreement. As the ink dried from our signatures, we learned about the investigation into* Doc Gray's *tonic and Lester's company. Bound from talking any further about the matter as they continued to build a case out of mounting evidence, we rode in silence on the street car back home. Oh, God! I hated tip-toeing around the house, quietly arguing with Garrett that evening after Mr. Darling fell asleep. It ripped my heart out to know that he felt betrayed by me not telling him the truth from the start, refusing to listen to anything I had to say. How can life be so good, yet take a turn and become so twisted and complicated?*

Garrett's words still rang in her ears. *"You chose to give your heart and body to me as you made love to me and yet you elected to keep those secrets from me? How could you? How can I trust you again? You know how much I love you. A part of me is so torn, Addie. I want you to come back to Hope. I want you to be my wife. But there's a part of me that needs to let you go so you can go to nursing school. Do you realize you are pledging yourself to be a single woman for the next three years? A lot can happen in that time. You may meet someone else. I may meet someone else. Can we wait for each other? Will we wait for each other?"*

When Mr. Darling and Garrett left to return to the farm

last week and the front door closed behind them, Addie stood alone in the hallway. *Now what am I supposed to do with myself?*

Whatever I do, I need to avoid running into Lester at all costs. The silence was deafening.

Is Garrett the one for me? Is it possible that I could meet someone new and possibly give my heart to another?

The squeaky, brass-hinged mail box swung opened and closed. She heard the sound of letters filling the container.

Addie ran to the box and retrieved two letters. Both were addressed to her. From the return address she could see that one was from Lena Hartman. The other was a letter from Sacred Heart Nursing School. "Gosh darn it!" Addie sulked and stomped her foot before returning to the parlor and sitting back down on the sofa. She picked up a brass letter opener off the coffee table and slid the envelope from Lena open. *Another day has gone by without a response from Garrett!*

24 February, 1914

Dearest Addie, My deepest condolences and sympathies are extended to you on the loss of Mrs. Gray. I know how much she meant to you and you to her. Though she never had a daughter of her own, I would dare say she loved and adored you as if you were her own flesh and blood.

I extend to you an invitation to join me for lunch on Thursday, March 5, 1914. I have a fellow nursing student who will be joining you in your class and I would like to introduce you to her before classes begin in April. Speaking of such things, you will also be receiving a letter from me on behalf of the nursing school.

Please RSVP for the luncheon at my apartment home by ringing me on the telephone at Main 36. Thank goodness I have my own private line and not a party line. I prefer my calls between relatives, friends, and hospital co-workers to remain between us. I have no use for nosey neighbors, bored housewives, and gossips!

Sincerely, Lena

Addie laughed out loud. *Oh, goodness! I don't even know the phone number to this house.*

I've never had to make a phone call before. I only spoke into the receiver once with Mr. Thompson when Mrs. Gray suffered her stroke. But that doesn't count as actually carrying on a real telephone conversation with someone.

Using the letter opener again, Addie slid open the top of the envelope from Sacred Heart Nursing School, removing the letter before tucking the letter opener away in her right skirt pocket.

Sacred Heart Hospital and Nursing School
John L. Williams, M.D., Medical Director
Lena Hartman, R.N., Superintendent
February, 24, 1914

Dear Addie, On behalf of the Board of Directors, Dr. John Williams, Medical Director, Leadership team, and myself, we welcome you to Sacred Heart Nursing School's inaugural class of 1914. We look forward to having you join us for classes beginning on Wednesday, April 1, 1914. You are instructed to report to Sacred Heart Nursing School located at 422 Spring Street by 9:00am. Be prompt. You are allowed to bring one trunk. Have it sent to Sacred Heart Nursing School prior to your arrival. Mark all your clothing, undergarments, and corset covers with name tape. Be sure to bring the following items: two large laundry bags marked with the name on the outside, black shoes (oxford or high shoes) with rubber heels (pumps and strap slippers are not permitted), bathroom slippers, washable kimonos, night gown, watch having a second hand, fountain pen, raincoat, umbrella, and overshoes.

Please complete and sign the enclosed form and mail it in using the addressed and stamped envelope provided no later than Monday, March 9, 1914. Failure to comply with this request will result in an immediate issue of ten demerits against your report card.

Before reporting for duty, have your teeth checked. If you have not been vaccinated for smallpox or typhoid (if not vaccinated within the last three years), please have this attended to immediately.

Demerits will be issued for tardiness and for inability to comply with the enclosed regulations.

The schedule for Wednesday, April 1, 1914 is as follows:

9:00am — Report to Sacred Heart Nursing School

9:15am — Introductions and dormitory tour

9:30am — Bed assignments (unpacking is permitted at this time)

Change into uniforms

11:30am — Lunch and hospital tour with Mr. Edward Alexander, Founder and Chief Executive Officer, Dr. John

Williams, Medical Director, & Clyde Posey, Chief Operating
Officer

    1:00pm — Report to Classroom A

    1:15pm — Overview of Program and Year 1 Classes

    2:00pm — Hospital Shift Assignments

    2:30pm — Break

    3:00pm — 5:00pm — History of Nursing

    5:00pm — Adjourn

    6:00pm — Supper

    9:00pm — Lights out

    Should you have any questions, please ring me at
Main 36.

    Yours Truly, Lena Hartman, R.N.

    Superintendent, Sacred Heart School for Nurses

Addie beamed as she flipped to the next page.

Sacred Heart Nursing School Contract, Term 1914 — 1917
This is an agreement between Miss (fill in the blank) and
the Sacred Heart Hospital Board, whereby Miss (fill in the
blank) agrees to participate in the Sacred Heart Nursing
School's three-year program beginning April 1, 1914 and
concluding on March 31, 1917. Sacred Heart Hospital agrees
to pay Miss (fill in the blank) the sum of $5 per month.

    Miss (fill in the blank) agrees:

    Not to get married. This contract becomes null and void
immediately if the nurse marries.

    Not to keep company with men.

    To be compliant with dormitory rules and regulations,

remaining on the hospital grounds between the hours of 8:00pm and 6:00am unless approved by Nurse Hartman.

Not to smoke or possess cigarettes.

Not to drink or possess beer, wine, or whiskey.

Not to be incompliant with uniform dress code to include dyeing of hair, wearing make-up or jewelry of any kind, keeping nails trimmed, and securing hair from face and off nape of the neck, and maintaining personal cleanliness.

Not to wear perfumes or scented lotions of any kind.

Not to wear dresses more than two inches above the ankle when out of uniform and to wear at least two petticoats.

Not to ride in a carriage or automobile with any man except her brother or father during time off.

Not to loiter in downtown ice-cream stores, bars or establishments of ill repute during time off.

This contract becomes null and void immediately if the student is found in violation of rules #1-10. Date:

Student Name (Please print):

Student Signature (Please sign):

With papers in hand, Addie ran upstairs to her desk. Using the pen in the black inkwell, she filled out the contract, dating and signing it. She flipped to the next piece of paper in the packet.

Sacred Heart Nursing School
Uniform Measurements
Please complete and return with the contract.
Name. Addie wrote. *Addie Rose Engel. Height. When I read*

my medical chart when Mrs. Gray and I were hospitalized at Grady because of Lester, I saw I was five foot, eight inches tall. Addie scribbled the number in the space provided. *Weight. I believe I weighed one hundred and twenty eight pounds.* Addie jotted it down. *Chest. When Mrs. Gray and I went to Rich and Brothers, I recall that the female sales attendant measured me at thirty-six inches. Waist.* Addie wrote the number twenty-six next to it. *Shoe size.* Addie penned the number eight.

The mailman darted across the street, catching Addie's eye as she glanced out the bedroom window. She folded the papers, securing them in the envelope provided as she licked it closed.

She ran back down stairs and out the front door.

"Wait! Wait! Mr. Postman. I have a letter for you to mail," Addie called out as she ran down the sidewalk. She looked both ways before crossing the street.

The mailman stopped, turned, and took Addie's letter.

"Thank you, sir." Breathless, Addie ran back across the street.

"My pleasure, miss." He replied as he tipped his hat to her.

"I'm off to go make my first phone call!" Addie waved back in excitement as she looked forward to finalizing lunch plans with Nurse Hartman.

"Good for you!" He laughed as he tucked the letter into his sable colored pouch.

Addie returned to the house, closed and secured the lock on the front door, and made her way to the kitchen. She picked up the phone receiver. There was a knock on the front door. "Coming!" She returned the receiver into the holder and hustled down the hallway. Believing it was the postman on the front porch, she began speaking as she opened the door. "Did I forget to do something?"

"As a matter of fact, you did. You can start by apologizing to me and my family."

Addie's neck and chest burst into red blotches. She immediately stepped onto the porch, shut the door behind her, and faced the uninvited guest. "I will do no such thing. What are you doing here? You have no business being here, Lester!" She took a step back.

His dark eyes sparked. He took a step closer. Addie felt his breath on her face. He wrapped his right hand around her neck and shoved her back against the brick wall, nearly toppling over a two-foot black, cast iron flower pot in the process. "Excuse me? I have no right to be on my dead aunt's porch? I have no right or claim to my inheritance? I have no business trying to get back what is rightfully mine? How dare you say that to me?"

If these are my last spoken words, I need to speak the truth. "Your aunt knew you were up to no good. In fact, it was the news about your antics that caused her to suffer a stroke. You broke her heart. She saw through your evil ways. You are reaping what you sowed, Lester. Do you hear me? As God is my witness, I have prayed that he would send a band of angels down to strike you from this world. You have no heart. You have no soul." She searched his eyes; they were void of any life. "I wish you were dead." She spat in his face and struggled to get free from his grip.

Lester's fingers tightened. "You first."

Addie gasped for air and tried reaching out for anything that could be used as a weapon. *Nothing.* Catching a glimpse of the postman across the street out of the corner of her eye, she tried to call out to him, but she had no voice. She tried pushing him away from her, but he was too strong and held his ground. Her vision speckled with flashes of light. As her arms dropped to her side, her right hand brushed against something hard in her skirt pocket. *The letter opener.* Fumbling to find it, she managed to withdraw it and partially stick it into Lester's abdomen.

"Holy hell! You bitch! What have you done to me?" Lester yelled out as he dropped his hand from around her neck and yanked out the brass implement. He stepped back to examine the tinge of blood on the end of it. "Jesus Christ!" He covered the growing crimson spot on his sage green vest with his other hand.

"Hey! You there!" the postman called out as he ran across the street.

Lester backed down the front walk, frantically making his way to his car parked in front of the house. "You wait, Addie. Your days are numbered!" he shouted while jabbing and pointing the letter opener at her.

Addie pointed at him and shouted back, "No, I believe that yours are, Lester!"

"Miss? Are you alright?" the postman asked as he ran toward her, holding his mailbag close to his body.

"I'm fine. It was just a misunderstanding." She retreated into the house, closing and locking the front door. She heard Lester's car tires squeal as he sped off down the road.

Thursday afternoon, Sixth Ward

Madam McGuire jumped off the street car and was immediately engulfed by exhaust and the winding blare of police sirens from two motorcycle units as they sped away from headquarters, south down Decatur Street. Once inside the bustling precinct, she made her way to the front desk. "I'm 'ere to see the Chief. I've got an appointment with 'im," she said in her Irish brogue.

The lean, tall officer nodded, pointing to an office down the hall. His black mustache wiggled up and down and from side to side as he spoke. "He's expecting you."

Madam McGuire found the door to the chief's office wide open. As she stood in the threshold, she watched the chief cut out an ad and an accompanying article for Doc Otto's tonic from the morning copy of *The Atlanta Dispatch*. He placed it proudly in the center of his desk next to a folder labeled Doc Gray's *tonic*. She cleared her throat. He looked up.

"Ah, good morning, Madam McGuire. Thanks for coming in today." He stood and extended his right hand.

"Top of the mornin' to you, chief. Please call me Amy." She shook his hand and then removed her gloves, pulling at one finger at a time before having a seat in an empty chair in front of his desk. "Sorry I couldn't see ya sooner. I've got a sick muthah in Chattanooga and she needed some lookin' aftah."

The chief closed the door and returned to his seat. "Not a problem. It seems like you may have some information for me about some officers that is worth hearing."

"Look, Chief. I know ye are tryin' to put the squeeze on businesses such as mine, so what's in it for me?"

He liked her direct nature and could see why Frank would choose her as a lover. As he studied her, he envisioned her lying naked on a bed of white linens. It could be so easy to get lost in her long, curly, red hair, ample bosom, creamy complexion, and sharp, blue eyes. He could drink her up like a cold cup of milk. "What's in it for you, you ask? Well, for your full cooperation, I won't shut your business down if you continue to run your operation as cleanly as I hear you have been doing. Otherwise, it will be curtains for you if you decide to clam up.

You'll find yourself and your girls in the pokey for sure."

"If I tell ye what you what ye need to know, ye promise to keep the riff raff out of me establishment?"

"What? Like Frank use to do?" He watched her ivory complexion drain as she bristled. He thought he saw her eyes moisten, but after a few blinks they cleared. He leaned onto his elbows that were already resting on top of his desk and waited.

Amy bowed her head; her lavender hat shielded his view of her face. She fidgeted with the gloves resting in her hands. After weighing her options, she raised her head and snapped, "How do I know yer men won't come back and hurt me again?"

"You have my word. I heard and I'm deeply sorry about that. It seems like I've got a few bad apples in the bunch. With March nearly upon us, it appears that I've got some spring cleaning to do."

She painted a hint of a smile on her face.

"Would it be easier for you if I asked you specific questions and you answered them?"

"Yes, I rather like that idea. I'm not sure exactly what yer lookin' for and I'd rather keep me cards close to me vest, if I can." She watched him snicker. "A woman like me knows a lot of secrets 'bout many powerful people in this town. I like to keep a few aces up me sleeves if you know what I mean."

"Fine. Tell me who you think killed Frank."

"Ye know who they are." She shifted in her seat. "They work for ya 'ere. After they roughed me up a bit and turned Frank's apartment upside down lookin' for somethin', I heard 'em talkin' to each other in the hallway as they left. I believe one is named Seth and the other Lamar. They weren't exactly wearin' their badges and formalities weren't exchanged when they punched me face and kicked me in the stomach."

He winced. "Understood. Again, please accept my apologies for their bad behavior. I need to establish a timeline. When did this occur?"

"It happened on a Saturday night, January 24th. Thank goodness I had the sense enough to mail Frank's package to Mr. Thompson that mornin'. I think that's what they were aftah."

The chief nodded in agreement. "I think so too. Do you know what the package contained?"

"No. I also make it my business to know when not to ask a lot of questions. Knowin' too much 'round this town can send you to an early grave. Frank knew too much, didn't he?"

"I believe he unknowingly walked into a hornet's nest. I've been called in to help with the extermination. Did he ever mention anything to you about Doc Gray's tonic or anything about Lester Schwinn?"

"No. But I'm familiar with Doc Gray's tonic. I actually carried some to me ailing maw last week. Me pharmacist told me they are comin' out with a new and improved version, called

Doc Otto's tonic. He said they were clearin' their shelves. He even gave me another bottle free of charge." She shook her head. "I don't know 'bout the man you speak of. Never heard of 'em."

"When did you last see Frank?"

"Monday, the fifth of January. I'll never forget his last words to me. He passed me on the staircase and said, 'If you don't see me in a week's time, please mail this for me.' He handed me a package addressed to the attorney, Mr. Jefferson Thompson. He kissed me good-bye. He was gone. I let the weeks slip by, hopin' he would walk back through me door again." She whispered. "He never did. I knew in my gut he never would." Her eyes welled up.

"I've heard enough. You're free to go. But please know that if I need anything else, you will cooperate fully."

Amy reached into her handbag and pulled out a few brothel tokens. She tossed them onto of the newspaper clipping. "Ye know where to find me."

As Amy exited, he picked up one and examined it. On one side of the bronze coin a Celtic harp was stamped in the middle. The border read, 'Erin go Braugh." He translated it in his head, *Ireland Forever*. Flipping it over, "Good for 1 screw-bath-grits" was imprinted in the center. The top edge read, "Madam McGuire's Emporium." On the bottom was stamped "Hulsey Street."

As he scooped them up and put them into his pants pocket, a commotion arose in the hallway outside his door. He jumped up to investigate. The chief found Amy sandwiched between Seth and Lamar.

"What the hell are you doing here?" Lamar pressed his

chest against hers. "Are you looking for more action or just more trouble?"

The chief interrupted. "Boys, I believe you have a meeting with me now? Please let Miss McGuire through. She was just leaving."

Lamar stepped back as Amy swung around stepped away from them. "Get your filthy paws off me, you two. Damn ye demons to the fiery pit of 'ell." She spat on the ground at their feet and disappeared behind three more uniformed officers who blocked their pursuit.

Seth screamed out after her. "Fuck you! What did you tell him? He won't believe the lies of a whore!"

Lamar panicked. He grabbed his revolver from his holster and fired a shot into the ceiling. Plaster sprinkled down on the officers like snow as Seth pulled out his gun and shot Lamar squarely in the chest. Blood sprayed all over the wall behind him. He dropped immediately to the floor.

The chief and the other officers responded, their guns drawn, all aimed at Seth. Seth waved his pistol around. "Chief, you can't believe a word she says."

The chief aimed his weapon at Seth's head and remained calm. "Why did you do it? Was the extra money that Lester paid to you and Lamar that important? Why didn't you come to me?"

"I didn't have a choice. My kids need new clothes and my wife is sick. Everything costs money."

"You always have a choice. You chose poorly." The chief stepped closer.

Seth's eyes darkened and darted wildly around. "Don't you dare, Chief! Don't make me do this!"

"I'm not making you do anything, Seth." He took another step toward Seth.

"Don't you fucking make me do this!" Seth cried out. He pointed his gun at his head. "Tell my wife I love her." He pulled the trigger. Pink mist, brain matter, and skull fragments spattered the hall wall behind him. He fell on top of Lamar.

The chief ran over to the bodies and secured their guns. "Shit!" He looked up at his officers. "Boys, do your best to take care of these men and clean up this mess." The Chief walked back to his office and slammed his door shut. "Fuck! Fuck! Fuck!" He dropped the bloody guns in the empty chair where Amy had sat and returned to his desk. He pulled out a flask from his jacket pocket and emptied it in one gulp. The phone on his desk rang. He picked up the ear piece and lifted the phone to his mouth. "Jesus, what do you want?"

A voice on the other line stumbled. "Uh, this isn't Jesus. It's Jefferson. Although, my wife does call me 'God' on special occasions!" He laughed. "What the hell is wrong with you? Having a tough day at the office?"

"You could say that."

"Did I catch you at a bad time?"

"No. No. I was just in the middle of doing some spring cleaning."

32

Lester burst through the front door at Newman's Painting and Supply Company, making his way through the bustling children as they carried paint cans filled hay and tonic bottles while others carried empty bottles labeled Doc Otto's tonic to the dispensing area. He clutched at his belly, which still ached from his altercation with Addie five days earlier. Ten stiches held his wound shut. The doctor said he was lucky for now. While the cut wasn't deep enough to nick any organs, prayers would be required to ward off pyemia. He needed to watch for signs of fever, redness, and pus around the site.

"Over here!" A man's voice called out from behind one of the brass dispensaries. "I'm just fixing two broken spickets. The knobs came unscrewed, tonic spilled everywhere. I've got a fresh batch waiting to be mixed for you."

"Great! I'll be sure to take those profits out of your paycheck this month. Do you have the samples of the new tonic for me yet?" Lester pulled out his pocket watch. *Two o'clock.* "I have to be at Alvin's store by three for a very important meeting."

"Not yet. I had to empty this tank to fix the problem. I'll whip up a new batch in a jiffy."

Lester pointed to the other capsule. "What's wrong with that one?"

The man peered around with a wrench in hand. "One of the pedestal legs loosened. We had to empty that one, too so it could be welded." Anticipating Lester's next comment, he added. "Not to worry, Lester. It will be up and running with the new formula by the end of the day. Today's been a bit of a jacked up mess."

"You think?" Lester pulled an old crate from the stack resting against the wall and had a seat.

A young boy all of ten years old pulled on Lester's coat. "I'm cleaning and disinfecting bottles for you today, sir. I just want to make you proud. Thank you for this job, sir." He lifted off his tweed cap and bowed. "Thank you, sir."

Lester glared at him. "If you stand here talking to me for much longer, you're going to find yourself out of a job and back on the streets." Lester shooed him away. "Now be gone with you!"

"Buddy, come over here, boy!" The boy ran to the man with the scarred hands. "Go upstairs and put the ingredients on the table into the coffers, just like I showed you how to do this morning."

"Yes, sir." Buddy ran upstairs to the second floor. He removed the lids from the copper vessels on the floor. He took a hose, turned it on, and let water flow into one of the basins. He stood on his tiptoes to pull containers, bottles, and bags off the table one by one, pouring the various powders and liquids into the vessels on the floor. He moved the hose to the other basin. He grabbed one of the bags of white powder and added it to the rest of the ingredients. He took the long wooden paddle, stuck it deep down inside each vessel, and stirred the mixture. Using the hose, he rinsed the residue off the sides. He ran back to the top of the stairs and called down. "The ingredients are in, just like you showed me. Tell me when to shut off the water."

The man with the webbed fingers looked at the rising indicator on the gauge on the side of the capsule. Ten minutes later, he called upstairs. "Buddy, you can shut off the water now."

"Yes, sir." Buddy ran back and turned off the hose. He replaced the lids, satisfied with his big accomplishment.

"What size bottle and how many do you need, Lester?" The man called out.

"Two large bottles should suffice." Lester checked the time again. *Twenty-one minutes after two.* He stood up and made his way toward the man rushing toward him, who held out two bottles of Doc Otto's tonic.

"Here you go. Sorry for the delay."

"As I said, you will pay for your mistakes today," Lester barked as he stormed out the front door. The bell tolled his departure.

Tuesday afternoon, Second Ward

Alvin glanced out the store front window looking for any sign of Lester. He pulled out his silver pocket watch as Dr. Williams took a self-guided tour of the pharmacy. *Ten minutes after three.*

"Ah, I see you have eucalyptus plaster." Dr. Williams pulled the green jar off the shelf for a closer examination. "I highly recommend this product for chest congestion. I have my patients spread this thickly onto their chest and cover it with a very warm, cotton cloth. The vapors and the heat open up even the most congested patient."

Alvin stuffed the timepiece back into his tan vest, shifted his attention, and rejoined Dr. Williams. "Yes, it's one of my top sellers, especially during the fall and winter months. It would be a good product to stock in the Sacred Heart pharmacy."

Replacing the jar, he said. "I concur. However, it's a horrible mess once it dries. I brought an Italian man to tears when my nurses and I tried to remove it. I ripped off all of his chest hair, leaving it as smooth as a newborn baby's buttocks. But he never coughed again!" he laughed.

The front door opened and the bell tinkled as Lester rushed into the store. "Sorry I'm late, gentleman. Traffic got backed up on Whitehall. There was a horrible accident involving a spooked horse, a wagon full of pigs, and a street car. It was a complete mess to say the least. There were still a few pigs running loose on the sidewalks when I drove by. You should have seen the women screaming. It was like they had never seen a farm animal before," Lester howled as he grabbed the doctor's hand and shook it vigorously. "Please accept my sincere apologies. You must be Dr. Williams. I'm Lester Schwinn."

The doctor regained possession of his hand and tucked it away into his pants pocket. "I understand from Clyde that Dr. Barringer has made improvements to the Doc Gray's tonic formula." He studied Lester. "While we were waiting for you,

Alvin showed me the research studies and findings of Dr. Barringer. I must say that the results are impressive. They're almost too good to be true."

Lester pulled out the two bottles of Doc Otto's he had tucked away in his coat pocket and set them on the glass counter next to Dr. Barringer's research study. "As you can see, this is the large bottle. It also comes in a medium and small size, too. I would expect that a hospital of your size would require large bottles for inpatient dispensing and small bottles for the patient to take home when they are discharged."

Dr. Williams picked up one of the bottles and read dosing instructions and the ingredients listing on the back. "Alvin told me that you are calling it a 'restorative.' I didn't see anywhere in Dr. Barringer's research where he used it on pediatric patients." He flipped the bottle around. "I don't see any directives on the bottle for use in children."

Alvin stepped up to answer. "While it's not recommended for use in little children, I would suggest that the youngest age to prescribe this medication would be ten years old. That's based on my professional recommendation, you see."

Dr. Williams nodded in agreement.

Alvin walked behind his sales counter and removed two shot glasses from a drawer. "Let's have you sample the product so you will know what it tastes like."

Dr. Williams threw up his hand in protest. "No, no thank you, gentleman. I prefer to take a bottle back to my lab at home so that I can personally analyze the ingredients. I'm not in the habit of putting anything into my body that I haven't tested and verified."

Lester turned his back and rolled his eyes at Alvin as he

unscrewed the cap from one of the bottles. He carefully poured out an equal amount of tonic in each jigger. Lester handed one glass to Alvin and kept the other. "Here's to your health!"

They toasted and threw back Doc Otto's new formula.

Alvin was the first to drop his glass. It exploded when it hit the floor, shattering into a hundred pieces. He clutched his throat. "Argh!" He gurgled and sputtered incoherently.

Lester did the same, falling to his knees, unable to speak. He threw up blood at Dr. William's feet. Horrified, Dr. William's jumped out of the way as white foam, stomach contents, and blood spewed from Lester's mouth. The conjunctiva of his eyes turned red. Alvin collapsed and clutched his belly, vomiting chunks of mucosal tissue and blood.

He ran behind the counter and grabbed the phone. "Operator! Operator! This is Dr. Williams.

I have two medical emergencies at Alvin's Pharmacy on Whitehall Street. Send two ambulances, stat!"

The operator on the other line acknowledged the urgent request, immediately dispatching police and ambulances to the apothecary. Dr. Williams dashed back around the counter to find Alvin and Lester in contortions as their lungs filled with blood. He watched, knowing they were in their final moments of life. He had witnessed death by poisoning before and knew there was nothing more to be done for them. It was agonizing to witness; he felt helpless.

Alvin gasped and reached up toward Dr. Williams. His arm fell across his chest. Bloody foam bubbled out of his mouth as he exhaled. His eyes rolled back in his head. Lester's eyes filled with blood as it ran out of his sinuses and through his tear ducts. Teeth unseated and dropped to the back of his throat, occluding his airway. He tried to roll over while a series of massive convulsions expelled some of the teeth onto the floor around him, then the seizures left him lifeless.

When Dr. Williams heard sirens, he ran out the front door to the street. He waved at the arriving motorcycle policeman and the approaching ambulances. "They're in here!" Realizing there wasn't a sense of urgency anymore, he lowered his arms.

The officer dismounted and ran into Alvin's Pharmacy. Dr. Williams followed.

As they studied the bodies, Dr. Williams introduced himself. "I'm Dr. Williams, the new Medical Director at Sacred Heart Hospital. There's no need to hurry them off to a hospital. Believe me when I say they're already dead."

The officer looked at the two men lying in pools of blood, vomit, and bits of red clumps. He bent over to make out the white objects in the mix. *Teeth*. He snapped upright, cupped his hands to his mouth, and ran out the front door. He threw up on the curb.

A red haired ambulance attendant said to his partner as they ran past the policeman, "Oh, it must be a good 'un." They found Dr. Williams with his black boot hiked up on one of the sales displays. They watched him clean spattered body fluids from it with his handkerchief. "Hey!

If it ain't Doc Williams. What have we 'ere my good man?" Brice McDaniel reached out to shake the doctor's hand. "This 'ere is me brother, Rob."

Rob, carrying the rolled up stretcher, shook hands with the physician, too.

"Good to see you both. Looking forward to working with

you boys more in a few months." Dr. Williams lowered his leg and walked back over to Alvin and Lester. In a matter-of-fact instructional manner, he said. "I believe these men inadvertently consumed some kind of a poison." He retrieved a pencil from his inside his breast pocket and used it as a pointer. "This appears to be a caustic ingestion. See the corrosive tissue injuries around their mouths, tongues, and gums?" He leaned over, poking and prodding the victim's mouths as the brothers took mental notes and nodded. "See how the inside of their mouths are burned and how their teeth fell out?" The men continued to shake their heads. Dr. Williams stood up.

The Chief of Police ran into the store. "I heard the sirens. I was just down the street herding pigs." He threw his hands up in the air. "Never mind, it's a long story. What the hell happened here?"

Bob pointed to Dr. Williams. "Dr. Williams 'ere was just giving us a lesson on the cause of death. By the looks of it, it appears as if they drank some kind of poison."

Dr. Williams pointed toward the two bottles of Doc Otto's on the counter with his pencil. "I wouldn't touch those bottles without wearing gloves, Chief."

The chief looked at the tonic bottles and the dead men on the floor. "What a fucking mess.

They died from drinking that stuff?"

"They did." Dr. Williams walked over to the Chief. "I'm Dr. Williams. I'm the new Medical Director at Sacred Heart Hospital." He extended his hand to the chief, who chose to not shake his hand and instead waved at him. Still using his pencil, Dr. Williams looked like he was conducting an orchestra as he spoke over each of the lifeless bodies. "I had a meeting with the owner of this store, Alvin Martin, who is also the new pharmacist at Sacred Heart, and Lester Schwinn about using Doc Otto's new formula at Sacred Heart Hospital. The men offered me a sample." The pencil stopped moving. "Thank the dear Lord above I don't make it a habit to consume products I've not yet tested and analyzed in my lab first." He twisted the pencil in the air as if he was punctuating and ending his lesson.

The chief looked at Dr. Williams in amazement, then back at Lester and Alvin's twisted bodies lying in a puddle of their bodily fluids. The stench from loss of bowel and bladder functions, tonic, iron in the blood, and emesis was becoming unbearable. The chief covered his nose with his index finger. Bending over, he asked, "Are those teeth?" The men nodded their heads in the affirmative. "Holy shit! I've got to shut their operation down immediately! To hell with the Feds! Doc, I need you to come with me. I'm going to need your help to identify what exactly poisoned these men. God, I hope no one else suffers the same fate from drinking that shit!"

The chief ran around the sales counter and grabbed the phone. He tilted his head from side to side as he impatiently waited for the operator to answer. When she did, he fired off, "This is the Chief of Police. Ring the precinct and tell them I need all available officers to report to Newman's Painting and Supply Company located in the Third Ward. We have a very dangerous and hazardous situation in progress and two dead bodies as a result. I'll be there in ten minutes."

He hung up the receiver. "Come on!" The chief grabbed Dr. Williams' arm and they ran out of the store. "Get in." He directed Dr. Williams to get into the passenger side of his patrol car. Dr. Williams grabbed a hold of the dashboard as the car weaved through the oncoming cars, horse-drawn wagons, and pedestrians crossing the street. They sped away toward the Third Ward. Horns wailed and lights flashed. "Hold on Doc."

The chief skidded into the parking lot of Newman's ten minutes later. He joined four other officers already at the scene. Three more patrol cars pulled up, blocking the street from traffic and onlookers. The chief and Dr. Williams got out of the car. His men rallied around him. "Here's what we got men. This isn't actually a paint store. It's a front for the production of Doc Gray's tonic."

Dr. Williams chimed in. "Chief, don't you mean Doc Otto's tonic?"

The chief eyed him. "Yea, yea. Whatever. I have reason to believe that the tonic they are making now contains a poison of some sort. Be careful and don't touch a thing. This here is Dr. Williams." He tilted his head toward the man standing on his left. "He's coming in with us to help us find the source."

He pointed to some officers. "You men secure the perimeter. No one is allowed to leave this place." He watched the men dart off and surround the building.

The front door bell jingled. Kids of all ages flooded the front porch upon hearing the sirens.

"Jesus, Mary, and Joseph! Get those kids out of here, now!" The chief yelled, directing another group of policemen to clear the porch. When the cops ran up the porch steps, the kids parted. They ran down the side steps into the street, where they disappeared behind neighboring businesses and cotton mills.

Four officers exploded through the front door, while others knocked in the back door. A moment later one shouted, "Clear!"

Another yelled back, "Clear!"

One peeled away and said. "I'm heading upstairs." Seconds later he called back down to the others. "It's clear up here, too!"

The chief and Dr. Williams entered the warehouse. "What do we have boys?"

"Looks like an empty warehouse with a pretty big operation, Chief. It appears that they use kids to fill bottles of tonic all day long from those big copper dispensers over there." The officer pointed to two shiny capsules where wooden stools sat, some overturned, under faucets.

The chief studied the area and looked up toward the ceiling where he saw pipes leading through the ceiling to the floor above them. "Hmm. That must be where they keep all of their ingredients." He motioned for Dr. Williams to follow him as he ran upstairs.

They walked over to find four covered copper coffers sitting on the floor. He observed a long, red rubber hose coiled on the floor that was connected to a sink faucet. Walking over to a rectangular wooden table, they found bottles of liquids, bins, and bags of powders that varied in color from white to green to reddish-brown lining the top. Dr. Williams carefully studied them all. He stopped at two bags filled with white powder. One was marked "cocaine" and the other, "chlorinated lime."

"I found it." Dr. Williams pulled his pencil out and tapped the brown paper bag with the chlorinated lime in it that also had a black skull and crossbones stamped below the label. "I believe this is what killed Mr. Martin and Mr. Schwinn. Do you know what this is?" he asked the chief.

"No."

"I bet they were using this stuff to clean their bottles. Chlorinated lime is used as an additive to treat our water supply. It is also used for disinfecting and bleaching purposes. In an effort to reduce the number of water borne pathogens such as dysentery, typhoid, and cholera, filtration and chlorinated lime were introduced into our water treatment processes over ten years ago."

The chief and the gathering officers winced as they listened to Dr. William's theory.

"Did you know that we use chlorinated lime in a special generator to create chlorine gas to disinfect hospital rooms?"

The police officers shook their heads.

Dr. Williams carefully opened the bags. "As you can see, they look very similar." The chief peered into the bags. "However, chlorinated lime, or bleaching powder is a greyish-white in color. It's a very subtle difference. I suspect they were teaching the older children how to mix the tonic. See those long paddles over there?" He pointed to two large wooden paddles resting against the wall. "It appears that they pour the ingredients into those bins on the floor, add water, and stir. The kids downstairs simply fill the bottles. Pretty ingenious and efficient, I must say. There's no lifting or toting of the product between floors. As a result, spillage is minimized."

"But if you're a kid who can't read...." one officer said.

"Then the mistake is deadly."

A man screamed out from the floor below them. "Let me go! Let me go, you bastards!"

The chief, Dr. Williams, and a few officers ran down the staircase to the first floor. They found two officers holding the arms of a man who had severe burn scars on his hands.

The officer holding the man's right arm also carried a black canvas bag in the other. He spoke. "Found him trying to escape in the tree line out back. He was carrying this bag filled with money."

The chief stepped closer. "What's your name, mister?"

The man spat at the chief's high polished, black boots. The chief hit him with a right hook, followed by a left.

"Did you poison the tonic that killed Alvin Martin and Lester Schwinn?" The chief reared back ready to strike again.

The man's cheeks swelled. He appeared genuinely confused. "What the hell are you talking about? Poison tonic? Alvin and Lester are dead? There has to be some kind of mistake."

The chief lowered his fists. "Why did you run?"

"I heard the sirens. I thought we were being raided for illegal interstate commerce. I just had one of the kids mix up a new batch of Doc Otto's tonic for a meeting Lester was having uptown. I don't know what the hell you are talking about. Poison?"

"Look, mister." The chief bit his lip. "Between murder and illegal interstate commerce, you're going to get sent away to the Atlanta Penitentiary." The chief paced for a moment then stood in front of him. "My father had a saying. 'There ain't no bit of difference between a hornet and a yellow jacket when they're both buzzin' in your pants.'"

Dr. Williams stepped in and joined the interrogation. "Do you use chlorinated lime to clean your bottles?"

"Yes. Of course we do."

"I found a bag of it sitting next to one marked *cocaine*."

"Holy hell!" the captured man exclaimed. "I told that boy to always put up that powder after he used it. I told him to make sure he read the labels."

"Jesus, Mary, and Joseph!" The chief shot off. "You're assuming that these kids can read?"

"He told me he could. He said he was good with his letters and his numbers."

"How was he with a picture of a skull and cross bones?" The chief poked him hard in the chest.

"Listen. Other than the bottles you gave Lester, have any more bottles left this premises?"

"No," the man said somberly. He stopped struggling.

"Book him," the chief directed the officers. They placed him in iron manacles and hauled him out the front door.

Dr. Williams pulled the chief aside. "Chief, these men were breaking the law, weren't they? You mentioned something about the Feds back at Alvin's Pharmacy. You knew they were doing something wrong and possibly smuggling this tonic out of state. You had them under investigation, didn't you?"

The chief remained silent.

"By the way, I don't recall reading *cocaine*, or any of their other sordid ingredients on the label. That's a violation of the federal Pure Food and Drug Act. No wonder these poor people get addicted to these horrible tonics. They're being sold a lie. This crap won't cure what ails them. It's complete hogwash!"

The chief turned to Dr. Williams and smiled. He patted him on the back. "Thanks, Doc for your help this afternoon. It looks like Alvin and Lester got a healthy dose of their own medicine!"

Clyde's phone rang. He rolled over Moira, who was in bed next to him, to answer it. "Hey," Clyde mumbled. "Who's calling?"

"Clyde? It's Edward. I've got some bad news to share with you. Is this a good time to talk or am I interrupting something?"

Clyde exchanged places with Moira. The alcohol and the drugs fogged his mind and slowed his speech. But the sound of Edward's voice served as a fog cutter. "Sorry Edward. You caught me sleeping." He looked over and winked at Moira. She smiled, jiggled her breasts, and winked back. "What's wrong?"

Moira leaned in, straining to hear what Edward had to say.

"Dr. Williams called me with some distressing news. It seems that our newly hired pharmacist, Alvin Martin, and a friend of his named Lester Schwinn were poisoned and died."

Clyde shot up out of bed. His tongue unglued and moved at lightning speed. "What? When? Where? How does he know?"

"It seems that he had a meeting at Alvin's Pharmacy this afternoon. The two men sampled the new Doc Otto's tonic and they died right in front of him. Dr. Williams even helped the Chief of Police identify the source of the poison. Evidently, they were using Newman's Painting and Supply as a front to make the tonic. Dr. Williams said a man with severely scarred hands whom the police captured confessed that they use kid laborers to make the stuff. A bad batch was whipped up today. Some kid mistook cocaine for chlorinated lime." There was a silence on the other end of the line. "Are you still there?"

"Yea, yea. I'm still here. I can't believe that. Did the police find out anything else?"

"What do you mean by that?"

"Were they doing anything illegal?"

"Funny you should ask. As a matter of fact, they discovered they were mislabeling the bottles and failing to disclose the real ingredients, like alcohol, cocaine, and God knows what else. They were even smuggling it to other pharmacies out of state in paint cans. Why do you ask?"

Clyde stammered, searching for the right words. "Well, thank God their antics were discovered before Alvin set foot into Sacred Heart Hospital. Can you imagine the bad publicity if we were tied to such a scandal?"

The scenario made Edward's head reel with questions. "When we met to discuss hiring staff for the hospital, didn't you say that Alvin was a friend of yours? You highly recommended him for the job. If I also recall, you helped set up the meeting with Dr. Williams and Alvin." Edward's stomach churned. "Clyde, are you in any way tied up with this tonic business? I swear, if I find out that you are...."

"No. No. Not in any way, Edward. You have my word. Thanks for letting me know. It sounds like we need to find a new pharmacist."

"Why don't Dr. Williams and I work on that project. You've got your hands full."

"Well, if you insist. Again, thanks for the call. I've got to go now." Clyde hung up the phone on Edward and quickly made another call.

"Mr. Chang? This is Clyde. Yes. I know. Yes, yes. I just heard about it too. Listen. I've got a job for your men. I need for you to destroy Alvin's Pharmacy and Newman's Paint Store. We don't need the police snooping around to find any connections back to us. When? It has to happen tonight." Clyde rolled over and inhaled the remains of cocaine on a hand mirror that sat on the bedside table. "How much? One hundred dollars? Fine. I'll be down there within the hour." He slammed the phone down.

"What's going on? What's wrong?" Moira sat up in bed, eager to hear the latest. She watched him pull on his trousers. He hopped around on one foot as he slipped on his boot in search for the other. He found it hidden under the bed.

Clyde filled her in as he finished getting dressed. "I'll be back in a few hours. Stay put." He ran out the bedroom door and down the stairs.

When Moira heard the back door slam shut and the car engine turn over, she scurried over to the phone. "Hey! It's me. Is it sunny out? Great! You aren't going to believe this. Boy, have I got some news for you. Got a pencil and some paper?"

Four hours later, a black car sped to Alvin's Pharmacy while another made its way to Newman's Painting and Supply Company. Two men got out at each location. They lit bundled sticks of dynamite and tossed them through the front windows. They ran back to the cars and drove off. Seconds later, roaring balls of red and orange flames exploded behind them, silhouetting their cars and the accomplices who made a clean getaway.

33

Thursday, March 6, 1914, Fourth Ward

Finding comfort in Mrs. Gray's traditions, Addie enjoyed a cup of coffee while reading the morning's edition of *The Atlanta Dispatch* quietly to herself. The brass clock on the mantel struck nine bells. She was engrossed with the headline story, *Explosive Ending to Toxic Tonic Scandal.*

"Lester's dead!" Addie dropped her coffee cup on the floor and threw the paper down on the coffee table. She ran to the kitchen phone. She rang the Schwinn residence.

A man's voice answered feebly. "Hello?"

Addie pulled the ear piece away from her ear. "Mr. Schwinn?"

"Speak up, please. I'm a bit hard of hearing."

Addie raised the volume of her voice and exaggerated her enunciation. "Mr. Schwinn. This is Addie. I just read about Lester in the paper. I'm so sorry for your loss. Is there anything I can do for you?"

"No child. You've already done enough," he shouted back.

Addie, unsure of what he meant, asked, "Can I speak to Mrs. Schwinn?"

"She's not able to talk. The doctor gave her a shot. She's sleeping now."

"Please let her know I called."

The line on the other end went dead. Addie hung up the phone. Knowing the Darling farm didn't have a phone, she grabbed the scissors out of one of the kitchen drawers and proceeded to cut out the article. She ran upstairs to her desk, opening the drawer that contained her stationary. Garrett's pebble rolled to the front of the drawer. She picked it up, bit her bottom lip as she smiled, and put it in her navy dress pocket. Addie scribbled a note to Garrett. Enclosing the newspaper clipping with the letter, she addressed, sealed, and put an extra stamp on the envelope. On the front, she wrote *Rush Delivery!* Upon hearing the familiar squeak of the mailbox lid, Addie ran downstairs. She threw open the door, stumbled across the threshold, and fell into awaiting arms.

"Morning!" Garrett steadied her back on her feet.

"Oh my goodness! Garrett, I thought you were the postman. What in heavens are you doing here? Did you hear? Lester is dead! I just wrote a letter to tell you." Addie held it up. Garrett took it.

The mailman tipped his hat to her from the sidewalk. He called out. "Morning, Miss. Do you have a letter for me?"

"No. Not anymore. Thank you," Addie called back. "It's just been delivered."

"Well, I can't beat that kind of service. Good day to you both!"

Garrett took a seat in one of the white wicker rockers on the porch as he tore open the envelope. Addie sat in the chair next to him. She watched him unfold the newspaper article and her accompanying letter. He read it in silence.

Addie waited until he finished before she spoke. "I'm so

sorry to hear about Lester's death." Addie hung her head and started to cry, still shaken by Lester's visit. "Truth be told, a part of me isn't sorry." Addie rubbed her neck, still sore and bruised from Lester's grip. Her high-collared dress covered the evidence. *I best not tell him what Lester did to me and I did to him. It doesn't matter now anyway.* "I tried calling your aunt and uncle to convey my condolences, but Mr. Schwinn hung up on me."

"Father and I received the news yesterday evening and we made our way to Aunt Mary's house straight away." Garrett refolded the letter and article and put them back into the envelope. "Look, we've been friends forever. I love you and I know you love me. I know you have made a commitment to pursue your nursing career. I completely understand," Garrett stammered. "Please forgive me for being a complete horse's ass. I was so mad at you for not being honest with me about your dealings with Lester." He fumbled for the right words. "For the first time, I felt left out of your life and I didn't like it. Not one bit. I hated the fact that I couldn't be there for you, to protect you and my aunt. I actually felt...helpless."

Addie placed her hand on his knee. He covered her hand with his. "I'm so sorry. I never meant to hurt you. I tried explaining everything to you in my letter," Addie said.

"I know. I just read it." He winked at her.

"Look, for some women, staying at home and keeping house is the right path. I'm not ready to settle down yet. I'm not a delicate flower that withers under the scorching Georgia sun." Her tone was emphatic. "I've discovered that I thrive, even under difficult conditions. I want to be right here. The aspirations of my heart and dreams are finally coming true as fulfilled wishes."

Garrett reached inside his coat pocket and pulled out a piece of paper and read. "Life is short, break the rules. Forgive quickly, kiss slowly. Love truly, laugh uncontrollably and never regret anything that makes you smile." He refolded it. "You make me smile, Addie. Do you know who said that?"

Addie flushed, reached over, and punched him in the upper arm. "Of course, I remember reading Twain's quote in the book you gave to me." Addie reached deep inside her dress pocket. She pulled out the pebble. "I plan to keep your stone with me everywhere I go. It's a constant reminder of you, my past, my Hope, and my tomorrows."

Garrett stared at it in disbelief. "I can't believe you kept it."

"I'm only just beginning. Life has so much in store for me. I'm ready to let go to see where life takes me."

"Can you forgive me, Addie? While a part of me wants to snatch you up and carry you back to Hope, I know that you long for more. I can't deny you that life." Garrett stood up and took Addie's hand in his. "I've got to head back to help the family with Lester's funeral arrangements. Before I go, promise me that you will write to me from school. I want to know that you are happy and doing well. That's my wish for you."

"I promise." Addie stood, cradled his face in her hands, and kissed him.

Garrett pulled her close, wrapped her up in his arms, and inhaled the familiar scent of lilacs. He whispered in her ear. "I love you, my dear, Addie. Come back to me someday."

Addie looked forward to seeing Lena and having lunch together. She couldn't imagine who the other guest would be. Deciding to take the elevator at the Ponce de Leon Apartments to Lena's place, Addie stepped aside to allow an elderly couple step out of the car and into the lobby. As she entered the car, Garrett's surprise visit and the unexpected news of Lester's death continued to consume her thoughts. The doors parted on the eleventh floor. *Lester sold his soul to the devil. There's no short cut to fame and fortune,* she thought. Addie recalled one of Twain's quotes: "Some men worship rank, some worship heroes, some worship power, some worship God, and over these ideals they dispute and cannot unite—but they all worship money."

Addie knocked on the door. Seeing Lena's smiling face comforted her. As they exchanged pleasantries, Addie walked into the living room to find the familiar face of a young girl with strawberry-blonde hair. Addie recalled admiring her chignon at the Alexander's Christmas party, and saw that it had now been replaced with long, spiral curls pinned high on her head.

The young lady stood and clapped her hands together. "Oh, I remember you! You're Addie Engel. It's a pleasure to see you again." She reached out and shook Addie's hand.

Oh my! The Alexander Christmas party fiasco! My plate fell, spilling food all over your sister and her friends. I passed out in your dining room. How embarrassing! Addie's cheeks and neck flushed. "Opal, it's so good to see you, too." Addie stammered. "Well...well, before we go any further, I must confess my profound apologies for passing out at your family's Christmas party. I was a bit overcome...*by Doc Gray's tonic and alcohol!*"

"Oh, don't think a thing about it. Please let bygones be bygones. Believe me when I say crazier things have happened at our parties. You just made it a bit livelier for us."

"I'm sure!" Addie remembered Mrs. Gray telling her about the time when Alderman Cotton dressed in one of Mrs. Alexander's dresses and was found in bed with a waiter at a New Year's Eve party. She smiled politely. *My antics pale in comparison after all!*

Lena stepped into the conversation. "Ladies, I wanted you two to become acquainted. Something tells me you have a lot in common, especially when it comes to your spirit and love of medicine. I have a feeling you will be my star students in nursing school." She waved her finger in the air. "But time will tell."

Addie and Opal pointed at each other. "You're in the first class, too?" they said in unison and laughed.

"What wonderful news!" Addie turned to Lena. "Thank you so much for giving us the opportunity to get to know each other before school starts. Since Mrs. Gray died, I have to admit I've been a bit lonely and have looked forward to meeting others like me with interests in medicine and nursing."

"It's my pleasure. I saw you from afar at Mrs. Gray's funeral at the Shrine of the Immaculate Conception. I could tell you were overcome with loss and grief. I knew that introducing you to Opal would help start this new chapter in your life."

The aroma of a delicious meal grabbed Addie's nose and attention. "What smells simply divine?"

"I've had lunch brought up from the kitchen downstairs.

Come. Let's eat and I'll fill you in on the latest about Sacred Heart Hospital."

Lena ushered the young ladies into her kitchen. On a silver cart next to the table covered with a beautiful pastel yellow lace table cloth was an array of finger sandwiches, fruit salad, soup, a tray of cookies, and a glass pitcher of fresh tea with sprigs of mint, lemon and ice cubes.

Addie delighted at the sandwiches which contained chicken and ham salad between the carefully cut triangular-sliced pieces of bread that were absent their crusts. She learned the soup was a chef's special, cream of celery. She spotted a familiar black wafer cookie with a white cream filling in the middle, the sort that she had seen on the Alexander's holiday spread.

Opal eyed them too. "Oh, these are my favorite! May I?" She turned to Lena, who nodded with approval. Opal picked up one, split it apart, and licked at the icing in the center. Lena and Addie did the same. "Oreos taste like heaven!"

As they filled their plates and enjoyed their meal, Lena updated them on the construction projects at the hospital and the nursing school. Addie was thrilled to hear about the three tunnels that were going to provide easy passage between the facilities and the school. Having never been in a tunnel before, Addie marveled at the idea that the doctors and the nurses didn't have to walk through the wind and rain between the complexes.

Lena also reviewed the members of the Sacred Heart leadership team, including the new physicians. "Dr. Randall Springer will be in charge of our pediatric ward. He comes to us by way of Children's Hospital of Philadelphia. He's currently on vacation in Europe and will be moving to Atlanta at the end of the month." Lena scratched her head. "We still have to find him a place to stay. He wants to rent a place before he decides to purchase a home of his own down here. I've been so busy interviewing and hiring nurses for the hospital, I've forgotten to make inquiries for Edward."

An idea struck Addie. She pulled her sandwich from her mouth, returning it to her plate. "I've got the perfect solution for him. He can rent Mrs. Gray's house."

Lena sat back in her chair. "Do you have permission from the family to do so?"

Opal leaned in to hear Addie's answer.

"As a matter of fact, I inherited it from her. During the reading of her will, I learned that her house and part of her estate were passed on to me and not her nephew, Lester."

Opal jumped in. "Really? I've been dying to ask you about him." Opal fumbled with her napkin and reached out to Addie. "Oh, I'm sorry, Addie. That was a poor choice of words. I just read about his tragic death in the paper this morning."

Lena leaned in, too, eager to hear more.

"It appears Lester was up to no good from the start. *I can't reveal too much. Be discreet like Mrs. Gray taught me.* "I believe Mrs. Gray had her suspicions about him. She and her attorney stopped him from using the Gray name for the tonic a few months ago. That's when he switched and used his sister's father-in-law's name. Doc Otto's was short for Dr. Otto Barringer, who was supposed to have developed an improved formula. I too just learned about Lester and his business partner's death in the paper this morning. I had no idea the extent of his corruption." *However, Mrs. Gray and I knew he was a bad man, a very bad man. As fate would have it, now a dead man.* Addie shrugged her shoulders innocently, refusing to reveal any more information.

Anxious to shift the topic back to Dr. Springer, Addie directed the question back to Lena. "So, if Dr. Springer needs a home, he can rent mine since it will sit empty while I'm in school. I would love to extend the offer."

"Marvelous! Thank you! If you ladies will excuse me, let me ring your father, Opal." Lena popped up and ran over to the phone to call Edward. Maddie found him in the Zoo. He was thrilled to hear about Addie's offer. He confessed he still had not found a residence for Randall either since he and Dr. Williams were busy searching for a new pharmacist for the hospital. Lena concluded the call and returned to the table.

"That settles it." She reached out and grabbed Addie's hand. "Thank you so much. Edward is pleased with the suggestion. He will speak with Dr. Williams. Dr. Williams will contact you to finalize the rent agreement and any other details on behalf of Dr. Springer."

Addie squeezed Lena's hand. "It's my pleasure. Having a physician and his family move into it..."

Lena interrupted. "Oh, he doesn't have a family. He's single and very dashing, if I may add that bit of information." The girls giggled. "I saw his photograph in his application file. He's quite the looker."

"If I recall, I just pledged my love life away when I signed my three-year agreement with Sacred Heart Nursing School," Addie added and sighed. Opal joined her.

"Yes, while you did agree to remain unmarried for the next

three years, the contract doesn't permit you from admiring handsome, smart men." Lena's eyes sparked as she laughed and tapped the back of Addie's hand, toying with her.

Addie raised her tea glass. Lena and Opal joined her in the toast. "To our new lives at Sacred Heart, to Nurse Hartman our instructor, to making new friends, to helping those who need us most, to making a difference in this world, and to admiring handsome, smart men."

Together, they replied. "Hear! Hear! Cheers!"

Thursday evening, Sixth Ward

The chief rang Mr. Thompson at the office early in the day with the hopes of meeting for a cocktail that evening. Mr. Thompson cleared his schedule and obliged the chief's request. He was anxious to get a summary about the recent events involving the demise of Lester and his tonics. Five hours later, Mr. Thompson toasted the chief and they tossed back their second round of single malt as they sat in the rathskeller of the Wincoff Hotel.

"I can't believe the turn of events this past week," Mr. Thompson leaned in and whispered. "It sure saved the city thousands from having to haul in Lester and his cronies into court and trying that bastard for Frank's murder, conspiracy to defraud, and smuggling, to name a few of his crimes off the top of his long list."

The chief motioned to the waiter to bring over the whiskey bottle. "It even helps out the Feds by saving them time and money for not having to prosecute Lester for breaking the Pure Food and Drug Act. Thank God we caught his right hand man at Newman's Paint Store before he got away with a bag filled with loot and Lester's ledger books. He sang like a little song bird when we put him behind bars."

They watched the waiter top off their glasses and set the bottle down in front of them.

"We found out that Lester was selling his tonic as far away as Illinois and Ohio. He sold his product to pharmacies and apothecaries all over and filled his paint orders using three colors. According to his ledger books, green was their top seller, which was masked as Doc Gray's Nerve and Blood Purification tonic. Doc Gray's Cure-all was coded and fulfilled as white paint.

Doc Gray's Restorative was sold as red paint."

"Really? That's pretty ingenious."

"Not really. It turns out that all of the tonics were derived from the same formula. The only thing that changed was the labels. Other than the undisclosed cocaine and alcohol, no other special ingredients differentiated them. Can you believe the balls on that guy?"

Mr. Thompson shook his head.

The chief tossed back his third shot. "Do you know what the difference was between Doc Gray's and Doc Otto's formulas?"

"Beats me. Bovine urine?"

The chief howled, sputtered, and slapped his knee. "That's a laugh!" He struggled to regain his composure. "Good one, but no. Lester simply added cinnamon to the new and improved Doc Otto's tonic. He even had Dr. Barringer fabricate the research study. Can you believe that?"

"The promise of fame and fortune can ruin a gullible, well-educated man, can't it?"

"That man's entire medical career just got flushed down the toilet. What a complete waste of talent."

"By the way, speaking about a complete waste, I'm sorry to hear about your two officers. That's a hell of a way to go."

"Thanks. That was tragic, to say the least. When I brought in Madam McIntosh for questioning like you suggested, they buckled at the sight of her and knew it was curtains for them." The chief hung his head as he recalled the terrible shooting incident between Seth and Lamar inside his precinct walls. Shaking his head to erase the memory, he looked up. "The rest of my men are really good and honorable. I just had a few bad apples in the bunch."

"Do you have any idea who blew up Martin's Pharmacy and Newman's?"

"I have a strong suspicion whose men were behind it. But for now I'm not going to pursue it any further. After all, they did the city a favor."

Mr. Thompson raised his glass. The chief joined him. "As promised, to happy endings."

"Cheers! To happy endings!"

34

Wednesday, April 1, 1914, Sixth Ward

Addie stood on the sidewalk outside 422 Spring Street at eight-thirty in the morning. The cresting sun illuminated the golden highlights in her hair while the morning birds sang from the citron tree tops. An hour and a half earlier she had closed and locked the door behind her on Houston Street after Dr. Randall Springer met her at Mrs. Gray's house to sign his rental agreement and pick up a set of keys to the house. Addie completely agreed with Nurse Hartman that Dr. Springer was a very handsome gentleman. He was the perfect pediatrician, soft spoken and gentle. She could envision him cradling newborn babies in the palms of his hands. Addie thought his blonde hair and blue eyes made him look like one of the angels she had seen in the stained-glass windows of the Shrine during Mrs. Gray's funeral.

In lieu of the street cars, Addie opted for a taxi to carry her uptown. She made arrangements to have her trunk sent before her arrival as the nursing school letter instructed. She looked up at the magnificent, white marble structure. The main entrance to Sacred Heart Hospital was flush with the sidewalk, void of any stairs. Four grand, square pillars supported the red ceramic-tiled, overhanging roof line that provided shelter over the wide front porch. Two columns closest to the center boasted a high archway overhead. Engraved in the keystone was the caduceus, a winged staff intertwined with two snakes.

Newly planted bright red and white azaleas bloomed. Bradford pear and dogwood trees scattered across the front yard. A few gardeners passed each other as they hastily cut the lawn with red, hand-pushed, rolling lawn clippers. Another man wearing a straw hat and overalls watered a row of boxwoods that bordered a red brick wall on the left hand side of the yard. The structure prevented Addie from seeing the white building with a brick façade being built around the corner.

Large arched, double doors opened as Addie walked toward the entrance. She looked up and noticed the tall windows, also arched, were gilded with wrought iron. A white cotton cloth covered the highly polished, brass hospital signage underneath. She knew it would remain in place for another month and a half, until the ceremonial ribbon cutting ceremony. Addie paused and closed her eyes to reflect for a moment. *What's behind me will not define me. It was just a lesson. It's what's ahead that will. For "the two most important days in your life are the day you are born and the day you find out why." Maw, I'm on my way to find out why.* Addie opened her eyes and stepped over the marble threshold.

"Good morning to you, Miss Engel. Welcome to Sacred Heart Hospital and Nursing School. Nurse Hartman is expecting you."

Addie beamed, recognizing the face and voice.

"Come on. We don't have all day." Nurse Scott grabbed Addie's hand. "Duty calls, Red."

About the Author

Katie Hart Smith loved writing as a child, creating her own story and picture books at a very early age. As a young adult, she pursued a nursing career and obtained a B.S. in Nursing from Georgia State University in 1987. In 2002, she received an MBA from Troy State University. Throughout her professional career, Smith continued to write and lecture for the medical community and even served as a guest speaker at Emory University, Nell Hodgson Woodruff School of Nursing for ten years. In 1995, Smith published, "In the Face of Disaster: Personal Reflections" in the *Orthopaedic Nursing Journal.* The article recounted Smith's work with the Red Cross to lead a group of volunteers from Atlanta to assist with the Flint River Flood recovery efforts. During the four-hour commute home on a city commuter bus, Smith wrote on scratch pieces of paper to journal the day's events.

Smith continued to expand her literary efforts and published and illustrated her first children's poetry book, *From the Heart,* in 2006. In 2014, she released a memoir, *Couch Time with*

Carolyn, for which Smith was nominated for the Georgia Author of the Year Award in the Memoir/Autobiography category in 2015 by the Georgia Writer's Association.

Smith is also working on a non-fiction book, collaborating with Fallon Coody, Georgia's second & fourth liver transplant recipient, to share her incredible journey and promote the importance of organ donation. This is a special priviledge and an honor for Smith, as Smith was one of the many pediatric nurses who cared for Fallon when she was hospitalized almost 30 years ago. To learn more about this miraculous story, visit Smith's Always From the Heart blog (katiehartsmith.wordpress.com).

In her spare time, she is an active member in her community and enjoys speaking to book clubs and community and civic organizations on a variety of topics.

CPSIA information can be obtained
at www.ICGtesting.com
Printed in the USA
FFOW03n1047291017
41594FF